Mums Like Us

Laura Kemp started writing to get out of doing a real job. A journalist for fifteen years, she turned freelance after having a baby because she couldn't get out of the house, washed and dressed, until lunchtime at the earliest.

A columnist and contributor, she regularly writes for national newspapers and magazines, such as the *Daily Mail*, and spends too much time on Twitter (@laurajanekemp). *Mums Like Us* is her first novel, which she hopes will strike a chord with exhausted mums who don't iron either.

Married with a son and a neurotic cat, Laura lives in the provinces, where she goes about her business ignorant of what's on-trend until it reaches her town, by which time it's out of fashion.

To find out more visit her website at:
www.laura-kemp.com

Mums
Like Us

LAURA KEMP

arrow books

Published by Arrow Books 2013

2 4 6 8 10 9 7 5 3 1

First published in Great Britain in 2013 by
Arrow Books
Random House, 20 Vauxhall Bridge Road,
London SW1V 2SA

www.randomhouse.co.uk

Addresses for companies within The Random House Group
Limited can be found at: www.randomhouse.co.uk/offices.htm

The Random House Group Limited Reg. No. 954009

A CIP catalogue record for this book
is available from the British Library

ISBN 9780099574583

The Random House Group Limited supports the Forest Stewardship
Council® (FSC®), the leading international forest-certification
organisation. Our books carrying the FSC label are printed on
FSC®-certified paper. FSC is the only forest-certification
scheme supported by the leading environmental organisations,
including Greenpeace. Our paper procurement policy can be found
at www.randomhouse.co.uk/environment

Typeset in Palatino by Palimpsest Book Production Limited,
Falkirk, Stirlingshire

Printed and bound by CPI Group (UK) Ltd, Croydon, CR0 4YY

To Paddy,
without whom this wouldn't have been possible

Acknowledgements

October 2007, I was sleep-deprived, tearful and desperate. A first-time mum of a seven-week-old baby, I was given the option of taking voluntary redundancy from my job as head of content on a Sunday paper after a huge restructuring. Returning to work as a career woman seemed completely at odds with my new position of zombie-in-charge-of-a-pram – I felt completely inadequate at achieving anything beyond the relentless feeds, nappies and worry. My husband spends weeks away working so I was pretty much on my own and I was terrified of failing, not just at motherhood but at 'having it all'.

So I took the money and ran. Well, more accurately, I wobbled. Even so, I was heartbroken. I was in mourning for my previous life as a journalist. More than a decade of chasing stories was gone. I thought it was all over. But as the months passed, words and ideas started coming to me, usually when I was wiping myself down after feeding time or panicking about being a useless mum. It led to this. I still can't believe it.

Here are the people who helped me make it happen . . .

Paul Dacre, *Daily Mail* editor, who responded to my emails, encouraged me to write and kindly called my pain-in-the-arse pestering 'tenacious'. Andrew Morrod and the Femail team at the *Daily Mail* for being the first national to commission and run my features. Not to mention the very fine art of toughening me up. I apologise for all those bloody emails.

The remarkable writer Allison Pearson, who gave me advice and support right from the off and beyond.

My fantastic agent, Lizzy Kremer, for plucking this clueless idiot out of nowhere and making my dreams come true. From the word go, she 'got me', and her input and ideas have been invaluable. I love her.

Thanks also go to Jane Graham Maw, Jennifer Christie, Julian Friedmann and Simon Trewin for giving me their precious time when I first began my search for representation.

My gorgeous editor Georgina Hawtrey-Woore, for her expert eye, hitting the nail on the head and being on my side by my side all the way. Spot-on Sarah Bance for her superb copy-edit. Plus everyone at Arrow for believing not just in this book but in the next.

Sparkly Milly Johnson, for her encouragement and for being the woman who's been there, done that and is not afraid to wear the T-shirt.

The legendary Mavis Nicholson for giving me the benefit of her experience.

Tim Gordon, from Media Wales, who lets me run riot every week as a columnist, and his Head of Features and Lifestyle Margaret O'Reilly, who got the ball rolling and shares my sport widow pain week in, week out. Also Tamsin Kelly at Parentdish for giving me a go. And everyone on Twitter for making me feel like I'm having a laugh in the office when in fact I'm in the kitchen by myself.

Web wonders Mash and Adam Walker, who translated my scrappy drawings into a website I'm proud of.

To my family and friends . . .

Mum, Dad and Cathryn, for always loving, laughing and listening – you are The Best.

My husband and son, who are the loves of my life. I won't ever let you go. Oh God, I'm going to start crying.

My father-in-law for his endless optimism and wise words – plus for doing the school run when I was up to my neck in editing. My mother-in-law and Grampy Tony for being the cavalry.

My best friend Jo, who is the other half of me, (the funny half).

To all the mums out there who've got me through the last five years, sharing my pain (and a few scraps of joy), particularly, wonderful Waler; the antenatal yoga girls Ceri, Sarah and Marie; and kindred spirits Claire, Stroppy Loy, Rachy Main, Sue, Loretta, Shezza, Jo, Angharad and Deb.

And finally, to all those – and there are plenty – who have intentionally or unwittingly made me feel incompetent – you have no idea how much you inspired me.

Mums
Like Us

If you struggle to juggle, join Stella Smith's Mums
Like Us revolution . . .

Week One

Inaugural Meeting of Mums Like Us
Stella's kitchen

Welcome, ladies. Or should I say lardies? We're certainly not as slim as we used to be, are we? Thank you for coming to the first ever Mums Like Us meeting. I know what a temptation it is to stay indoors at this time of year.

Some of you are friends we've met along the way; others have come because you identified with the dog-eared, coffee-ringed advert for the group I put up on the library noticeboard a couple of weeks ago.

You're here for a variety of reasons, which include: you don't live in Notting Hill, you haven't got a nanny or a second home in Somerset and you don't go to the Caribbean for New Year. You struggle to juggle work with motherhood; you drink far too much at home; and you've lost your libido. It's probably at the bottom of the dirty washing pile, but seeing as you'll never get there, you're unlikely ever to find it. Nor do you really want to.

My name is Stella Smith – aka MUMMYYYYYYYYYY YYYYYYYYY – and I am the chairwoman. But please don't think I'm going to make you feel inferior with tales of how I make everything work. In fact I am the most inadequate example of motherhood you'll come across. The aim, each week, is to tell it how it really is for mums like us, who are normal, ordinary and thoroughly provincial.

Look around you and you'll see the evidence: fluff-balls, encrusted food remains on the worktop, pants drying on the hall radiator, toys everywhere and loads of empty bottles of wine in the recycling bin of shame.

The purpose of the club is to bring our kind together, to celebrate our slovenliness and to offer a shoulder when we want to let off suburban steam when the rest of the world is putting on a Mother Superior face. Each week we'll discuss issues that affect us; for example, how to cope with competitive mums, what on earth you're going to cook for the kids' tea and whether it's worth picking a fight over whose turn it is to put out the black bags.

You may wonder if the club is your kind of place. Over the next three meetings I will give you lots of information so you can decide if you want to join. There will be an explanation of our motto and mani-festo, but at this first meeting, I'll begin by telling you a bit about myself.

Before I start, though, just one thing: if at any point you feel yourself nodding off, I'll quite understand – I'm as knackered as you are. The minutes of each meeting should be available at some point in the future, possibly written on a piece of paper smeared with peanut butter – that's if I get round to it.

Oh, and help yourself to tea, coffee, double chocolate muffins and death-by-hydrogenated-fats biscuits. Please note, we do not do cupcakes here because they are Mother Superior fodder; by which I mean they're easy to smudge across a plate to make it look like you've had some. Here, when we eat cake, the plate should be licked clean.

So . . . I'm a thirty-six-year-old married mum-of-one who tries to earn a living as a writer. I'm a Work From Home Mother; my office is the kitchen and I rope in my husband, mum and friends to help out while I'm up against a deadline. I write when our son goes to bed, but I also rely heavily on the state providing free preschool nursery for our three-year-old. I cover anything from press releases to personal features for papers, magazines and websites, and I love my job. It's my escape and my sanity-saver.

Looking back, I never longed for parenthood because I was so wrapped up in my pre-baby career as a journalist, chasing stories and bashing out copy, and I just assumed it would happen. At the age of thirty, having had the misfortune to date a bunch of idiots, I met Mr Right You'll Do, we got married and then an enormous hormonal surge took me hostage and told me it was time to reproduce. That magical little blue line emerged on a wee stick after about six months of trying and so I gave up fags and booze cold turkey-style, which was utter hell, not helped by the daily hormonal weeping sessions. I believed my mother when she told me labour was quick and easy and then as soon as the first contraction started, I went into shock. Three years later and I am still stunned by the ridiculousness of motherhood.

No annual appraisal, no right to strike, no pay, no holidays and no sign of the earthquake subsiding.

I've been shocked at each stage of my son's development. When he actually started sleeping through, leaving me awake half the night checking his breathing. When he began sticking marbles in his mouth. When he was able to turn the telly on by himself. When he cried his eyes out for the first month of pre-school. And I can only imagine the shock that will come when he leaves home and I have no idea what he's doing, what he's eating or if he's done a poo.

All I will have left by then is an even weaker pelvic floor, more wrinkles and more grey hair, as opposed to the unwashed talcum-powdered roots that you see today. On the upside, I'll be able to go to the pub for an all-dayer like I used to and perhaps have a conversation with my husband – if we ever recover from baby-bomb walking-wounded status, that is.

I came up with the idea of this club as a result of the myth of yumminess.

Everywhere I went, I saw women smiling through gritted teeth, talking an excellent game. They told me how much they loved being a mum, how they mourned the end of night-time feeds because they missed the midnight cuddles, how they wept when their precious bundle grabbed a sugar-toxic biscuit behind their backs and how it broke their hearts when their babies didn't look back when they dropped them off at nursery for the first time. Then, as soon as maternity leave was over, I heard these same mums telling me how much they loved their career and how much easier it was to go to work than look after a baby all day.

It's called self-preservation – pretending everything is brilliant and great. But if only we could admit that we're in denial – that way we wouldn't lash ourselves every second of every day.

Along the way, I met three wonderful mums, who I'll introduce to you over the coming weeks as our secretary, treasurer and events co-ordinator, and together in this very kitchen, over four bottles of wine in-between tales of stretchmarks and sex-dodging, we gave birth to Mums Like Us.

It's a safe haven where we can say unmotherly things like, 'I was so grateful when my son started preschool; finally, two and a half hours to myself every day so I can finish a cuppa while it's still hot', or, 'I really, really hate my job and wish I could spend more time with the kids, but we can't afford for me to stay at home.'

Whatever it is you want to say, you can say it and no one will judge you. Ever.

Apart from if you scoff all the muffins – then you'll get it big time.

The plan is we meet here once a week for an hour or so, covering whatever's on our minds followed by a general chit-chat, either after drop-off or before peace is shattered. We'll arrange the slot as we go, because stuff always comes up, like work and kids.

Anyway, I've rambled on far too long. It's almost pick-up time, and I've got to go and get some milk and a shit Valentine's Day card – my husband and I pride ourselves on the tackiest ones we can find – so if you don't mind shooting off, I'll see you all next week.

Dads United

The lounge

Email to: davidsmith70@hotmail.com
Subject: long time no email
Date: 12 February, 21:06

All right, Dave?

How's life in Silicon Valley? What you been up to? Spending that enormous salary of yours on women, booze and iStuff and blowing the rest?

Sat in the lounge, telly blaring, nothing decent on. Stella's gone to bed, so thought I'd give you a shout.

Life here is same old, same old, that's why I haven't been in touch for a few weeks. Don't think you're that interested in my boring, unsmug married life! Work is work, computers, blah blah blah – not as exciting as your career but it pays the mortgage. I'm pretty much stuck in the job until the big knobs leave, it's just a question of being patient. I thought about applying for some positions elsewhere but when I looked they were (a) non-existent and (b) miles away. How the feck did you end up being the hotshot? You bunked off school, whereas I went to every lesson and even lunchtime chess club. You went out with that girl in the sixth form when I was squeezing my spots and loading the ZX Spectrum in my bedroom. When I'd started work on one of those graduate schemes, you were getting chucked out of uni. You always were a risk-taker and I was such a square. You bastard!

The little one is brilliant, at that stage of asking 'why' every five seconds – cute until he asks, 'Why doesn't Mummy have a willy?' He's full of it, exhausting as ever. We'll have to do Skype soon so you can see your nephew – that's if I can get him to sit still for long enough for you to have a chat.

Stella's her usual self – going round like a fart in a thunderstorm. You know how she loves a good moan? Well, I came back home the other night after a session in the Feathers with some of the lads (more of that later) and the house was a wreck, covered in paper, wine glasses and empty bottles.

Stella had been drinking with three of her mates, who've all set up a mums' group. She'd hosted the first meeting that afternoon and 'the committee' just had to get together that evening for a – cough – debrief. Any excuse.

It's funny, because I've sort of done the same thing too. At the pub, after a few pints, me and the boys decided we needed to get rid of our beer/Greggs/curry bellies so we're going to start doing football training. I think we're all having a collective pre-midlife-crisis crisis; I've become obsessed with dying and death, definitely inspired by all the responsibility of fatherhood.

I'm captain because it was my idea, plus, being forty-one, I'm one of the oldest and greyest (although Stella says I've got salt-and-pepper hair, which she reckons is a sexier way of putting it). It's called Dads United and I hope we'll get to play a few local teams. Might knacker me out but it'll get me out of bedtime once a week. Seriously, it's hard work being a modern dad – I work hard all day, then when I get home, Stella expects me to do my bit. I'm not complaining, I know she gets the brunt of it, but I get ball-ache if I leave a sock on the floor while I'm entertaining the little one in the bath as I make a quick work call and get out of my suit.

Right, better go, lots to do. I'm planning a surprise Valentine's Day meal. We don't usually do anything for it, but I've started doing a bit of cooking here and there. Yeah, I've reached that age when men get into farmers' markets and wine and shit. Pathetic.

Mum says can you give her a ring.

Cheers,

Matt

Week Two

The Mums Like Us Motto: Perfection is Impossible, So Don't Bother Trying

Stella's kitchen

Lovely to see you all again. Ooh, and some new faces too – word must be getting round. How are you? Come in, come in. No, no need to take your shoes off, the carpet is a right state anyway, don't worry about it.

Doughnuts over there, tea and coffee on the side, just help yourselves. A cake will definitely help to fight off the four p.m. blood sugar dive when you end up stuffing the kids' crusts and crisps because you're so bloody starving.

I hope you've all had a good week. Mine's been total crap.

My son was ill, waking up every hour or so in the nights, poor little thing. Seeing the most precious thing in the world to you doubled over, throwing up and whimpering, surely is one of the most harrowing parts of motherhood. You know it'll pass, you know it's boosting their immunity and 'all part of life', but life is shitty enough when you become an adult – why do they have to suffer when they're so small? There's something just so heart-wrenching about a hot, fitful little body.

Jesus Christ, looking after a sick child is so draining. The endless Peppa Pig episodes numb your brain. And why is it that they hate the sight of their dads and only want their mum? My husband, Matt, took full advantage and went down the Feathers most nights because he said there was no point sitting on his own in the house while I was upstairs spooning Calpol and scrubbing vomit off the carpet. This is one of those differences between men and women: we wouldn't dream of going out when we've got a poorly child. Dads don't think they could be useful, like bringing tea up on a tray or getting some housework done or feeding the cat. You're just left to sneak down for a round of toast, hoping they don't wake up, having noticed your cradling arm has disappeared and it's the end of the world.

I left the house twice in six days: once to go to the chemist and once to take the little one to the doctor. Both times, Matt helpfully pointed out I looked like a cross between Rod Stewart and Courtney Love.

Of course, I humiliated myself in front of the GP and burst into tears.

She asked me if I was depressed. I said, 'Yes. Of

11

course I'm fucking depressed. I'm knackered, my son's ill, I feel really guilty that I couldn't do any work to bring in some much-needed money, my skin is dreadful thanks to hormonal rosacea and I'm just so tired, so very, very tired.'

She gave me the 'children are hard work but you must find time for yourself because a happy mum makes a happy child so why not go for a run' lecture. I would've punched her had she not been printing out a prescription. Yes, lardies! A prescription for antibiotics! How many times have you begged for those magic pills and they fob you off with the 'it's just a virus' line? Not just one for my son's chest infection but another for my patchy red face. Result!

So anyway, he was fine after that. Today is the first day I've put on make-up since Monday. I didn't even bother for Valentine's Day. Matt made this amazing scallops thing with chilli, which was lovely, but I was so knackered I wolfed it down and then went straight to bed. Alone!

Life is returning to the normal standard of shittiness rather than utter shittiness, and I feel a slight sense of independence after being permanently attached to my boy for the last few days. Hell, I've even been able to go to the loo by myself.

Right, better get on with this week's topic. Tesco beckons after this, then it's pick-up. Matt was brilliant at keeping us stocked up with the essentials while I was housebound, but I had to point out to him we really didn't need forty-eight Scotch eggs or a bumper box of Fruit Flakes, which he thought counted as one of your five-a-day. I had to give him a lesson in basic nutrition, bless him. He's also asked me to get him a water holder thingy for his Thursday-night football training with strict instructions that it must not have any 'twatty logos on it which will make me look a poser prick'. A *Ben 10* one it is then.

What was I talking about? Oh yes, this week's topic – our motto, which is 'Perfection is Impossible, So Don't Bother Trying'.

If you don't get to grips with this then you'll never truly be a Mums Like Us member. Let me explain. Perfect is a fantasy, an illusion, a mirage; one that is peddled on a daily basis, whether it's a famous mum on the front of a magazine telling us how sexy she feels with baby sick on her top – pictured obviously with no baby sick on her top – or the cow at Baby Milkshake who told you she loved having cracked nipples because it made her feel like a 'proper mum'.

It's all lies designed to make you feel inferior. Pursuing perfection, therefore, is a waste of time. Instead, being good enough is what we need to aim for, be it as a mother, a wife, a friend, an employee, a boss or a moaner.

The only way to reach this state of mind is to surround yourself with a gang of like-minded mums; those who will not talk of organic foodstuffs, baking, television stunting a child's development and how many circuits they did at Power Punch at lunchtime.

The quest to find these women is fraught with difficulties. You will meet some total nightmares at playgroups who will suck the life out of you, compete with you and lean on you so hard that you are physically on the floor by the time they've finished with you. But, let me tell you, once you find your girls, they will be there for you through thick and thin. More thick than thin, to be honest, seeing as you don't get a chance to exercise these days and frankly, you'd rather sit on your fat arse than work that butt.

You don't need an army of women – my support network is small but very strong. Having a wobbly? No worries – we're always just a text away, give or take a few hours because we're always mid-something, like the school run, but that's fine.

Obviously, my gang is here today. This is the mother of all mothers, sensible brunette pixie-haired Alex, a forty-year-old teacher married to Stu, who has one of each and is the master of boundary-setting. She is firm but fair, consistent and focused, and she inspires me to say 'no' to my son rather than give in because I'm a walkover. She is also secretary of the club, owing to her awesome list-making skills.

Then there is Lucy, thirty-three, our club events co-ordinator, who is a librarian, married to Dan with a son. She is laid-back, optimistic, and you can tell she's cool by her Jessie J-style black bob and fringe. She never panics, goes with the flow, mops my neurotic brow and laughs in my face when I have anxious, weak moments over some trivial worry. For example, when I wonder out loud if my son is watching too much telly because he knows the words to the Harpic loo cleaner advert, she says my son's future wife will be very grateful that he crossed the cleaning gender divide at such an early age.

Last is redhead Maggie, thirty-nine, the club treasurer. She has two girls with her husband Si and leads a chaotic life as a marketing whizz, being the family breadwinner, who is busy, busy, busy but always has time to text a mountain of advice, like 'Fuck them', 'Don't let the bastards grind you down' and 'Don't feel guilty about sticking on Nick Jnr – kids get enough stimulation and need to wind down, plus you watch telly when he goes to bed, so don't be such a hypocrite – either that or start learning Japanese.'

We all met at one of those God-awful church hall mum and baby groups where you get a cup of foul coffee made from three instant granules and a slice of white buttered toast for a quid. It was a Wednesday morning and each of us turned up alone – save for the babies – and we just happened to sit in the same corner. We swapped furtive, sympathetic smiles when one of the toddlers pulled a bag of Quavers out of my handbag and I loudly pretended the crisps were for me not my son just in case there was a Mother Superior within sniffing distance. Our cover blown by each of our children yelling 'Wavers!' at the tops of their voices, we started chatting, and by the end of the session we realised we'd met kindred spirits. We had all known another sense of self prior to motherhood and we had all found the shift incredibly bewildering, going from a woman who can go out to the cinema at a moment's notice to one who considers a trip to see a film as a huge luxury, because it involves the excellent forward-planning skills we had once used for projects at work and going on those early dates with our then-to-be husbands.

The strands that bind us are as follows: we are exhausted; we are in disbelief that anyone would dress up for the school run; we embrace fish fingers, chips and peas, pizza, spag bol and roasts because at least we know they'll get eaten; we only wear heels when we are without the kids; we never did baby yoga; we only really fancy sex once a month mid-cycle; we loathe the Nasty Childbirth Trust for telling frightened first-time pregnant women that if you take the drugs and don't breastfeed then you've failed; we do not get Brazilian waxes – in fact, we have hairy legs most of the time; we love our kids with every ounce of our body fat and would kill for them but there are times when motherhood really gets on our tits; and we daydream about a wild affair but in reality we would much rather go to sleep in a bed by ourselves.

We are, in essence, the antithesis of yummy, the anti-yummy, if you like.

Oh, and we've all got crêpey, saggy, finger-swallowing mummy tummies.

That's it for now. Next week I'll tell you all about the rules of membership. In the meantime, remember: perfection is pointless.

Week Three

The Mums Like Us Mummyfesto

Stella's kitchen

Hi, everyone. Glad you could make it here today in this pissing rain. No, I haven't been outside in it – I just have awful frizzy hair. The house is a total mess – I'm not going to apologise for it because that would undermine the Mums Like Us 'good enough' ethos. On this point, however, I'd like to add that a bit of tidiness is not a hanging offence. We'd all love to put our kids and husbands in straitjackets to preserve the orderliness after a clear-up. Unfortunately, it's probably against the law.

I remember the days when I could clean my old flat in five minutes and then settle down with a book or a magazine, knowing it would stay clean until I messed it up. Now the housework is a never-ending task, just like those bridges that need repainting as soon as they're finished, and the only time I get to read is before bed – and then I often fall asleep after one page.

Anyway, my shithole of a home is where you get to make your mind up. This week you decide: are you in, or are you out?

You'll know if you want to sign up for life by the end of today. Here is the Mums Like Us mummy-festo, our thirteen rules of membership, crafted by me and the girls over the months and months that we've sat in one another's houses, wondering when we'll get the elaborate joke that is marriage and motherhood.

First, appearance. It's lovely if you get to have a shower and do your hair, but scruff-bag is completely acceptable. Food on your clothes is fine by us, particularly if it's ketchup, ice cream or chocolate. Fruit and veg don't count.

Make-up is good for the soul, but don't worry if you only have one set of eyelashes coated in mascara thanks to a small person distracting you at the critical moment by pouring a packet of rice onto the fluffy rug that grabs onto food particles and never lets them go.

Footwear is mainly sensible and handbags must contain a size-too-small nappy, dried-up wet wipes, half a rotting banana from two weeks ago and a mobile for emergency child amusement purposes. Body hair will probably be visible – either your top exposes a hint of armpit shadow or your swimsuit (not bikini) line is threatening to apply for protected status with the Forestry Commission. Nail varnish, if you get the opportunity, can be chipped, and you're allowed rough patches of skin on your ankles and knees, inevitable after time spent on all fours searching for lost toys and administering cuddles to wailing prostrate infants.

Second, playgroups. If you've ever been to baby origami, baby pilates or baby gardening, you won't get in. However, if you regularly attend germ-infested soft-play sessions and your child wrecks the local library's rhyme-time when all the other kids are sitting very nicely, you get the thumbs up.

Third, nookie. Regular sex is only happening if you're trying for another. Recreational sex for pleasure is allowed but you can't recall when you last did it – although probably it was when the kids were on a sleepover. Beds are first and foremost for catching up on that precious sleep you crave every other second of the day.

Fourth, moaning. Anyone caught not having a whinge at their lack of sleep/irritating in-laws/bosses who tut when you nick off early for Calpol duties will be handed a life ban. Voicing life comparisons BC (Before Children) and AD (After Delivery) are compulsory. For example, you might say you used to spend hours packing your holiday suitcase, planning every night's clubbing outfit and taking fifteen pairs of emergency shoes. Now, for God's sake, you spend hours packing the kids' stuff in the holiday suitcase and then the morning you're about to leave – say three a.m.

– you remember you haven't sorted your own stuff so you grab whatever comes to hand from the drawers and you get there to find you have three jumpers for thirty-degrees-plus weather and a dress that fitted five years ago but now makes you look like you're expecting, which sets off a physical shiver because you've done your bit in providing this country's next generation of taxpayers.

Fifth, diet. You're allowed to be on one, just try not to lose so much weight you make us feel even more insecure. Please try to shed any inches around your bust rather than your thighs or stomach. Scoffing eclairs while complaining about your muffin top is positively encouraged.

As for your child's food intake, you will probably have puréed your way through the supermarket's organic vegetable counter in the first stage of weaning. It's nothing to be ashamed of; we've all had butternut squash spat back in our faces. From now on, just make sure your trolley contains chicken dippers, Mickey Mouse-shaped pizzas, crisps and Haribos.

Sixth, cultural awareness. Your grasp of world news must be pitiful, you must have no idea what is on telly after nine p.m., and when it comes to fashion, your wardrobe contains not on-trend trousers but chunky knits from George at Asda which you panic-bought while en route to the nappies. Your uniform is yesterday's jeans with a fresh top – if you're making an effort. Clothes must always be able to double as a tissue, flannel and muslin square. However, when it comes to knowing the identity of every CBeebies character ever conceived or what this year's must-have Christmas toy is, then you're on it.

Seventh, breastfeeding. Great, fine, do it. But do not be a hardliner – lots of women don't want to do it or can't do it, and if that's the case, leave it up to them. Anyone caught spouting any Nasty Childbirth Trust nonsense about non-breastfeeders being selfish or breastfeeding being the only way to ensure your child can join Mensa at the age of eighteen months will be instantly sent home without their usual two doughnuts. Please note, this also applies to snarky comments from bottle-feeders who slag off walking, talking kids on the boob. Mammaries are a mum's business, nobody else's.

Eighth, your mum status. Whether you fit the description of a stay-at-home mum or a working one, members will agree that both terms are ridiculous. We all work hard, be that in an office or at home, often both. Whatever reasons you have for how you decide to live your life are valid: you need to work for your sanity, you choose to stay at home to be there for your kids, you have to work to afford the mortgage, you wish you could go to work but there just aren't the hours out there for you. Whatever. Mums are in this together – snarkiness reduces us to cartoon caricatures of career bitch on one side versus housewife on the other. And inevitably, both parties fail at motherhood – the working mum is deemed to be selfish and neglectful while the stay-at-home mum is smug and lazy. The truth is, we'll be see-sawing from one end of the scale to the other throughout our lives, so get over it.

Ninth, friendships. Post-baby, your pals must be divided into those who have kids and those who don't. Those who have them will suddenly be your best mates, while the thoughtless childless friends who have known you since school will be relegated to pests. I mean, who on earth phones after seven p.m.? Don't they know we're midway through bath, book and bed? And do we look as though we're interested in your tales of pulling that married bloke from sales? Oh, he's got an eleven-month-old baby daughter? You don't happen to know if she's walking yet, do you?

Tenth, communicating with your partner. Membership is guaranteed if you've (a) sobbed uncontrollably when hubby asks you to show him how the pushchair collapses; (b) laughed hysterically when that idiot you married politely enquires if sexual relations can resume now the baby is nearly two; or (c) contemplated divorce but come to your senses when you realise you'd have to do everything, even the minuscule amount of housework/shopping he does, if you gave him his marching orders. Matt and I always try to reserve a night each week so that we can chat about what's happening in our lives. It usually means we sit and watch a film in total silence over a Chinese. But that's fine, we're both too tired to talk anyway. And to be honest, if we did chat we'd probably have a row. For example, I would resentfully compare him to my dad, who, despite not doing much round the house because that was what men were like thirty-odd years ago, still played with me and my sister far more than Matt does, because laptops and Sky Sports hadn't been invented, so when we had him, he was completely focused on us and gave us all of his attention. He was also excellent at DIY and would have a go at fixing stuff even if he didn't know how. Not like today's pathetic excuses for fathers.

Eleventh, exercise. Only ever to be taken in the evenings so you get out of the witching hour. Membership of gyms, hardcore circuit sessions and trendy dancercise classes should be avoided because you'll be the wobbliest there. Instead we recommend a little bit of jogging in tracksuit bottoms round the block, boot camp club where you can hide at the back but chicken out if it's too cold, and yoga in a draughty community hall with dust bunnies and dirty flooring, because it's basically bendy sleeping.

Twelfth, spreading the gospel. You must swear to tell every woman pregnant with their first child that labour is utterly hideous but it will pale into insignificance compared to the sleep deprivation that follows;

super-duper trendy buggies may look nice but they don't stop you ploughing through dog poo in the park and wheeling it all over the hall carpet; mothers-in-law may be a pain but without them you'd never get dinner made; weeping over your child starting school is completely normal for a day or so, but really, their growing independence is to be embraced, otherwise you'll be wiping bottoms, spoonfeeding and tucking in till they're fifteen, when your kids will have even more reason to hate you.

And finally, rule number thirteen. Whatever is mentioned at a meeting or a gathering of our members is confidential so that we can speak freely without fear of retribution. Any breach will result in disciplinary proceedings.

OK, everyone, I'm not going to ask you all to sign up here and now. You've got a week to think about it. If you decide you do want to be a perfect parent, then that is completely fine, and I wish you well.

For those who do not aspire to spreadsheet your children's extra-curricular activities, hoover daily, host a seven-course dinner party for your husband's best client, boast to others about how bright your child is or resemble Gwyneth bloody Paltrow, Claudia effing Schiffer and Elle blimming McPherson, then I'll see you here next week at the different time of seven p.m. – so you get out of the final insult of the day that is bedtime – for the initiation ceremony.

We'll be celebrating, so bring a bottle. Actually,

make that two bottles, because I'm always reading about new studies that show desperate mothers binge-drink every night. We have a reputation to maintain.

Dads United

Matt's office

Email to: davidsmith70@hotmail.com
Subject: Dad
Date: 21 February, 08:16

All right, Dave?

Mum's been trying to get hold of you – you gone AWOL? She says can you remember to call Dad because he's going in for that hernia op, and even though it will obviously be a pained conversation about his groin area, apparently he will appreciate it.

And I'm sure he'd love to hear about your new bird. Spare him the details, though, it might excite him too much. How did you get to pull a model? I bet the conversation is riveting. You are such a jammy git – I still haven't forgiven you for nicking That Woman off me.

Do you remember? Bet you don't, you've had so many birds. I'd spent ages charming her, being sensitive and understanding and funny, we'd just started going out, then you came along to that indie club night where I was DJing. (By the way, did you know that club is now a café frequented on Saturdays by dads with baby carriers? Dreadful place.)

I'll never forget it. I looked across the dance floor and saw you and her not only noshing each other's faces off but sneaking off before the end of my set! I was gutted. Remember I walloped you one on the nose and Mum went mad? Then, unbelievably, after you'd shagged her, you dumped her. I'd never even got past the snogging stage! She tried to get back with me, but by then I was heartbroken. And it would've been weird to 'go there' after you.

Funny thing is, she's also in IT now, runs a big company, so we sometimes nod at one another at conferences and stuff. Still sexy. Not that I fancy her. Well, I do, a bit. In an ironic, new man kind of way.

Still, if you hadn't done that, I'd never have ended up with Stella. So I've got you to thank. Or hold responsible, depending on how you look at it.

Anyway, all fine here, although I've been working my balls off, twelve-hour days on this pitch to a potential client, so hardly seen Stella and the little one.

My days go like this: sleep, shit, work, conversation about shit, sleep, shit, work, etc. Stella laughs when I ask about the little one's bowel movements – she thinks I'm trying too hard to be a cool dad. But it's my way of knowing what's going on – if his bum is up the junction then something's wrong. Like father, like son. So she's all sarky and explains in graphic detail about how many lumps he's had, but I actually want to know. It means I'm still in the loop, not just the bloke that snores. You're well out of it, mate.

Mums just love being the martyr – they're all 'my life has changed and yours hasn't' and when I ask her about what they've been up to, Stella just says 'the usual', as if I'd find it boring, but I don't. Why do mums think they've got a monopoly on parenthood?

Every time there's one of her fishwife meetings and I go past the door if I'm working from home and they see me, all their hooting and shouting stops and I just want to tell them: 'Look, I was at the birth, I saw my wife go through hell, I cut the cord, I hardly slept either, I cooked every night for months to make sure she had enough strength to get through the early days, as well as building a career, I sleep on his floor when he's full of a cold, I sob at the thought of someone bullying my son at school and at the prospect of how shit he'll feel when he's dumped for the first time – no, I don't want a bloody medal, I just want you to know us dads go through it too.'

Wouldn't dare say that, obviously.

I have no idea why I'm telling you all this – the closest you've ever come to a meaningful relationship is with your iPad.

By the way, scored a goal at football training the

other night just like Maradona's 1986 goal against England. I went from inside my own half, through five players plus the goalie to crack it low in the net. I was buried under a pile-on of fat teammates. It was brilliant.

Don't forget Dad.

Matt

Week Four

The Initiation Ceremony

Stella's kitchen

Oh my God, what a turnout! I didn't expect so many of you to come back, and wow, there are loads of new mums who've come along for the first time too . . . This is brilliant. It'll be a bit of a squash, but if you dump all your stuff in the hall, I'll get the garden chairs in. We can just take it in turns for a seat.

The bottle opener is over there next to the wine glasses on the side. I've done a few nibbles – gone a bit upmarket this week with Tesco Finest, but nothing home-made, obviously. Don't worry, there are no Scotch eggs – my husband finished them off in a final purge. He's captain of a crappy football team of dads, so he's on a health kick, and he thinks he's got to set an example for the lads. It's like they're trying to convince us they don't just play football to go for a few pints afterwards.

And sorry about the smell; he made a chilli last night for the team, which they're going to have

31

tomorrow after training – he insists it's always better when it's been festering in a stinking pan on top of the hob for two days. The landlord of the pub has agreed to reheat it because they hire a room off him for their so-called post-training analysis. He must have to get it fumigated after they've been in there.

By the way, I have no idea why I'm whispering. Habit, I suppose, at this time of night. The house is ours – my son's in bed and my husband will be late from work and he'll come straight in and hide under the bed until we've finished, because, frankly, he's terrified of big groups of women.

I still can't believe there are so many of us! There are even mums from our neighbouring counties – give me a wave, there you are, thanks so much for coming all this way! They emailed in the week to get directions and I had to double-check they weren't taking the piss.

Sorry to go on, but I'm gobsmacked. As you'll have guessed, I've never been one of those popular people – I was the quiet, dull, unremarkable, bushy-eyebrowed, mousey-haired, late-developing boring one at school who was terrified to speak in class because I was (a) flat-chested when all the other girls were in lacy bras and (b) I thought everyone would laugh at me. At university, I hid away, watching all the mad and crazy and irritating extroverts with horror. I've spent my entire life being square and unremarkable, watching the 'in crowd' with morbid fascination. So it's amazing to have found a bunch of like-minded souls.

I was also fearing the worst because someone who came last week, that really skinny dietician, saw me in the high street the other day and she actually made the effort to cross the road to tell me the club was a pathetic celebration of frozen food and Fruit Shoots and filthy clothes. I couldn't have put it better myself. I'm not surprised – I knew she wasn't one of us when she started going on about her and her husband taking their nine-month-old on a windsurfing holiday to Morocco, where the baby not only ate every scrap of tagine put in front of him but also learnt to speak French by the end of the two weeks.

She isn't joining, obviously.

Anyway, not to worry. As I said, this club isn't about slagging off others. It's about refusing to do the self-loathing thing when we haven't been for a run for two years, when we stuff the *Mister Maker* art comic down the back of the sofa if we can't face crafts or hide from the kids between tea and bed, actively choosing to clear out the bathroom cupboard, because we can't take any more bloody role play.

So, tonight I'll collect all of your email addresses and mobile numbers and then circulate them to all of you so you can get in touch with each other. Feel free to contact me if you can't make it one week, if you want to suggest a topic to cover or have any queries, whatever.

OK, before we get shitfaced, we'll quickly do the initiation thingy.

Fill your glasses, everyone, raise them to the ceiling and repeat after me:

'I do swear – a lot – that I will be faithful and bear true allegiance to Mums Like Us, her members and successors, according to the rules.

'I promise not to self-flagellate when I:

1. serve up oven chips three times in one week;
2. groan at the thought of the school holidays;
3. write my own kids' thank you letters with my left hand;
4. stick the same socks on my children's feet two days in a row because the washing is still in the machine;
5. prefer to watch some reality show shite with a bar of chocolate rather than go to Zumba;
6. take the kids to Pizza Hut if I can't be bothered to cook;
7. tell my husband when I'm not in the mood rather than make up some crap excuse;
8. arrive at and leave work exactly according to my working hours;
9. open the wine before six p.m.; and
10. stick a DVD on if the kids are still complaining of being bored after we've played hide and seek, got out the Playdoh and I've been the tickle monster and I'm desperate for a break.

'Finally, I pledge I will not break our code of secrecy regarding confidential matters.'

That's it! We're all sworn in! Let me just explain a few things about tonight now.

Anyone who fancies a crafty fag is very welcome to go out the back. There's a brolly by the door, and watch out for cat poo in the garden because she's getting a bit old and doesn't always make it to the borders. I've provided chewing gum if you've told your husband you never, ever, absolutely no way would ever smoke ever again.

Any spillages, don't worry. Frankly, there's nothing that hasn't been on this kitchen floor. Tears are fine, too. If you're having a meltdown, feel free to drink too much and weep huge, snotty sobs of despair at the injustice of it all – I've put Tesco Value eye-make-up remover wipes in the loo if you want to mop up the mascara from your chin.

Confessions of any kind are also welcome. For example, Lucy told me that if her son wakes up too early she'll put CBeebies on downstairs and give her son some milk and toast then go back to bed. Maggie lies to her kids about how many Easter eggs they get so she can eat a couple behind their backs. And get this, Alex actually has a 'like it or lump it' eating policy, so if they don't like what she dishes up, they go hungry. How amazing is that?

As for me, I admit I once put Ken Bruce on at full volume so my son couldn't hear me puking my guts up after a night out. Oh, and I am also prone to an afternoon nap when he's in pre-school.

Before you go, make sure you all have a mug of builder's tea, three paracetamol, a packet of crisps and two rounds of toast so your head doesn't hurt too much in the morning.

I'd really appreciate it if you could dump your paper plates and bottles in the recycling – I'll leave the dishwasher open so you can stick your glasses in at the end of the session. If anyone pukes, there's a bottle of bleach by the toilet for a quick rinse round (for the loo – remember, there's chewie for you). And remember, what goes on in here, stays in here; this is your safe haven and your umbrella to protect you from the downpour of drudgery.

Next week's meeting, when we'll revert to our usual daylight-hours slot to be decided by consensus over email, will be about surviving mum-upmanship.

We'll tell you how to bat off undermining asides from that breed of woman who see child-rearing as a competition.

Cheers, and flabby bottoms up!

Dads United

www.dadsunited.co.uk

CAPTAIN'S BLOG

See what I did there? Captain's log/blog, geddit?

Right, lads, seeing as I'm an IT geek, I thought I'd set up a website so we don't have to spoil pints after football training with shop talk.

Bit pissed, been on the wine at home. Stells was pouring in a hair-of-the-dog way because she got wrecked last night with her club.

I crept in at half ten after working late and went straight upstairs, and you should've heard them. They were cackling, crying, shouting, smoking in the back garden, even puking in the loo. Stella came to bed completely out of it with a stripe of guacamole on her arm – the bloody guacamole I'd made to go with a chilli I'd done for post-training, but they scoffed the lot. And when I went to turn over she said, 'Don't even think about it.' As if! I told her wine breath and avocado bodypaint did nothing for me.

37

This morning the house was a total tip. Stella says I'm untidy, but Jesus Christ, those women were like a herd of toddlers; the floor was covered in missed mouthfuls of food and wine and there were sticky blobs everywhere.

I didn't say anything to Stella because she was hideously hungover. She emerged from her stinking swamp just after I'd got our son up, tidied everything and was about to leave for work. I'll save it up as a 'get out of jail free' card for another time when I'm in the shit for something. That makes it sound like she's a monster, which she is, obviously, but – and I know I'm pissed now – but I love her being a moody cow. She is the most amazing woman I've ever met. A brilliant mum, too, although she thinks she's useless, but you should see the way she is with our son – totally devoted and will give up her last mouthful of chocolate for him (not for me, but that's the way it should be). We met years back at a party; she was gorgeous, all long blonde hair and laughing blue eyes, she loved the Smiths like me, and she was funny and feisty. But at that time she was knocking around with some nobody, who, get this, later tried to win her back when we'd started going out. I'd just dumped someone else after she'd shagged my brother; he was always much better-looking and more charismatic than me, so it wasn't that unexpected. Anyway, I was just enjoying the single life and didn't want anything serious.

But a year later, I heard she was single and so I emailed her to ask if she fancied going to a pub quiz together at the Golden Lion – you know, that brilliant boozer in town. The pub we used to live near before we went mental about schools and had to move or we'd ruin our son's entire life. It sounds really dull, doing a pub quiz, but when we'd first met at that party, I'd asked her to tell me something really boring about herself, because I've always hated those fake 'small talk' situations, when people go on about how wild and crazy they are.

She'd admitted she liked crosswords, jigsaws, Sudoku, even building Ikea furniture, and I thought she'd enjoy the quiz even if she didn't fancy me. But we clicked, our team, 'Mine's A Stella', came first and we were inseparable. When she said she wanted a baby, I was over the moon; I felt like the luckiest man on earth. I still do – looking at her and our son together, cuddled up on the sofa, just makes me want to cry. Fatherhood has completed me, completed us. Whenever I tell her that she says, 'Oh, that's good because the lawn needs mowing.' That's her all over. But that's why I love her, she makes me laugh.

It's easy for me to say this because I'm not as involved as she is, being the mum, but it feels like we're in it together, on the same team. A bit like Liverpool in the early Eighties: I'm Kenny, obviously, she can be Rushie, without the 'tache. Oh Kenny, King Kenny . . . I used to parade around the back garden in my Liverpool kit, making my mum call me Kenny, and I'd hold up a plastic cup, some naff trophy I'd got at school or something, and pretend I was at Anfield.

Sorry, drifted off there. Seriously, before I became a dad I could hold my drink, now Stella can outdo me quite easily. And I get the worst verbal gushy diarrhoea. As you can tell.

Right, the point of this was to tell you that next week I'm away on business in the Midlands, so training is cancelled.

Cheers,

Matt

Week Five

How to Survive Mum-upmanship

Stella's bed

Email to: mlumembers@yahoogroups.co.uk
Subject: Meeting
Date: 1 March, 21:06

Dear members,

I'm afraid I've had to cancel this week's meeting because I've got loads of work on and not enough hours to do it.

On top of that, Matt is away for the week – no idea where he's gone. In the old days I'd have known his hotel room number, sent him millions of 'missing you' texts and spoken to him five times a day. Not now, though – too exhausted, but he's fine with it. He knows I trust him, and there's always so much to do when he's away. And, frankly, I don't want to hear if he's sick of yet another five-course meal.

His absence means I have no time off from running

the house (plus side: no snoring, no enormous T-shirts to wash and occupy every radiator for a fortnight while they dry, no Sky Sports and no post-Dads United drinking when he comes in pissed and deliberately makes a noise getting into bed so I wake up and he can tell me in this really excited voice about some goal he's scored).

Obviously I have factored in me-time: 'Loose Women', hot chocolate breaks, ringing my sister to discuss the irritating practice of dads calling it 'babysitting' when they're in charge, and staring out the window at the garden which is slowly coming back to life, wondering how I have become this lump of nothing, this married single mum, this flattened piece of beige.

God, it seems unbelievable, but there was a brief moment in my mid-twenties when I seemed to have cast off the shackles of my inferiority complex because I had discovered the joys of hair bleach. I was doing well at work, I had a small but tight circle of brilliant friends and I had some self-esteem. I also went jogging three times a week, bought fuck-me shoes, and I was always on the piss or eating out and really loving life. Back then, I never knew what responsibility was; I mean, no one was depending on me to keep them alive. Now I'm lucky if I go to the hairdresser once every six months. Catching up with my mates consists of liking their Facebook statuses and I only ever go out during the day.

I'm sure you understand.

Seeing we're at such a crucial point in our club's fledgling history, I daren't miss a week, so instead of getting you all over here, I thought I'd email you with the club guide to mum-upmanship – the peculiar practice of getting one up on the sisterhood.

To explain what I mean, here's an example. When I was pregnant, I went to Nasty Childbirth Trust classes and the course leader announced to everyone that she had popped out her three kids without a puff of gas and air. At home. By herself. And she dished up her placenta for dinner.

I was awestruck at the time and believed my own journey towards motherhood would be as easy. But then twenty-two hours of hell ensued. I had gas and air, then pethidine, which felt like I was off my tits in a tequila way. Then I asked the midwife for an epidural and she told me I wasn't anywhere near established labour. So I waited and waited and waited until my body was ready and then I shouted, 'Where the fuck is the anaesthetist?' and suddenly he appeared. The loveliest vision of manhood I'd ever seen because he was about to take the pain away. I didn't care he could see my veiny nawks which were the size of watermelons, and I didn't care that my nethers were on public display. All I wanted was for the torture to stop. After an episiotomy, my beautiful son was delivered by forceps (salad servers still give me the fear) but I struggled with breastfeeding, hit the baby bottle after three weeks and two days and sobbed and sobbed and sobbed, feeling such a failure.

A month later, the Nasty Childbirth Trust group met up again, with the beaming course leader asking us each to tell our stories. Out of twelve of us, just two had had no pain relief; we were an assembled rabble of painful fannies and C-section scars, sharing haunted looks. The leader congratulated the two who had straightforward births and pitied the rest of us. But then she added spitefully, 'It's a pity none of you experienced the joy of a home birth – maybe next time, eh?'

Hang on a minute, I thought, this isn't a competition; you aren't a better mother because of the way you did it. I put it down to my hormones, which were yo-yoing between deliriously happy and breakdown tragedy.

Then when I started going to mother-and-baby groups, I encountered more women like her.

Those who claimed their babies were sleeping through after six days – mine wasn't. God, what's wrong with him, what's wrong with me? He obviously hates me.

Those who were returning to work at six months because they felt ready – I'd gone freelance (having calculated the cost of childcare would've left me with £17 a week) but I was so sleep-deprived I panicked at the thought of stringing a sentence together. I could barely write a shopping list.

And those who told me they had already enrolled

44

their child at the local primary because places are so hard to get – Oh Christ, I haven't and my son is going to grow up an idiot, I'm such a SHIT mum.

It reminded me of school, when all the cool girls sniggered at me and my flat-chested Clarks shoe-wearing friends. They were all shaved legs, highlights and rebellious short skirts. We were all boyish and desperately conscientious, frightened by their know-it-all tales of snogging the boys from the Lower Sixth. We were so innocent, still in knee-high socks, dreaming over some pop star and being content to go home to watch 'Grange Hill' rather than hang out until six p.m. in the park with some bum-fluffed adolescents.

Motherhood took me back in time to that same feeling of awkward inadequacy.

Slowly, I began to realise what these mums were up to – bigging themselves up at my expense. I was bedraggled and inept at motherhood, freaking out at the prospect of having to take my son somewhere in the car – 'What if he poos on the way?' – and mentally rehearsing putting the pram in and out of the boot.

These other mums, meanwhile, were catching planes to far-flung destinations with their babe in arms whereas I was quaking over the petrol station dilemma: should I leave him in the car when I go to pay or should I take him with me and risk waking him up?

Worse, I admitted it to these other mums.

They could have sympathised with me, but no, they piped up with something designed to make me feel worse. If I confessed to wanting to lock myself in the loo after yet another hour-long screaming-baby session, they would stare at me Bambi-like and mouth: 'I can honestly say I've never felt that.'

I thought as first-time mums we were all in the same boat. I was wrong.

How you deal with these women is to cut off all ties with them. Avoid their coffee shops, take the long route to the park rather than walk down their street. Or hide behind a post box if you see them coming (they usually travel in packs with very trendy buggies).

If you have the misfortune to be in a corner and they spot you, there is only one way to emerge with your pride intact.

'Where have you been? We haven't seen you for ages,' they'll say.

Tell them casually, 'Lovely to see you. I've been away at an Indonesian yoga detox mother-and-baby sanctuary where we had to forage for food while carrying our children in slings on our backs.'

When push comes to shove, mum-upmanship is the only language that type of woman understands.

There is a footnote to the above, however: we do support one form of competitiveness here, and that is trying to outdo each other with tales of awful parenting.

For example, when Alex says she ditches the kids at the leisure centre crèche and then goes for a coffee in the café rather than a swim, Mags responds, 'That's nothing – I put mine in the Ikea crèche and then go and stuff my face with two hot dogs before insisting they have something healthy at home.'

Or if I admit that I once smacked my son because I lost it when he ran out of the park, even though he got over it two seconds later, Lucy will say, 'So what? I felt so awful after I walloped my youngest for some misdemeanour which I can't even remember, so it can't have merited a whack in the first place, I went out and bought him some Lego out of sheer shame and guilt.'

Anyway, hope this has all been useful. Next week, we'll talk routine versus laissez-faire parenting – which way do you do it?

Must dash. I've been commissioned to do a funny feature for the *Daily Mail* entitled 'Embrace Your Mummy Tummy'. It's an open letter to mums all over the country inviting them to join our good enough revolution. I'm nearly done but I need to finish it tonight, because tomorrow is a ball-breaker with the dentist and shopping and stuff.

Who knows, the piece might get us a few extra members?

Your chairwoman,

Stella

Dads United

Matt's hotel room

Email to: dadsutd@yahoogroups.co.uk
Subject: Meeting
Date: 1 March, 21:06

Dear team,

So here I am in a faceless hotel in the Midlands, being bored to tears at this conference by IT geeks who only seem capable of conversation if it includes letters and numbers, as in 'Have you seen the new 344az software model of the such-and-such?'

How the fuck did I end up in this job? At times like this it feels like a life sentence with Metal Mickey.

Obviously, I realise I'm lucky to have a job in this climate, and as a dad, I can think of nothing more horrifying than redundancy. There are perks: good money, and I get to be a grown-up ten-year-old with a technology-induced stiffy. It's just that the people in this industry are so dull.

That's why I've sneaked upstairs from yet another dinner to send you the attached schedule of times and dates I've booked for training at the leisure centre; my laptop has more personality than Colin from Network Solutions Ltd in Tamworth.

If only Stella could see me sitting up on my floral quilted bed in a slightly damp room overlooking a noisy main road – she thinks I'm out having a laugh and a banter, enjoying posh meals and fine wines. The initial bit of any business trip is good, I'll admit – a bit of breathing space, a swim and a fry-up – but for the majority of the time, it's like being Alan Partridge. Awkward smiles in the lift, waking up in the night wondering where I am and sleepwalking to the bathroom looking for my son. Once I actually wandered out of my room and down the corridor in just my boxers (inside out as they were on the second day of usage) and I came to when the door slammed shut. I had to go to reception to ask for a key to get back in. Humiliating, I can tell you.

Being a dad, you want to provide for your family. I know women are our equals these days, and thank God, otherwise us men would have even more of a panic about job security, but I for one feel the pressure of wanting to bring home the bread, doing well for us and giving our son the best we can afford. But then when we get home we get a bollocking about not taking some junk down the tip within five minutes of being ordered to do it. If I had any ego at all I'd be brought back down to earth with a bump every time I stepped back in the house. Stella doesn't even know where I am half the time. I must admit, it's hard sometimes to accept I'm below the cat in the importance rankings. Sometimes it would be nice to chat about what I've been up to when I get back, but she glazes over and yawns and then walks out the room to do something, saying, 'I am listening, I've just got to put the washing in the airing cupboard.'

What I'm saying is, it's a hard transition to make, from respected career man to the bloke 'who doesn't do any bloody housework'. Though there are men out there who seem to be able to do it effortlessly – they breeze in, having cycled twenty miles home from work, put the kids to bed, make dinner and then seduce their wives with a waft of their Alpha Male armpits. I met a few of those types at our antenatal classes. We did the Nasty Childbirth Trust classes that every middle-class couple does, thinking, we'll make new friends! We'll share lazy Sunday afternoons in the park with a Jamie Oliver-inspired picnic! And we'll be in it together forever!' Except that just didn't happen. The dads on our course were grinning buffoons with a sideline in superiority complexes.

In the car park, they bleeped their huge 4x4s and strutted into the building in designer sunglasses and trendy shirts tucked into their trendy jeans while I locked up the rusting Honda saloon wearing a band T-shirt (the Sex Pistols, I remember), a pair of threadbare cords and shades held together with Sellotape.

They were all firm handshakes, white teeth and healthy physiques, introducing themselves as recruitment consultants and lawyers. When it came to group discussions about birth and babies, they seemed to know everything about it, announcing they'd discussed the birth plans with their wives and were 100 per cent behind their 'no pain relief' status. Stella announced that hers said 'every drug going, please' and I pissed myself laughing – but no one else did.

It was hideous. These couples were just not like us. They had it all planned, nurseries set up (ours was the spare room and we had the cot still in a box); parents were banned from visiting because they wanted to bond exclusively with the baby (Stella's mum insisted on moving in with us for a week to make sure we remembered to eat and do the washing and stuff) and they talked about their buggies as though they were discussing cars – rather apt, as their pushchairs probably cost the same as our shed-on-wheels.

If I hadn't met you lot, I reckon I would've found becoming a dad even more overwhelming, particularly that shift from relatively carefree husband to responsible family man.

I remember one night when my son was barely eighteen months and he fell down the stairs – just a couple of them, but he started yelling and I thought, that's it, I've killed him. Stella was out on a job. I tried to ring her but her phone was switched off because she was doing an interview and so I automatically rang the lads. God, I was sobbing down the phone while my son was howling. Danno rushed round to help, Si kept trying Stella and Stuey gave me the best piece of advice ever – as long as they're bawling, they're fine.

Each of them saw me ride the rollercoaster, crying and losing it and everything, and then when Stella got in, they took me for a pint and we had a heart-to-heart. Mostly about fatherhood but also about football, cricket, work and whether we should go for a curry or get a kebab on the way home. And they understood that it had to be a kebab because I wanted to get back as soon as. Those other bastards would definitely have made me go to a poncey coffee house.

But you lot, well, you're gents, and I'm proud to be on your side.

Right, got to go. I've just had a call from downstairs – turns out that old mate of mine is here and she wants to know if I fancy a nightcap. It would be rude not to, eh?

Cheers,

Matt

Week Six

Routine Versus Baby-led Parenting
Stella's kitchen

Hi, girls, come in! So lovely to see you all – it feels ages since we last met. Mind the wellies and waterproofs – I put them there to dry three days ago after my sister and I forced our kids to go for a healthy walk in the drizzle and . . . well, they're still there.

Yeah, Matt's back. I made sure I got three lie-ins in a row to compensate for him staying in luxury for a week. He tried to make out he'd been working hard, putting in twelve-hour days, talking shop non-stop. Well, guess what, I was on duty twenty-four/seven and I didn't get my meals made for me, my dishes magically cleared away, my bed turned down or an ironing service.

I felt a bit sorry for him, though, when I gave him a kiss hello and then announced he was going to be in charge for the next couple of days because I needed a rest. Love him. It really didn't bother him – if that was me I'd have gone mad. But then I was still doing all the meals and the tidying up, I just needed some head space.

Christ, before our son came along we would've jumped into bed after any absence; it was like that from the moment we got together. Even though I had read all the mags which said 'never sleep with a man on the first date', I did and it felt right.

We had talked for hours, laughing our heads off, flushed with that feeling of 'oh God, me too, I think the same'. And it was two a.m. and we'd both admitted we were fed up with meaningless relationships, we loved the Smiths, we'd both grown up in suburban boxes and fucking hated the conservatory aspiration of our parents, and we'd realised that we didn't have any award-winning talent which would turn us rich and famous.

Besides, we did know each other, having met at a party a year beforehand. I was loosely with someone at the time; he'd just dumped someone, so he says. So that counts as 'waiting' in my book! Anyway, we just ended up in bed, having brilliant sex.

Now all I can think of is wanting to curl up alone.

Anyway, before I go into one, let's get down to business and talk about parenting methods. There are so many books out there telling mums what to do and how to do it, it's really confusing.

Take me and Alex, who went by the routine

mantra. We turned to *The Baby Whisperer*, *Contented Little Baby Book* and *Do As I Say Or Else, You Idiot Parent* because we didn't have a clue what we were doing. We'd had careers that involved working to deadlines, meeting targets and managing people who followed orders. So we approached motherhood as if it was a project and plumped for the routine method because it would give us a – wanky word alert – framework.

Controlled crying (ours), timed feeds, weaning schedules, consistent nap times, the naughty step; the baby instruction manual was going to turn us into supermums and answer every question we had.

Except it didn't. It turned us into raging control freaks, fuelling our anxiety and relegating our instincts to somewhere below the to-do list of fixing the squeaky cupboard door and writing thank you notes for the mountain of presents we received post-partum.

For instance, if the book said nap time, I'd put my son to bed even though he was wide awake and wonder why he was screaming his head off. If the book said give three days of puréed pear to test his tolerance and we only had bananas, I'd shout at Matt: 'Go and get some bloody pears from somewhere, anywhere, I don't care, but they must be organic, perfectly shaped and a particular shade of green or he is going to die.'

Matt and I would only take the baby out in the car

if it was a designated sleeping slot – all hell would break loose if our son fell asleep when he bloody well wasn't supposed to.

I would look with envy at Mags and Lucy, who followed the baby-led route of feeding on demand, weaning according to what they had in the cupboard, random naps and all that.

But then they told me that wasn't a bed of roses either.

Unsure of when their babies would want a feed, they would go out and have the misfortune to start spurting milk over people in the post office as their babies started wailing for milk NOW. They would begin a desperate quest for somewhere to derobe – usually a manky greasy spoon or a freezing park bench – and then panic, frantically patting their boobs, because they couldn't remember which breast they fed from last time.

Naps struck at the most ridiculous of times, usually around about four p.m. – which spells utter catastrophe because they wake up horribly grumpy and hungry and then can't sleep until midnight.

It took us a while, but eventually we came to the same conclusion: whatever method you choose to follow, your child will do the opposite. Why? Because it has a will, a mind and a personality of its own which, combined with an energy level way beyond yours, means you may be the adult but they are ultimately in charge.

The little devils are probably gurgling about it when they're at playgroup or nursery or with Granny. 'You'll never guess what, my idiot mum only shoves a bottle in when I'm asleep because she's read some book about dream feeds – for God's sake, how stupid can you get? And she wonders why I wake up at five a.m. every morning but refuse to feed – I've got to get my own back somehow.'

'Silly cow. Mine reckons I'll be ready for my own room soon. What a cheek! It's as if they're bored of me now. To teach them a lesson, I've started waiting until they're just about to drop off and then I make these horrible choking noises to give them a fright. I reckon I'll be in there for a few more months yet.'

If any of you are feeling fretful because your chosen method of baby-raising isn't quite going to plan, then take heart – eventually you'll get into the groove and find your own pattern. It's hard to believe, but you will learn what makes them tick and what bribes work best. There's also a lot to be said for thinking: 'Oh, for goodness' sake, they are loved, warm, dry and full, so stop bloody worrying.'

OK, so that's this week's topic covered.

The other thing I wanted to raise was the amazing response we had from the *Daily Mail* piece. I had hundreds of enquiries from women all around the country wanting to sign up, even though they can't physically get to the meeting. The online comments beneath the feature were incredibly positive, too – there were so many, I lost count at 942!

Alex, our secretary, who does the minutes and is working on a newsletter for us, has suggested we draw up a membership document that mums can sign and return to us so they can join in spirit. What do you think?

Great, you all agree. Alex will respond to the enquiries and sort out all the paperwork.

One last thing: you'll never guess what, but hilariously, we've been invited onto *This Morning* to talk about the club. YES! With Phil and Holly! A researcher rang me to ask if I'd go on in a couple of days. I told them I certainly wasn't going to do it without asking you all, and we may decide to nominate another member – just because I'm chairwoman doesn't mean it has to be me. She said that was fine and if whoever appeared couldn't get childcare they could take their kids with them.

What do you reckon? Would anyone like to do it?

No? Oh. Really? Oh God, that means I have to, then. We can't exactly turn down the best daytime programme on telly, can we?

I'd prefer not to, I'll be a bundle of nerves, but I suppose it could be good for the club's profile – and just think of all the mums out there who might identify with our Good Enough message. I feel sick already. What if I go blank? What am I going to wear? Anyone got anything not stained that I can borrow?

Right, I'll get back to them and tell them I'll do it.

Wish me luck! It's rather apt that next week's topic is How to Deal with a Crisis.

See you then, lovelies.

Dads United

The Feathers

Lads. LADS! Before you start getting pissed, can I just have a quick post-training word to cover some Dads United business?

The skipper of another team of dads in the area has contacted me asking for a match. They're called Fit Fathers and they heard about us through the pub. Are you up for it?

OK, how does a week night sound? Not when there's football on the telly, of course. Weekends are off for us because Stella insists on family time, by which she means I take the little one off to the park and she has a nap.

So, looks like it'll be a Friday. Nice one, I'll arrange it.

Fuck, we need to shift some weight, I know I do. A week in that hotel and I must've put on a stone.

By the way, thanks for all those sniggering emails after I said I was going for a nightcap with a 'she' in the hotel. You lot are a load of saddos to get excited about a man having a drink with a woman who's not his wife. Grow up. Admittedly, she was an ex, the one I dumped after she snogged my brother. Yes, I know what you're thinking, but that was years ago and it was just a friendly drink. I have no feelings for her whatsoever. We just talked about business. No, she isn't married. What's that got to do with it? Lads! Calm down! I can't help it if I've got sex appeal.

We happen to be in the same business, that's all. We share a passion for computers. She's done really well for herself – she's got her own company – and I'm a nobody who needs to develop some contacts because I will die a long slow death if I stay where I am forever. She might have an opening for me. Oh God, will you stop it with all the fnar-fnars?

We didn't even mention the past. Seriously, it was all industry talk, and we had a right laugh. She told me to keep in touch and she'd look out for work for me. The drinks were on her, anyway, can't turn that down. I haven't mentioned it to Stella, so keep shtum. I don't want her to know I'm desperate to leave my job or she'll panic – she's got enough on her plate as it is.

Right, who fancies getting the captain a pint?

Week Seven

How to Deal with a Crisis

Stella's kitchen

Oh. God. Please don't tell me you watched 'This Morning'.

By the looks on your faces, I can tell you did. Awful, wasn't it? Honestly, I've never been so humiliated in my life. Actually, I have – when the midwife asked to see my stitches a week after I'd had my son. It was the first time in my life I'd taken my pants off in front of a near-stranger without the aid of alcohol or Barry White on the stereo.

Oh, and there was also the time at work when my boss called me in after IT alerted him to the fact that I'd been sending pervy emails to this twat I was kind of seeing, and every time I walked past the techie blokes, they would make orgasmic noises and ask me if I wanted any help 'turning on' my computer, ha bloody ha.

Anyway, I'm devastated I brought shame on the

club by losing my temper, trying to run off the set and swearing on live telly. I promise you, I was completely together in the green room – they had free Danish pastries, bacon sandwiches and loads of women's mags, and I was really enjoying myself. It started to unravel when the make-up man asked me if I had been to a dermatologist about my acne – acne, at my age? – and if I minded if he used an entire can of dry shampoo on my roots. Then I was asked, very politely, if I had brought anything to change into because I looked a bit 'casual'. I was crestfallen – it was my only trendy dress teamed with leggings, so I just shook my head and asked if they had anything in the wardrobe I could borrow. But apparently they didn't go up to my size.

Then they ushered me towards the studio and miked me up, which involved shoving a wire up under my top, and the techy person suggested I stick the microphone thing over the blob of pastry grease I'd managed to get on the neckline of my top.

There was so much going on: floor managers, cameramen, make-up people carrying handbags of products to give guests a final touch-up. When I was pushed towards the sofa, I started having one of those out-of-body experiences. I could see myself fake-smiling and touching my hair and trying to keep it together.

The advert break finished, the music started, the cameras rolled and then I heard Phil introducing me and I panicked and had a meltdown; it just came tumbling out that sometimes I start drinking when CBeebies is still on air. In my defence, I did add that I meant sixish, but Phil spoke over me and it made me look like I'm a three o'clock wino. It's just that there was so much going on in the studio – the lights were blinding, it was hot, people were moving around off-camera – and I was completely distracted.

I've watched it over and over, hoping it will change somehow with each replay.

They didn't tell me I was going to be up against the chairwoman of a group called Mothers Superior as part of a debate on the changing face of motherhood. Well, they might have done, but all I heard was, 'Blah, blah, blah, we'll pay your travel expenses, pick you up in a car, blah, blah.'

I didn't even know about Mother Superiors. Well, I knew they existed, obviously, they're everywhere, but I never knew they were represented like our kind are. Had you heard of their group before 'This Morning'? No. Good, that makes me feel less stupid.

Their dreadful chairwoman, Hattie Hooper, was being all 'every mother should take time to look after her appearance or her kids won't respect her and her husband will leave her' and that's when I said she was talking 'a load of bollocks' and children and other halves were not as shallow as that. I mean, what planet is she living on? Planet Supermodel With A Nanny? That's when I tried to get up and leave, but Holly grabbed my hand and mouthed 'I'm on your side', which was nice of her. Because Hattie bloody Hooper with her glossy hair and dewy skin and bags of energy was that annoying.

I'm still having flashbacks now to Holly's bosom and Phil's concerned face. Naturally, the girls all texted me straight after. Mags thought I was 'hilarious and didn't look that fat'; Alex said, 'It was a set-up. Hair looked gorge, tho', and Lucy wrote, 'You were very human – lots of warmth and appealing to TM's demographic of non-supermodel mums.' Matt, however, just keeps taking the piss out of me but says not to worry because everyone will forget it, and it's not as if the club is world famous or anything. So supportive of him.

Still, Alex says we had lots of queries after the show went out. They kindly put our contact details on screen when I was on, so at least we got something, albeit something minuscule, out of it.

Honestly, I feel such an idiot. My nerves still feel shot to bits. Just hearing the theme tune to *This Morning* makes me feel weird now. Which, seeing as I have fresh first-hand experience, brings me quite nicely to this week's discussion: how to deal with a crisis.

A crisis can be anything from running out of milk when you're home alone with the kids and they're all in their pyjamas and there's only enough petrol in the car for the school run, to your husband changing the subject when you ask, 'Do I feel different . . . down there . . . you know, after having kids?'

We are not here to judge – if you believe it's a crisis, then it is. Some days you can keep it together when you've spent an hour going round Tesco only to find you've left your purse at home and there's no way you can go and come back before pick-up time and there's fuck all for tea. Other days you'll weep uncontrollably if you run out of dishwasher tablets.

Of course, PMT and idiot husbands play a part in your reaction, as does utter exhaustion, being asked to work late when it's parents' evening, worrying about how you can afford a camping holiday in Wales when everyone else is going to Tuscany, the car breaking down, being unable to fit into anything in your wardrobe and only realising you've run out of wine when the kids are in bed and your husband is away and you are stuck sniffing round for last Christmas's Baileys.

So, how should you deal with a disaster? Lucy has come up with the club Crisis Action Plan (CrAP for short) which has got us through domestic disasters on many occasions, be it finding your kid watching porn on YouTube on your iPhone or having no ham when the kids want it and want it now in a sandwich cut in triangles with no crusts.

First, count to ten. Take a deep breath and then shout 'FUCK!' at the top of your voice.

Then pick up the phone and leave a message on your husband's phone (he won't pick up because you only ring when you want something and he knows that) blaming him for everything, from putting an empty carton of apple juice back in the fridge to our patriarchy-by-stealth society which tells us we can 'have it all' but really we're enslaved from the day we're born, thanks to work, children, being paid less than men for the same job and the constant bombardment of images of size-four women.

After that, text all your mates, telling them in minute detail how you have been spurned, including the she saids and he saids in the incorrect order so it makes no sense whatsoever. They will respond with the appropriate you-are-absolutely-right-in-every-way messages and suggest you tackle the problem head-on that night with a bottle of wine and an enormous family bar of Dairy Milk.

A huge calorific intake and consuming your weekly government recommended alcohol allowance in one night will not tip the situation back in your favour but it will make you feel a fuckload better. The aim is to pass out so that the memory of the day's catastrophe is just a blur and you can get up with your head held high with very little recollection of the dignity-damaging incident.

Hopefully, your husband – who came in late for fear of being the target of your vented spleen and slept in the spare room – will have got the kids up, fed them and lined them up by the front door ready for school by the time you emerge.

Which is exactly what happened after I went on *This Morning*.

Don't worry if you didn't get all that. Lucy will type out the CrAP guide and Alex will send it out with the minutes so it's to hand if you ever stupidly feel tempted to think rationally, take the blame and want to apologise.

Next week, we'll do a question and answer session because a few of you have emailed me – asking to remain anonymous – over some guilty thoughts you're having. All I'll say is that you are not alone; we've all suffered sordid Mother Superior aspirations at some point or other. Don't worry, we'll discuss it and lay to rest those despicable urges we all get to join Curves, start a no-carb high-protein diet and consider bettering ourselves either through learning a new skill or having fillers.

Just to let you know, several members have suggested a sponsored event so we can raise some cash for the club because they're a bit sick of the same old cheapo biscuits. Lucy is co-ordinating, so please send your ideas to her. Nothing too ambitious is necessary, just enough to get us branded cakes.

Have a good week and enjoy Mother's Day – those wonky beautiful scrawled cards are just the best, aren't they? See you, and take care.

Week Eight

The Q&A

For those struck down with the current lurgy who couldn't make it, here are the secretary's minutes of the meeting:

9.30 a.m.: Chairwoman welcomes everyone. Apologies from various members who are ill due to a vile new springtime virus sweeping the playground. Chairwoman points out that she's got a huge new wrinkle on her forehead and then confesses that she didn't get a chance to get cakes in because Matt is apparently dying with said virus and so she's had to do everything – even her own breakfast in bed on Mother's Day – but she does have five pizzas in the freezer, if that's OK with everyone. No objections raised whatsoever. Oven set to 200 degrees Celsius.

9.31 a.m.: Round-up of what everyone's been doing (generally not much of interest but shitloads of dull stuff that everyone nods at, for example, Mags found a sausage under the sofa the other day which looked like it had been there for weeks).

9.45 a.m.: Calling order, chairwoman reminds members that this week's session is a compilation of questions that have been raised by mums (who wish to remain anonymous due to the distressing nature of their enquiries), all of which refer to momentary lapses of imperfection. She says she will read them out and respond in turn. Chairwoman puts the pizzas in the oven.

Q. 1: I am so ashamed to admit this but the other day I went to lunch with a Mother Superior mummy friend and because she was having salad I did the same. How do I resist the temptation next time?

Chairwoman's response: Don't feel ashamed, this happens to us all at one point or another. Consider it a blip; renew your commitment to the Mums Like Us cause, move on and make sure you order a burger and chips next time.

9.52 a.m.: Discussion of what toppings are on the pizzas because they smell lush.

9.55 a.m.:

Q. 2: My husband has invited a client over for 'supper' on Saturday and I'm sorry to say I'm actually considering making an effort. What should I do?

Chairwoman's response: Dish up quails' eggs with truffle

shavings, an Asian-American fusion of venison with a jus d'orange and Eton Mess for afters. Joke, lardies. You have two options: host just this once and serve M&S Dine In for Two food. Your second option is to tell your husband he can bloody well do it or you'll dish up fish fingers and smiley faces. And it's not supper – only Mother Superiors who have personal trainers, drive 4x4s in the city and have children named Tarquin and Lottie call it that.

10 a.m.: Pizza break. Group salivates at sight of pizzas which are passed round. No one says anything apart from 'mmmm' and 'Thank God, I was starving. I had breakfast hours ago, at 9.'

10.09 a.m.: Chairwoman finds a Penguin, three chocolate coins and some Haribo sweets in the saucepan drawer, and distributes them while wondering how they got there, then realises she did it just in case she gobbled the contents of the treat drawer and there was nothing left for her son at a crucial bribing moment.

10.10 a.m.: Teas and coffees.

10.17 a.m.: Back to business.
Q. 3: A mum at the school gates told me the other day that in order to get your child into the best secondary school in the area you have to go to church. Should I do it?
Chairwoman's response: This is a tricky one because we

all want the best for our children with the least amount of effort from ourselves as possible. I would suggest that the best way of coping with this is to get your mother-in-law to do it.

10.20 a.m.:
Q. 4: I've been fantasising about wearing a bikini on holiday. What should I do?
Chairwoman's response: The club rule on this one is straightforward: we encourage the flaunting of mummy tummies so that the cover-girl illusion of perfection is seen for what it is – a damning falsehood which puts women under enormous pressure to aspire to an unrealistic role model. Please note, sub-section b, clause ix adds that it is not compulsory but a sarong is very handy should you suddenly find yourself sat next to a twenty-something with pert breasts, flat stomach and peachy bottom.

10.25 a.m.: Toilet break. Discussion of those long hairs that have appeared on the backs of thighs post-reproduction.

10.35 a.m.:
Q. 5: I feel so guilty because the other day my four-year-old daughter wanted to do some painting and I told her the paints had run out because I couldn't face all the mess. Did I do the right thing?
Chairwoman's response: Don't beat yourself up about this. Most of the time, mothers will give their children

the freedom to express themselves when and how they want. But we're human and sometimes we simply can't be arsed with the hassle. You've taught her a valuable life lesson that we can't always get what we want. Besides, she'll do all that at pre-school, so chill out.

10.38 a.m.:
Q. 6: I had a pang of envy recently when I spoke to a Mother Superior who told me she received an enormous baby diamond for pushing out her fourth child. How do I keep my pecker up?
Chairwoman's response: Oh dear. This is an easy trap to fall into. Women like us tend to get a takeaway as a baby diamond. But tell yourself a Mother Superior's lot is a one-dimensionally empty materialistic one. Finally, never speak to her again.

10.45 a.m.:
Q. 7: Why do I feel such resentment towards my husband for simply breathing when he works so hard and I really love him?
Chairwoman's response: This is a very common feeling with which I am very familiar. I too suffer feelings of hatred towards the man who basically keeps the household afloat financially. My father did virtually nothing domestic around the house and yet I worshipped him. But I cannot seem to apply the same thinking when it comes to my equal – my husband. There is no answer to this and never will be. Just try

not to let the kids see you seething when Daddy comes in and flops down and gets out his laptop when they are desperate to mess about with him and you've got dinner to make. This, lardies, is life. Get used to it.

Chairwoman continues in the same vein for ages and ages.

11.25 a.m.: Chairwoman apologises for banging on about her husband. Then announces that next week will be about sex. Lots of snorts, howls of laughter and a few admissions from women with weak pelvic floors that they've just weed themselves a tiny bit. She says not to worry, she hasn't done it in ages and the thought of it makes her feel a bit scared and sick, but she will endeavour to do it before the meeting so she knows what she's talking about.

11.30 a.m.: Chairwoman thanks members for their fundraising suggestions – although she expresses surprise that someone has come up with the idea of a sponsored fun run. While it is incredibly worthy, it is considered at odds with the club philosophy. Having spoken to many members, the events co-ordinator reported the majority would like to do the sponsored sleep. All funds raised will go towards a charity close to our hearts – the cake fund. Incidentally, treasurer has asked for a list of favourite snacks so she can price them up and see if she can get them cheaper at Costco.

Thanks and goodbyes.

Week Nine

Sex

Stella's kitchen

Email to: mlumembers@yahoogroups.co.uk
Subject: Sex Survey
Date: 1 April (sheer coincidence, not trying to make a joke of it, honest), 14:27

Dear all,

After that hysterical chair-wetting reaction to my announcement of this week's topic last time, I thought I'd replace a face-to-face meeting with an email asking you to fill in the following anonymous sex survey so that no one gets embarrassed. Don't worry, before I print off the emails to collate the results, I'll delete all your names so I don't know who is who (I really don't want to know precisely who is having more sex than me, thank you). Then I'll present them at next week's meeting.

The purpose of this survey is for us to get things

off our chests and be open about a topic that some of us (probably most of us) spend a great deal of time worrying about. But not doing anything about it, obviously. My train of thought often goes like this: 'We hardly do it any more, everyone else is doing it more than us, why has it become so difficult to be intimate with my husband when we are so close in every other aspect of our lives, God I'm tired, zzzzzzzz.'

In fact, I'm convinced he doesn't fancy me any more. I can't blame him – I feel so disconnected from my body these days, like Mr Blobby with tits. And I eat so much garlic that I only notice it when I don't have garlic breath.

The weird thing is, I still really fancy him; he makes me laugh all the time and he's so tender with our son and he seems more confident now he's a father. But I just can't seem to turn that mental connection into a physical act; it's like I've lost my confidence.

I wish he would just come in from work – obviously after working late so our son is in bed – and grab me and bend me over the kitchen table. I would rather there wasn't any build-up, like suggestive texts or whatever, because I get all self-conscious and distance myself from him – which is the reverse of what I want to do. Take last night, for example. We haven't done it for ages, and he came in, gave me a big hug and kissed me on the lips, which was lovely because it was so unusual – a peck is the norm – and then he whispered,

'God, I love you', which was so nice, but I had to get the washing in because it was starting to rain.

I mean, why did I do that? Couldn't the clothes have waited for once?

As I pulled away he said he'd make dinner and make it something special and then when I got back inside, he was already chopping away, singing along to one of our favourite albums, something erotic like *The Queen Is Dead*.

Why didn't I just relax and enjoy it? Instead, I tensed up and felt all nervous at the prospect of What It Meant and drank three glasses of wine before he'd even dished up the pasta (a delicious bacon, mascarpone and broccoli thing he'd got from one of his cookbooks), so by the time we came to eat I couldn't focus on my knife and fork.

I felt so mortified, I tried to start an argument by asking if he had to make such a bloody mess when he cooks. Then I cried because he looked so hurt, we ate in silence and at the end I feebly tried to apologise without using the 'sorry' word. He forgave me, which made me feel even worse. I actually found myself thinking he only did that because he wanted sex. I am my own worst enemy – why am I so frightened of intimacy? So I decided, after two more glasses of wine: right, if that's what he wants, he can have it. I am bloody well going to have sex with my husband. I'm going to show him I love him and I desire him. But I'm not sure I want him to see it just in case I bottle out.

So I got up from my seat, grabbed a tea towel out of the drawer and tied it round his head as a blindfold. He started to say, 'What the fuck are you . . .' and I put my finger to his lips and whispered 'Shhhhh'. I went to the cupboard and took out the olive oil (Tesco own-brand, not extra virgin, appropriately) and I stripped down to my unmatching comfy bra and M&S size fourteen pants. Another good reason why I blindfolded him. I told him to hold out his hands and poured some oil onto them. Then I sat on his lap (poor bloke) and told him to 'put the tail on the donkey'. I couldn't believe it, it just came out. He burst out laughing and I got all embarrassed and went to get up but he grabbed me and well, it happened: foreplay, snogging – with tongues. Yes, tongues – when was the last time we actually got off with our blokes?

Even an attempt at oral (abandoned by both parties due to overwhelming taste of olive oil and very shiny faces) and then we did it. It was fan-bloody-tastic. Honestly, I couldn't believe we were capable of it. On the kitchen floor.

Afterwards, we were both in shock. Lying there, covered in oil and bits of fluff because the floor hadn't been swept in weeks, like two Turkish wrestlers, with the greasiest hair you can ever imagine. And Matt's blindfold had migrated from his eyes to his forehead so he looked like the Karate Kid. We were relaxed, happy and agog with it all.

But when he went to get up, his foot slipped on the

tiles and he skidded across the floor in slow motion, trying to twist himself onto his side so he could break his fall with his hands. He landed with a thud on a piece of uncooked penne pasta, which speared him in the buttock. He started swearing really loudly and obscenely and the next thing I knew, our son appeared all bleary-eyed in the doorway, asking, 'Why's Daddy crying, Mummy?'

Then he pointed at the offending piece of pasta, remembered he'd come home from nursery the day before with a robot picture decorated with painted farfalle, and said, 'Mummy, is it because you won't let him do crafts?'

We nodded solemnly and marvelled at our son failing to notice his parents were naked, covered in oil and on the kitchen floor.

It was one hell of a night, all round. And one that will not be repeated for aeons because (a) it took me ages to mop the floor of slime, since Matt put our son to bed and then had a shower and fell asleep, leaving muggins cleaning up and (b) putting out like that has earned me a get-out-of-sex card that lasts decades and the next time can be a 'Lie back and try not to think how soon the alarm is going to go off but if at all possible, hurry up, I'm knackered.'

So I suppose the moral of this is 'don't be afraid'. Sex doesn't have to be *Fifty Shades of Grey*; just have a go. Once in a while. If you can be arsed.

Anyway, here's the survey. Please be as honest as possible.

1. When you hear the word 'sex' do you:
(a) Assume the conversation is about whether you decided to find out what flavour your baby was before it was born – it's not as though you come across fornication much in your line of work as wife and mother.

(b) Recall that you have done it recently but can't remember when. It was probably the other weekend when you got drunk and your husband fell asleep on top of you. Or was it when the kids stayed over at your mum's last month? God knows, but you did do it, you're certain of it.

(c) Fantasise about your man coming home tonight, then rip off his clothes as soon as the kids are in bed.

2. What does your sexy undies drawer contain?
(a) I haven't got one. All my undies are greying and ancient, mostly from supermarkets. Oh, but I have got a breastfeeding bra that peels open and my husband has asked why I don't just cut off the flaps and turn it into a naughty one.

(b) One minuscule pair of knickers, last worn BC.

(c) A huge supply of Agent Provocateur lingerie, massage oil and vibrators.

3. How touchy-feely are you with your husband?

(a) We give each other a peck on the cheek when we go to work, if we remember.

(b) We cuddle up on the sofa when the kids have gone to bed but then I move to the other chair when he breaks wind. We also snog during sex.

(c) We are always touching – French-kissing whenever we get the chance, holding hands in public and we fall asleep wrapped in each other's arms.

4. What does your pre-sex prep consist of?

(a) I Jolene my upper lip once a month, that's about it.

(b) DIY waxing strips, a spray of perfume and a quick downstairs stand-up wash.

(c) Botox, fillers, threading every single body hair, blow-dry, suspenders, crotchless knickers and high heels.

5. What's your favourite position?

(a) On my back, with my eyes shut. By myself. Sleeping.

(b) On top.

(c) On all fours.

6. Do you ever engage in dirty talk?

(a) I turn the air blue when I find out my husband forgot to put the recycling out yet again and we end up needing an extension to house all those fucking boxes for glass, cans, paper and plastic.

(b) Only if I've had two bottles of wine.

(c) Yes. I know how to say 'fuck me' in French, Russian and Arabic.

7. How many partners have you had?

(a) About five.

(b) About ten.

(c) Hundreds.

8. Is your husband the best lover you've ever had?

(a) Yes, the best sex I've ever had was when we conceived our children. I just knew I was fertile and threw myself into it because I was desperate to fall pregnant.

(b) No, I once bedded a younger man who kept me up all night, but I wouldn't swap my man because I wouldn't be able to keep up with a toyboy these days – sleep is too precious.

(c) So far.

9. When you go on holiday, do you have more sex?

(a) No. We go camping and we're all in together.

(b) Yes, the sun really gets us in the mood.

(c) Twice a day – either before the kids wake up or when they're in the kids' club and once they've gone to bed.

10. Would you rather have a cup of tea and a bar of Dairy Milk?

(a) Yes.

(b) I wouldn't want to give sex up completely but once a month is enough for me.

(c) No; sex is an essential part of a relationship.

Right, there we go, I hope you didn't find that too excruciating.

Results next week.

Your chairwoman,

Stella

Dads United

Matt's office

Email to: davidsmith70@hotmail.com
Subject: stuff
Date: 3 April, 14:07

All right, Dave? Cheers for the email, good to hear you've had yet more promotion – you are the jammiest sod on the planet.

Look, got to be quick as supposed to be working but something's on my mind.

I'm worried Stella is doing the dirty on me. We did it for the first time in ages the other night (just wait till you're married with kids and you'll understand) – I was brilliant, obviously – but it was different to normal, not pervy or anything, you know me, man of the world and all that (cough), but she was really up for it. She's never really up for it. She doesn't even fancy me. Well, not like I fancy her.

She practically ripped my clothes off. Then she asked

if I wanted 'to pin the tail on the donkey', I mean, WTF does that mean? She has got to be having it off with someone else to come up with that, it was just so out of character. I even got a sex injury thanks to a piece of penne pasta (uncooked) – don't ask.

Then the next day she was all smiles, and I thought I'd tell her about a camping holiday I was thinking of booking to see if it tipped her over the edge, you know, triggering one of those 'you don't know me at all' conversations and forcing a confession.

But she just clapped her hands and said she couldn't wait. It's all so weird.

What do you reckon? By the way, Dad says can you give Mum a ring.

Cheers,

Matt

Week Ten

Sex Survey: The Results

Stella's kitchen

Welcome, everyone.

I apologise for my stern face. Don't panic, no one's having loads of really erotic and fulfilling sex. That's not why I'm all serious.

First, I must confess I have brought you here under false pretences this week. You see, I've had a feeling for the last few weeks that all is not as it seems in our lovely club.

I had an inkling things weren't right when someone suggested the sponsored run for our fundraiser. It was thoroughly out of character for a member to come up with that when we do not believe, as a group, in running. Plodding, yes, but not running. Then the Q&A revealed that same person was experiencing feelings of envy of a Mother Superior and I wondered if the two were linked.

I decided to find out for good by asking you all

to fill in the sex survey. And that same person was the only one of you all to tick all the 'c's; the ones that only a Mother Superior mummy could possibly pick.

My dear members, this may come as a shock but we have had a mole in the club.

You may remember her – Jess Wright was her name – she was dressed as drably as the rest of us apart from her gel manicure. It seems our mole, Jess, couldn't entirely abandon her superiority when she was dressing up as one of us.

You'll be relieved to know she is not here today – I have spoken to her and she has admitted everything and will never darken my front door again.

I know, I know, it's all very shocking. Why on earth would someone want to sit here with us and listen in to our most intimate thoughts when they have nothing in common with us? I asked her that very same question when I emailed her to enquire what she was up to. She asked to meet me for coffee in a neutral location to explain.

I was five minutes late because I had to take the cat to the vet for her booster jabs plus do the shop, but the second I saw her across the café, I knew she had been pulling a stunt.

While she had dressed down for our meetings, Jessica, for that is how she asked to be addressed, was sat there in the café with just-stepped-out-of-the-salon hair, a full face of barely there make-up, skinny jeans, heeled boots, a breathtakingly clean shirt and, of course, her perfect talons.

I gasped as I saw the full scale of her treachery. She heard me from her table and put away her iPhone into her Alexa bag and took a slow sip of her skinny decaf latte.

I marched over and asked her what on earth she'd been up to.

Looking genuinely upset, she told me she was really very sorry, she hadn't meant to go this far and that she regretted everything. It turns out she was secretary of Mothers Superior and had been sent by her chairwoman Hattie bloody Hooper. 'Jess' was only supposed to come a few times, but after *This Morning*, Hattie's curiosity turned to seething obsession. Apparently my passion for slovenly mumminess really rattled her; she fears Mums Like Us could eclipse and even threaten the existence of the Mother Superior movement.

Jessica told me their chairwoman suspected we were out to woo women to the dark side. Her mission was called Operation Daylight Slobbery, and she was to report back to the chairwoman with her findings so they could launch a counter-attack at the school gates.

Incidentally, I managed to wheedle some info out of her on the other club. Like ours, it's just been set up, meets weekly and has a committee. But the similarities end there. They get together over a Dukan-approved lunch in a boutique restaurant and points of discussion cover anything from how to burn calories when in a conference call to the very best educational after-school clubs such as Accountancy for Future World Leaders, and from grooming tips to getting your new eco-orangerie featured in *Livingetc*.

The trouble was, the mole said, she had actually started to enjoy herself and began to see how appealing our way of life was. How to be free of daily blow-dries, protein-only diets and personal trainers could lead to liberation; and how her desire to please everyone but herself resembled a prison. It was then she started sobbing quietly, and began apologising profusely, but even then there was no red face or snotting, which is what happens to me when I have a loud cry.

She said that while she knew she could never truly be one of us – she just couldn't ever endure naked nails – she had stopped going to Mothers Superior because she was distressed by the change in the tone of the meetings. Discussions about best hair products have been replaced by battle cries emanating from her chairwoman, who wants to polarise the two camps of women.

I admit I sympathised with Jessica and I still do – she is a devoted mum-of-two who naïvely agreed to do what she thought was harmless research but ended up being used by a truly frightening woman. I forgave Jessica her treachery and then once I had finished my slice of New York cheesecake and washed it down with a double chococino I told her to pass on this message to Hattie:

'We do not want a war. We believe we can co-exist as two clubs, because whether women are Mums Like Us or Mothers Superior, we all love our kids with a ferocious pit-of-the-stomach maternal instinct. There is room for all types of parenting in this world. But if you get nasty, we will deprive you of your beauty fix by block-booking every spa appointment within a fifty-mile radius of your house and show you up in front of your members by arranging for a bulk-buy box of value-brand fish fingers to be delivered to your door during one of your meetings. We will not let intimidation hamper our campaign to walk with our greasy-hair-heads held high and to revel in reality rather than the mirage of perfection.'

With that, I got up, gave a triumphant little flourish of my head and then completely ruined it by tripping over my Tesco bags and then spending five minutes finding an onion that had rolled all the way over to the other side of the café – but do you know what, even though I looked a total twat, I was proud to be myself. I was proud to be your chairwoman and I will continue to be so for as long as you will let me.

By the way, if anyone is interested in the results of the survey, once I'd discounted the mole's answers, fifty per cent of you picked mostly 'a's and fifty per cent of you picked mostly 'b's. You either don't do it or you don't do it very often, but then that's no surprise. We're saggy, tired and far too busy thinking about what we've got to do tomorrow to do it tonight.

Incidentally, my husband followed up our night of passion by telling me he wanted to whisk me off to – wait for it – only North Wales to go camping for the weekend! Do you know what, I'm actually really pleased that he's organising something for us to do as a family, even if it is freezing our tits off under canvas. I think he's a bit stunned by my reaction – I don't usually respond so enthusiastically to his suggestions – but he's probably still on a post-coital high, you know how straightforward men are.

Next week I'm talking regrets. I've got more than a few. Probably starting with inviting my mother to stay for the week – we don't exactly get on. You see, I was a total daddy's girl – we just seemed to have an easy relationship – whereas it was a bit strained with my mum. She always seemed to be cross about something. Obviously I love her loads and depend on her more and more as our son grows up, I just wish my dad was alive to see his grandson. Maybe I even take my grief out on my mum still, angry that he isn't around.

Oh, I don't know. God, I do go on.

Anyway, that's it this week. Thanks, and stay strong.

Week Eleven

Regrets

Stella's kitchen

Right, that's enough nattering – I think we've established we've all got some dodgy-looking veins which could possibly or possibly not go varicose. Besides, we've got to be quick, because I made my mum go out to town for the day so we could vent our spleens. Yes, she's still here. And she hasn't mentioned leaving yet. I caught her in tears the other day when she was handwashing her undies – why do women of a certain age do that? – so I haven't broached the subject of her departure as yet. I asked her if she was OK and she pretended she had some dust in her eye, which I think was rather mean, insinuating that my housework isn't up to scratch. But does anyone actually dust any more?

OK, settle down, lardies. Pile up your plates and top up your mugs, this week's topic is a big one. Let me begin . . .

Ask any Mother Superior if she has any regrets and

she will smile, play with her hair and then say, 'Of course not, I'm really happy, and if I hadn't followed this path then I'd never have every Friday morning at the five-star spa for my weekly facial and massage.'

But the majority of mums like us are stalked by regrets. From the second we wake up, when we catch sight of our figure in the mirror and wish we hadn't eaten a McDonald's for lunch and a takeaway for tea on Saturday, to the moment we close our eyes, wondering how we ended up in bed with this snoring man mountain.

Even then it doesn't stop. Our dreams are haunted by people and moments in our lives which we never forget. And these dreams are what I want to tell you about. I can go about my day getting on with stuff, counting my blessings and thanking my lucky stars for a great husband, a beautiful, bright and healthy son and a fulfilling-ish writing career. But at night, during stressful periods of my life, my regrets come alive in my dreams.

My dreams are always about the way I let myself be used by a particular man in my life – something I really do regret. If only I'd stood up for myself, not slept with him immediately and engaged in pathetic sex texting. I look back, feeling ashamed at my desperation to please and to be loved.

The dreams always go like this: I'm having sex with this man and then he disappears and I spend the rest of the dream trying to find him. I call him the Man

Of My Dreams because he's always in them, not because I have feelings for him any more. I did used to, though, big feelings. He was just one of those sexy blokes, do you know the type I mean? Funny, chatty and at ease with himself. Sparkly is the way he was. Not that he was devilishly handsome, but he was good-looking: thick, dark, messy short hair, big brown eyes, olive-skinned, tall, good physique and really smiley.

I spent a year of my life in what could loosely be called a relationship with him. He promised me nothing but I believed he'd come round eventually. When he did – because he found out I had met Mr Right, who was to become my husband, and obviously then wanted me because he couldn't have me – it was too late. I'd realised he was a waste of space and had met Matt, who showed me what a proper relationship was all about. But despite the happy ending, I am still haunted by the Man Of My Dreams, because when I feel insecure about stuff, my good old low self-esteem likes to remind me of how it felt to be unloved and desperate.

It's strange, because he wasn't the first man to make me feel rubbish, there were a few who did that.

Take Mr Cool, to whom I lost my virginity at seventeen. After six months together, he dumped me for a skinny horsey-type blonde in the Upper Sixth who was going to Oxford, even though he said he was anti-establishment. Clearly his dick wasn't.

Then there was Mr Mistake, a public-school crusty who completely ignored me after a one-night stand. Followed by Mr Good Time, who drew me in with his handsome looks but then would pop out to the shops and not return for four days. Mr Dangerous was a fiery sort who covered me in kisses then left me with genital warts. Mr Gorgeous was worth the heartache of being ditched because he was physically perfect and eight years younger than me. On the other hand, Mr Sleaze was completely not worth the tears because he was three-timing me.

Perhaps the Man Of My Dreams got to me because that was when I started to feel like an adult, like my time had come to settle down with a MAN as opposed to a boy. At the end of the day, he was a good person, he just wasn't ready to settle down. I wasn't The One, I suppose. I ignored all that, though, because we had such a laugh and we had chemistry. And now I realise that, if it wasn't for him, it would've taken me even longer to understand what makes an equal relationship, like the one I have with Matt.

Regrets, however, don't have to be about men. Oh no, and Alex begged me earlier to tell you about hers to prevent anyone repeating the same mistake. She once made friends with a group of Mother Superiors after she foolishly went to baby signing. I say foolishly, because what is the point of getting a baby to mime the word for milk when they can do it already with the very adequate breast-dive? Their lives were all Boden, Bikram and pop-up bistros. Some were on their fourth child, others were on twelve-week maternity leave from their trendy jobs designing organic children's clothing.

When the classes were over, Felicity, who was the 'head girl', suggested they all take it in turns to meet at each other's houses. They lived in enormous town villas which had glass atrium parquet-floored kitchens-cum-wet rooms, a floor for the nanny and walk-in wardrobes. Alex was terrified her son was going to vomit all over their nude throws. Refreshments were herbal teas and raw vegetables. She would worry herself sick every week with what to wear. She had to watch what she said, and she invented this double life for herself, telling the girls each week that she couldn't host yet because she had builders in. The truth was that her house was a two-up two-down terrace and she was ashamed of it. I know, I know, pathetic, but she'd been sucked into their world, believing that some of their 'success' would rub off on her.

In the end, when she could put it off no more, she had to host. She gave them the address of a house two streets away and then hid inside her home with the curtains closed and didn't go out for the day. She has never seen them since. And then we met – at the church hall place, when I tried to pretend I wasn't feeding my son Quavers and she boldly asked if her son could have one. Within a few weeks she had confessed everything. Alex had become confused, because she was a really organised, together person and she thought she fitted in – the Mother Superiors thought she did too, thanks to her tiny figure, which they endlessly cooed over through plumped up lips. But Alex realised afterwards that those women had help to run their lives – nannies, gardeners, personal trainers, chefs and the like – and she was doing it all by herself. The important bit about Alex's story is that she has managed to deal with this regret, which is why she is now one of the best members going.

Maggie's is an interesting case, because she regrets working her arse off to get to such a high position at work that she ended up being the breadwinner. It meant that she had to go back to work after six months with both kids because they needed the money, and now she uses her lunch hour to do the pre-school to nursery drop-off, her online shop or present-buying for yet another kids' party. Her husband's salary isn't enough to support them, although she admits she could've scaled her spends down a bit – but when you're used to having two cars, a holiday abroad plus a massive mortgage, there's no option but to get back on the nine-to-five treadmill. Being high up – both in the leggy height department and being head of regional marketing at a bank – means there are very few women up there with her, so inevitably there are raised eyebrows whenever she has to escape work early for parents' evening or whatever, but they seem to forget she's always at work first. So even though she knows things will change when she reaps the benefit of a pension and all that, at this stage in her life she regrets being successful because it's just given her a major headache and a huge heartache at having to leave her kids.

That is not to say that every mum like us has regrets. The club's events co-ordinator, Lucy, is one of those rare creatures who believes they are a waste of time – she says she eats too much, drinks every night even if she doesn't really feel like it and hardly ever walks anywhere. But she reckons when her son gets to big school, she'll be able to sort herself out. I am in awe of her 'life's too short' mantra. In fact, lardies, that will be the lesson for today: life is too short to regret things. We should accept who we are and what we've done, because it was all part of our learning, and thank the Lord we have each other to confide in.

But I bet I go to bed tonight and the Man Of My Dreams makes an appearance. Damn him.

Dads United

Matt's office

Email to: davidsmith70@hotmail.com
Subject: camping
Date: 21 April, 06:57

Yes, it is that early – got a presentation to do after lunch and I haven't started it yet. Don't worry about your impoverished brother not having time to eat, though – Stella's mum is staying with us for a bit and she got up early to make me a fry-up sandwich. She is brill, a proper old-school mum, doing my ironing, making my packed lunch and telling me to go to the pub because it's important I relax!!!! Stella HATES it.

By the way, thanks for your very sensitive response to my concern about Stella having an affair. 'LOL' was not very helpful. I'm thinking I might have jumped the gun a bit, anyway, she's so knackered all the time I can't see how she'd fit in an affair. That bloody club of hers is the rival for my affections, that's what it is. It's all she cares about. She must be getting funny sex ideas from her harem of cackling mums.

Hey, I forgot to tell you, you'll never guess who I had a drink with a few weeks ago? That Woman! She was at a conference and we had a good chat about work and stuff. I was thinking, I bet she still secretly fancies me, because she was so chatty and open, and then boom, she casually asked if you were still around. God, I hate you. She was looking good, no kids, bit of a high-flier. Come to think of it, she looks a bit like Cheryl Cole. Really into her sports and adventure travel. Living a completely different life to me.

Right, quick one – do you remember the name of that brilliant beach we went to in North Wales that year we went camping when we were small and it was sunny every day? Asked Mum and Dad but they couldn't remember. We went crabbing there, loads of caves, we made friends with that French family and you had your first kiss with the daughter and got a stiffy and we all laughed at you. Ring any bells?

After it being all shitty with Stells of late, I want to take her and the little one away somewhere special, somewhere meaningful, where we can play on an amazing beach – the sand was white, remember? And the sea was so clear. We can go to nice pubs for lunch and have barbecues by the tent at night. I want them to see the porpoises go past on the horizon, which

Dad always told us were sharks, and the rock pool where we found that octopus – do you remember that, when we put it in Mum's sleeping bag and she went mental?

Cheers,
Matt

Week Twelve

The PM's Letter

Stella's kitchen

Wow, it's getting quite a crowd in here now. Thank you all so much for coming along today. Did you realise we're three months old already? Check out the huge coffee and walnut cake to celebrate – big thanks to Lucy for making it. Oh, you bought it. Good. It wouldn't be right if it was home-made.

It seems we have already made something of an impression. And I don't just mean with the thousands of mums who have become members via email over the last twelve weeks. You know we all thought I'd blown it big time on *This Morning*, swearing my head off and generally looking unhinged? Well, it appears someone very important was watching. Only the Prime Minister!

We've had a letter from his Communications Department asking if we would be interested in a visit from him to discuss – and I quote – 'real women, real lives, real politics'. The letter is actually from the Zeitgeist Team within the Communications Department, whose job, a quick search on Google told me, is to 'pick up on new trends and lifestyle changes, which the Government can manipulate in order to retain power and look really on the ball'.

I'll read out the letter and then you can let me know what you think.

Dear Mums Like Us members,

I am writing from the Zeitgeist Team, which is part of the Government Communications Department.

Our hub (which is like an office but we don't like to use that term because it's so twentieth century) is in a really swanky building in London, which has no desks, just iPads and comfy sofas, so we embody the fluidity of creativity.

Our drive (which is what we call work, a word that reflects toil rather than our zestful joy, which brings us into our hub every day, on bicycles, naturally) is to identify new movements that we think will improve the Government's standing among 'ordinary people' and then grab hold of them and suck the life out of them. Then we brief the Prime Minister, with whom we have direct twenty-four-hour access.

We believe Mums Like Us is one of the hottest ventures around. The PM saw your chairwoman's appearance on *This Morning* (posted on YouTube, loads of hits by the way) and was energised by her energetic energy.

In these recessionary times, we believe that her passion and common sense is very now – it totally works with our 'make-do and stop moaning, proles' ethos. The PM's wife couldn't identify with it all because she has a nanny and her own line in handbags, but she pointed out that normal women, who look slightly grubby and grey from not enough sleep and too many dowdy clothes, would identify with you all, and that if we aligned the Government with you lot then we might just win their votes at the next election.

The PM wishes to visit to meet you all to get some feedback on a new campaign he is frontlining to re-engage women with politics – it's called 'real women, real lives, real politics'.

Our ultimate wish is to find a face to front the project (must be in thirties or forties, have lifeless hair, tired eyes and a defeated look about them) and then wheel her out every time the shit hits the fan when the Government is accused of riding roughshod over Mrs Joe Bloggs, her kids, child allowance, schools and hospitals.

Please let me know the dates the PM could visit.

By the way, would it be possible for the entire Zeitgeist Team (there are fifty-six of us) to come too?

We'd like the opportunity to sit at your kitchen table, because we really miss sitting at a desk to work. And as we are banned from having anything non-organic-eco-carbon-footprint-monitored to eat or drink in the hub, could you get in some PG tips and custard creams?

Catch you later, respect,

Ivan

Trend-spotting manager, Zeitgeist Team

So, what do we all think about that?

Can we have a show of hands please. All those in favour of the PM visiting?

None.

All those against the PM visiting? All of you.

Mags has offered to draft our response because she's ace at that sort of stuff, and then if we're happy with it, we can ratify it next week.

By the way, we're not in a rush this week because my mum has gone. She and I had a bit of a set-to a couple of days ago, relating to her crying incident, which has already been deleted from our family history because my mother can't admit to having any emotions. It doesn't sit well with her M&S trouser suits, her perfectly made-up face, Hillary Clinton hair and statement jewellery.

It happened when I asked her if she was OK after 'the other day'. I made sure we were occupied with something, I think we were making lunch together

– or at least, I was doing it and she couldn't bear not to help and muscled her way in – so it would mean no eye contact and therefore would appear a more casual cross-examination and would make her feel less on the spot. She said breezily, 'The other day? Oh that, I told you, it was some fluff. Do you want me to do some salad?'

I said gently, 'Mum, you were crying, I know you were, you know. You were, so just tell me if there's anything troubling you. You're perfectly entitled to cry, you know. You're human – we all are – and I'm not a child any more, you don't need to protect me.'

She just laughed, called me ridiculous and tried to change the subject. So I started to get angry and asked her directly – banging the knife down a bit too hard – if she was lonely or missing Dad, or was she ill or what? And I went into this big diatribe about how I thought about Dad every day and how I was still grieving five years after his heart attack and how he'd been robbed of being a grandparent and how wonderful he was.

Then she turned to me, pierced me with her blue eyes and said, 'I don't want to talk about your father, Stella. Enough. I think it's time I went home.'

And she walked out of the room, packed her stuff and then came back down as though nothing had happened and asked if she could pick up her grandson from nursery so she could say goodbye, and then she'd go. I was still in shock, so I just nodded and we ate while she nattered on about the garden and her pensioner's discount at B&Q and then that was that. It all became clear then that my only act of rebellion in life has been to spill my guts because she never has; I have confessional diarrhoea whereas she is emotionally constipated.

I'm just so confused by her reaction to me bringing up Dad. He was amazing, really loving and full of joy all the time, a big bear of a man, with huge puppy-dog brown eyes, a shocking head of chestnut hair and a perma-tan from playing golf and being out in the garden. I just don't get why she won't open up – it must be her way of coping with the loss.

Right, bile expelled, let's get on with the cakes.

Week Thirteen

Our Response
Stella's kitchen

Busy week, everyone? The usual running at 100 miles per hour to stay on the spot – work, shopping, cooking, cleaning, scraping baking trays, paying bills, Vanishing skidmarks on your husband's pants?

Me too. After all that, I was told the night before last that my son had a fancy dress day at school and the theme was 'inappropriate clothing'. I considered pyjamas, but all of them were in the wash, so I put him in a dress one of my friend's daughters left behind the last time they visited and I'd forgotten to send back. He ended up winning first prize in the Equality/ Transgender category, much to Matt's disgust. He really is such a bloke.

Right, let's crack on.

Here's Mags' letter to the Zeitgeist Team after our 'no' vote last week:

Dear Ivan,

Thank you very much for your letter regarding the Prime Minister's request to visit our club.

Unfortunately, the members voted overwhelmingly against your suggestion. That's not to say we weren't flattered by the PM's interest; we are thrilled to be thought of as on-trend when we have no idea what's in or out these days. The problem is this: we just haven't got the time to fit you in. Our meetings are sacred and we're on too tight a schedule to squeeze the PM in. What's more, we find it thoroughly patronising to be targeted by London-types who get paid a fortune from the public purse to then be perceived as political fodder in a desperate attempt to win votes.

Being courted by you lot is like being flirted with by the dishy whippersnapper at work, who's ignored us since day one but has realised we may be useful in his ascent to the top because we know the boss's wife through the PTA. We were tempted to play along, bridle even at those luscious eyelashes batting in our direction – it's been a while since any man other than our husbands has paid us a compliment and that was ages ago – but we can see right through it.

Therefore, we are not impressed at all by your desire to hijack our sacred organisation for political point-scoring. This is our refuge, the place where we come to discuss matters that no politician deserves to hear. We are time-poor and information-overloaded – why on earth would you think we would want to take part in a campaign that would make us even worse off? We simply don't want to be disturbed.

We are not token mummies who want to talk recessions or hospitals or unemployment for your benefit. Indeed, our thoughts on such matters are guaranteed to be diametrically opposed to yours anyway.

Finally, we do not want to be dragged into the squabbling world of politics. We spend our domestic life playing umpire, adjudicating between 'he hit me first' and 'well, she stuck her tongue out at me'. If you and your colleagues start behaving as we ask our children to – play fairly and by the rules, treat each other with respect and NO SHOUTING because we've got a headache – then we may be interested at some point in the future.

To show no hard feelings, we enclose a Costco crate of custard creams, paid for by the members, which we have wrapped in brown paper so you can smuggle them in for elevenses.

Collectively yours,

Mums Like Us members

Is that OK, everyone? Well done, Mags, spot on. I'll make sure I stick it in an envelope, carry it around in my handbag for a week, find it at the bottom covered in ink from a leaky biro and then eventually post it.

Do you know what, I never used to be like that: I was known as the most organised person on the planet before my brain got mushed by responsibility. Blimey, I used to get promoted, be trusted to manage people and fulfil the requirements of my job description. Now look at me. What the hell happened?

Oooh, next week I want to introduce you to a project the committee has been working on to reach out to all our UK-wide members who'll be able to access the club twenty-four/seven, for those times when you need some sisterly advice or support. It's really exciting.

Shit, there's the phone. I'm waiting for a work call and that's probably it. I'll take it upstairs but you're very welcome to stay. Help yourselves to anything, not that there's much in.

Bye!

Dads United

www.dadsunited.co.uk

MATCH REPORT: Dads United v. Fit Fathers

Dads United's first foray into match territory delivered an impressive debut from our first XI.

The heat was on from the off when the Fit Fathers arrived in a professional coach and emerged with kit sponsored by Organic Vegetables Co. Ltd. We had come by battered cars and wore our usual jumble of tracky bums, swimming shorts and multi-coloured T-shirts.

But appearances can be deceptive. In the leisure centre, Dads United pulled together, winning the toss, and getting off to a cracking first 20 minutes with Stu scoring his first goal after a dramatic scissor-kick in the area, supplied by a sweet pass from Dan. Our pre-planned goal celebration – pretending to eat a Greggs pasty – left the Fit Fathers staring open-mouthed.

Unfortunately, we were pissing ourselves so much that we didn't hear the whistle go and the opposition capitalised on this by immediately drawing level with a goal that no one saw and we went into the break with the psychological edge. A minute of extra time was added after Si twisted his ankle like a girl at 37 minutes.

We had water and oranges in the break while Fit Fathers opened their cool boxes and had proper sports drinks and a palm each of organic nuts and seeds.

They got off to a brilliant start in the second half, with their captain Jez Huntingdon-Small (who had a One Direction haircut) nutmegging the captain and making him look a total fuckwit by scoring at 47 minutes. Their inflammatory celebrations – miming putting on a designer cardigan and coloured skinny jeans – spurred us on until Matt accidentally clattered into Jez and we faced a penalty at 65 minutes.

We watched as Si stood tall, spread his arms and did that bendy legs thing that Grobelaar used to do. Jez stepped up to the spot, took a strike, going for top-left corner, and the ball bulleted in as our keeper went right. Three–one to the visitors.

Realising we had to dig deep, we started shouting at each other, swearing and stuff, to try to intimidate the Fit Fathers. It worked! In the 89th and 90th, Stuey rattled through their defence twice in two minutes to bring us even; one a glorious header from a corner (taken by Danno) and the other a Bobby Charlton-esque shot from the halfway line. Four minutes of extra time (due to the captain challenging Jez to a fight outside if he carried on pulling my T-shirt) proved testy as we tried to keep possession.

The whistle blew and our relief was audible. Three all in our first match was a respectable result seeing as we were really unfit.

Man of the Match: Stuey due to heroic hat-trick.

Donkey of the Match: The entire Fit Fathers team for that cardigan celebration.

Please note, there will be no training for ages due to the entire team pulling hammies – should give us time to recover and prepare for our game against the sales boys at the captain's place of work, who reckon they are going to destroy us. Fair enough, they're all twenty-five and read *Men's Health*.

Week Fourteen

The MLU Website

Stella's kitchen

Hi, everyone, fab to see you again, I'll stick the kettle on, you lot pass round the eclairs. Mags has done us proud with these, thanks to the proceeds of our sponsored sleep, which went remarkably well considering we have children who like to wake us up with their fingers up our noses. Alex raised the most due to her critical planning of spare room, ear plugs and sympathetic husband. My contribution was meagre because the little one kept having bad dreams and he ended up squashing in between Matt and me and didn't stop wriggling all night.

God, these cakes are lush, aren't they? Just love the way . . . they . . . ooze cream and . . . the chocolatey bit is . . . mmm . . . gorgeous. Thank the Lord for wet wipes.

So, the project we've been working on is this: the Mums Like Us website.

Many of you have said the weekly meeting sometimes isn't enough. Perhaps you can't get to as many meetings as you'd like, or you find yourself cornered by a Mother Superior preaching the merits of home-grown papaya at a mums' night out. Where do you turn if you've sent your apologies or you stumble in drunk at half eleven and you need sustenance?

The website, that's where.

After an enormous amount of input from members and a collective brainstorm by the committee, Mags put it together with a little help from my geek husband with the coding and whatnot.

So, if I just go to the computer and tap in www.mumslikeus.co.uk then . . . wait a sec while I just click here . . . here we are.

It's a bit basic at the moment, but let me show you round the site. Right, we've got different sections; for example, there are non-beauty tips, cooking ideas and a forum so you can chat online.

If we click on Non-Beauty Tips, there are really helpful pointers like, 'Never, ever use eyelash curlers once you get hooded eyelids because your mascara will give you panda eyes.'

Go to Get Cooking and I've put in a few of my favourites to start it off, but the aim is for everyone to stick their own up too so we have a catalogue of cheap, easy, nutritious meals.

My first recipe is for fish fingers and chips, and you can see the instructions are very simple – turn on oven to hot, open freezer and put fish fingers (five per person) and chips (two large handfuls each) on oven trays, put in oven, set timer for twenty minutes, sit down for fifteen minutes, heat up tin of beans then serve.

I can also recommend Lucy's recipe for surprise mince. Basically, start off by frying an onion with some mince. Then panic, look in the cupboard to see what you've got and add either tinned tomatoes and Colmans sachets for spag bol, lasagne, chilli or moussaka, or add gravy for cottage pie. Kids love the surprise element – until you dish up, when they say 'not that again'. But by then you've got them to the table and you can threaten them with no pudding.

The site also has a Useless Bastard of the Week, in which we can vent our anger at any man we choose, from our husbands for forgetting to buy some cheese on the way home so the kids have to have Marmite sandwiches in their lunchboxes again, to builders who never wolf-whistle us any more.

Heroine of the Week is for anyone who comes across a brilliant example of mummy tumminess – for example, you could nominate a mum you know who takes her kids swimming so she doesn't have to do bathtime or the mum who sticks a storytime CD on because she's too knackered to read any books after a day on the run.

Women's health is of the utmost importance to us, too, hence the section called Mummy's Having Her

Milk Now, which is about alcohol intake. Like all of you, I am in denial about how much I drink – I actually can't believe I survived nine months without wine during my pregnancy. Waking up without a fuzzy head and dry mouth after three-quarters of a bottle the night before is very rare, I can tell you.

But we feel we ought to at least remind you all of how many units we are supposed to be restricted to. Unfortunately, I've usually done my weekly allowance by Tuesday. I blame it on the stresses and strains of life; by the time I've done bedtime, the carrot tempting me downstairs as opposed to getting into bed and collapsing is a cold glass of white wine. There are various suggestions on how to stick to the recommended levels – diluting with soda water, hiding it in the garage behind the death-trap lawnmower which is certain to chop off your arm if you move it, and not buying any at all. I have asked my husband if he thinks I have a problem and he says, 'If all of us are doing it then it's normal, so you're fine.' Not convinced, but at the moment I cannot bear the thought of sobriety. I have cut down on the number of abusive texts I send once I've had a few – probably because I can't focus on the bloody buttons and I'm doing it with one eye closed. But in my book that's a move in the right direction.

My favourite bit of the site is My Top Tip, which allows us to share hints on anything from time-saving to cutting corners. We've compiled all your suggestions into a top ten, so just click on the 'feet up' icon and you'll see . . .

1. When it comes to dusting, washing the car and ironing, do not fucking bother. It's a total waste of time.

2. If you're having trouble getting your kids to sit at the table to eat, lay a tablecloth on the floor and call it a picnic and they'll love it.

3. Don't waste money on a spa treatment – simply run the kids' bath and sit in the bathroom with them. You'll get a great facial steam and you can squeeze your blackheads while they're getting clean – talk about multitasking.

4. As soon as your child can control his or her fingers, give them a Thomas the Tank Engine/Dora laptop – computers are an essential twenty-first-century skill and they give you a bit of space to make a cup of tea. And drink it. Hot.

5. Allow grandparents to spend as much time with their precious grandchildren as possible – a Saturday-night sleepover at their house is highly recommended.

6. Encourage your other half to spend quality time with the kids. Watching Sky Sports is barred, as are trips to PC World and their mum's house – that's cheating.

7. Pets are useful for introducing children to concepts of death and responsibility. But make sure the hamster has actually perished and is not hibernating before burying it in the garden, because if the kids see it scrabbling its way out of the grave ten minutes later like a *Thriller* extra, you'll never convince them that people do not 'come alive again'.

8. Save any rubbish presents your kids get and then dish them out as gifts for all those random children's parties you get invited to. Same goes for plastic crap that comes with comics, which are ideal for party bags.

9. Make sure your children have piggy banks – you never know when you're going to need £15 to pay for a takeaway delivery.

10. Save up your Tesco Clubcard points and get a Wii. When it rains, you will be so grateful.

Excitingly, Mags has been in touch with a dry shampoo company which is interested in sponsoring the site – which means money for future ventures and cakes. Remember, it's your site, so please get involved, send in your ideas. If anyone wants to do a blog then that'd be great. Mags is the one to talk to, because I'm shit at techy stuff.

By the way, did you all notice that photographer in the street on your way in? He was there when I put a stinking bag into the food caddy this morning. I asked him if he was after a celeb – I love a bit of showbiz gossip. I do know there's a reality TV star whose mum lives up the road. But the snapper just laughed and said, 'Sort of!' I can't wait to see who's been up to what.

Okeydoke, that's us done. If you need to go, see you next week. If not, do hang around for a bit.

Hey, did anyone see that new detective thing last night, with that really tasty actor in? Whatshisname, you know, he was in that other thing last year, that medical series with . . . that woman who was in . . . Oh, never mind.

Week Fifteen

Special Meeting

Alex's lounge

Hi, everyone, I'm so sorry this is such short notice, I'll explain in a minute why we're meeting a day earlier than usual. I'm really glad you could make it and that you found your way here. This is why Alex is our secretary. She is excellent under pressure and her directions were spot on – marking the way via the park with the resident weirdo, Tesco Express, the bakery and the offy was genius.

And check out her so-called last-minute supplies – defrosted doughnuts. Only Alex would have just-in-case cakes in the freezer.

Anyway, you'll be wondering why we're at a different venue and why I'm wearing make-up, a too-small career-bitch suit and four-inch heeled boots from my pre-tummy days.

It's because I had to escape my house this morning, in disguise. I reasoned no one would recognise me if

I slapped on a full face and wore smart gear. The mud on my boots and chin is because I left mine via the back door so I wouldn't be seen leaving and had to jump over the fence to get into the alleyway. Unfortunately, I split my skirt in the ascent and lost my balance and landed head-first in some weeds, which is why I'm sporting a Territorial Army-style smudge of dirt camouflage on my face.

This morning I received a phone call from my sister, Sophie, who set in motion this emergency get-together.

'Fucking hell, Stells – did you really turn down the PM?' she said, safely turning the air blue because her two girls were in school.

'What? How do you know?' I replied.

'Because your club is in the *Daily Mail*. Haven't you seen it?' she hooted.

So I went online and there, right at the top of the sidebar of shame – you know, the column on the right with all the celeb stuff in it – I saw a picture of me in my pyjamas, with the headline 'Mums Like Us Chairwoman "too busy" to meet PM'.

That bloody photographer I mentioned last week was only after me. The photo is awful – no make-up, hair scrunched back, faded pyjamas, and I've got this sour look on my face, which was because of the smell of the bag of veggie peelings and rotting meat, but they don't bloody say that in the piece so I just look a cow.

I just can't believe it.

Two seconds later, the phone started ringing and ringing and ringing – it was every paper on the planet after an interview, and the doorbell started going nuts too with reporters. I said 'no comment' to everyone, took the phone off the hook, texted Alex and legged it over here so we could at least work out what the fuck we're going to do now.

Basically, our letter telling the PM to bugger off was leaked after it was emailed to everyone in the Zeitgeist Team, got forwarded right round the Communications Department and then the entire Government. I suspect none of you will have seen it because we don't exactly get a chance to read anything – calorific content labels and shopping lists aside – until bedtime. On my way here, I nipped into the newsagent and bought the paper, and look, we're on page five.

Let me read the story to you. The headline is 'PM bellyflops with tummy mummies'. It goes like this:

Mothers today are always complaining they have too much to do and not enough time to do it. And that's precisely the excuse the Prime Minister was given by a group of women who said they were too busy to meet him.

Mums Like Us, a club set up for mums who believe in being 'good enough' rather than perfect – has snubbed a request from the Government to talk politics with our leader. The advance came from the Zeitgeist Team, a Communications Department unit which monitors social trends. The team hoped to find a face within the club for a new campaign to engage more women in politics.

Even though the publicity would have enabled the club to get their message across at the highest level, the members decided against it. But to soften the blow – or perhaps stick a cheeky tongue out at the Government – the women sent their apologies with a crate of their beloved biscuits.

The letter, from members led by chairwoman Stella Smith, a thirty-six-year-old married blonde with a three-year-old son, went viral on the internet after a civil servant emailed it to colleagues. Mrs Smith's coven, who explained their meetings were 'sacred', gather in her kitchen once a week to eat calorie-laden treats and plan their social revolution.

It is not the first time Mrs Smith has caused controversy. She was responsible for a foul-mouthed tirade during a live appearance on ITV's *This Morning* to discuss motherhood, when she was up against thirty-eight-year-old Hattie Hooper, the chairwoman of Mothers Superior, a group in favour of intensive mothering.

Last night, the well-groomed mum-of-four, who works in PR and counts Elle Macpherson and Claudia Schiffer as personal friends, said,

'MLU really is a disgrace to motherhood. How on earth can anyone be too busy to meet the PM? Perhaps they should have told him they couldn't do it because they were washing their hair – God knows they could do with it.

'None of them have pedicures, they decorate their homes without an interior designer's personalised mood chart, they do not carry mummy cards that they can exchange to set up play dates with their children, and they think vintage is wearing clothes from seven seasons ago.

'They just sit there and moan while stuffing their faces with tea and cakes. No wonder they moan about the impossibility of "having it all". If only they stopped eating, then they'd realise it's a cinch.

'They have a laughable plan to convert mothers across the country to their way of thinking, which means denying physical contact with their husbands, wearing the same clothes for several days running despite gravy stains, not getting their hair done for sports day and leaving their children to entertain themselves. It really is a scandal – if this idea catches on, then we could have a generation of young people who miss out on extra-curricular activities such as cooking the N16 way and learning Russian. They will have free time and God only knows where that will lead.'

Mums Like Us stands in stark contrast to Mothers Superior, whose members must set the alarm for six a.m. every morning to go for a ten-kilometre run with their personal trainer, wear full make-up at all times and cook organic from scratch for every meal.

Mrs Hooper, who lives on a sprawling country estate in the home counties, said she would be 'absolutely delighted' to assist the PM, suggesting he contact her through his wife, because they attend the same book group.

The Prime Minister's spokesman said the PM 'fully understood' the time restraints placed on modern women and 'hoped Mrs Smith would be able to help in the future'.

What happened to the biscuits is the subject of an internal investigation, the spokesman added.

Mrs Smith was unavailable for comment yesterday.'

Then, blah de blah, there are some bits from our letter and more snotty comments from Hooper.

My initial reaction was OH FUCK. But, get this, when I went online, the comments underneath the story were overwhelmingly in favour of us. By ten a.m. there were 1,056 posts, and loads of them were asking how they could join. Mags has told me the website has crashed due to an unprecedented level of interest from yet more mums like us!

I'm completely shell-shocked by all of this. As are you lot, by the way your mouths are hanging open! Do you think we're onto something here? Shall we work out a plan of action – a strategy, as Alex would call it?

I'm floundering at the moment, so how about we have a good think before the next meeting and see what we can come up with?

Good, you're all nodding.

You may have noticed there are some chopped slices of lemon on the worktop. Alex has taken the decision to do away with teas and coffees for refreshments today. We need something stronger – I know I do – so help yourselves to a gin and tonic.

For now, if anyone approaches you from the media, it might be an idea to refer them to the website, which Mags said she's sorting out as we speak.

Right, I'm going to attempt to get back into my house without being followed. Just a quick double G&T, then I'll be off.

Dads United

Matt's shed

Email to: davidsmith70@hotmail.com
Subject: Fucked off
Date: 23 May, 13:01

Mate, have you seen that link I sent you earlier? The one from the paper with Stella in it?

I'm working from the shed today, because there are reporters camped outside our front door, yelling questions through the letter box about our family life and our marriage. I tell you, I'm fucking furious about it.

Stella, on the other hand, is bloody delirious with it all and trying to convince me it's a good thing her cause is national news. I have to book five seconds with her to talk about something, anything. I mean, I'm only the bloke who pays the bills.

Yes, I know I'm an adult and I should be dealing with this in a grown-up way, but Jesus, Stella has gone too far this time. I can take care of myself but I'm worried about her. She's on such a high, the only way is down, and she's drinking like a fucking fish. I can see in her eyes she's off on one – it's like she's got this buzz on, this mission, and she's in a trance and I can't seem to get through to her.

Obviously, there's a bit of jealousy there, I'll admit it. She never wants to do anything with me these days. Sometimes, I can spend an evening in her company and not actually exchange a word. She'll be working on some idea for the next meeting so I'm left to just catch up with people on Facebook or watch the telly.

It's no surprise then that the camping trip has been postponed – indefinitely, I suspect. She just can't spare a moment, she says.

In other news, That Woman has been in touch. She's emailed me some names and numbers of her contacts, not with the promise of anything leading anywhere, but she says I should be networking a bit – probably right.

Cheers,

Matt

Week Sixteen

Members' Plan of Action Handout

Stella's kitchen

Sorry for making you all come in over the fence and through the back door – our doorbell batteries are knackered after all the journalists pounding the door last week, and we haven't got a knocker so I'd never have heard you, what with the telly being on so loud.

The committee got together at the weekend, at Lucy's, who event-co-ordinated beautifully for us with some Pinot and a Chinese. That's why some of the handouts we've prepared for you have a few black bean sauce stains on them – apologies.

Taking in all your ideas and proposals, we produced a Plan of Action, detailing our next step in the light of the many approaches we had from the media following the *Daily Mail* story. Principally, our aim is to capitalise on our new profile as an alternative to the Mother Superior way of life. Not only have we had a huge amount of interest from newspapers, magazines, TV and radio, but also, and more importantly, we've heard from normal mums across the country. We've had hundreds of thousands of hits on the website, so many emails and letters and . . . for once, I'm quite speechless. It appears we've tapped into something big. I don't want us to get carried away, but it's clear we've got some hard work ahead of us.

Right, let me take you through what we've been offered.

Daily Mail: From Muffin-Top to Mothers Superior – a makeover transforming members from dull, baggy jumper status to gorgeous glamorous mums who repent their formerly scruffy ways and vow never to eat cheese in blocks again.

The *Daily Star*: Sexy shoot in which members wear saucy underwear while dishing up spag bol, eating cakes and cleaning the loo.

Channel 4: Old-style reality show where Mums Like Us members swap homes with Mother Superiors à la *Wife Swap*.

ITV2: New-style reality show like *The Only Way Is Essex* but called *The Only Way Is No Sex*, featuring us lot being filmed with our families with the camera there when we're supposed to be having 'private moments', such as when I have to explain to the little one why women don't have willies and me having a go at Matt about him never noticing there is congealed food on the floor.

Grazia: Members reveal how little sex they've had in the last year with the headline 'Why you should never have kids'.

Woman's Hour: Super-intelligent feature examining whether the Mums Like Us v. Mothers Superior battle is detrimental to womankind. Plus debate on custard creams.

FHM: Are you married to a Mother Superior or a Mums Like Us member?

Nuts: Would you rather shag a Mother Superior or a Mums Like Us member?

Observer: Nasty Childbirth Trust invites MLU to watch a forest birth to marvel at mother nature over mother NHS.

Sunday Times Style Magazine: Tummy Chic – how to get that worn-out look even if you have a nanny.

Wine Lovers' Monthly: Panel of members decides best bottles under £6.

The *Sunday People*: What's in their bin? We rummage through members' black bags to see how many bottles and plastic takeaway containers they've deliberately not recycled to show their DEPRAVITY.

Playboy: five-pound offer to club kitty for entire group to strip off.

Daily Express: How mums could learn a lesson from Princess Diana; members receive lessons in royal motherhood etiquette.

And, finally, here's the one that has piqued my

interest. One of the broadsheet weekend magazines wants to feature a member in their 'How I Make It Work' section, which means there's no angle. One of us just has to talk through the routine of their day, and that way, people can make their own minds up about us. I have to say I favour this because it's rather more low key. We're not pitting ourselves against anyone, which is something I think we should avoid. We don't want to start World War Three, do we?

Who wants to do it then? Anyone? Oh . . . you think I should do it because I'm chairwoman? Well, I'm not entirely sure it should be about me, yet again, because this club isn't about one mum, it's about all of us. Having said that, I am happy to do it because it won't take long. It means an interview and a photoshoot. But I'll make sure it's inclusive of you lot. I need to run it past Matt, because he's still fuming about last week. Well, when I say 'run it past him', I mean tell him we'll do it. He's such a spoilsport, it's like he's jealous of the club.

I'll give a polite 'no' to the rest then fix up the broadsheet thingy. It should be straightforward and pretty harmless.

In the meantime, what do you think of us going on Twitter? Yes, I know 140 characters amounts to an awfully small number of words when we've got so much to say, but there are millions of mums on there and it's a great way to reach out to them. Mags says she'll sort it.

Fantastic, we're all agreed then.

Motions carried, blah blah blah. See you all next week.

Week Seventeen

Don't Ever Knock Being Happily Miserable

Stella's kitchen

Fellow mums, I am in the shit.

Not the usual kind we're used to – wiping bottoms or chipping away at the bowl after the other half has had a dump. But deep, deep shit.

That interview three days ago was a disaster.

Let me tell you about it. You'll need a full cup of tea and several biscuits to see you through it, so get yourselves settled.

OK, deep breath, I'll set the scene. I arranged it for when Matt was away on business and my son was with my mum for the day and night so I could get the interview done without any interruption. I spent ages neither doing my hair and make-up nor tidying the house. I thought, the interviewer can find me as they see me, and by being minus foundation, primer, blusher, mascara, eye shadow, lippy and whatever else Mother Superiors apply to their skin, I would be liberating womankind across the world. Well, not really – but I have to say, our website has had hits from the unlikeliest of places, where women are generally thought of as immaculate and gorgeous, such as France, Italy, Venezuela, LA and Rio.

So, anyway, I was in the clothes I'd worn for three days running, pony-tailed and in my green Ikea Crocs rip-offs reading *Closer* when the doorbell rang.

I arranged my best 'go on, come and have a go if you think you're hard enough' stare as I prepared to dazzle the interviewer with my messy house – I'd deliberately not picked up the coats, shoes and bags all over the hallway.

I opened the door and there before me, standing on the step as though it was the most natural thing in the world, was the Man Of My Dreams. Yes. HIM. The one I told you about, who haunts my dreams, the one who refused to commit when it came to the crunch after a year of would-he-wouldn't-he. To me, it seemed we had everything going for us – chemistry, obviously, and, despite him turning out to be a bit of a user shitbag, we had a really close friendship too. He would always pick up if I was ringing, all miserable and dribbling, and listen to my woes or come round at a moment's notice to have an impromptu picnic in the park or a night in the pub. It seemed he was there for me – he was 'the one' before I came to my senses and realised that he wasn't going to commit to me since he 'wasn't ready'.

I'd always imagined if I came face to face with him again I'd be fine. As much as I hate to admit it because it sounds so smug, I'm deeply happy to have ups and downs, a boring life, the usual stresses and strains, because I've got the little one, Matt, a job and you lot.

But whoomph, him standing there at my door hit me right in the stomach – the rejection all those years before came back to me in a split second. While I thank him for teaching me a lesson never to put out if a man doesn't stay over or text every day about nothing, just to be in touch, I could've done without his unexpected appearance. It took me back to the demeaning time and place where I had begged him to be my man. He came close many times, but at the last minute, usually after sex, he would tell me he wasn't sure things would work out.

You already know the rest of the story, when I got together with Matt and the Man Of My Dreams decided he'd made a huge mistake and wanted to go out with me. As you know, I told him to bugger off, but we did stay in touch for a while, as we had been such great friends. The contact gradually fizzled out and the next thing I knew, a few years later, he texted to say he was getting married and had a baby on the way. I was pleased for him because I felt nothing for him romantically by then – I was married and had had my son, and I felt like we'd laid stuff to rest.

Even though I'd heard on the grapevine that he was now working for one of the quality newspapers, it didn't even cross my mind that he would be the interviewer. Holding open the door at that moment, I dropped my stare as my mouth fell wide open at the sight of this bloke who had once been on my soulmate hit list. He hadn't changed dramatically – the dark hair had a few greys and there were laughter lines around his eyes – but then men do age nicely. I felt myself trying to cover my wrinkles with bits of hair, suddenly self-conscious, hoping I didn't look the old bag I feel.

But when his face relaxed into a smile, I remembered how that wide, warm, sexy, funny, teasing mouth had me hooked, lined and sunk; it did when we first met, about six years ago, when we worked at the same newspaper. We were in different departments – him in features and me in news – so we only properly met at someone's leaving do. We both got drunk and ended up talking the whole night, and from then on, we'd email each other all day every day, and before I knew it, I was head over kitten heels – I used to make a bit of an effort with my footwear back then.

So, as you can understand, I was in shock when I saw him at my door.

'Hello, you,' he said, using the two words he always used to begin every conversation he had ever had with me during our fling. 'You weren't expecting me, I take it,' he laughed, his eyes creasing gently in the way that years ago would have had me eating out of his palm. Or more aptly, his crotch.

'No. No, I wasn't,' I said, wishing I'd at least worn something that wasn't stained or baggy. Not because I wanted to impress him but . . . I wanted to impress him.

Fuck, fuck, fuck.

I quickly recovered my composure and thought, just brazen it out, just do what you do, pretend you're confident and couldn't care less what anyone thinks. Anyway, he's seen you with your fingers down your throat, mascara down your cheeks, naked and blubbing, I told myself.

'Come in, great to see you! I've made a special effort to dress up, you do realise,' I said.

So he stepped inside over the mess, explaining that the magazine's editor had allocated him the task of 'having a crack at the miserable, fat cow who was giving mums ideas, my wife included, about not bothering to wax their foofs'. He had almost tried to get out of it but then decided what the hell, and said he was curious.

Then he came towards me with both hands reaching out to my waist, and his full lips, his beautiful pouty lips, kissed me on the spot just by my lips but not on them. He still smelled the same, a sweet saltiness which used to make me go giddy. Oh God, it made me shiver and I could feel a stirring in my woman's bits. No, no, no, I told myself, you don't fancy him, he's a prick, he always was, he's got a completely average willy and he has no right to kick-start that activity in your knickers. Get him into the kitchen now.

I offered him coffee (knowing he hated it) but he called my bluff as he always did, telling me the train journey had been a nightmare and he wanted a drink. I went to the fridge and pulled out a bottle of wine – it was four p.m., by the way, so it was five p.m. somewhere – and poured us both a large glass.

We sat down at the table and over two hours we talked and talked and talked. He was really happy; so was I. He loved being married; so did I. He had found parenthood really hard at first – him and his wife had a daughter – but had grown to live it and breathe it with utter devotion, as had I. It was just as easy as it had always been. The conversation flowed back and forth, skimming over our time together, agreeing it would never have worked, but peppering our memories with references to the nights that had ended up with us in bed. Both of us would occasionally say, 'We'd better start the interview or we'll be here all night,' before getting sidetracked.

By this point it was sixish and I hadn't eaten since lunch, so I was getting drunk. I suggested I cook something and he asked if I still crucified pasta, a crude reference to the time I'd invited him round to my flat and burnt the bloody home-made spaghetti when we'd got carried away and ended up having sex in the kitchen while the pasta burnt black. That was one of those nights he had seduced me with talk of what life would be like if we got it together. I thought I was in, clear and dry. We had sex there and then, with me sat on the floury worktop where I'd made that bloody pasta. Half an hour later, he went, saying he was going to get a takeaway for us, but he texted me to say he'd bumped into a contact and he had a story for him so he was very sorry but . . . I was left to wipe up my own floury bum-shaped crescent and pushed some baked beans around my plate, trying to make excuses for him, ignoring those creeping thoughts that circled in my head about his pathetic behaviour.

The memory jolted me back to reality. Bastard. Suddenly, his flirting made me angry, and I told him he had to go and could he email the questions and I'd get back to him. I'd been drawn back in, my stupid ego enjoying the attention, and now I felt a fool. A fool with a flabbier tummy and more wrinkles than in the days when I had been so desperate for love that I'd allowed myself to be used.

I stood up, took our glasses to the dishwasher and hoped he'd let himself out.

But he came up behind me, pulled my hair to the side and began kissing my neck, his hands exploring my shoulders, then my hips, and my seething turned to longing. I turned round and stared into his eyes, wondering what the fuck was going on – I mean, men only do this on the telly.

I am ashamed to say I wanted to kiss him, to lose

myself in his mouth and forget I was a wife and a mother.

Then he told me, 'Stella, I just can't forget you. I want you, I always have, can't we, you know . . . No one needs to know, this can be our thing, our escape.'

His mobile rang on the table. Thank God. He looked at the phone, then at me, then he went pale. It was his wife. He had a brief conversation with her as his hard-on drooped, like a tent coming down in his trousers. 'Yep, just finished, on my way back, won't need to stay over at the hotel now,' he told her.

'I think you should go,' I told him, furious that he had actually planned an excuse ahead of his visit, thinking I'd be just as easy as I'd been all those years ago. Bastard.

'I'll email the stuff for the piece,' I said. 'Don't ever contact me again.'

He nodded and then fussed about with his bag, his laptop, his tie and his pants – obviously rearranging his meat and veg – and then he walked out.

'I meant it, Stella, every word,' he said to the door when I'd slammed it shut.

What the fuck just happened? I asked myself. I wandered back into the kitchen, dazed, and finished the bottle of wine. I sobbed my heart out at my near-treachery, torturing myself by looking at our wedding album. Remembering what a beautiful and quirky day we'd had five years ago, on that crisp, winter day. My lovely dad walking me down the aisle in our local church, having the reception in a marquee decorated with glitter balls and leopard-print chairs in the garden of the Golden Lion, where we went on our first date. We had silver service for fish and chips and champagne, our cake was a six-tier chocolate-orange-Bailey's thing and we danced our first dance to 'Can't Take My Eyes Off You' by Frankie Valli and our second to 'Rock the Casbah' by the Clash, when I had to hitch up my ivory puddle train to have a proper mosh.

God, I wondered how I could have wanted someone else and couldn't believe how close I'd come to being so stupid – I adore my husband and our son, and I wouldn't ever want to wreck what we have. That day when I gave birth was the most wonderful day of our lives – actually, the build-up wasn't wonderful, I was foul-mouthed and abusive – but when that little boy came into the world, Matt and I were sobbing with joy. Even though in the weeks leading up to the birth he'd said he didn't want to cut the cord, he changed his mind when he saw that bawling, scrunched-up little body, waving his fists about, fighting the light and noise and even our kisses. Our son was the embodiment of our love; we'd never been happier.

And I'd come that close to wrecking it.

When my husband and son returned the next morning, I still felt so guilty. Even though I hadn't done anything, a part of me which I thought I'd grown out of had wanted to. Then he asked how the interview had gone. 'Fine,' I said and disappeared to put some washing on and have a cry over the Fairy Non-Bio.

So, members, there you have it. I've almost sinned and also, yet again, wrecked our latest shot at convincing the world that our Mums Like Us ways are the perfect riposte to Mother Superiordom.

I suppose what I want to say is that even though I spend my life moaning about motherhood and marriage, in actual fact I am happily miserable and we should all take time to thank our lucky stars for our good fortune.

Next time, I'm sure I'll have bounced back. Women like us always do. It's thanks to something called self-preservation, which really means self-doubt, as in, he was desperate and I must have looked desperate . . . I'm just a silly old fool. Thank God what goes on in here stays in here.

Week Eighteen

Minutes from a Meeting at Maggie's House

7 p.m.: Treasurer welcomes members, expressing thanks for their flexibility after Stella cancelled the meeting at HQ. Offers tea and coffee and then apologises for lack of treats as her online shop is scheduled for tomorrow but she does have a few Kit Kats and Mint Clubs going if anyone is desperate.

7.01 p.m.: Treasurer waves her hands around at the mess, which includes hardened splodges of ketchup on the tiled floor and a piled-high basket of ironing. Explains she hasn't had a chance to do any housework. She used to have a cleaner but then her husband lost his job and they had to make some cuts. She says she knows members will not give a toss about the detritus but for some reason, even though she is the breadwinner and gets a maximum of six hours' sleep a night because she has to catch up with all the kids' stuff as well as work at home most evenings, she still feels the need to excuse

146

herself. She wonders if a man would ever feel the need to justify his domestic surroundings then adds 'unlikely' and 'definitely not my husband, anyway'.

7.03 p.m.: Treasurer reads out an email from Stella detailing her absence:

Dear members,

Apologies for letting you down tonight. The thing is, I'm struggling a bit at the moment. I seem to have lost my oomph. It's probably all the excitement of late, and my body is telling me to slow down. Booze doesn't seem to be helping, either, but I seem to be in some sort of six o'clock cycle – I have a drink to make myself relax, finish the bottle, wake up in the middle of the night and promise myself I won't drink until the weekend, feel crap when I wake up next day, spend all day feeling flat then at six p.m., I find myself pouring a glass, which makes me feel better.

I blame the shock of what happened, or didn't happen, with the Man Of My Dreams. I feel stupid, naïve, old and fat.

This whole episode has knocked the stuffing out of me. It's reminded me that I am nothing special. It has taken me back to the brief time when I thought life was amazing and I was on my way somewhere – I was single, happy in that happily-shagging-round-because-I'm-bound-to-end-up-with-a-great-husband way. The sex I was having was brilliant and I remember thinking, Oh my God, I can't wait for my mid-thirties when I'll reach my sexual peak – but now look at me, equating sex with duty, like something I should be doing with my husband, and then having spontaneous and involuntary knicker tinglings over a shit who walked all over me.

Before him, I had no cares in the world and I was on the crest of this huge wave. I didn't realise it then, of course. The world was exciting and I was confident for once, working my way up the ladder and being respected.

And then I met the Man Of My Dreams and slowly but surely, he made me feel small, needy and desperate. And he's done it to me again. It probably looks like I'm being a drama queen but I genuinely want to curl up in a ball.

I feel ugly. I feel as though my existence as a sexual being is over and I'm going to spend the rest of my days as a thing, and one day I'll wake up and find I have absolutely nothing between my legs. It's not just about the sex – it's about desire, something I'd forgotten all about. Feeling it again so unexpectedly has unnerved me and left me wondering why it is that we crave 'the one' but then desire evaporates the more settled we are. And these days the pressure is so rampant to be a Mum I'd Like to Fuck. My parents were married for thirty-six years and they still seemed in love, although they would have huge rows every now and again – I never knew what about – but they always made up. Then they'd have moments when they would be swimming in each other's eyes and my sister and I would feel totally excluded, but in a nice way, knowing they loved each other and our family fortress was impenetrable once again. But me and Matt don't argue like that. We love each other, unquestionably, but we just seem shattered, even too shattered to express how we feel.

I have drawn a line under this whole thing by sending my How I Make It All Work diary to the Man Of My Dreams with no 'hello, how are yous' included, just the words. He must have realised how angry I was because he got the magazine secretary to email me to say it's going in this weekend. That took every ounce of energy I had; the rest of the week I have functioned at a bare-minimum level.

That's why I can't be there tonight. I'm sure you understand. Course you do, you've been emailing me and texting all week – what would I do without you?

Your support has been amazing. Lots of you have been really honest with me and confessed a simmering saucepan of affection for old flames. A few have even been in my slippers and know how it feels to confront feelings of desire for men you are not married to.

I am sincerely grateful to you all.

Your chairwoman,

Stella

7.10 p.m.: Treasurer wishes the chairwoman a speedy recovery, a comment which draws murmurs of agreement from members, who nod their heads in an exaggerated fashion as if miming 'poor old Stella'.

7.11 p.m.: Treasurer informs members there will be no meeting next week because the PTA midsummer ball is on and with many of the mums attending, there is bugger all chance anyone will be capable of conducting club business for days afterwards. Greeted by vigorous nodding from all corners of the room. Treasurer reminds them of last year's ball when the deputy head started drinking at four p.m. and by seven p.m. she was slow-clapping the headteacher's welcome speech before grabbing the microphone and singing 'Like A Virgin' a cappella.

7.15 p.m.–7.25 p.m.: Group discussion of who shamed themselves at last year's ball, including one of the mums who got off with a teaching assistant – female – as a dare and the PE teacher fighting, and squashing, a dad who claimed he had bigger muscles.

7.26 p.m.: Treasurer says she doesn't want anyone to feel their evening has been wasted for a quick chit-chat, so she introduces the club guide to Loud Parenting.

(She went on forever so highlights as follows.)

- This is a brilliant way of working out if a mum in our vicinity is 'one of us': You may be happily chatting at a soft-play centre or a children's party, sharing stories, admiring one another's roots, when bang, she starts talking to her children in a very loud voice, congratulating them on something banal such as, 'OH YES, DARLING, YOU'RE RIGHT! MUMMY IS WEARING HER NEW BOOTS. WELL DONE, GOOD SPOTTING.'
- If this happens, step away immediately because she is a Mother Superior in disguise – our enemy in sheepskin Ugg boots clothing.
- The reason she is (a) talking at 100 million decibels and (b) doing that really annoying positive praise thing of 'good shouting' or 'good weeing' is because she wants everyone to notice what a good parent she is. They say it's the emptiest vessels that make the most noise and they're right.
- This trend for positive praise gets right up the club's nose. Yes, kids respond to it, but the applause for breathing is completely unnecessary. Talk about setting them up for a big shock when they enter the big bad playground and then the

world and they find out no one is going to give them a gold star for behaving themselves.

- To conclude, Loud Parenting has no place in the Mums Like Us mummyfesto – good enough parenting is conducted by stealth, in a manner that doesn't undermine anyone else within range, either openly or passive-aggressively.

8 p.m.: Treasurer wraps up and receives a standing ovation from members, who then dash out to get back in time for *EastEnders*.

10.16 p.m.: Committee members finish their third bottle of wine, toasting the chairwoman every third glug.

10.42 p.m.: Treasurer's husband asks for them to keep the noise down as he's got a busy day tomorrow. Treasurer heckles him down with an 'AS FUCKING IF' and the meeting is officially brought to a close.

Dads United

MATCH REPORT: Dads United v. the Flash Harries

Dads United's second ever match was a total shambles, thanks to the supreme fitness (and childlessness) of the Flash Harries, a team made up of sales boys from our skipper's place of work.

They arrived at the leisure centre in Audi TTs and Gold Mini Coopers and it took them bloody ages to get ready for the game because they all had to do their hair with gel beforehand. They emerged from the changing rooms with flamboyantly sculptured creations attached to their heads which we were lucky to see, because we were almost blinded by their white teeth and glinting Rolexes. Their captain, Harry 'Geezer' Mills, won the toss – obviously, because he is a total tosser. Their kit, sponsored by some trendy IT creative company, was pink to prove they were not just comfortable with their sexuality but also handsome testosterone-filled fanny magnets.

Before the whistle, they actually went into a huddle and started swearing and shouting, 'Let's smash it!' while we stood there awkwardly, scratching imaginary itches and exchanging nervous glances.

There is no point describing the actual match, because we were utter shit. They beat us 12–nil because they are fitter, younger, better looking and higher earners than us. Also, they are not fathers, and any sleeplessness they have is because they are shagging loads of birds and not doing night feeds.

Their goal celebrations were an art in themselves. Each one told the story of a Ryan Giggs infidelity, from Imogen Thomas to his sister-in-law, and their final goal was marked by getting a superinjunction. The smart arses. Half-time saw them do tequila shots using the dentist's chair formation. Honestly, what a bunch of pricks.

The result summed up a hideous few weeks for the skipper, who then proceeded to get really pissed after the game and tell everyone he was completely miserable because his wife had gone weird. Not only has she gone really quiet and withdrawn and failed to do any moaning at him for ages now, she has also started Tweeting every random thought that comes into her head, and occasionally breaks her silence to tell him how many followers she now has. He said he just didn't get it, because he was there to talk to, and she would rather communicate with strangers about trivial matters.

Oh, and he said his job was starting to get him down and he was thinking of asking That Woman he had a nightcap with WHO HE REALLY DOESN'T FANCY AT ALL if she had any positions going (oo-er). Then he said his wife had started wearing make-up and paying a little bit more attention to the hairiness of her legs because she's always being photographed for pieces in the paper, and he was so confused because she wasn't the woman he'd married, he barely saw her let alone got a blow job, and then he cried and had to be carried home.

Man of the Match: Harry 'Geezer' Mills for beating us before we'd even kicked off.

Donkey of the Match: The entire Dads United team. So useless, if we had failed to turn up, we'd have lost by a smaller margin.

Week Nineteen

How I Make It All Work

www.mumslikeus.co.uk

LATEST NEWS ... LATEST NEWS ... LATEST NEWS

You may have missed it, so here's the link to chair-woman Stella Smith's piece in one of those wanky weekend London-centric broadsheet mags which have recipes for stuff like fig truffle on fried partridge eggs and meeja agony aunts who always recommend expensive therapy:

> *Mums Like Us chairwoman Stella Smith, 36, who lives not in London but in nowheresville, like many millions of mothers, reveals How I Make It All Work.*

The alarm goes off at 5 a.m. and I bounce out of bed, delighted to be alive, and while I do my dawn yoga burpees, I wonder what adventures will come my way. Yeah, right.

What really happens is this: the human alarm clock, our three-year-old son, races into the bedroom, usually between 6.30 a.m. and 7 a.m. and subtly hints it's wake-up time by bouncing on my head.

My husband and I lie there in our silent stand-off – the rule is whoever flinches first has to get up with him. I usually win because I actually can't move until caffeine has been administered with a syringe to my eyeballs.

Breakfast is whatever fad my son is currently obsessed with but hasn't informed us what it is, so we get a bollocking for not being mind-readers. Sometimes it is eggy bread, other times it is a ham roll, it could be a supermarket cellophane-wrapped chocolate crêpe or a brioche, the fussy little so-and-so. We have given up telling him in our day it was Weetabix and we could only open the Shreddies once the Weetabix was gone.

The TV is always on – we get to 'come to' at a more leisurely pace. And it means he is more likely to finish his breakfast rather than take one bite and dash off to find something to break. I am obsessed with the fear of him being hungry because if he is, he gets like me, irritable, angry and prone to crying at the drop of a jar of coffee.

Once I've cleared away the crumbs, we get dressed. My son in something gorgeous a relative has bought him, and me in whatever smells

157

cleanish around the armpits from the floor, usually what I've been wearing for the last two days. Clean pants always, though – I do have standards, you know (one standard, actually).

Ten a.m. is the time we aim to leave for whatever activity we've got lined up. So we leave about half past. It can be the library to return some hideously late books (children's, so thank God there are no fines) and then a café. Or perhaps we go to meet friends at the park and then a café. Anything as long as there is always a drink and a cake involved (for me).

Midday is lunchtime. Whatever my son eats, it always involves broccoli and at least four other fruit and veggies because I am PARANOID about him not getting his vitamins. I think that's because, like most mums, we hate it when our kids get ill (distressing and also hideous due to disturbed sleep). It is also an irrational attempt to keep bugs at bay, because it is horrendous having to ring work to say we won't be in and receiving a huge sigh of, 'Oh well, we'll have to cope without you today, bitch,' from the boss.

Once I've dropped my son off at pre-school, I head home to catch up on work. I'm usually pitching to newspaper and magazine feature desks, most of which never respond due to my shockingly desperate ideas. If, for some bizarre reason, I do get a piece commissioned, I'll do it then over a cup of coffee and a packet of biscuits. While doing the washing, tidying the house, emptying the dishwasher, etc. I work in the kitchen and always set the oven timer so I remember to get my son, because I get so immersed in my writing.

But my priority is always Mums Like Us business. There is daily admin to do, website content to write, membership enquiries to answer and committee planning meetings on how best to get mums to strive for good enough rather than perfection. Social media is very important too and must be updated daily, even hourly. Twitter is proving to be a very useful tool for getting the word out; we are connecting with downtrodden mums across the entire world. At present we have some 250,000 followers.

If we have a meeting, I'll be arranging the cakes and trying not to eat them before the members arrive at my house.

Sometimes, I don't even do any of that. I simply set my alarm for fifteen minutes before pick-up time and go to bed for a nap.

Once school is over, my son and I go to the park and then it's teatime. I always make it a rule to eat whatever is left on his plate because it just wouldn't do to lose any weight.

My husband comes in from work and does bathtime, which gives me enough time to sink my first glass of wine. Then we take it in turns to do bedtime, because frankly, we both brought him into this world and I'm bloody exhausted by then and sometimes the whole battle of getting my son into bed after 5,000 stories can be the final straw.

Sharing two bottles of wine (sounds nicer than saying we sink a bottle each), one of us will cook dinner – mostly me, because I have a pair of tits, so obviously that's my department – and then we'll settle down to sit in happy silence in front of the telly for an hour or so until he falls asleep with his laptop surgically attached to his groin and I realise the washing needs to be brought in or I have a feature to finish for the morning.

Bedtime is my favourite time of day. I love shutting off the world with a good book or a nice row over the fact my husband never bloody thinks to change the sheets, and why is it always my turn?

Sometimes we fall asleep as early as 9 p.m.; parenthood is so rewarding but it is exhausting.

And we're usually pissed, which helps.

Week Twenty

Back to Business

Stella's kitchen

Hi all, I'm much better, thank you. I'm back to normal, have pulled myself together and everything is fine, FINE. It's all fine. A trip to the doctor for a good cry helped too. A big thank you to Mags for holding the fort – I've had lots of feedback from members, who were really impressed.

Right, let's crack on. I think I can say that we are getting our message across.

Four months on since we started this little club, we are now in the position of being 'on the radar'. At first there was a trickle of requests from the media for quotes from the club, but in the last few days, I've been approached by TV, radio and newspapers to give 'our view' on any story they're running that is vaguely mum-related. I've been asked about all sorts, from those stupid daily reports that come out saying, 'Working mums are responsible for ninety-nine per cent of the

161

world's troubles' to celebrity-inspired body-obsessed features on 'Should you ask the midwife to perform a fanny nip and tuck while they're down there?'

My standard response is always to (a) answer the question along the lines of 'what our members would say', which usually involves a howl of laughter then a stern mouthful of common sense, and (b) push the imperfect message.

It's doing wonders for Mums Like Us – you should see how many hits we're getting on the website every day. We seem to have online members joining up at a huge rate – they're in their hundreds of thousands now. And Twitter is going amazingly well – our followers include Oprah, Michelle Obama and Richard Madeley. Unfortunately Russell Crowe has blocked us because I sent a drunk tweet asking if he would do my housework naked for me.

Excitingly, the American press is showing an interest, too. *USA Today* put us at number three in its 'Top Fifty Subversive Women' piece, and the *New York Post* has done a spoof cover of *Vogue* using that photo of me with eyes-like-pissholes in my pyjamas putting the food waste into the caddy by the front door, asking, 'Is this woman the greatest threat to the beauty industry today?' Not forgetting *The New York Times*, which, in a piece about the effects of the recession on Mommy Superiors, called me 'the spokeswoman for a generation of ordinary mums' – how hilarious is that? They could have invited me over for an interview

– I fancy a seven-hour flight by myself to read and sleep.

Anyway, the only problem with it all is that Hattie Hooper is getting a bit shirty; there have been several interviews in which she's hit back at us. In one the other day she called me a 'disgusting role model', responsible for husbands having affairs and children having snotty noses. I'm sick to the back teeth of her attacking us when we have explicitly told her she's picking a fight with the wrong women.

I tell you what would get right up her nose – a march. So, this is what I wanted to talk to you about. I wondered what you all thought about us holding a demo – a peaceful one, obviously – to get our message across.

We need to rise above those who are spreading the Mother Superior myth that we should be aiming to 'have it all'; we need to tell women across the world that you can go for whatever you want, but if you can't manage it or you don't get there, you will not be branded a flop or pictured in the papers with a smidgeon of cellulite on your thigh which is cited as evidence you've let yourself go.

We must stand up for our beliefs, for the right to be good enough, to be average, normal, ordinary – to be as unremarkable as we want without being accused of slobbiness.

But for this to happen, we need to pool our ideas, because there'll be so much to organise. For example, where should we hold it? How should we go about it? What do we want to get across? What should we wear? And most importantly, what should we take in our packed lunches?

Lucy is in charge of the details – the time and date and transport and stuff. Alex will co-ordinate the legal side of it, being spectacularly scary when it comes to communicating with officialdom, such as arranging insurance and notifying the police and council of wherever we decide to hold the march. And Mags will look into the costings of travelling up en masse. It makes sense for me to sort out the publicity, get a buzz going and prepare a speech for the rally, which I only hope will get on the local news – they've got fuck all else to cover.

So, please send all your feedback to us as soon as possible, because the end of term is looming and we all know how impossible it is to have a quiet poo during the holidays. Talking of which, school sports day is on the horizon, and I just wanted to run through our position on this event which Mother Superiors live for.

The kids' races are all fine – feel free to shout your heads off for your little ones, ideally at a notch significantly higher than any Mother Superiors. Your aim is to drown out their 'Run, darling, run! Mummy is so proud of you!'

But the parents' races are what we really go for. I know the Mums Like Us mummyfesto spells out our position on exercise. But sports day is the exception to the rule. Mother Superiors will have been training for this from the day they gave birth. We haven't. But do not fear – our bodies are so unused to running that when we do, we will be carried along by adrenalin. It's only a small run, after all. Plus we have girth, which can be used in very effective ways. For example, we can swerve over into a Mother Superior's lane and knock them over.

You will know who the Mother Superiors are by their very expensive trainers, running leggings and very brief skin-tight vests which show off their washboard stomachs. In contrast, we will be in flip-flops, Primark leggings and something floaty which makes people wonder if we're pregnant again. Usually I would say make-up is up to you, but because sports day is so special, I recommend raiding the kids' face paints and applying war markings which will stun the opposition into submission.

Ahead of the race, give yourself a pep talk. Go through every snub you've ever received, every look that could've killed. That is your motivation to beat the Mother Superiors. At the starting line, kick off your flip-flops and start saying 'c'mon' really loudly, then at 'go', run like you've never run before. Imagine there's a bottle of wine waiting for you at the end, use your elbows, dig in those heels and go for it.

If victory is yours, feel free to roar with delight, pumping your fist and shouting 'YEEEEEEEEEEEEEEEEEEEEEEEEEEEES' in the faces of

165

Mother Superiors. If you can see you're going to lose to a Mother Superior, pretend you've twisted your ankle and pull up. Simple as.

That's that covered. We're nearly done, but just before you go, I wanted to let you know that a holiday company has been in touch. They're called OM Holidays – the OM bit stands for Only Mums, and the blurb on the letter they sent says OM also stands for the meditative state we will achieve after a week on one of their breaks.

They want four members to go away to one of their Mediterranean retreats for four days in three weeks' time to – and I quote – 'relax, unwind and forget about domestic duties', and in return we just have to do a piece about it on the website. It's what they call a 'bung' in the business.

It's very short notice to arrange childcare, so sadly some of us will be unable to go at all. It's such a shame, as every single one of you deserves a rest. Having had a think in the bath last night, I reckon the best way of working out who goes is for every member to email me with the name of whoever they want to nominate. It goes without saying we can't vote for ourselves, and if you absolutely can't make it, let me know and I'll strike you off the list.

Next week, we'll look at those suggestions for the march.

Sorry for kicking you all out, but I've got a hairdresser and beautician coming to make me look less revolting for a photo shoot for *Red* mag, then I'm going on the BBC News Channel to talk about our movement, and then a radio interview. Honestly, I do hate all the fuss for a photo shoot, but if me wearing a bit of lippy gets us in the news, it's a sacrifice I've got to make.

Week Twenty-one

Operation March

Stella's kitchen

Members, I am delighted by your response to the suggestion of the march.

Your ideas are stunning – you've blown me away. It appears we are all of the same mind – of course we are, that's why we're here! But to see you back the proposal, to know we're all behind it and willing to take our movement to the streets is simply breathtaking.

Having co-ordinated your thoughts, the committee has prepared a top secret handout, which I will pass round and read out so we are all on message . . . there you go, take one and pass it round.

TOP SECRET *** TOP SECRET***TOP SECRETE
(oops, typo, but sums up my bladder nicely)

Our Mission: The Mums Like Us March.

Our Message: To inspire mothers across the world to embrace our Good Enough philosophy.

Our Marching Ground: Westbourne Grove, Notting Hill, AKA Mother Superior HQ, where you will find exquisite skinny lattes, Smugaboo pushchairs, interior designer boutiques, bespoke jewellers, trendy cafés selling 'air sandwiches' (i.e. no bread, just salad), dog trainers, personal chefs, concept stores (whatever the fuck they are), an organic mattress shop (I kid you not), a beauty spa, an oyster bar, plus 4x4s and straw boaters as school uniform. This location will deliver maximum impact.

When: TBC but definitely midday on a Saturday.

Getting There: Coaches, so we all get there together and no one has a panic attack on the underground. Departure will be at 8 a.m. the day of the march. Lunch must be eaten before the midday start – on the coach, please – so we don't have any low blood sugar levels making us all dizzy and angry.

The Schedule: We will gather at the junction of Westbourne Grove and Portobello Road and then walk slowly down Westbourne Grove towards the junction with Queensway then back again. We'll continue this until we need a coffee and a sit-down. The pavement may have to do. Maps of the route will be provided so no one gets lost. The chairwoman will select a place on the day to make her speech (she will bring a cool box to stand on, plus a loudspeaker, or if she can't find one, either a kitchen roll tube or her son's ZingZillas microphone). Then we will have some cake. Then we will go home. We aim to return in time for *Doctor Who*.

Chants: We need some kind of catchy chant – off the tops of our heads, how about 'What do we want? Cake! When do we want it? Now. Or when we get a bloody minute' – plus slogans to write on our banners. This will be confirmed nearer the time. Suggestions welcome.

Outfits: We must appear as one to make sure (a) we present a united front and (b) our message is as powerful as possible. Therefore, the usual not much make-up, greasy hair, black velour hooded top and jogging bottoms set priced £2.99 from George at Asda, your most battered pair of shoes/ sandals/flip-flops, plus your Black's/Peter Storm waterproof jacket which you take everywhere just in case it rains.

Bring: Carbohydrates (such as sandwiches, crisps, sausage rolls), drink (flasks of coffee, Diet Coke and wine), a Shepee (the portable female urinating device), plus the usual crap you always take with you in your handbag. Phones are essential for remaining in contact should we lose any of you; bring cameras too so we record the march for posterity.

Publicity: Chairwoman to contact local TV, radio and papers. March announcement to be made public on our website 24 hours before demo to avoid any counter-action from Mothers Superior.

So there's the plan, hope you like it, you made it!

Next item on the agenda is the holiday. We had tonnes of votes through, and I'm really embarrassed to say the four people with the most votes were . . . the committee.

We just can't believe it. Many of you said we deserved the break because we'd worked so hard on the club, and I'd just like to say how touched we are. We could stand here and do some fake bluster and refuse to go, but we're not like that – we're really bloody grateful and we want to thank you from the bottom of our hearts for giving us the opportunity to leave our kids and husbands for a few days.

We promise we'll use the time together to plan loads of club stuff. In between dribbling on a sunbed, that is.

Thank you once again.

We'll send you a virtual postcard via the website in

lieu of a meeting, but we promise not to attach any of those really annoying photos of blue skies and cocktails by the pool because we don't want to rub your noses in it.

Week Twenty-two

Note To Self #1

In front of Stella's bedroom mirror, while
packing for holiday

Right, Stella, here's the thing – you're about to go on
holiday with the girls and you seem to have developed
a bit of an over-reliance on a few things you're not
supposed to.

I don't mean booze, although you are heading that
way and we'll discuss that at some point in the future.

But you need to talk to yourself about that brand-
new Lancôme foundation you've just secretly packed
in your suitcase, twice-wrapped in Tesco bags, which
you've told yourself is 'just in case they spill' – which
is highly commendable – but we both know there is
also a fear that you will be discovered by the girls.

It's OK, don't panic like that, you're not about to
deprive yourself of them. Every woman has a drawer
full of expensive beauty products they bought at one
time or another, usually if they're feeling bad about

themselves or they have met a new man or they're entering a new phase in life.

Yes, you've had an awful lot on of late and you wanted to treat yourself, and yes, you kind of got used to looking nice for all those photo shoots and TV cameras and all that. But just remember that you are the chairwoman of a club whose members see you as the epitome of good enough. Your job is to love yourself for who you are – and if they catch you with just a little bit too much make-up on, or see an expensive Mac lipstick poking out of your bag, or you go to the loo and that greasy forehead of yours has disappeared under a puff of powder, you will be rumbled and deemed a fraud.

There is nothing wrong with make-up per se, Smithy, the club does not outlaw it. Indeed, the Members' Handbook does have a list of permitted products such as ten-year-old mascara, crumbling blusher, blunt eyeliner and really unfashionable eyeshadow palettes. A bit of slap so you don't frighten the children is fine. But one step beyond lies a slippery slope. The ultimate conclusion is getting up at six a.m. to go to the gym, eating just protein and claiming your son loves spinach/pre-school pilates/behaving. You will be living a lie – and you know what that means: you'll have become a Mother Superior.

This is the first time ever in your life that you have found something that you completely believe in. What started as a personal gripe has turned into a crusade and women are listening to you, they understand where you're coming from and they agree with you. Their heads are at bursting point with a jumble of words from experts on how motherhood 'should' be done and pictures of mummy celebs looking immaculate in adverts for stuff, even though we know they're wearing hair extensions and false eyelashes. They believe they're inadequate – the truth is they are anything but.

The club is a breath of fresh air.

You are the woman who doesn't do zumba but if she did she would be painfully out of step to the beat.

You are the woman who advises wearing M&S Magic Knickers under a swimsuit because you don't see the point in dieting when there is support underwear on the shelves.

Don't forget that. There are plenty of people out there who would be willing to swap places with you.

Now chuck all these clothes into your suitcase and go and enjoy your holiday.

Dads United

Email to: davidsmith70@hotmail.com
Subject: Out of office
Date: 12 July, 15:34

Thank you for your email.

Fortunately, I am out of the office for a week on holiday.

Unfortunately, I am in sole charge of my three-year-old son while his mother goes away to a sun-drenched Mediterranean island with the girls to sit and read on a sunlounger with no interruption or requests for an ice cream, a trip to the beach or a play in the pool.

If your request is urgent, please ring the switchboard number below for assistance.

If you have any advice on how I can entertain my son, then please contact me on my mobile number below because I am not sure I can cope alone and I have no idea how my beloved wife does it and I'd really like a week off to myself for once.

I will respond to your email on my return. That is,

if I'm not signed off with stress, thanks to a child who is going to bed later these days because he needs less sleep, while I am going to bed earlier because I need more sleep.

Kind regards,

Matt

Week Twenty-three

Virtual postcard

www.mumslikeus.co.uk

Dear all,

So here we are! On our first day of holiday! Without the kids! Holy shite, it's fantastic.

We're on a secluded and remote beach resort in Ibiza somewhere, no idea where exactly because there really is no need to know. Our every whim is catered for, the sun is shining and mirrors are only available on request, so we're all imagining we've got super-duper tans and our bosoms are as pert as the day they sprouted.

Our journey here was terrible, obviously – a packed six a.m. aeroplane full of dads drinking double rum and Cokes and kids screaming. Luckily, OM Holidays laid on a bottle of champagne for us, so our edges were blurred, and we were whisked away from the airport in a limo, driven by José, a gorgeous male representative from the company. Five minutes into the drive, we all fell asleep and woke up dribbling two hours later in paradise.

First impressions? Put it this way, each of us wept with gratitude. Apart from the cicadas, there was silence. The no-shoes and no-clocks complex was immaculate, with lush gardens, three pools, a path to a private stretch of beach, and we each have a white-brick villa to ourselves. And there were no kids anywhere.

Once we'd finished jumping up and down and saying we were never going home, we noticed the staff. Every one of them was a handsome young man dressed in a uniform of thigh-skimming white tennis shorts and a huge smile. And the service? Anything we want is served with a loin-achingly good flirt – not OTT, but just enough to make you feel amazing. Thanks to her smiley Kylie elfin looks, Alex is quite the hit of the holiday – so if we need anything we get her to ask for it because they attend to her more quickly. She looks better in her bathers than we do. Must be all that Military Fitness she does, stomach crunches in the mud and all that.

The way it works is this: wake up in enormous king-size bed, breakfast is on the dazzling bougain-villea-filled veranda and you can choose to sit at either the 'chirpy' or 'don't speak to me until I've had three cups of coffee' table areas. Alex and Lucy go 'chirpy', Mags and I grunt until we've had caffeine. Seats are chaises longues so that the boys can feed you whatever you choose – from pastries to fry-ups, plus a bit of fruit if you need to keep your bowels going. Then once they've wiped the goo from your face, you're free to sit by the warm-as-a-bath pool – where assistants instinctively seem to know when you need a G&T or a bacon sandwich for elevenses. If you fall asleep, they gently rouse you if you look like you're getting burnt – that's not likely, though, because they have men to put sun cream on you. If you want to read, the staff will hold the book and turn the pages for you.

There is a spa where you can get the usual treatments, but there is also a brilliant one called 'sleeping' where they cover you in warm towels and you can drop off for as long as you like. The gym is fantastic, too – there are no exercise machines, just beds with attached fridges containing wine and chocolate, and your personal instructor will give you a foot massage.

Lunch is wherever you want it – again, fed to you so you can carry on doing nothing but masticate – and the afternoons are spent on the beach, where the assistants will plonk you on a lilo for a bit, making sure you don't fall off, and then return you to your luxury sunlounger with a plate of foreign chips, which as we all know are the most delicious thing in the world.

Then it's back to the villas for a snooze, a shower

and to get changed before we congregate at the bar and start our nightly ritual of drinking loads. Which is what I'm about to do, will continue this tomorrow . . .

So, it's day two and I will carry on from where I left off yesterday. Let me tell you about dinner. It's the most scrumptious banquet you can imagine – fresh fish, paella, more chips, whatever you fancy – and then the sweet trolley comes out. It's more of a sweet train, actually, there are that many to choose from. To make sure we give this place the most comprehensive review possible, we each have three puddings and then have a bit of everyone else's. The favourites so far are Sticky Toffee Banana and Death by Chocolate with Coconut Ice Cream.

In the evenings the resort hosts events such as wine-tasting and cocktail-mixing classes. I had a go at flamenco dancing lessons last night, which was great, because I was masterfully led around the dance floor by one of the staff who had the body of Nadal and the face of, well, I wasn't really looking at his face, to be honest. There is nothing like copping a feel of a beautiful stranger's muscles after a skinful.

Then they wheel you back to your room, where they take out your contact lenses, give your face a wash, get you a big glass of water and then switch off the lights.

The word on the resort is that they also offer 'special

services', such as a good shag, but none of us is in any fit state to copulate after such an exhausting day.

Indeed, we have been working very hard on club business, discussing our direction and long-term plan. Alex has drawn up a SWOT analysis spreadsheet detailing our strengths, weaknesses, opportunities and threats, which she will present to you all at some point. She is so on the ball, it's frightening.

Will finish this up tomorrow as can't stop yawning. Need a post-afternoon-nap pre-dinner snooze. OMG, OM Holidays is, quite frankly, the best invention ever . . .

Morning! We had a bit of a disaster last night. We decided to go on the resort's VIP Pasha trip to the world-famous club, which saw us behind the ropes on our very own table with endless Dom Pérignon, courtesy of OM. The four of us were having a great time, dancing away, when Lucy disappeared. We didn't notice for ages, assuming she'd just gone to the loo. But then there was a giant whoop from the crowd and all of a sudden, we spotted her up on the podium, stripping off down to just her bra, wearing her pants on her head, and thrusting and waggling her bottom at people. Security were having none of it. They clambered up onto the podium, but Lucy was too quick for them. She took off her bra and started waving it round her head, and then jumped into the crowd and legged it to the loo.

Obviously, we all panicked and followed her in hot

pursuit, managing to push her into a cubicle when the beefburger doormen barged in. We pretended we didn't know what they were on about and when they left, Lucy came out, still with her pants on her head, and asked why there was such a fuss – after all, wasn't this where they had live sex shows?

After we had corrected her – Manumission was where people did it on the stage, not here – she got dressed and asked if we could go and get a kebab before splattering the entire bathroom with sick. So we carried her out (luckily security didn't recognise her with her clothes on) and José drove us back to the resort, with Lucy's head shoved out of the window just in case she did an encore.

This morning, day three, Lucy admitted she smoked something someone gave her a few minutes before her strip. Fair enough, sometimes we forget we're responsible adults and it's very tempting to get carried away and try to roll back the years to those wild and crazy times we had before we had kids.

And that is sort of what we've learnt. While sometimes we crave time alone, time to have a bath with the door locked, time to temporarily waive our responsibilities and stride out into the world without having to check everyone's had a wee, what happens when you actually get a chance to do this is that you feel a huge hole in your heart, a heavy load at the pit of your stomach and as if a limb is missing.

We are all now sick of the sun, the staff and the

buffet. We miss our children. Even though we know the onslaught will resume the second we walk back through the front door – the sibling fights, the 'Have you seen my plastic thingy? You know, the red one from two Christmases ago, I need it NOW!' and the mess – we can't wait to go home and bury our noses in their necks, kiss their perfect skin and wonder at their little ways.

We even miss our husbands – well, apart from Mags, who says she would be happy to swap Si for José because she's sick of living with a mouse, not a man. In fact, I really, really, really miss Matt and I can't wait to see his gorgeous, missed-a-bit-shaving, stubbly, laughter-lined, weathered, forty-something face. This holiday has reminded me how much I take him for granted and how lucky I am to have him – I'm going to make so much more of an effort when I get back.

It's also made me think about my mum and how hard it must be at her age, having done her child-rearing and feeling this gap where her family used to be. I really need to be more welcoming and appreciative. Her lot was very different to mine; she had no career other than housewife, and my sister and I adored Dad when she was the one doing everything for us. That must've irked her – well, something irked her, and it still does, and I just want to make her happy.

We leave tomorrow at the crack of dawn, so see you at next week's meeting.

We are all going to spend the rest of the time here sleeping, just to make sure we are properly rested before our return to domestic un-bliss.

Adios all.

Your chairwoman,

Stella

Dads United

www.dadsunited.co.uk

Dear all,

There's no training this week due to childcare issues. By that, I mean I'm in charge, because Stella's gone away for the week.

Yeah, would be great to have a holiday – women seem to be able to justify getting away with needing a break, as in 'just a few days with the girls'.

Men rarely get away with 'I just need some time with the boys'; if we do, it's usually a stag weekend, and you know what wives think of those.

So I've taken a week off work and any thoughts of having a moment to myself, you know, to play some golf or go to the pub, well, they were beaten into submission by this list that Stella left.

I thought I'd share it with you:

INSTRUCTIONS ON HOW TO COPE WHILE I'M AWAY

MORNING: When you get up (or when you're woken up!!!), he likes a beaker of milk to start with. Then, he likes a play, which means with YOU and not by himself. Favourite games are the train set thing and hide and seek.

Don't put the telly on yet (you'll need that later when he's a bit bored) – otherwise he'll zombie out. I know this from bitter experience – he goes into this weird starey-eyed trance and his co-operation levels plummet even further. For breakfast, make sure you give him something with protein in it – protein (such as meat, eggs, cheese) fills you up, so it means he'll be less likely to have a meltdown when you're out (yes, you have to go out with him, too). For example, eggy bread, cheese on toast, bacon sandwich. Get some fruit down him, too, like a handful of grapes – not black ones, he hates them, and make sure you don't include manky ones, because he'll chuck them at you.

While you're making breakfast, put on a wash (programme E for dirty stuff, L for less dirty stuff).

After breakfast, get him dressed – no need for a vest, or he'll overheat and have a meltdown when you're out. Stick with shorts and T-shirt; don't let him wear his Lightning McQueen racing driver suit because it's fleecy and he'll overheat, etc.

Clean his teeth!!! Brush his hair, wipe his face. Oh, and you might want to get dressed too.

Before you go out, hang out the washing. Pack a bag with some tissues, water, banana and something like Mini Cheddars in case you get stuck somewhere and he starts melting down.

Ask him fifteen times if he needs a wee. Make him go if he still refuses.

Things to do in the morning:

1. Jazzy Pirate's Play Barn Fun House is good, free Wi-Fi and nice coffee, opens 9.30 a.m. every day.
2. If the weather is nice (and seeing as it's summer it won't be), you could go to the rec; remember sun cream and hat. There's a café there but the toilets are mingin, so make him go in the bushes. Remember antibacterial hand gel stuff.
3. There's soft play from 10 a.m. to 11.30 a.m. at the leisure centre on Mondays, Wednesdays and Fridays – cheap but no coffee, so take a flask.
4. You could take him to the library. His books need renewing, they're in his room on the side. He will refuse point blank to return them so just renew them to save a meltdown, look for new books which feature cats and trains.
5. He loves Ikea, so you could have a mooch

there. He might go in the crèche, but don't force him.

6. He quite likes going to the garden centre to see the aquatic fish, so if you're really stuck, go there.

Aim to be back in the house for about 11.30 a.m. so you can get lunch on. You need to get him to eat a proper lunch or he will crash out at nursery. For example, spag bol, meat and gravy, pasta, gnocchi, pizza etc. Make sure he has three lots of veg – such as broccoli, peas and sweetcorn, or green beans, leeks and spinach – plus fruit for afters. Once he's had that, he can have a yogurt or some chocolate or sweets.

You can stick the telly on now while you make lunch. Btw, NOT *Ben 10*, even if he asks for it, because it really scares him.

While you're doing that, give the loos a once-over with some bleach, wipe the surfaces and tidy up his toys as you go along. Put like for like in the same boxes or you will never find what he is after. He usually has a poo after lunch, so keep on at him to try. He will deny it vehemently but you'll know he's holding it in by the smell. He will relent and then you have to put him on the toilet seat, close the door, give him his privacy – he'll get upset otherwise – then when he's finished he'll shout for you. Do not let him take off his trousers when he sits on the loo or he will leg it once you've wiped his bum and you will be chasing him for ages trying to get them back on and you'll be late for nursery.

AFTERNOON: At 12.50 p.m., you need to leave the house, so make sure you start getting him ready at half past. Yes, it does take that long to get his shoes on and schoolbag sorted.

Pop him up to school. You have to go in with him to make sure he gets his name badge and hands his bag to a teacher, then you have two and a half hours to yourself.

Not really. You'll have the washing to bring in, the dishwasher to load/unload, sheets to change, hoovering to do, ironing, shopping etc. (I have arranged for a Tesco online shop to come on Wednesday between 8 a.m. and 10 a.m., so DO NOT GO OUT UNTIL IT'S ARRIVED, also there's loads of stuff in the freezer. But keep an eye on milk and bread – you don't want to run out of milk at critical moments such as breakfast time.) Think about what you'll be making for lunch the next day and if necessary, take something out of the freezer to defrost.

At 3.20 p.m., leave the house to do pick-up. Take a snack and drink and then go to the park afterwards. All his little mates go there after school so you can do half an hour or so there while he plays.

The ice cream van goes past at 4.17 p.m., so

make sure you leave beforehand or he'll have a meltdown when you say no, he can't have a lolly. I bet you say yes!!

EVENING: He needs his tea at about 5 p.m.. Do sandwiches (ham, cheese, chicken or peanut butter, but not egg, he'll puke that up), plus cucumber, carrot, celery sticks, but not tomatoes, he will not eat them if he can identify them, and don't bother reasoning that they're in pizza etc., he will refuse point blank. Aim for fruit, too, like grapes or apple cut up. I don't insist on sitting up at the table at teatime, he can have it on his lap in front of the telly. Give him a bag of crisps and something out of the treats drawer when he's finished.

He will be refuelled now so you have to play some energetic games, like hide and seek, races, football, tag, whatever he fancies.

Run the bath for 6 p.m.. He will only get in once you've played Monsters – that game where you have to chase him naked saying 'Monster Munch' over and over again. Get him to do a wee before he gets in. Wash his hair every other night. Make sure you clean his bum.

He will happily play in the bath for twenty minutes, but don't wander off just in case.

You could clean the bathroom while you're in there.

Check if he needs new pyjamas (sniff the crotch, if it smells of wee, change them), get him out of the bath and dry all the crevices or he'll get sore. Let him have a run around naked if he wants, helps dry him off. Slap on some of that dry skin cream that's in the cabinet and then get him some milk. Also an ideal time to check you've got a bottle of wine in the fridge.

Now he'll want a cuddle and some books. Try to encourage him to identify letters and numbers. You have to do the characters' voices too. He may ask for supper, like a little old man, so give him cheese and crackers. He can have some telly, too, or some games – get down on the floor with him and play.

At 7 p.m., take him up, clean his teeth, get his night-time nappy on (check willy is tucked in or he'll wake up wet) and give him a made-up story. Leave the hall light on, turn his night-light on, make sure he's got Puppy and Fluffy. Yes, I know you know all of this bit, but just a reminder. He'll be out of sorts with me away, so stick to the routine.

Hopefully, he'll go straight to sleep. If not, leave him chattering away – don't go back in unless he's crying. If he gets out of bed and comes down – very rare – then he's usually upset about something, so don't bollock him straight away, find out if he's hot or needs a wee or whatever. If he's got a temperature (thermometer in the first aid thingy in the bathroom), give him 7.5 ml Calpol to bring it down. Strip him off and let him come in our bed with you so you can keep an eye on him – put towels down wherever he is in case he pukes.

When he's asleep, you'll need to give the house a tidy – pick up all the Lego or you'll tread on it later and it'll kill. The cat will need feeding now. She needs lots of cuddles, too, having been hiding under the bed all day to get away from the Three Foot Tyrant. She needs three sachets plus bickies.

The bins go out on a Tuesday night – food waste in the green bags goes into the caddy thing; recycling all goes in together in the white Ikea boxes in the utility room, and it's also black bags this week. Stick it all on the pavement – when you go outside to do it, wedge the front door open or it'll slam on you and you'll be locked out. And hysterical.

You need to give the garden a water if it's been a hot day – I'll be gutted if my tomato plants die while I'm away!! You'll probably need to do some more jobs, like some ironing – never do this while he's up, just in case he pulls the cord and the iron lands on him.

Umm. Think that's all. Check in the diary for anything – don't think he's got much on apart from Mum's, when she does pick-up and gives him tea, so you might be able to fit in a pint!

I've left the doctor and dentist numbers on the kitchen noticeboard just in case. Easy, innit? Just thank your lucky stars it's not the summer holidays, because then you'd get no break whatsoever.

Love you, see you in a few days xxxxxxxxxx
xxxxxx

Lads, I am unsure if I'm going to survive this week – I'm stressing a bit, to be honest. Please spare me a little prayer if you get a chance. I might have to give my mum a ring and get her to visit. She's three hours away, but this is an emergency. See you on the other side.

Your captain,
Matt

Week Twenty-four

Survival Course: Wine & Chocolate
Stella's kitchen

Hi everyone, lovely to see you all! We've missed you so much. Wow – check out your pram tans! Looks like you've had some nice weather – such a relief to be able to take the kids to the park in the holidays, isn't it? Help yourselves to some of this lethal liqueur stuff we brought back for you. It's a traditional Ibizan drink – best to just neck it, because it tastes vile, but it does give you a bit of a kick.

So . . . yes . . . I have been crying.

Matt isn't here. He's away on business, but the way things were left, it feels like he's walked out. So I'm on my own. It's just me, my son, a box of tissues and these hideously puffy red eyes.

If I start weeping at any point, ignore me. I keep getting these waves of uncontrollable panic and sadness, punctuated by anger at Matt, followed by doses of 'I've-just-got-to-get-on-with-it'. Well, with a three-year-old there is no other option, thank God I've got my little man.

It all happened last week. When I came home from Ibiza, I walked towards the house with my heart soaring, desperate to see my two boys. I opened the door, shouting 'I'm home!', expecting to be squeezed breathless in a massive group hug. But as I came in, the first thing I noticed was another woman's smell. It was my mother-in-law's perfume – she'd clearly been here to help out, which is basically cheating. That got up my nose straight away.

Then I saw the mess. Shit everywhere. Millions of toys on the floor, plates piled high in the sink, books scattered across the carpet, dirty spoons lying in pools of congealed milk, single abandoned shoes and pyjamas and pants draped over the backs of chairs.

There was a note from Matt. He wasn't there. It said: 'Work called while you were away and said I needed to go on a course, some new product development thing. I can't get out of it. It's a residential whatsit, so I'll be gone for a few days. I didn't want to tell you before and ruin your holiday. Quite looking forward to it – last few days have been a nightmare as I had to do some work from home, even though it was my week off. When do I ever get a rest? The little one is at your mum's because I had to leave first thing. Dunno when I'll be back, ring you later.'

No kisses, no 'so glad you're back'.

I started to feel bewildered. Upset. And angry. This

wasn't the homecoming I'd expected. Yes, selfish of me, I know, but Matt's words were so . . . mechanical, so distant. Everything started reeling, my head went fuzzy. I knew something was up but I couldn't put my finger on it, I still can't.

I mean, I'd rung him every day while I was away and I'd ended every conversation with 'I love you' – but come to think of it, he'd always ended the call with an excuse why he had to go and he had seemed off with me. I'd just assumed that was because he was finding it hard going being alone with our son all week – I'd kind of thought, well, now you know how I feel most days, and left it at that. But as the silence of the house engulfed me, I stood there, frozen, trying to take it all in.

The phone went and I thought it'd be him telling me he loved me and not to worry, he was just tired. It was my mum, asking if I needed her to give my son his tea. I went into auto-pilot, telling her I wanted to do it because I hadn't seen him for a week, and then told her I'd been surprised to find Matt had gone. She said in clipped tones he had a very demanding job, it was no surprise he'd have to go away on business; he'd have so much to catch up on after I'd dropped everything to go on a jolly.

I lost it. 'A jolly? A bloody jolly? Yes, I've been away on club business – the first time in years and years without Matt or your grandson, might I add – but that doesn't give him the right to up sticks, with some vague explanation of "work". He has a responsibility to us. He's a grown-up, he's a father, he lives under this roof, we are entitled to know what's going on.'

The line crackled as she paused, then told me very simply I was living in a daydream world.

'I don't mean to sound harsh, love, but what did you expect? Women can't have it all. No matter what people say, or what modern women want, men, husbands, need to be looked after – they need a meal on the table, they need to feel special. Trust me, Stella, I know. Look, I've got to go, there's someone at the door. I'll see you later.'

I put the phone down. Mum was acting as if it was my fault, and worryingly, that it was more serious than I had thought. And then I cried huge bubbles of snot.

When she dropped off our son, dashing off because she was meeting a friend, I hugged him as if my life depended on it, as if his warm little body would give me strength. I told him Daddy had gone away and he just looked at me unblinking and said, 'I know. He's going to bring me back a present. Did you get me something from Ibeefa?'

The rest of the week has been a blur. During the day, I've gone into 'Everything's fine!' mode. There's no time to get upset because it's the school holidays and I can't let on I'm unhappy. We mums are great at this, aren't we? The evenings are the worst. I'm not sleeping and I'm drinking too much, and I'm swinging between confusion and insecurity. I know I'm not the best wife on the planet and I know I've been working hard lately with the club, but I love Matt so much, and I'm just really stunned he didn't tell me how he was feeling. And amazed that, if Mum is right, he could be so, well, old-fashioned and jealous because I'd found something outside of him and our son and work to be passionate about.

Matt called that first evening to say the hotel was fine. It was only half an hour away, so I asked why he didn't commute from home, but he said there were night seminars and the company was paying, so why not? And he wasn't sure when he'd be back because there was a chance he might have to go on a job, installing some new system somewhere miles away. He rings every day, but any attempt I make to ask how he is or what he's thinking, he clams up.

It's driving me mad. Obviously the committee has been very supportive, providing hot meals because I can't face eating – I've lost four pounds already, a very minor bright side to it all – and wine and chocolate, which, funnily enough, I manage to hold down.

I'm not sure what's going to happen. The club will not suffer, I promise you. In fact, it just makes me even more determined to see it prosper. I'm working my arse off on various projects to get our name out there. One of them, which is today's topic for discussion, is my idea for a zero-airbrushed naked calendar. You know, like the Women's Institute did, in which they hid their ladies' bits with jam jars and iced buns. Lots of organisations do it these days, but ours will be the only one that shows real women's wobblies without being Photoshopped. Our thighs will not be rid of cottage cheese dimples, our wrinkles will run free and our stomachs will not be wiped of stretchmarks. It's guaranteed publicity because it will create so much debate: are these women mental for doing it? How do other women feel about it? Do people actually want to look at unairbrushed images? I can see it now: we'll be loved and hated in equal measure, and we'll be invited to discuss it on every platform possible. We'll keep it simple, calling it the Mums Like Us Calendar, with all proceeds going to a women's charity of some kind. Perhaps we could even start up our own charitable trust, so people feel good about buying it.

Us lot on the committee have agreed to do it, which means that's four months taken care of, so I need some volunteers to come forward. It would be brilliant if we could get as many as possible to do it, because a huge group shot would make a fantastic cover. Ideas for each month, with a seasonal theme, include:

January: My New Year's Resolution Is To Be Good Enough – a member in bath of wine. Rude bits covered with screw-tops.
February: Take Me As I Am, Valentine – a member lying on the kitchen table. Rude bits covered by heart-shaped chocolates.

March: The Perfect Mother's Day – a member with feet up being waited on by naked hunky male. Rude bits covered by home-made cards.

April: Spring Cleaning Is Pointless – a member chucking cleaning products in the bin. Rude bits covered by feather dusters.

May: The Tummy Mummy Gets Into Shape For Summer Diet – a member bodypainted with chocolate, stuffing cream cakes into her mouth.

June: Summer Nights – group shot of members drinking Pimms in country garden. Rude bits covered by strawberries. Could double as cover.

July: School's Out – a member lying in a darkened room. Rude bits covered by Nurofen pills.

August: Love Your Mummy Tummy – a member on the beach. Rude bits covered by cocktail umbrellas.

September: Back To School Rules – member making up lunchboxes. Rude bits covered by Dairylea Triangles.

October: Hallowe'en – a member stuffing her face with her kids' 31 October sweetie stash. Rude bits covered by Haribos.

November: Bonfire Night – a member setting fire to white jeans and a Smugaboo pram. Rude bits covered by jacket potatoes.

December: Goodwill To All Tummies – a member engulfed by Christmas puddings, Turkish delight, yule logs, Christmas cakes and platters of smoked salmon, cheese, grapes and nuts. Rude bits covered by chocolate oranges.

Is anyone interested? Oh my goodness, you all are. Fantastic. Remember, no dieting, no trips to the gym, no stomach crunches in front of the telly. We'll be doing this for real women everywhere. If you're all happy, I'll sort a photographer and get us a beautician – I never said we had to go foundation-free, we've got to make the most of what we've got!

Right, that's it for this week. See you in a fortnight – it's my son's birthday next week, so there's no chance of hosting a meeting. I'm far too weighed down by the thought of making the party bags. In our day, there was no such bloody thing, just a piece of cake and a balloon if your parents were loaded. These days, the kids expect Lego Minifigures, sweets, bouncy balls and other plastic claptrap.

So, how about a shot of this Ibizan snifter? Who wants one, or is it just me?

Dads United

www.dadsunited.co.uk

END-OF-SEASON REPORT

Lads, it's been an emotional season, our very first as a team. As your captain, I would like to express huge and sincere thanks to every member of the squad, particularly those who did sweet FA on the pitch. You know who you are. We all know who you are.

We have only played two games, but we can be proud of ourselves. As Stuart Hall never said, it is not the winning that counts but the drinking. So, because we can't afford to have an end-of-season dinner – I'll be arranging a fundraiser at some point so we can hold a belated one at Christmas – here are the awards:

Player of the Season: Danno, for his never-ending enthusiasm for the beautiful game; for his optimism when we're losing; for his inventive goal celebrations (personal favourite was the Zumba Dance when the other half of the leisure centre hall was hosting a class and the teacher went mad at him for distracting everyone); and for introducing the club tradition of a post-match tequila chaser with our first pint.

Plonker of the Season: Stuey, for forgetting to wash our kit when it was his turn; for reminding us every week of his 'I could've been a professional if I hadn't broken my ankle in the Lower Sixth' story; for his secret warm-ups in the car park which he thinks we haven't noticed; and for his debatable football skills.

I hope that's inspired you all to greater things for next season. Pre-season training begins in a couple of weeks, see you there.

By the way, that week flying solo went OK, bar a few hitches. Put it this way, I'm glad to be away on business for a while. Stella isn't happy I've had to go away on a training course, but she seems to forget this is my job. Someone's got to pay the mortgage. I wouldn't mind, but she chose to be a work-from-home woman because she wanted to be there for the little one. Having to work away is part of the deal; it's as if she's taken it personally that I'm away. I'm actually surprised she's noticed I've gone.

Your captain,

Matt

Week Twenty-five

CrAP Emergency Meeting with Committee
Stella's kitchen

So, so sorry for getting you over here tonight, just really needed you three. Mags, there's wine there, I've had a bottle already, let me get you some glasses. Alex, there are some crisps somewhere and Lucy, if you're driving, we've got squash and bugger all else, sorry.

I've been feeling dreadful about Matt. The whole thing's been playing on my mind; something just hasn't been quite right. He's been gone about ten days and I've seen him once, on Saturday when he took the little one out for the day. His course finished that morning and then he was off on a work trip that night.

He seemed flat and angry with me and said mysteriously he hoped things would be sorted soon. I waited for an explanation, but our little boy rushed in and any chance of finding out what he meant was gone. Once they'd gone, to football club, a new thing Matt's started taking him to, then lunch and the cinema, I decided to look on the bright side. I told myself he was working really hard; he's under loads of pressure, he's missing us; he just can't afford to dwell on it because he has no choice – he has to get on with it because the mortgage is down to him.

But then an hour ago, I went on the computer to check something, and once I'd moved the mouse, the page that came up was Facebook and Matt's wall was up; he hadn't logged off. So naturally, I had a nose, not expecting to find anything but wondering if there were any clues on there. I found lots of posts by his uni mates and his brother living it up in LA, plus a few funny status updates on how his solo parenting stint was going and YouTube videos of funny goals and bands and stuff.

Then I went to his messages and . . . well, my blood runs cold and I feel sick just thinking about it . . . he's having an affair. When he said things would be sorted soon, that's what he meant – he's preparing to leave me . . . us . . . and this course and work trip are just lies. It's all so spineless. I never suspected he'd do this to us. I thought he was different.

Sorry, I'm rambling. Let me explain. Right at the top of his messages was a conversation he'd been having with That Woman. He'd just dumped her when we first met at a party, when I was with the Man Of My Dreams. She'd done the dirty on him with his brother and he was really upset because he was really into her. They'd been friends for a while – he'd known her since school, and then they started going out and he was head over heels. He told me when we first got together that they'd never had sex and it'd taken every ounce of strength to finish the relationship because she'd had a fling with his brother. He knew that was the right thing to do, but you know what it's like when you really fancy someone and it's there for the taking – she was really sorry, she'd been hammered when she'd gone off with his brother and she was desperate for him to take her back. I asked him back then if he felt they had any unfinished business – I wanted to know if he'd go back to her if he got the chance, and he was adamant that no, he didn't feel like that. I fell in love with him for that; he seemed so decent and honourable. But from bitter personal experience with the Man Of My Dreams, sometimes you do wonder what things would've been like had it all worked out.

So I clicked on the message – it was from a few months ago, and there was a string of chit-chat between them. She said she was really pleased they'd got back in touch after so long, he said he'd really enjoyed their drink, and they'd swapped mobile numbers. I didn't know he'd even seen her, let alone that they'd had a drink together. Why didn't he tell me? They've obviously been in touch since then because of their number-swapping. How fucking cosy. It's been going on behind my back and I just thought he was being off with me because I'd been away and working so hard on this club, and all the time he was betraying me.

I've tried to ring him tonight but his phone's off. I'm stunned. I never thought he'd do this to me. I still can't believe it. Matt and me were going to be forever, but obviously not. How am I going to explain it to my little boy – Daddy's buggered off with the woman he's always secretly loved? So now what do I do? Sit and wait for him to tell me it's over?

I'm dreading the birthday party tomorrow. He's said he's invented a 'quick job' so he can dash off from where he's supposedly been posted so he can come, which makes me realise how good he is at lying and covering his tracks. I can't bring any of this up tomorrow – I don't want to spoil the little one's big day. I'm going to have to ignore Matt because I know myself, I'm likely to cause a big scene. Thankfully, it's only two hours at that manky soft-play place on the industrial estate, and it'll be busy.

Shit. This is one of the worst days of my life – right up there with Dad dying. It's all so clear in my mind still – the call at lunchtime from Mum, when Matt and I were still aglow from getting married, to say that he'd collapsed at work and had been taken to A&E with chest pains, then all that hope, all that reassuring myself and my sister that he was a fighter all the way on the journey to the hospital, and then getting there and seeing Mum's face, looking old and haggard and pinched and pale and haunted, telling us he was already dead. I'll never forget her howls as long as I live. The doctors gave her some Valium or something and we all just went home and lay on their bed and sniffed the sheets and hugged his jumpers and tried to keep hold of him.

I'm feeling that same disbelief now. I look about me, my head in a spinning mess, the tears making everything all blurred. Everything we had just two weeks ago is suddenly on very shaky ground. At this very moment I hate him. I hate him so much for letting me down. But I'm trying to work out why he went to that cow – did I do something wrong? It goes against everything I've ever believed to say this, but maybe it's partly my fault. Have I let myself go a bit? Maybe my mum was right, maybe men need their wives to be adoring and dressed up, waiting for them with a hot meal and . . . but this isn't the Fifties. Women have changed, men don't seem to be able to accept that. Why do they have to be so fucking predictable? Why do they have to feel neglected and threatened?

Well, fuck him. I'm not standing for it.

You'd better go; it's late. And you'd better tell the members about my situation. They deserve to know, because my ups and downs keep interfering with the club.

Thanks so much for coming over, I'll let you know what happens. I'm fine, honestly, you've been brilliant. Seriously, go, I think I'm about to puke.

Week Twenty-six

Big News

Stella's kitchen

Lardies, come in, come in. I have some news. Some bloody ridiculous news.

I have been invited to the White House to meet the First Lady! Yes, you heard right. I am bloody wetting myself! Can you believe it? Six months ago, we had our first meeting here in this very room. Little did we know we would create a movement so massive that we would have the ear of the wife of the President of the United States of America. I tell you what, it puts my shambolic marriage into perspective. More of that later.

I received a phone call from her private secretary yesterday evening. I thought it was one of those crank calls and I started effing and blinding at this woman who, it has to be said, was very patient. After she'd convinced me – putting me through to the switchboard, who said yes, it was a genuine call – she told me the First Lady was holding a private afternoon tea for a number of women who were making a difference in their communities worldwide. Apparently, she'd read about us in the American press and was very impressed with our campaign for women to get real rather than dressed up.

I tried to get out of it – I said selecting me was against our democratic constitution and the way we did things was to select our own club representative. That's when she got shirty and did the 'may-I-remind-you' speech – she was calling from the White House and what the First Lady wants, the First Lady gets. She said if it wasn't me, it was nobody. So what should I do? Do you want me to go? It's up to you . . . you do. Fine. I'm happy to go, delirious even, just to get away from my shitty domestic situation.

One other point – the White House is hosting the event next month and suggested I contact its press office to see if I wanted to get involved in any other media opportunities on my visit. She said chat shows were the obvious route. Oprah would've been ideal, but she's not doing hers any more, so she suggested Piers bloody Morgan. It's worth a go, I reckon. Imagine if we break the States? This could be huge.

I'm not sure it's going to help my marriage, but frankly, Matt can do one. The woman said there was a crèche at the White House so I could take my son. Seriously, if Posh can travel with four kids by herself on a plane, give or take a nanny or three, then I can do it with one. I hope. Isn't this surreal? But that's the way my life seems to be going at the moment. The club is keeping me going and I owe you all so much.

My other news is that I have cancelled wine o'clock chez moi. The reason for this is because I hit rock bottom last week. I've been necking a bottle of wine every night for the last God knows how many, spending the days feeling so tired because I don't sleep properly, and being tipsy before my son's even gone to bed. I'm really ashamed of what I did.

Let me just boil the kettle and I'll tell you what happened. As the committee will have informed you, Matt and I are unofficially separated as he's still pretending to be on a job miles away while he prepares to dump me. Our son is the thing that keeps me going, but the other night after his birthday party, I did something so stupid and so selfish, it was a like a wake-up call to grow up and take responsibility for the little one and our happiness.

I was emotionally exhausted after avoiding Matt and pretending to be happy and smiley all day when inside I was worried sick about how the break-up would affect my boy. I'd rather kill myself than let That Woman be around my child, playing happy part-time families with Matt. So I hit the bottle big time. I felt I could get away with it because my son was staying at my mum's that night. I have no recollection of what happened next. All I know is I woke up naked in bed with a note from the Man Of My Dreams on my pillow.

I know, I know, I was as shocked as you all are now. My mobile and the note helped me put some of it together, but there are certain things I still don't know. There were a load of texts I'd sent the Man Of My Dreams – awful, cringey, desperate, self-absorbed and needy texts. I'm mortified. I am not shifting the blame here – I clearly contacted him first – but it was obvious I was drunk, and after how things were left last time between us, he should've just told me to go to bed. Instead, he texted me to say he was in town seeing a mate from our old paper and he was on his way over.

I remember opening the door to him but after that, nothing. From the note, I can only assume we ended up in bed together. I may as well read it to you, because I have lost all my dignity anyway.

Hello you,
    Did tell you last night I couldn't stay, so don't get your knickers in a twist. That's if you can find your knickers.
    Hope your head isn't too awful.
    Me xxx

So, I have no idea what went on, what we talked about or if we did anything. Anatomically speaking, it didn't feel like we'd had sex – sorry to be gruesome. But there's no point giving myself the benefit of the doubt. It doesn't matter if we did or not – what matters is that I acted like a twat. I used drink as an excuse to behave irresponsibly and I got myself into such a state that anything could've happened to me. And the person who would've suffered would've been my son, which is why I have stopped my six p.m. Sauvignon Blanc.

Obviously, as soon as I'd read the letter, I vommed. Then I unhooked my knickers from one of the bedside lamps and I rang the Man Of My Dreams. It went to voicemail, so I left a message telling him I never wanted to see or hear from him again. For the second time of late.

Then I showered and scrubbed and sobbed and vowed I wouldn't waste a second more feeling sorry for myself or wondering what could've been with Matt. I also went to Boots and got myself a morning-after pill, just in case. Then I promised myself no more solo self-pitying boozing.

My focus from now on is my child and this club. Men can go to hell. By the way, that's not my chin wobbling. It's absolutely not.

Dads United

Email to: davidsmith70@hotmail.com
Subject: Party
Date: 17 August, 23:10

All right, Dave?

Just a quickie. I've attached some pictures taken today at the nipper's party – brilliant presents, by the way. The Darth Vader costume was very well received. He wore it all day and I think he went to bed in it. I say think, because he's staying at Stella's mum's tonight. Thought I should tell you that Stella and I are going through a bit of a rocky patch.

I had to go away on business the second Stella got back from holiday and she took it really badly. The company put me up in a hotel for a training course, and now I'm installing a new system an hour up the motorway and I'm on call 24/7, so I haven't been properly home for ages.

I stupidly told her I had to leave for a while because I needed to give this job my full concentration and she took it the wrong way, telling me to leave her alone. You know what a shit she is when she's angry, so I backed off, and I've only been ringing to talk to the boy. It's ridiculous – a simple misunderstanding, a bit of rubbish communication, and now it feels like things are on the edge.

I'm a fuckwit. I just was so knackered from work, and then Stella went away with her mates, and the week without her was unbelievably hard. I never knew how tiring it really was to look after a kid 24/7. I should've told her that, but I just stewed over it all and thought how men have it hard, too, and there's never any support for us, we're just expected to deal with it. Obviously I've buggered it all up.

I tried to talk to her, but she kept right out of my way at the party today. I could tell she'd been crying – she gets a little red blotchy patch on her neck. No one else would've noticed. But even so she looked amazing. She looked glam – she has done of late, come to think of it, sort of in a 'made-up not to look made-up' way. I blame the club for that – it's changed her.

The stupid thing is, all of this came about because I'm trying to do the right thing. It's too complicated to explain now, will fill you in as soon as I know, but get this, it involves That Woman.

I can't believe I've been a dad for four years – the time has flown. I hardly remember the early days; the tiredness wiped out all the memories. I'll never forget seeing him for the first time, how he was plonked on

Stella's chest, bawling at the indignity of it all.

Anyway, cheers, give Mum a call, she wants to talk to you about Christmas – yeah, she's started on about it already and it's only bloody August.

Matt

Week Twenty-seven

Matt's Back
Stella's kitchen

Right, you know I said 'men can go to hell'? Well, it turns out I am in fact going to hell myself, because Matt is back and he has done nothing wrong. I repeat, nothing wrong. Whereas I am now the guilty party, having spent the night with the Man Of My Dreams. Obviously I haven't told him anything, and I'm so glad our code of conduct includes the Official Secrets Act or I'd be in the shit. Not that any of you would grass me up but . . .

He came home at the weekend. He looked dreadful. There was a knock at the door and when I opened it, I had to stop myself from saying 'no, not today'; I swear he looked like a tramp. He was white as though he was sickening for something, he'd blatantly had a cry and he stank of booze.

I froze and automatically stepped back so he could stagger in. I also stepped back because he smelt really horrible. I tried my hardest to stay rational and calm – he'd been a complete wanker and I wanted him to know it – but the sight of him made my heart gasp. No matter what had happened, he was still my husband and the father of my son. I went into 'poor lamb' mode, told him to come in, sit down and have a cup of tea. Once our son had covered him in kisses, I switched the telly on and told him to let Mummy and Daddy have a little chat.

Matt just blurted out, 'She lied to me. She told me there was a job going at her company, but she lied.'

Feeling strangely calm – not how I'd imagined I'd bring it up during all the hours I'd spent planning how I was going to throttle him – I told him I'd seen his Facebook messages and put it to him straight: 'Has That Woman dumped you then?'

He looked up, incredulous, staring at me as though I'd wounded him. 'What? Do you think I was . . . with her? When I've got you and . . . No, no, no. No. Oh my God, no.'

He explained everything. He really had been off at a course then on business, having a shitty time in faceless hotels, being schooled in a new revolutionary load of crap then afterwards giving a bunch of incompetent members of staff lessons in how to switch on their computers. The drink with That Woman happened at a conference he'd been at in March. They'd talked shop all night – he was desperately unhappy at work and she'd offered to find an opening for him at her place. Later she asked him to come to an interview – she's a big-shot company MD and he'd thought she was going to offer him a job. He hadn't wanted me to know any of this because he didn't want me to worry about how hard he was finding everything, he'd wanted to fix it all himself and come home the reliable breadwinner, surprising me with a shiny new job and salary.

Instead, she set him up with the intention of having her wicked way with him. I have to say, he was a bit naïve – the interview took place in a hotel room, not in an office. He claims he thought it'd be in a conference room or over dinner, but she took him up to her room and laughed when he asked about the job she had going. I can imagine his innocent little face, his inner panic, his stuttering excuse to leave. The poor thing. So he did what any man would do – he went and got shitfaced and then slept it off in the car in the pub car park.

But why the hell he didn't discuss with me the tiny matter of changing jobs is beyond me. He says he didn't want to tell me until he'd had a firm offer. He didn't want to get my hopes up, because I had so much happening. And then he said all he'd ever wanted was to give his family a better life, to be able to build a future, to give our boy a good start, to set us up for retirement. He said he'd felt so useless of late, like he was the one who got under our feet.

Jesus. That was when I burst into tears, not only for

him but for my stupidity. Both of us have been fools, both of us have lost our way. I felt relief: relief he hadn't done the dirty on us and relief he was the man I thought he was. But also a huge sense of loss, at how I'd let him and our son down – everything I'd falsely accused Matt of doing, I'd ended up pretty much guilty of myself. I even felt sorry for That Woman, to go to those lengths to entrap someone else's husband. She must be really miserable to do that. On the surface, you'd think she has it all. Her own business, amazing holidays, an exciting social life – I know this, because I've been stalking her on Facebook, particularly her photos of scuba-diving in Nicaragua and trekking in Nepal – but underneath, she must feel like a piece of the jigsaw is missing. Or maybe she's just a lunatic. Makes me realise how lucky I am.

Matt and I just sat and hugged for ages until our little boy came in and got jealous and started punching Matt, telling him to leave Mummy alone. Then he asked if Daddy was home again now and I quickly said, 'Yes, Daddy's back, we're all together again.'

I can't deny I'm feeling horribly guilty. I considered telling Matt all about the Man Of My Dreams, but what would that achieve? It would only appease my conscience. I'm better off keeping it quiet, learning from it and making sure I count my blessings every day.

Apologies to all who've had to witness my

breakdown and descent into a moral vacuum. Sometimes I wonder if I'm the right person to be chairwoman. Anyway, you're stuck with me for now. And thanks to you lardies, this weekend we're all off to America to do the White House. Matt is coming – we all need a holiday – so there'll be no meetings for a fortnight. I'll be writing on the website so you can keep up with what I'm up to.

Finally, things seem to be going right. It's even been maxi dress weather – how brilliant are those dresses? No need to shave your legs at all.

The next time we meet, the kids will be back at school – bliss, eh? Although my son starts reception next month and I am having massive wobblies about him leaving me. This is typical of me: I spend most of the time trying to peel my son off me then the thought of him going to school all day makes me feel empty and sad. My mum told me this is the start of empty nest syndrome; I presumed it came on when your kids leave home. I never realised it started so early. Luckily we have each other, and I'm sure many of you who have gone through this will tell me sagely, 'You'll get over it. After a week you'll find the three twenty-five p.m. pick-up arrives too soon.'

Besides, we have a march to occupy us. Not to mention getting our calender together – shooting starts next month. And after that, it's Christmas. Ha! Don't all moan! You can bet Tesco has its festive lines in the stockroom and they're just waiting for the first leaf to fall from the trees to put them out to torment us. With that seasonal rant over, make the most of the holidays, and if you're going away, remember to wear those tummies with pride on the beach!

Dads United

The Feathers

Yeah, that idea of mine to do pre-season training was a bit shit, wasn't it? Glad you all emailed to give me a bollocking and to suggest we meet here instead. What on earth was I thinking? Much better to have a pre-season pint instead so we can discuss er . . . tactics and stuff.

Some of you might have heard me and Stella were having a few problems. Well, we did, but it's all sorted out now. It was a bit up and down, but we're back together and it's all good. I feel awful for putting Stella through it – the funny thing was, it was all a bit of a comedy of errors. Can you believe, she thought I had a bit on the side! I know, I'd never do that, not my style. Women frighten the shit out of me, frankly. I could have an affair with *Match of the Day*, but never another woman.

You see, That Woman, well, I thought she was after me going to work for her. She dangled this carrot in front of me, suggesting we hook up, and I thought she meant making me a director. She said she'd interview me at a hotel because their boardroom was being redecorated.

I made sure I was all suited and booted, expecting to meet some of her other company execs. When I rang her number she told me to go up to her room. It was an odd time, come to think of it, about 7 p.m., but I just assumed she wanted to give me a pep talk, you know, a guide of what to say to impress the others. I thought she might give me a tip or two, a warning about who I was going to meet, that kind of thing.

I knocked on the door and she shouted, 'Come in!', so I did, and there she was, in bed, with a bottle of champagne, in her undies. Then she got up and jiggled towards me in this black lacy thing and suspenders and she told me she had an offer to make me.

I just froze. Stop laughing, you lot, it was awful. No, I didn't have a stiffy. Any appreciation of her female form just disappeared there and then – she's a bloody nutter. So when I stood there with my mouth open, she took that as a come-on and pulled me towards the bed and told me she'd been waiting for years and years for me to come round. She said she'd always wished things had worked out between us, she'd felt so awful about shagging my brother and she wanted to make it up to me. I just started babbling – 'Oh my God, Stella always said you were unhinged for choosing my brother over me, she was right about you' – which was the worst thing I could've said, because she suddenly went off on one.

'Stella? Stella? Why are you bringing her up? You can't back out now. You said you wanted to be with me, you said you were ready for a new start,' she screeched, her eyes flashing – she's got these green eyes, and they went all lizardy and mental.

'I didn't mean with you . . . like this . . . wearing that,' I said, stammering by this point. 'I meant as a business partner. I thought you were going to offer me a stake in the business, I thought . . .'

She started weeping then, saying she loved me and Stella didn't deserve me, and she begged me not to go, so I couldn't walk out.

I felt really bad that I'd got myself into this situation and, really pathetically, that I'd hurt her too. I waited until she'd stopped crying and then I told her I wouldn't mention it to anyone in the industry, wouldn't dream of it, I'd look a right idiot. She asked me not to say anything to Stella, but I told her that'd be impossible because we'd always been honest with each other, well, most of the time. Then she started going on about how lucky Stella was and how she didn't appreciate me – I had to agree with her at that point – and she said she'd 'show her', whatever that means. I suppose I should've walked out, but we've been mates for years, so I gave her the 'you'll meet someone and fall in love' chat. She was adamant she already had – me. I tried to put her off, told a few shit jokes, belched the word 'bollocks', and then I gave her a hug goodbye – I'd made her get dressed by then and no, I didn't have a peek . . . well, maybe a little one. Eventually I managed to unwrap her arms from around my neck – it was like pulling off a velcro octopus – and I walked out, feeling gobsmacked by what had happened.

I got in the car and drove around for ages, trying to process what had just happened, then I went to the Golden Lion, where Stella and I had our wedding reception, got shitfaced and slept in the car. Next day, I went home and I came clean about everything with Stella, apart from the naked bit.

Stella was amazing. I thought she was going to hit the roof, but she accepted my apology and told me she didn't want some ball-breaking megabucks husband, she just wanted me as I was and that was that. She even said she'd been neglecting me and apologised. I mean, this woman never says sorry, she's always right. It was like some kind of breakthrough.

She really is an incredible woman. She was so calm and forgiving – talk about inner strength, and God . . . I can't believe she's mine. Then she told me about America and I was just blown away.

So, we're off in a couple of days, just the three of us. It's a quiet time at work now, anyway, so the boss let me have some leave. I can't wait to get away with my family. Yes, Stella will be going to the White House

227

– I can't be arsed to explain why, it's to do with that club of hers – but it's only for a few hours and the rest of the time we can just hang out and go sightseeing and eat and argue. It's going to be wicked.

Cheers to that, boys.

Week Twenty-eight

Virtual Postcard from America

www.mumslikeus.co.uk.

Dear all,

OMG! We're in America! It's big, it's loud, it's like an all-you-can-eat buffet! Needless to say, I am loving it.

So we arrived two days ago, flying to New York, which was pretty painless, I have to admit, because we were flown over by the White House in First Class. FIRST BLOODY CLASS! The stewardesses were amazing. They took our son off us and played with him so we could sit back and eat our seven-course meal with real cutlery and china plates, and we even managed to get a nap in too.

The complimentary travel bags were incredible. I made sure I nicked a second one, too – they're so nice, they'll do for a Christmas present for my mum. Inside, they had Bulgari perfume, soap and body lotion, plus posh chocolates and diamanté ear plugs. Matt's was fantastic, too – designer aftershave and ruby-encrusted nose hair trimmers. I nicked his off him before he had a chance to use it, so that'll do for his dad, who is yet to be persuaded to drop the Brut, bless him.

When we landed in New York, we were ushered off through customs – no two-hour queue for us; we were treated like proper VIPs. A stretch limo took us to our hotel, where we checked in, dumped our stuff and headed off to Fifth Avenue to just walk and gawp at everything. We'd promised the little one we'd go in search of *Star Wars* toys, too – it's his new fad, lovingly cultivated by his father, who is a total *Star Wars* geek – so we tramped around for ages for that, anything to keep him a bit quiet! The total highlight so far is dining out: ginormous portions, free refills and loads of cheese on everything.

In a couple of days we go to Washington – First Class once again – for the tea party, then we come back for a round of interviews with the American papers and magazines. Then I'm appearing on a few talk shows – still waiting to see if I make *Piers Morgan Tonight*; depends on how I'm perceived in the media, I suspect. But I have a trick up my bingo wing, so you'll just have to wait!

The First Lady's office has been in touch quite a lot, outlining the etiquette of the tea party. Apparently, I need to dress up and get my hair and make-up done, because that's the way things are done here, so if you see me in any coverage, that's why I'll be resembling a Mother Superior – it's not what I want but it's something I just have to do. I will be channelling my inner tummy, don't you worry.

This break is just what Matt and I needed, it's like the last month never happened. We're getting on brilliantly – we've even had sex. Proper sex, not we-ought-to-do-it sex but we-want-to-do-it sex. Don't get me wrong, it wasn't brilliant, but it happened, and that's good enough for me. Our hotel room is a suite (not like our usual holidays when there's one bedroom and Matt ends up on the sofa bed in the lounge because me and the boy end up in together), so once we've put the little one to bed we can relax, getting room service and drinking Manhattans – I'm allowing myself alcohol in company, not alone – looking at the skyline from our balcony. The view is incredible. We can see for miles around – the lights of New York are never-ending. It's, dare I say it, very romantic. It also helps that I don't have to make the bed, clear up, do any washing, think of what I have to cook or pick up Matt's wet towels. I'm so relaxed I'm even dropping my wet towels on the floor too.

Must go, we've a schedule to keep to – doing the Empire State Building and the Statue of Liberty this afternoon.

Wish you were all here.

Lots of love,

Stella

Week Twenty-nine

What the Papers Say
The *Telegraph*: 'Mums Like Us' takes America by storm

Eight months ago, no one had heard of Stella Smith.

Today, the chairwoman of Mums Like Us is the talk of America after upstaging – and then winning over – the First Lady with a semi-naked protest at the White House.

Before hundreds of guests at a tea party to celebrate women making a difference in the world, including the Duchess of Cambridge and Lady Gaga, Mrs Smith took a huge gamble, challenging the United States' prudish reputation. But the mother-of-one's near-naked stunt, to draw attention to what she called 'a generation of invisible women', appears to have paid off, with newspapers, magazines and TV stations reporting a national outpouring of heroine worship for the 36-year-old from nowhere.

Throwing off her sober midnight-blue trouser suit as the First Lady went to shake her hand, Mrs Smith said that stripping down to her greying bra and armpit-warmer knickers to 'flash my wobbly bits' was designed to highlight the unseen millions – women who have had kids, who are struggling day to day to keep up with the spectre of Mother Superior motherhood, who feel disengaged, uninvolved, worthless and ignored by a society which values youth, pneumatic breasts and tight buttocks over experience.

The tour de force, including the moment the First Lady ordered her security guards to stand down after they tried to grapple Mrs Smith to the floor, was captured by rolling White House cameras, which record events for Presidential archives. The footage was released yesterday, on the First Lady's instruction, and instantly went viral, registering millions of hits worldwide.

Her private secretary last night paid tribute to Mrs Smith, saying, 'Stella is a remarkable character. Throughout history, campaigners have resorted to drastic measures to force a spotlight on their beliefs. Stella knew nudity remains a taboo in the United States and so she used it to put across a point about women being accepted for who they are and what they are, not who they should be or what they should be doing. This brave act will be remembered for a long time to come and I celebrate her courage.'

Capitalising on her new-found fame, Mrs Smith flew to New York to appear on CNN's *Piers Morgan Tonight*, wearing clothes this time, where she called herself an 'everywoman', confessing she had given up alcohol because wine o'clock had turned her into a drunk. She also admitted she is on anti-depressants, claiming 'virtually every mum I know is or has been on them' because mothers don't have the time, money or inclination to attend talk therapy, thanks to their gruelling daily schedules.

Mrs Smith is due to return home to Britain this week.

Her nemesis, Hattie Hooper, who is chairwoman of Mothers Superior, which encourages mothers to make an effort on the school run, expressed disbelief at Mrs Smith's behaviour. 'This woman is publicity-hungry. She will do anything to get her name out there. And have you noticed she was looking exceedingly well groomed at the White House? Her usual attire is drab and unironed, but in America, she appears to have had some kind of transformation. I do not trust her and I implore mothers to seriously consider their support for her club,' said Mrs Hooper, who was speaking from her second home in Tuscany, where she is holidaying with her husband and four children.

She's still got her mummy tummy but the question is: has Stella Smith had work done?

The 36-year-old, who streaked at the White House, was last night accused of betraying her worldwide following after cosmetic surgeons gave their verdict on her suspiciously fresh-faced new look.

Here's what the experts said:

Teeth – appear whitened and less coffee-stained than previously.

Eyes – her crow's feet look softer, probably thanks to Botox.

Forehead – her frown lines have been smoothed out, suggesting fillers.

Hair – blow-dried and streaked, the brassy cheap blonde colours have been replaced by warmer hues of honey.

Skin – her pasty complexion looks sun-kissed, fake tan smudges visible on ankles.

Hattie Hooper, chairwoman of Mothers Superior, reacted with disgust. 'Her figure is unchanged – dumpy and flabby as usual – but her face is remarkably youthful. If she has had work done, then she should admit it. Her followers deserve the truth,' she said. 'If she has, then she is lying to everybody, and her club will be exposed for what it is: a giant ego-trip for Mrs Smith and Mrs Smith alone.

'It is obvious from her dependency on alcohol and anti-depressants that she is unstable. She is behaving like a wailing banshee and leading astray many unsuspecting women. Medication and the taking thereof is not something that should be made public. This woman has no grasp of what should be kept private. I pity her and my heart goes out to her long-suffering husband and son, who must be deeply traumatised.'

Club secretary Alex Walker last night said an internal investigation would be launched because members 'have a right to know' the facts. She insisted Mrs Smith was the 'unlikeliest mum in the playground' to have dabbled in surgery and she was sure the chairwoman would be vindicated.

Week Thirty

Stella 'Fesses Up

Stella's kitchen

I swear I was going to tell you – I swear on my life. It completely slipped my mind and I kept meaning to bring it up. Please believe me, I didn't intentionally mislead any of you. I completely understand you're disappointed in me – I would be too if I was you. But let me say you're not in full possession of the facts, which is entirely my fault.

The emails and tweets and messages I've had in the last week, well, they've been brutal. Rightly so. Many have come from members, even mums sat in this very room, and I only have myself to blame. Your shaking heads and angry faces tell me how furious you are, but I can explain.

A month ago I was approached by a TV production company commissioned by BBC Four to take part in a documentary with a twist. They asked me if I was prepared to undergo a transformation into a Mother

Superior for a week. I was instantly smitten with the idea, because I felt it would give me, us, an insight into their lives.

I suggested a few things I could do – such as having a personal trainer and a nanny, as well as dressing up each day, making sure my hair looked immaculate, that kind of thing. Then they suggested a range of beauty treatments such as Botox, fillers and teeth-whitening. I was dead against it at first. But they told me I'd have to go the whole hog if I was to make the documentary credible. Yes, I'll admit there was a tinge of vanity involved. I'd seen how ragged I'd looked on telly and in the papers, I was even beginning to wear more make-up to try to make myself look less of a pig's ear. I told myself it was a necessary evil.

So just before I went to America, I went to a cosmetic surgery place, where the secretaries had the freshest of foreheads and most dazzling of smiles and I was bewitched. I wanted to get it done quickly so I could cross it off my list of things to prepare for filming, which was due to start this week. After all, the effects of the cosmetic stuff would last for months, so it didn't matter that I got it done weeks ahead of the fly-on-the-wall filming. There was so much to organise. I did have help from the production team to get me a Mother Superior wardrobe and compile a shortlist of nannies I could choose from, but it was up to me to get my face done. So I did it. The cameras rolled while I sat in the chair with black marker pen and needles and gum shields. The footage captures my nerves and reluctance to do it, and indeed there's a scene which shows me wrestling with the surgeon after he's done the crow's feet on my left eye. I freaked out and told him this was against everything I stood for, but once he'd pinned me back down again, he told me I'd look a freak if I didn't finish the job. So I relented. It was bloody horrible, too, like being at the dentist, getting poked and prodded, and I was quite puffy afterwards. Puffier than normal anyway.

I wish I'd never done it.

For this catastrophic error, I sincerely apologise to you all. I can only say my intention was true – to expose the heartbreaking betrayal of one's morals in the pursuit of perfection. I don't even think I look any better or younger, just weird. To be honest, I feel like the Joker, my features are paralysed and it'll take a while before the wrinkles come back. Obviously, Matt didn't notice any difference whatsoever, so he doesn't even know. He doesn't read the papers any more because they make him angry, he just sticks to the Channel 4 news.

But I fucked up. I've pulled out of the documentary – and yes, I paid for all the work myself so there's no suggestion I benefited financially from it. You'll be wondering why I didn't say anything. Well, if you remember, I was in a bit of a state a month ago. My equilibrium had been shattered; it felt like I was walking on a bouncy castle. My judgement was shot to shit. I was like a chicken, flapping around and walking in random directions; I'd meant to bring up the documentary but I forgot. Then once I'd had the facial freezing, I felt guilty and embarrassed and I hoped no one would notice. I was a coward.

Then we went to America and I conveniently left my treachery at home; I hoped my achievements for the club would overshadow my misdemeanours. Weakly, I hoped you wouldn't notice. I convinced myself you'd be proud of me. I couldn't wait to come back here victorious, to tell you the First Lady had told me in confidence she would've become a member if she wasn't who she was. To tell you I'd been stopped in the street over and over again after going on Piers Morgan's show. To tell, you I'd been asked to go on *I'm A Celebrity . . . Get Me Out Of Here!* and *Strictly Come Dancing* and a load of other programmes.

But that means nothing now you know what you know.

I will obviously put all this in writing in a statement for the press. I am quite prepared to be dragged through the mill. But I also know I can turn this negative into a positive, that's if you'll still have me. I really think I can use this experience to show a wider understanding of what we're up against.

OK, if anyone wants to come up and give me a slap, then go for it. Alternatively, you can save it up and have a go at me after the meeting. I deserve it.

One thing I'd like to add, though – I'm not ashamed of being on anti-depressants. I started taking them after the Man Of My Dreams encounter. You'll recall I bounced back after a trip to the GP. Well, that's why. I refuse to feel bad about taking these tablets – if I had some traditional physical condition, I'd take the pills to keep me healthy, and it's the same with my mind. It's not the first time I've been on them; I've had a series of depressive encounters, and each time, the pills have got me back on track. Taking anti-depressants is a response to a chemical imbalance in the brain – far from being weak, it is a sign of strength to admit it and do something about it.

I wouldn't dream of asking for those people in this room or our members around the world or the now two million-plus who follow us on Twitter to stand up and be counted unless they were comfort-able with it. Just remember, one in four of us will experience mental health problems at some point in our lives; it's an incredibly common thing, and if it isn't happening to you then it will affect someone you know. Yes, I could ask the doctor to see a psychi-atrist, but I can't face raking over emotions and feelings which would divert what little energy I have away from my son, my marriage and you. I'd rather neck the pills and get on with it, thanks very much.

Moving on, I do have some good news. We have been contacted by the Department for Culture, Media and Sport because the Minister wants our input on new guidelines on airbrushing. Plus, a cross-party group of MPs has asked us to advise on the viability of a new Cabinet position, that of a Minister for Motherhood.

This is definitely the direction we need to head in – and I'm very proud we have been considered. But I realise the club is now charting choppier waters and you may yearn for the early days when our meetings were more straightforward. What I would say is, this is the nature of life and of relationships; change is inevitable and it is impossible to improve our lot, to push for imperfection if we stick to sitting around discussing biscuits and muffin tops.

This club is finally getting somewhere. We are the first port of call for many organisations now, be it for comments for stories in the media or being consulted on Government policy. We are at the forefront of a big change; one day, our sons and daughters will thank us for this.

I will make it up to you all, I promise. Gone are the flirtations with beauty products and fluffy features. It is time to get hardcore.

Next week, we've got our first photo shoot for the calender. Also, we'll be meeting at the event co-ordinator's house, where we'll be finalising details of the march. We'll be making banners, so bring sheets and cardboard and stuff. Lucy's husband, who plays with Matt in his football team, will be doing a barbecue for Dads United and Mums Like Us members, so bring your other halves and the kids.

See you then, I hope. And please, give me the chance to prove myself again.

Dads United

www.dadsunited.co.uk

Lards, we're having a Start of the Season barbecue at Dan's house on Saturday, from noon. It's a joint one with Stella's cronies from her Mums Like Us club, so bring the family.

Please note, this is a fundraiser for Dads United, because your captain does not resort to publicity-stealing stunts like some clubs I could mention (joke – they have loads more members, so not as skint as us and we need cash to pay for our Player of the Year and Plonker of the Year trophies). Entry at your discretion but don't take the piss.

We all need to contribute to food, and drink, but there will be a trampoline and face-painting for the little ones and karaoke/music system for later on.

Here's a list of what would be very welcome on the barbie:

Burgers – the women specifically requested that any put out for the kids must NOT be cheap ones due to dubious nutritional value. They said it was fine for us to eat them, though.

Sausages – ditto.

Pork/Lamb – women request thin escalope-style cuts otherwise they'll burn on the outside and still be raw in the middle.

Chicken – don't even go there, we don't want food poisoning.

Fish – if you want to bring fish, then you clearly shouldn't be a member of this team. Fish is all well and good from a chippy or in a nice restaurant, but on a barbie, it disintegrates and is a pig to scrape off the grill.

Veggie options – bring your own plus disposable BBQ to avoid contamination.

Bread rolls – loads of them, baps and hot dog ones, because they help soak up spillages when we run out of kitchen roll.

Kitchen roll – see above.

Paper plates, plastic cutlery, pint and wine glasses.

Mayo, ketchup, relish – women say low fat stuff where possible.

Magnums – women say plan for two per head.

Salad – putting my foot down and banning it because no one eats it at a barbecue. Please note, do not bring salad servers; Stella says a few of her members had hideous births and if they saw a pair, they'd lose it.

Potato salad – same as salad.
Coleslaw – bloody loads of it.
Drinks – squash, juice, lemonade, wine, lager, cider and any odds and sods of spirits you have in the cupboard so we can make up a cocktail.
Look forward to seeing you there,
Your captain,
Matt

Week Thirty-one

March Mastermind HQ

Lucy's garage

Well, what can I say? You're amazing. I've had so many cards and emails and texts and stuff telling me I'm just about forgiven for my Botox fuck-up; many said they've secretly considered getting their wrinkles done in moments of weakness. That means a lot.

It's certainly given me a boost after my son started school this week. I was really down in the dumps. It broke my heart, seeing him in his school uniform on his first day. He was so proud of it and only had a tiny wobble when he lined up in the playground to go in. I thought I'd be OK, you know – he needs to be there now and it's a new chapter in our lives – but I had a lump in my throat when I walked away.

To me, it feels like the start of a new academic year for us, too, with this march to plan. I feel really positive this week. This Indian summer is helping – it makes life so much more bearable. Just listen to the kids out there in the garden – they're loving it. It's nice they're getting some quality weekend time with their dads too, which is always a good thing. Gives us a chance to get on with this.

So . . . I can officially reveal the demo will be held a week today. Times and details will go out this week in a confidential email, so keep your eyes peeled. The committee has worked very hard on getting every-thing ready, but if there are any oversights, let us know ASAP. Incredibly, a few thousand international members are coming over especially to join us, while others are going to hold sofa sit-ons to show their solidarity on the day.

Thanks go to Lucy for letting us trash her garage while we make our banners. She has raided her crafts cupboard for our benefit – you'll find everything you need to decorate your sheets and cardboard and wood placards. There's paint, glitter, pipe cleaners, sequins, feathers, ribbon, glue, felt, pom-poms, googly eyes and spray cans, so feel free to come up with your own slogan and get making.

If you're stuck for ideas, you could perhaps try Tummy Mummy And Proud, We Heart Our Wobbly Bits, even Bellies and Tellies – anything that you can think of that sums up our message of who we are and why we refuse to feel ashamed of our bed-hair and untidy houses.

Alex, as you can see, has gone a bit full-on with her placards. I can't fault her enthusiasm with that photo of Hattie next to the words 'Mothers Inferior'. It's . . . quite personal.

Chants are very important, too. Committee members will have loudspeakers so we can start them off, so we suggest the following:

'What do we want? A nap! When do we want it? Now!'

'We're mummies, with tummies! Don't take us all for dummies!'

'Gin not gym! Gin not gym!'

Then we have some songs which include:

To the tune of Dodgy's 'Good Enough': 'We're Good Enough At Work, We're Good Enough At Home, We're Good Enough Full Stop And We Really Love A Moan.'

To Christine Aguilera's 'Beautiful': 'We're Invisible, No Matter What They Say, Wrinkles won't bring us down, We're Invisible, In Every Single Way.'

There's also Amy Winehouse's 'Rehab': 'They try to get us all to go for Botox, We say NO, NO, NO! They try to get us all to eat just protein, We say NO, NO, NO!'

To 'I Predict A Riot' by the Kaiser Chiefs, we can do: 'Quiet! All we want is quiet, Diets! We don't want to diet!'

Don't worry about remembering them now, we'll print off sheets which you can lose in your own time, and we'll also practise in the coach on the way to Notting Hill. By the way, I've made a start on the rallying speech at the march. I've Googled 'inspirational speeches', so a few cheers here and there would be marvellous.

OK, let's get cracking. We can do this in an hour or so, I reckon. Just to remind you, afterwards, the men are providing refreshments in the form of a barbecue – that means we won't get to eat for hours, but there'll be plenty of nibbles and booze.

Up the revolution, lardies!

Dads United

Big thnks everone for coming today. Just did a count-upp and we raised well over £300. It was packed in the end.

Fucking brill!!!!!!!!!!!!!!!!!!!!!!!!!

Writng this having just got in from bbq, Im a little bit watsde so apols.

ill bring it up before anyone else does – yes, i did forget the barbecue and charcoal and firelighters, which was why it was a few huors before we ate. But was wothr it in the end!

See you next week at traininnhg.

Jessu, my head is going to hrt in the morning.

Matt

PS Love you, not just saying it becaue Iv had a drunk

251

Week Thirty-two

The March
Sky News Channel Breaking News: Riot breaks out on 'Mummy March' . . .

We're getting reports from our helicopter over West London of a riot breaking out on the streets of Notting Hill. Police sirens and armoured officers are believed to be on their way to the scene of a march, organised by Stella Smith, the chairwoman of Mums Like Us, an organisation for mothers who are disgruntled at the modern phenomenon of Mother Superiors.

Eyewitnesses have told us the all-women demo calling for 'Good Enough Motherhood' started off peacefully at around noon today on Westbourne Grove, many arriving on coaches chartered from across the country, carrying placards and banners in the glorious September sunshine, blowing children's whistles and making their voices heard with those plastic echo microphones and voice-changer masks.

There was initially a party atmosphere, with

impromptu picnics and lots of singing and laughter, but it turned nasty when a group, which we understand is led by Hattie Hooper, chairwoman of the opposing Mothers Superior, began jeering Stella Smith while she was making what her supporters labelled 'a truly inspirational' speech in favour of being Good Enough rather than Perfect.

I believe we have mobile phone footage of that speech, which we will bring to you as soon as we can.

Reports suggest shoppers were forced to flee to safety when a mass brawl involving thousands broke out between the two groups of women.

One witness told us Stella Smith and Hattie Hooper began shouting at one another through loudspeakers, even though they were face to face, and then one of them looked as though she was pushed forward by a surge and the other, thinking it was an attack, retaliated with a shove. Then they dropped their loudspeakers and started scrapping, with Stella pulling at Hattie's hair and ripping her false nails off while kicking dust onto her white trousers. Hattie responded by getting a hairbrush out of her designer handbag and attempted to brush Stella's hair, shouting, 'You should be ashamed of yourself!'

You can see now from our live pictures that the fighting is still going on. There are high heels and sensible shoes being lobbed across the crowd; the contents of handbags are scattered on the street; sausage rolls and packets of crisps are being thrown back at healthy-eating joints of beef and other protein-rich foodstuffs. The women are ripping each other's clothes; there are abandoned velour tracksuit tops and designer jackets lying on the pavement; some are splatting cream cakes at each other and . . . yes, I've just seen a Shepee fly across the tops of some parked 4x4s.

This really is a shocking development on a normal Saturday afternoon in a well-heeled part of London, the heartland of the Mother Superior camp, which presumably is why Mums Like Us held their demo here today.

The police have arrived, here they are, they're wading in, pulling the women off one another and bundling them into vans, where they will be driven to the local station and dealt with. We can see a water cannon being deployed. Yes, the women are being hosed down, mascara is running all down the Mother Superiors' faces; the Mums Like Us members look like drowned rats. Mounted police are being thrown off their horses by some of the Mother Superiors, who have clambered onto the saddles and are performing dressage movements up and down the thoroughfare.

And in a remarkable unprecedented response, officers are using Nerf guns with foam bullets to try to restore order.

Local traders are locking up, fearing they may be looted. We're getting word that Smythson, purveyor of luxury leather goods and stationery, is being occupied by some Mums Like Us members, who are staging a sit-in – no, I'm being told it's actually a lie-down. I'm also hearing from reporters on the ground that some Smugaboo buggies have had their tyres slashed and some doughnuts set alight.

We now have the footage of Stella Smith's speech:

Members and mums like us! We are gathered here today to celebrate motherhood. Not the glossy-haired, airbrushed, skinny, toned, organic and telly-free version we are bombarded with the minute we open our tired, tired eyes. But the 'good enough' variety. The type of motherhood the vast, huge, enormous majority of us experience; the one we are living and breathing; the one we achieve day in, day out. The one in which we give our very best according to the resources, energy, time and money available to us.

Yes, there are days when there's too much TV, chocolate or toys and not enough fruit and veg, books at bedtime or one-to-one time with each child. But there are many more days when, despite the pressures of our jobs and our marriages and our gigantic pile of ironing, we run ourselves ragged to meet the standards we set ourselves as mothers.

This march is a celebration of a movement born in the humble uncleanliness of my kitchen. It is an acknowledgement of a movement that has meaning for millions of ordinary mums up and down the country and all around the world. We, the members of Mums Like Us, are here to call on mothers to reject perfection, to give guilt the elbow and to embrace one another with mutual support.

With apologies to Martin Luther King, I have a dream that one day, the daughters of Mother Superior mummies and the daughters of Mums Like Us mummies will be able to sit down together at the table of motherhood to agree to disagree, to not judge the other and to let every mum choose the way they want to go about motherhood.

I have a dream that one day, even newspapers, which are sweltering with the heat of 'look who's got stretchmarks', sweltering with the heat of 'how to lose your baby weight in a week', will be transformed into an oasis of features on how to be good enough.

I have a dream that our daughters will one day live in a nation where they will not be judged by the sagginess of their skin but by the content of their characters.

In the words of suffragette Emmeline Pankhurst, I come to ask you to help to win this fight. If we win it, this hardest of all fights, then, to be sure, in the future it is going to be made easier for women all over the world to win their fight when their time comes.

To paraphrase William Wallace in *Braveheart*,

aye, fight and you may die. Run, and you'll live at least awhile. And dying in your beds many years from now, would you be willing to trade all the days from this day to that for one chance, just one chance, to come back here and tell our enemies that they may take our lives but they'll never take . . . OUR BISCUITS!

Barack Obama won't mind me saying, if there is anyone out there who doubts good enough is possible, today is your answer.

Or as some French bloke once said, the flame of the Mums Like Us resistance must not be extinguished and will not be extinguished.

To borrow Harold Macmillan's words: the Mother Superiors think we cannot beat them. It will not be easy. It will be a long job; it will be a terrible war; but in the end we shall march through terror to triumph.

And while I'm at it, I'll do a bit of Churchill too: We shall fight in the aisles and car parks of the supermarket, we shall fight in the playgrounds, we shall fight on the school run, we shall fight at the coffee mornings and at the PTA meetings, we shall fight in the M&S changing rooms; we shall never surrender . . .

What we want is peace – we know we may have to fight to get it – but peace will bring us tolerance. Today, we want to redress the balance. Tomorrow we want to be left alone to be good enough.

Jesus, is that you, Hattie? There really is no
need to scream abuse at me through that bloody
thing. What are you doing here? Have you come
to join us or fight us? Oh God, what on earth . . .

The mobile phone video then cuts off there. You'll
have seen Hattie Hooper's arrival – she is the brunette
in a sleeveless Burberry ruched blouse and white
Joseph capri trousers, waving an Anya Hindmarch
handbag – but it is impossible to see who is responsible
for the first shove.

I am just hearing now police confirmation that both
Smith and Hooper have been arrested by officers on
suspicion of public disorder offences and they have
been taken away. They have been handcuffed, they've
been bundled into a van, the same van, in which they
will be driven to the nearest police station for
questioning.

This really is a remarkable story, and it is the latest
in a series of outlandish and flamboyant confrontations
between these two women, who share very opposing
views on motherhood. There is absolutely no doubt that
tomorrow's newspapers will be leading with this story.
We seem to have lost our aerial pictures, we'll try to fix
that and bring them back as soon as we can . . .

Week Thirty-three

The Aftermath
Stella's kitchen

Looks like we all made it back in one piece – eventually! To be honest, I'm still reeling from the march, so there's no agenda as such today, just a sort of a feedback 'what-did-we-all-think-of-it' chat, much like those conversations we used to have after a big party in our twenties when we'd pore over who snogged who.

You might have seen on the news that both Hattie Hooper and I were given a police caution because we were first-time offenders unlikely to get into trouble again. On a personal level, I'm actually quite proud of it, having been part of a day that made such an impact. On a parental level, I'm a bit mortified; when my son is old enough to understand it, he'll think he can misbehave 'because Mum did'.

Some of you have been asking, who threw the first punch? Well, it was neither me nor Hattie – it was in fact Alex. She told me she made a beeline for Hattie as soon as she realised she'd turned up and she ground a doughnut into her trousers. Alex made it clear to me she is a bit hacked off that she didn't get arrested too. She isn't here today because she had a strop when I told her violence was not acceptable. She hasn't sent her apologies.

Being carted off by the police was all rather exciting. As this officer cuffed me, he started apologising, saying he was sorry but he had to do it. He was only in his early twenties, bless him, very good-looking, so I was quite happy to just go along with it. By then, I was knackered anyway, from all the shouting and the marching, as was Hattie, who was also cuffed, and we were put in the back of a van together. I was just relieved to get a sit-down and get away from the noise. My blood sugar level had dipped a bit because it had been at least an hour since I'd eaten, so I thought I might as well enjoy being arrested.

The journey in the van to the station took about fifteen minutes; we were crawling through the crowds. Loads of women had seen us getting in and they were banging on the tinted windows, even though they couldn't actually see us, and shouting, 'Free Stella Smith! Free Stella Smith!' – I felt like Deirdre Barlow.

At first, Hattie and I avoided each other's gaze; we were enemies, after all. We looked everywhere but at one another; at the dented metal floor, at the scratched plastic seats, at the black wire mesh on the windows. Then, all of a sudden, Hattie snorted, threw her head back just like a horse, and started guffawing.

I asked her what the bloody hell she was laughing at and she said, 'You, darling.' I stared at her open-mouthed and then looked down at myself. I'd lost a flip-flop, my feet were filthy black, my jogging bottoms were ripped on one side all the way up to my thigh, an arm had been torn off my T-shirt, my hair resembled a bird's nest and I could feel my swollen mouth smarting from a random punch.

In-between roars of mirth, she said, 'Sweetie, I know you've had Botox but I didn't know you'd had your lips plumped as well. You must give me the number of your surgeon.'

Well, that was it – I was off; pissing myself and hooting at the utter ridiculousness of it all. I took her in: her expensive hairdo was a complete mess, with flakes of sausage roll pastry stuck to her scalp, and she had a false eyelash hanging off her chin. She had managed to keep her shoes, but one of the open-toe wedge heels had come off, her pedicure was scuffed, her trousers were smeared in doughnut jam, she'd lost an earring and one of the shoulder seams of her blouse had split, making the material droop diagonally down to her tanned midriff, exposing one cup of her hugely expensive white bra which now had a dirty handmark on it.

'Bloody hell, Hattie,' I said, gulping for air, 'you've really let yourself go.'

She stopped dead – blinking the tears away from her eyes – and launched into a laughing fit so hard, she confessed through gasping squeals that even though she'd had C-sections and had a very obedient pelvic floor, she'd wet herself 'a smidgeon'.

Once we'd stopped rolling around on the seats, clutching our middles with our handcuffed hands and wiping snot onto our arms, we wondered aloud what our kids would make of us, arrested and on our way to be fingerprinted and have our mug shots taken.

She said to me, 'Stella, none of this is personal, you know. In another world, I think we'd get on but we both know that is impossible. I rather admire you, bumbling from one calamity to another, always getting back up, no matter what happens. You think it's easy to look effortlessly chic, but so much work goes into this . . . this façade. I get up every morning at six a.m. and go for a five-kilometre run with my personal trainer, come rain or shine. Then I have to tidy up the house before the nanny arrives – I can't let her think I'm not coping – the mess four children make is absolutely horrendous. I then have to have a shower, exfoliate, moisturise, apply my make-up, style my hair and get dressed before hubby surfaces at seven-thirty a.m.. Yes, OK, I don't make the children's breakfast, but that's because I have to make sure I'm ready to sit down with hubby every morning, to look relaxed and fresh and ready for the day, to show I'm in control, otherwise he'll consider me weak and lazy. Once he's left for work, I do the school run, timing it so I'm seen with Elle and Claudia – it's networking, sweetie, pure and simple.

'After that, I trot off to start work. By that, I mean, my appearance. If I'm not going for a facial or a spot of Botox, I'm at the hairdresser or having my nails done, or I'll be getting my legs and armpits and arms and toes waxed or my teeth polished. Perhaps I'm with the nutritionist, desperate to find a non-fattening, calorie-free, magic ingredient which will, for once, fill me up and get rid of that nagging, empty, hungry feeling I carry with me during my waking hours. Then there's the house, which needs to be updated according to whatever is in vogue décor-wise, so I spend hours trawling interiors websites, magazines and shops to check we have the look du jour.

'Then there's "being seen". I have to make sure I'm seen at the right places, carrying the right organic bags, perhaps having lunch with the right women – mumpreneurs, barristers, City high-flyers and A-list mums.

'After that, I may be organising a dinner party, drawing up the guest list, sourcing Michelin-starred chefs and organic, sustainable local produce menus, or I could be arranging a weekend away for two years' time to ensure we are holidaying at the same place as the Prime Minister.

'Then there's my career to run – I have my own PR business, specialising in promoting charities with celebrity patrons. I went back to work after eight weeks' maternity leave on each child – it's crucial to my image that I was seen to be coping. There's nothing more empowering than being a businesswoman breastfeeding at a meeting while discussing figures and so forth. I obviously had a great team: a yogi for my antenatal meditation, a doula for the post-C-section lifting of babies and pelvic floor pump sessions, a night nanny, my personal trainer, and we also brought in help for meals and cleaning.

'So I'll head to the office for meetings, which take up the rest of the afternoon. The nanny does the pick-up because if I was spotted doing it, tongues would wag and questions would be asked: shouldn't she be somewhere more important?

'Club business is dedicated to anything from setting up reading clubs for mothers who want to give their six-week-old babies a head start, to encouraging parents to buy web domains in the name of their newborns just in case they turn out to be City whizz kids.

'If the children aren't flexi-boarding at school – sometimes they stay overnight when hubby and I have a function to attend – I help with homework and supervise their extra-curricular activities. They may need to be taken to Arabic lessons or a lacrosse match.

'Then I'll jump into the shower again to freshen up and change; we might have a kitchen supper to host. By this time, Jeremy is back, so he'll need to be soothed and pampered. If we're not going out, one of us will try to do bedtime, then we'll eat, a little gourmet speciality I learnt on a cuisine course, and we'll go through the family diary so we know what's happening the next day. There might be some business to attend to – we're often on our iPads of an evening. Then we might watch a film or a box set – this is usually something Scandinavian – and after that, I am expected to be fragrant and alluring for bedtime, even though we rarely have sex. Our marriage is more of a business arrangement, which suits me. I suspect Jeremy is having an affair – most husbands within my circle do have track records – and to be truthful, I am pleased his needs are catered for. I have a little 'agreement' myself with a twenty-something masseur who visits once a month, he's wonderful.

'I can see by your face, you're shocked. But this is my life, this is my job. I am the most extreme version of a Mother Superior I know – the vast majority are Mother Superiors in spirit. They may not have the money to participate in Easter skiing trips with Royalty but they approach the park with the same mentality: look fantastic, stay calm, smile and cope. Even if it's raining in their hearts, they never let on how they really feel. It's all a performance; we are, in essence, the stars of our own show. Now can you understand why I find your way of doing things so . . . drab?'

I couldn't believe my ears. Hattie was a full-time Mother Superior, in much the way I'm a

265

full-time Mums Like Us member. Her dedication was awe-inspiring. Her honesty was breathtaking.

'But why are we even on your radar, Hattie? Why did you send a mole to my club? Why do you slag me off, every opportunity you get?' I asked, bewildered.

'Because, darling, you are a threat. Your club makes a mockery of mine: I do not want my daughters or anyone's daughters growing up to believe in dishevelled indignity. Mothers are not just mothers: we are women, thoroughbreds even. We have a duty to make the best of ourselves, to show some self-respect. Get up early and whack some slap on and you can take on the world; run late in your pyjamas underneath your coat and you are on the back foot.

'Mother Superiors also understand the way men work. They don't want to wake up next to someone resembling the cleaner; they want illusion, they want it all. And by giving it to them, we can look them in the eye and be their equal. I understand your reticence. You see my life and think it is all surface. But let me tell you, there is power in looking good. It is life-affirming. You may say it's only possible with money, but I would argue that aspiration and ambition are free of charge. We can only better the world and better our children by keeping up appearances and maintaining standards. Good enough, I'm afraid, Stella, simply isn't good enough.'

Then she threw a grenade in my direction.

'That's where you come in. I have an offer to make you: come over to my side, Stella. Join me; together we are stronger. You can reach out to the women who don't have nannies. Listen to me, we are all in this together; we can show that motherhood is only a part of what defines us as women. I can see you're tempted. You've had a taste of Botox – remember how good that felt, how amazing you looked when those crow's feet melted away, how empowering it was. How attractive you felt. You can have it all, Stella. I will share the Mother Superior spoils with you,' she whispered.

Then the doors of the van opened and we were whisked off to be questioned. It was fine – we had tea and sandwiches and everyone was very polite. I used my call to ring Matt to say I'd be home, God knows when, and I was allocated a duty solicitor. We received our cautions and were told we could leave.

Three hours had passed when we stepped out of the police station, by which time it was dark. Hattie was looking immaculate once again, her million-quid-an-hour lawyer had brought her a change of clothes. She air-kissed me 'mwah' goodbye, told me to think about what she'd said and asked if I wanted a lift anywhere – there was a driver for her, which her husband had arranged. I refused, feeling dazed and confused, and as she swept off into the night, I made my way, hobbling and aching, to the station to catch the last train home.

In that stinking carriage, full of drunks and weirdos,

I sat and stared at my reflection in the window; the woman who looked back at me was bedraggled, dirty and tired. I admit I could empathise with Hattie's point of view: her words had been intoxicating, her argument had legs. Had she highlighted the crux of the matter? Was I underestimating myself, and millions of other women, by telling us to aspire to being Good Enough? Was I letting down my husband? Was I teaching my son to accept what life dishes up?

It's true, I had been seduced by the makeovers for television and photographers; I had secretly marvelled at myself when I watched my television performances or picked up a newspaper or magazine. I had become thinner as a result of the trouble with Matt, and on a few occasions I had caught myself admiring my slimmer hips and flatter stomach in the mirror. Then there were the blow-dries which had bullied my wavy hair sleek, the foundation which had ironed my imperfections sheer, the mouth guard which stunned my teeth white . . .

As the train pulled into suburbia, I got up from my seat, feeling the sticky floor beneath the foot that had lost its flip-flop.

There, waiting for me, were Matt and our son, who was fast asleep in his arms; they'd been waiting on the platform for an hour, checking every train because, by then, my phone had run out of battery.

'Thank God you're safe, we've missed you,' he said. 'We're so proud of you. Welcome home, Stella.'

I knew then I would never turn to the dark side.

I must admit I have a deep respect for Hattie, even though she is the enemy. It made me realise that we're certainly a force to be reckoned with. To have her ask us to join her shows we've rattled the Mother Superiors. And at the very least, despite the arrests and the bruises, we know we have brought our debate to the nation's consciousness and showed there is an alternative to the Mother Superior way.

Our website is doing extraordinarily well. We had a deluge of hits after the march, and so many supportive messages. Of course there are lots of trolls on there, too. There's one particularly vicious person who goes by the name of 'Tattoo' – very spiteful and personal, who has clearly seen a lot of me judging by the attentive level of criticism. I haven't reported them to the cyber police because I believe censoring views makes us look touchy. The phone has been going mad, too – so many offers and requests for quotes and things, but thankfully, because I tend to respond to the media, they don't bother knocking at the door any more.

Anyway, all of this is flabtastic news! I think we deserve a standing ovation. Well done, everyone. Oh, and I nearly forgot to tell you – shooting has finished for our calendar. I can't wait to see the finished product.

Now I've got to run. Matt is cooking a birthday curry from scratch tomorrow night, so I have a mountain of ingredients he has asked me to get. He's forty-two this week and we're having a family soirée on the night; we won't be eating it for another couple of days because he's gone all *Masterchef* and says we need to let it rest to develop its flavour. Obviously if it were up to me, I'd ring the Indian and ask for 'the usual'.

So I'll see you next week. Have a good one, bye!

Week Thirty-four

How Not to Host a Party

Stella's kitchen

Has everyone got a cuppa and a cake? Great, let's start then, shall we?

This week I wanted to talk to you about family gatherings. This is inspired by our completely disastrous party for Matt's birthday. Getting everyone together is fraught with difficulties – our do was a textbook 'how not to', which I'll tell you about as we go.

Mother Superiors love hosting because it gives them a chance to show off their domestic goddess skills, from home-made crudités and stylish aperitifs to latest interior acquisition.

Mums Like Us members, on the other hand, should know better, because it equals work, stress, tidying and wishing everyone would just bugger off home because we've got to get up early the next day.

I have no idea why Matt offered to cook for everyone.

271

He knows I have a meltdown whenever we have family over because it's always so much work. I think he thought it'd be different this time as we've been getting on so well. I foolishly did too.

So, the club's take on hosting is this: if at all possible, do not do it. If you can't get out of it – say, you don't think up a reason quickly enough – then make it as painless as possible by following these rules . . .

Coats get chucked on the banister because you don't want guests wandering off to find theirs in the spare room, since they'll notice on their snoop round upstairs that all the junk from downstairs has been relocated up there.

Nibbles are minimal – think Value cheeseballs and sticks of celery. You don't want to stay up half the previous night making your own because you'll only be even grumpier at the party. Wine must be cheap and nasty and in limited supply. Drunk people don't stop talking and they stay really late.

Serve the meal really quickly, no starters, something simple like a help-yourself lasagne and garlic bread. Pudding should be sickly, so people feel nauseous and go home earlier, and absolutely no cheese or coffee.

Don't let children go to bed – you want them screaming so your guests can't wait to get the hell out of there.

As soon as you've cleared the table, start tidying away glasses and chairs so you make it obvious you are expecting them to go. Then nip upstairs, get your pyjamas on and start yawning, mentioning very loudly you're on with really heavy bleeding, which will embarrass everyone over the age of fifty, who will make their excuses five minutes later.

Unfortunately, we did none of the above. With us still in our 'back together' honeymoon period, I wanted Matt to have an amazing party and, accordingly, I switched my alarm bells to silent.

I really should've woken up when he suggested a *Star Wars* fancy dress theme, spent £300 on booze and took over the kitchen to make fifteen different types of starters and three varieties of curry, and created a cocktail which he christened the Death Star. But no, I made the fatal error of letting him have what he wanted. He was so happy doing it all and it had been so long since we'd hosted a party, I just let him get on with it.

We had twenty-five guests coming, including his parents and aunts and uncles, plus my mum, my sister and her husband, plus a load of mates. Everyone turned up at the same time, so it was manic – big hugs, hellos, drinks, fancy bhajis and samosas which Matt had made, all to a background of music he'd spent ages compiling in that teenage anally retentive way men never get over.

I went as C-3PO, wearing a gold lamé catsuit I found in the dressing-up box, which I'd previously worn to an Abba-themed party way back when, with gold face paint and scraped-back hair, doing the jerky hand movements. Matt was Yoda, wearing his manky old brown towelling dressing gown and a wig that he found online which had the ears and wrinkled scalp, and painting his face and hands green. Our son was in his Darth Vader costume, waving a lightsaber around, because he was allowed to stay up for a bit before bed.

My mum came as Princess Leia, in a white gown and brown doughnut-ear wig. Matt's dad came as Darth Vader, as did seven others, including Lucy. Matt's mum said she was Chewbacca, wearing just a brown fluffy jumper because she doesn't really like 'this sort of thing'. We also had two Han Solos and an Obi-Wan Kenobi. Mags was Leia as Jabba's slave but wore a swimming costume over tights rather than a bikini. There were three Lukes, one of whom was my sister Sophie; three Stormtroopers; and a Darth Maul, at whom Matt took umbrage because it wasn't strictly old-school *Star Wars*, which he had specified on the invites.

Showing off her teaching skills, Alex came as R2-D2 in a decorated-with-foil cardboard box held over the shoulders with braces and swimming cap complete with holoprojector and camera eye. We had a Boba Fett, who Matt secretly wished he'd thought of; a Jawa; and a Spock – one of Matt's uncles got the wrong end of the stick.

About an hour into it, I nipped off to put the little one to bed and was only gone about fifteen minutes but when I came back down, I noticed how drunk everyone was already. I decided then that I'd keep a lid on my drinking – I know, shock horror, but I tell you I'm determined not to be such a drunk these days. I also had a funny feeling things were going to go awry.

The meal was absolutely delicious – a bit hot, which meant they were all necking glasses of Death Star, which didn't taste alcoholic at all even though it contained rum, vodka, gin and tequila. Everyone was having such a fantastic time, loads of laughter, jokes and stuff. It was brilliant – until Chewbacca – my mother-in-law – loudly asked Princess Leia – my mum – if she would ever consider marrying again. God knows why she thought it was an appropriate time to enquire – she's usually really discreet and lovely, but obviously not after a pint of Death Star.

A very pissed Princess Leia stood up and pushed her chair back too hard so it fell backwards, which made everyone stop dead. Her wig was by now minus an doughnut ear – it had fallen off into the biryani when she reached over for a naan. 'Is this what you've all been thinking?' she slurred. 'It is, isn't it? When is that sour-faced old cow going to couple off so we don't have to feel responsible for her any more? Well, let me tell you once and for all, I would never marry again – I had thirty-six bloody years of it. Thirty-six-bloody-years. I'm well aware life could be easier for all of you if I did meet someone else. Perhaps it would be for me too, but I'm happy being by myself, happy not to be facing the prospect of wiping someone's bum when I'm old and grey. None of you need to worry – I've sorted out my finances, and I won't be a burden on any of you when I'm infirm. So, I hope that answers your question. C-3PO, I mean Stella, another Death Star, please.'

As she bent over to pick up her chair, I made the mistake of telling her she'd probably do better with a cup of tea.

She turned around, her eyes flashing at me, and she exploded. 'How dare you tell me what I should or shouldn't do! You're just like your father – he thought he could behave as he wished one minute and then occupy the moral high ground the next, doling out advice, when he was in no way fit to do so. You're the same, Stella,' she snarled.

That was it then. I started defending Dad and Sophie was desperately trying to calm us down. Mum stopped me in full flow with a trump card so heartbreaking, I was stunned into silence.

'Your father was an adulterer. A serial adulterer. He betrayed us. This isn't the ideal time to tell you, but I've had enough of you hero-worshipping him. He was a man, not Superman. Yes, he was your dad and you rightly adored him, but he was a human being, one who made mistakes, plenty of them. I never ever wanted to influence how you thought of him because you were a child, but now you're an adult, you need to deal with the truth.

'I loved your father deeply. There was never any question of us divorcing – it wasn't the done thing in those days, and we would've been financially destitute, so I stuck it out for you girls. Besides, he loved you both so much, I couldn't have taken you away from him. And on the whole, he was worth it. I was enthralled by his charisma and charm, but when it came to his infidelities – there were several, I'm not going to go into it with you because that was between us – well, they were too much to bear, so I shut down emotionally. He was a boy who never grew up. Working at the bank, he had so many opportunities to . . . to sneak off. He was loved by his staff and his ego just couldn't resist the flattery. They all knew what was happening – the events I had to go to, knowing they were whispering behind my back. It was the humiliation, looking at someone he was talking to, or indeed a woman I'd be small-talking with, and wondering if it was her. Things calmed down in the last ten years of his life. We reached an understanding that what was in the past was behind us, we fell in love again. But then he died, so suddenly, and it felt like I'd been abandoned all over again. Girls, I'm so sorry he wasn't who you thought he was. I think it's time I went.'

The party broke up then, obviously. Mum left in a cab. Everyone sobered up. I was handed tissues, and my sister disappeared under a series of hugs. Matt tried to get everyone going again, producing the

277

karaoke machine and belting out 'Careless Whisper', but I think the sight of gold face paint and mascara and snot running down my chin was enough to convince everyone the fat lady was well and truly singing.

I've been in a daze ever since, lardies. Matt's been brilliant, letting me talk it through over and over, patching together memories here and there like a jigsaw, thinking back to the times when Dad was away for birthdays and school concerts, and trying to work out if he had been acting suspiciously. Then I'll be trying to remember if his return home was met with an icy 'welcome home' by Mum. I get these little flashbacks, looking back and wondering if a hushed argument I recall between my parents was over an affair or something trivial. Soph and I have pulled together over this: we're on the phone a lot. Initially we were angry that Mum hadn't told us about Dad – we're not kids any more. Although I guess we'll always be kids to her. Maybe that's why she tried to protect us?

My heart goes out to Mum every time I think about it – how she must've felt, how she kept going for us, how dignified she always was. I've spoken to her a few times since, but she hasn't mentioned the party once. I don't blame her – finally I understand this is her coping mechanism.

So, there you have it. That is the Mums Like Us guide on how not to host a party.

I won't be around next week. I've got a heap of work on, plus a whole load of research I need to do, because I've been asked to go on *Newsnight* in ten days. Opposite Hattie. Yes, that old chestnut. I'm utterly terrified of showing myself up but . . . courage.

Courage.

See you in a fortnight.

Dads United

www.dadsunited.co.uk

MATCH REPORT: Dads United v. Landlord's Lads

The Dads took on the Lads in a friendly last night to mark the Dads' captain's birthday.

Skippered by Fat Larry, the Lads arrived on foot, having had a cheeky pint at the Feathers, which is within staggering distance of the leisure centre, and were wearing kit sponsored by our local. We unveiled our new matching strip, a rip-off of Barcelona's because we refuse to have a capitalist emblem on our chests. That last bit is a lie – no one wants to sponsor us.

Before the game began, the ref – our landlord – held a minute's silence round the circle to mark the passing of the Dads' captain's youth.

The Dads won the toss and opted to kick off; the Lads chose to defend the goal known as the Bogs End, which is closest to the conveniences.

Ten minutes in, a free kick was given to the Lads

and a swinging delivery into the penalty area from the right-hand side by Terry Five-Bellies was met by the head of Fat Larry, who nutted it in for a goal. The ref let everyone stop for a breather, some of the Lads popped out for a fag, and then the game was resumed with the Dads producing a promising run of possession but resulting in bugger all.

At half-time, the ref insisted everyone knock back five double tequila slammers to mark the first meeting of the two sides. The Lads began to get a bit tasty with their challenges, earning the Dads a number of penalties. No one can remember how many, but the Dads only managed to score one goal, courtesy of their captain.

Twenty-five minutes in, the two captains agreed they were both knackered and abandoned the game, which ended 1–1, so they could get pissed in the Feathers.

The Dads' captain, who was made to attempt to drink his age in alcohol units, was eventually escorted home by three of his team and put to bed by his wife, who went mental when she saw the state he was in. 'Didn't his teammates realise he had to get up for work in the morning?' she asked them.

Man of the Match: Fat Larry for his goal celebration, which saw him pretend to urinate over the Dads.

Donkey of the Match: The ref. Unanimous decision.

Week Thirty-five

Stella Visits Dad's Grave

Hi, Dad, sorry I haven't been here for a while. Beautiful day, isn't it? The last week of October, and I can't believe it's so sunny. I hope you're warm in there – expect so, you were always like a hot water bottle. I remember when you'd surprise Soph and me and pick us up from school, whether it was freezing cold or boiling hot, your hands were always toasty.

Things have been a bit hectic of late. I've started this club and it's going really well. Actually, it's going amazingly and, well, we're sort of . . . famous around the world. Ridiculous, I know. It's almost like a full-time job. You'd be completely confused if I explained what it was all about and you'd laugh at me, so I won't bother. And then there's my writing and your gorgeous grandson. If only you'd got to meet him. He's got your spark, Mum says that all the time. And Matt, too, we're all fine. We've had a few ups and downs this year, which is kind of why I'm visiting.

Mum must've been here recently; those roses are gorgeous. God, I miss you. Shit, I wasn't supposed to start sniffling so early on, I promised myself I'd be more like Mum, more restrained and stoic, a bit more grown up. But it's easier said than done. The other night, Mum told me and Soph that you'd had some affairs . . . It felt like the rug had been pulled from under my feet. No, I hadn't been drinking, before you ask. I've kind of decided to cut back and . . . anyway, the rug went from right beneath me. Dad, I felt so let down. I couldn't, I still can't, believe it. You're my hero, you were the one I looked up to. Why did you do it to Mum? Why did you do it to us?

The thing is, I sort of know why. I'm so ashamed to admit this, but I've been kind of unfaithful to Matt and my beloved son. I don't know how it happened, well, I do – I was feeling neglected and unappreciated and invisible, and then this prick, this old flame of mine, made a play for me and I fell for it, and then Matt and I had a few problems and I turned to him. It's all by-the-by now. You didn't ever meet my ex – good thing, really, as you'd have probably seen right through him – anyway, he's melted back into the past again and I doubt I'll ever hear from him again. I hope not, anyway.

It was so stupid of me. Adults don't do that to one another, they don't go off for some love like a fucking puppy just because they feel ignored. I've realised that now. I've been acting like a teenager, not like a mum or a wife or a woman. Not like Mum, who kept us all together, putting herself last because she knew that actions have consequences.

She said I was like you. She doesn't know this stuff I've told you, but I've been thinking she's right. My most private fear, one I can't tell Matt or Mum or Soph, is that maybe I'm destined to take after you – maybe I'm genetically programmed to betray those who love me. Perhaps I've set in motion a weakness I can't contain. I hope not, and now that I've found out about your other side, I can only try to be more aware of myself. I don't want to be unfaithful. I want to be with Matt forever.

I do forgive you, Dad. I was so angry at first, at how you lapped up all our love then spat it out every time you went off with some fancy woman. I suppose, like Mum said, you were only human. I understand how the expectations and pressures of parenthood and marriage can make you want to throw off the strait-jacket sometimes and go a bit mad. I do get that. I feel the same every now and again. But if this has taught me anything, it's that I want to work harder on my relationships rather than just think, what the hell, and let some bastard massage my ego for his own benefit.

Here I've been banging on about being Good Enough, and I've realised I haven't been anywhere near Good Enough.

You'll always be my hero, Dad. Your fall from grace is only temporary, and I expect I'll cope better with this over time. But I've got a new heroine now – my mum – and just like I've got to accept you did the dirty on us, I have to accept her way of dealing with your dicking about. I have a new-found admiration for her.

Anyway, I've got to go, I need to start thinking about what's for tea. Matt has got the little one this afternoon and took him out for a glory pizza for lunch, and it'll be my job to make sure he gets some vegetables down him. Why is it men think they're doing us a favour when they offer to sort out lunch? What child is going to grumble about eating something unhealthy? I have no idea why I'm asking you – you were completely guilty of taking us for a rubber burger at Wimpy on the rare occasions you took me and Soph out for lunch, and you never cooked, apart from making a five-minute cake in the microwave that first Saturday after we'd got it, some time in the Eighties. It came out wonky and smelled of soap.

And there's some of my club paperwork that won't go away. I have a stack of emails to reply to, from across the world, would you believe. You'll never guess what – I'm on *Newsnight* with Jeremy Paxman next week – yes, I know, me! Your favourite programme! Will try to do you proud, obviously, but will probably embarrass myself.

Plus I've got some writing to do. Yes, I'm still at it – not a proper job, but then you'd only have been happy if I'd got myself behind a bank cashier window and worked my way up!

Look, I promise I won't leave it so long again to visit you. One day, when your grandson is old enough not to freak out about it, I'll bring him here. At the moment he is obsessed with death and thinks I'm going to die every time I leave his side. I talk about you all the time, telling him you're up there looking down on us from heaven. Unfortunately, his teacher told him she'd just come back from Devon, so he thinks you're going to come and stay for a bit. If only you could.

Right, must go. Love you, Dad.

Week Thirty-six

Newsnight

'Exhausted or exhilarated? Harassed or having it all? Never before has motherhood been so scrutinised – polarised by experts, politicians and even mums themselves, at loggerheads over how the job of raising our children should be done.

'In a special edition of *Newsnight*, broadcast at seven-thirty p.m. for the very first time for the benefit of millions of women who cannot stay awake past nine o'clock, we'll be examining twenty-first-century motherhood.

'With me here is Stella Smith, who is the chairwoman of Mums Like Us, which campaigns for a good enough approach. And Hattie Hooper, the chairwoman of Mothers Superior, which celebrates the pursuit of perfection.

'If I can come to you first, Stella, why do you think motherhood is so hotly debated?'

'Thank you, Jeremy. Good evening, or should that

be happy wine o'clock? In my opinion, and in the opinion of our millions of members, motherhood has become an industry. The "having it all" diktat was pushed throughout our education in the post-feminist age; it took us into the workplace, then frightened the life out of us when we became mums. Instinct, or the "mum knows best" mantra, was swept aside in favour of analysis and control. We were encouraged to treat motherhood like a career, which meant finding an objective, keeping an eye on the competition and being brilliant at it. The trouble is, all of this doesn't go hand in hand with the actual experience of having a baby, because babies turn us into emotional cavewomen who will do anything to protect their offspring. This has opened up our metaphorical stitches and produced a gap between what we are doing and what we think we should be doing. Even the hardiest of mums feel the pressure from the industry that has grown up around us – spouted in newspapers, magazines, on TV and in the social media – which has turned us into navel-gazers, worrying we're not only letting our kids down but looking like a mess as we do it. And chief cheerleader of this is Hattie Hooper.'

'Hattie, that's a damning criticism – apparently you're responsible for upholding an ideal which hard-working mothers have no hope of attaining. What do you say to that?'

'Jeremy, darling, lovely to see you again! The last time we met was at the summer fundraiser for the

Wild Trout Trust, of which you are vice-president, and a wonderful cause it is, too. Regarding motherhood, Stella talks about pressure and worry, whereas Mother Superiors like myself see it from a different perspective, one of opportunities and standards. What we should be doing is absolutely what we should be doing. We do not want to fail our children, our husbands and ourselves, we want to give them the very best we can. This juggling act they moan about, well, juggling is fun, is it not? It's all about fulfilment and making the best of what we have. Stella's view is very depressing, very insular. The reason motherhood is so discussed is because it is important – the most important job in the world. We need to make sure women realise their responsibilities and their potential, and so I see the discussion as immensely empowering. Every day, every minute, we need to be reminded of how good so-and-so looks after a traumatic birth captured by *Hello!* magazine. It spurs us on to great things.'

'Given the level of interest in parenting and family life, which is a central political platform these days, do you think there is a case for a Minister for Motherhood, Stella?'

'Yes. Our society has rightly embraced the fight against racism, sexism and homophobia, and the push towards equal rights, so it is about time an entire invisible generation of our population is represented within Government to monitor and legislate where necessary to stop this silly notion that mothers must be perfect. Look at the media – countless studies report a negative effect on girls from as young as four from the size zero images on television and in films and on billboards. The same must surely apply for mums who are bombarded with pictures of celebrity skinny mummies losing four stone in four weeks post-birth. Is it any wonder record numbers of mothers are taking anti-depressants and hitting the bottle? How on earth is this affecting our kids, when they are being brought up by exhausted mothers who are being told to strive towards an unrealistic and frankly damaging aspiration? This is why a Minister for Motherhood is vital.'

'Oh, Stella, to suggest we need Big Mother to tell us what to do, how to think, and to protect us from . . . what, a silly magazine which shows a photo of Victoria Beckham looking delicious when we all know she has access to childcare and dieticians and chefs? No. A Minister for Motherhood would assume we mothers are brainless automatons who cannot distinguish between reality and celebrity. As millions of us show day in, day out, we are very capable of running our own lives, believing in our own gods, be it having it all – which, by the way, is the only way to live your life, to ensure your children have the very best of everything – or as Stella believes, being too lazy to get off one's backside to make the most of oneself. In my view, we need nannies but we do not need the Nanny State.'

'Some people watching this will be thinking you

mothers never stop moaning. Is that true, ladies? Stella?'

'I don't think mums complain enough! It is true our mothers' generation subscribed to the like-it-or-lump-it school of thought, giving up their jobs to have babies without any question of returning to work. But then, guess what happened, the next generation came along and started to complain. Yes, they may have been trivial things, such as why are there no changing stations in the men's toilets? Why are there no crèches in shops or leisure centres so I can have an hour to get something done? Why are there no parent-and-baby parking spaces close to the supermarket entrance? My mother always tells me how hard it was in the days before the difficulties of motherhood were acknowledged. These changes only came about due to complaining. Of course, we mums do like to moan about personal matters when we meet up on a play date. Obviously we love our children, worship them, but it is a very tiring, demanding job, which is not nearly as well recognised as it should be. The work-place is a prime example of our voices needing to be raised: raised eyebrows at leaving at four p.m. to pick up the kids is not acceptable. We've probably worked through our lunch hours because we fear we'll be considered flakey.'

'Stella makes it sound like motherhood is a chore. It isn't – it's a delight, from that first life-affirming contraction to the charm of those night-time cuddles.

Tiredness is a state of mind, I firmly believe that, and exercise and looking after yourself are essential to combat that 'poor me, pour me another drink' attitude. I found every stage of mothering my four children the most rewarding achievement of my life. There really is nothing to complain about – watching your progeny discover the world around them is a joy.

'As for complaining in the workplace, I think it's a big bad world out there and no one is going to do you any favours. Women who squeal discrimination are generally the ones who are caught updating their Facebook profile or doing the weekly shop during office hours and they have only themselves to blame. Work hard, stop moaning and get on with it.'

'Hattie! You had yours at the Portland and you have a nanny. How on earth can you relate to ordinary women who are so tired they cannot cry straight? Have you ever wept into a bowl of baby rice? I sincerely doubt it, but even if you have, you'd never admit it. Your stiff upper tit is damaging to the vast majority who feel they are failing on those days when they are not coping. As for the favours bit, you're friends with the Prime Minister's wife, you share the school run with celebrity mums and your business benefits from these associations. You have no idea what ordinary mums go through every day. That dreadful alarm clock beep when it seems we've only just got to bed means jumping out at a hundred miles on hour to get everyone dressed and fed, making lunchboxes, finding lost gloves before legging it to school. Then we rush to work and try our absolute hardest, even though we have been up half the night with a crying child. At lunch we race around getting birthday presents or returning library books or taking the dog for a walk or picking up the four-year-old from school and delivering them to nursery, then it's back to work, eating a sandwich at our desks, followed by doing the pick-up, making dinner, checking home-work, playing with the kids, housework, cuddles, bath, bed, husband time, TV, ironing, ringing a poorly or heartbroken friend, collapsing into bed, only for it to start all over again. You can add financial troubles or the we-haven't-had-sex-for-ages worry or the 'I feel such a fattie so why did I just eat that Twix?' torment, and it becomes very clear why we complain. This is why Mums Like Us membership is soaring and this is why your exclusive clique is so very out of touch.'

'This bout of verbal sparring begs the question, surely mothers would be better served by stopping this infighting?'

'Jeremy, I asked Stella this very same question on the afternoon of our arrest after the march, and she has yet to answer me. Is this because she knows I am right to suggest mothers of the world should unite, to keep our moans and embarrassing bits to ourselves because it doesn't do our cause any good? Well-groomed, effortless and size-ten perfection is the only thing to aim for in life – if we don't, we become depressed and fat and old before our time. Stella only has to say the word and we can share a platform, standing tall in our Kurt Geigers – after all, you did have Botox, so you're halfway there, sweetie.'

'I am all for solidarity. I am all for finding a common path. I am all for the sisterhood. But I am afraid I cannot see how we can worship at the same altar when we are so very different. In the police van on our way to the nick, you did indeed ask me to turn to the dark side. I cannot say I wasn't tempted; after all, I would much rather look at my face in the mirror and be pleasantly surprised at my youthful reflection. But that is a lie. It is surface. Hattie, there are many more things to worry about than keeping up appearances. My club is for the kind of woman who knows that deep down. If you and I became one, I would be letting down every single one of them. There is more to life than starving oneself, flogging oneself at the gym and delegating cuddles to the nanny. But do you know what convinced me most of all? That in the early days of my club, you sent in a mole to find out what we were up to. Had you asked to meet me, I would've been more than happy. But you went behind our backs, sneaking past our muffin-tops, because you felt entitled; on reflection, it made me realise how very low you are. This exchange of words has only confirmed my gut instinct – and my gut, due to its size, has made itself heard, loud and clear. I am not perfect, I have done things I am not proud of but at least I admit them. Since then you have attacked me at every opportunity in the press, whereas I have tried to refrain from retaliation. This, Hattie, is why I will never be your bitch.'

'Yeeees . . . on that note, we'll have to leave this discussion. We'll be back tomorrow night at the normal time, thank God. Goodnight.'

Dads United

Email to: davidsmith70@hotmail.com
Subject: Stella's birthday
Date: 2 November, 13:25

Dave,

It's El Stel's birthday on the 5th and I need you to ring home at 5 p.m. to wish her the very best.

You need to tell her you've just heard from me. Say the battery on my phone has gone dead – I tried to ring her mobile but it went to voicemail, so I rang you instead with what little juice I had left.

Explain to her my car has broken down and she needs to pick me up from the office. Tell her you've rung Mum and she's on her way to babysit. Got a brilliant surprise lined up for her.

Cheers,

Matt

Week Thirty-seven

Fireworks

Stella's kitchen

Thanks for all your birthday texts and cards and tweets and emails – you're a lovely bunch. I had an, um, interesting day. Parts of it were brilliant, other parts not so brilliant. But then what did you expect? Nothing in my life seems to go smoothly.

I was brought breakfast in bed – the little one's contribution was a chocolate coin he had saved from trick or treating, bless his cotton socks – sausage sandwich, pint of tea and a stack of cards that had arrived in the previous few days. As usual, Matt didn't give me anything in the morning – we always leave it till after work to do presents – but the little one handed me a card he'd made. It was heartbreakingly rubbish (a work of art in my eyes, obviously), a few *Star Wars* stickers and a scribble, but he had managed to write his name backwards. Matt dashed off to work then so we had a lazy hour or so, got ourselves ready, wrapped up warm, and went for a lovely walk to the park. The sun was shining and the leaves were all crunchy and we were so happy the two of us, him on his scooter, me yelling, 'Mind the dog poo!' Mum came and met us for lunch, bringing me a huge bunch of flowers and some vouchers – she knows I would rather shop online in the evening than perform the race-against-time in the two and a half hours I get to myself of an afternoon.

Mum was high as a kite because she'd booked herself a New Year cruise for 'independent mature travellers'. She's doing the Canaries for a week, sounds perfect for her. We scoffed steaming plates of fish, chips and peas and then we said goodbye so I could do drop-off. I kissed my rosy-cheeked angel and walked home with a huge smile on my face.

At the front door, there was a huge parcel, a perfect square, about the size of a large box of washing powder, covered in luxurious silver wrapping paper fastened with silver velvet ribbon, with a label attached bearing my name in swooping elegant letters! I squealed with excitement and carried it in, collecting more cards from the doormat which the postie had delivered in my absence.

I settled down with a cuppa and began wading through the pile, feeling like I was the luckiest woman on the planet. I saved the box till last, going through my mental list of sweet-hearted suspects, wondering which of my beloved friends or family had gone to so much trouble.

I carefully pulled off the ribbon – putting it aside to use again, perhaps on a Christmas present or more likely in some half-arsed crafts session with my son – and opened the box. Buried within a snowstorm of those polystyrene white wotsits was a transparent bag of doughnuts – thirty-seven of them. My age in jam doughnuts – how brilliant! I searched around the lucky dip for a clue of the sender and I found a card with writing on it.

And I froze. In that looping handwriting, it read, 'You can't have your cake and eat it. Tattoo.'

What the hell was that about? It slowly dawned on me this was no gesture of kindness from a friend but a nasty threat from an enemy. Someone who knew where I lived and had waited until I'd gone out, someone who had been watching me. Who the hell is this Tattoo, this nutter who is regularly abusing me on the website? Who hates me that much? I wondered. And who's got a tattoo that I know?

Shit – if I remember right, the Man Of My Dreams has one, a Celtic cross thing on his wrist. Well, it's true he's a prick, but he's not spiteful, at least I don't think he is. Who else? Hattie? Yes, she showed me a dolphin on her ankle from her wild university days when we were in the police van. But this isn't her style. She wouldn't touch a doughnut, let alone thirty-seven of them, would she? What about someone in the club? There are loads of mums with tattoos on the small of their backs, we compared them once on a night out, but it can't be one of them. I've made mistakes but I've always been honest and tried to face up to them. It must just be a loony. Not that that is any consolation.

A Catherine wheel of panic whizzed round my heart and I tried to ring Matt at work. But he was in a meeting so I tried to occupy my mind, remembering I needed to get my favourite dress out of the wardrobe to get it dry-cleaned, because it was still covered in wine stains. It wasn't there. It had gone, and I started gasping with fear. Was I losing my mind? A pair of shoes had gone, too, as had my make-up. Oh God – what on earth was going on?

By then, it was time to run to the shops to get some birthday fizz and then do the pick-up. When I left the house, I pulled my hood up, peering out with eyes on stalks to see if there was anyone out there following me. My pace quickened and I was so relieved to get my son and lock the door behind us. At five p.m., the phone went, making me jump. It was my brother-in-law telling me that Matt had asked him to ring me since his phone was out of juice. Apparently Matt needed picking up as the car had a flat battery, and their mum was on the way over to babysit. As soon as she turned up, I told her not to answer the door to anyone and I'd explain later. I dashed out into the darkness, locked myself in the car and began the drive.

My racing heart was helped neither by screaming

fireworks going off in the sky around me nor by the fog of smoky gunpowder air which seemed to close in on me. I pulled into Matt's car park and there he was, with a bunch of flowers and a bottle of champagne.

He ushered me, stunned, into his car and bellowed, 'Surprise! We're off for the night to that really posh hotel you always talk about. I've booked us dinner which – get this – is in the hotel's glass atrium restaurant which overlooks the river, and while we eat, there's a huge fireworks display, and then tomorrow, we don't have to check out until midday so we can have a lie-in!'

I sat there in the passenger seat, speechless and wide-eyed.

Then I started shouting at him: 'WHAT THE BLOODY HELL IS GOING ON? I'VE HAD THE WORST DAY, YOU'VE HOODWINKED ME INTO COMING OUT HERE FOR YOU, AND OUR SON COULD BE IN DANGER. STOP THIS FANNYING ABOUT AND LET'S GO HOME.'

Matt went pale as I jumped into my car and sped home, jumping lights all the way. Matt screeched in behind me on the drive. I ran into the house, pushed him inside, and slammed the door shut, locking up, before checking the back door was secure.

He was fuming by now because I'd ruined everything, and it was my turn to explain the doughnuts and the missing dress, shoes and make-up.

After I'd gone through it, we had a chance to calm down. There was no point calling the police; they had proper criminals to catch. Could it be a joke that I wasn't getting? Was I getting uptight and oversensitive in my old age? We both agreed it was better to ignore it. I have my reasons, as you will know – 'fessing up to the Man Of My Dreams would not go down well. And Matt, being a man of sense, said that if the hate-mail story got out, it would be like oxygen for the stalker. He has a point – but I can't pretend I don't feel uneasy. At least this person is targeting me, not my family. But if it comes to that, my God, I will hunt them down and go full gorilla.

I was also reassured because the missing stuff was down to Matt – it turned out he'd packed an overnight bag for me, having secretly dry-cleaned my dress last week, and it was in the boot of his car. Anyway, we never made it to the hotel. Matt cancelled, blaming illness, which is partly true if you think about Tattoo's mental state, so we weren't charged. We invited his mum to bring her overnight bag in from her car and stay for a Chinese takeaway. When it came to watching the displays from the upstairs bedrooms, I gave it a miss. I'd had enough fireworks for one night.

Since then, I've spoken to the committee and we would like you all to stay vigilant, because we don't know if this is a personal campaign against me – let's face it, I'm excellent at making enemies – or if it's going to spread to other members. Please let us know if you see anything suspicious, and of course, if anyone else is affected we will go to the police.

Whoever this sicko is, we will not be frightened into silence.

OK, moving on, Lucy's had an idea about setting up some Mums Like Us antenatal workshops to prepare mums-to-be for the baby bomb. We could call them The Truth Hurts, or something like that. The aim would be to offer an alternative to the bile delivered in the Nasty Childbirth Trust courses. It is vital we try to recruit members at the pre-birth stage; it will save them a lot of trouble in the long run. Any feedback on content would be wonderful, so please have a think and get back to Lucy.

Right, that's the meeting done, feel free to stay for another cuppa. If you need to rush off, then thanks for coming and we'll see you next week. There's lots of club business brewing at the mo – we'll fill you in then.

Dads United

Matt's head, jogging

Right, Smithy. You've done your stretches, the ones you saw when you sneaked a look at one of those twatty men's magazines in the dentist's waiting room, so no excuses. Get your fat arse running or you'll never lose those moobs. You need to lead the lads by example. Today's target is five kilometres in half an hour. Let's do it.

Off we go. Feeling good, iPod on shuffle, first track is . . . here it comes . . . oh brilliant, 'Bat Out of Hell' by Meatloaf, that'll get me going. Mind the dog shit – why the fuck don't people clear it up, filthy bastards? OK, I think I'll turn left down there, head out towards the rec, do a couple of laps then I'll be back in time to do the little one's bath. God, it's cold; nips out weather.

I'm quite enjoying this. I reckon I look quite good, you know, for my age. Not bad, son, not bad. Keep it up. Wonder what's for tea? I'm starving. Could kill one of those doughnuts Stella got yesterday. I can't believe she threw them out – what a waste. Watch the kerb, there, it's wobbly, you don't want to twist your ankle and look a complete girl in front of that woman walking her dog. I mean, I know this person is a nutter, but I hardly think they'd contaminate them. Stella didn't think it was worth the risk. If she hadn't squeezed washing up liquid all over them, I'd have dug them out of the bin and had one last night.

I'm glad we didn't ring the police. I don't want Stella getting all het up – a visit from the plod would've worked her up and she'd have started to get obsessed about it. I don't want her dwelling on it. Oh God, here comes the hill, this is going to be unpleasant. Don't look up, just focus on the pavement in front of you.

Could the doughnuts have come from That Woman? I dunno. It's weird how the first person who came to mind when Stella told me was her. Would she do something like that? I did notice she had a tattoo on her hip, which would've been covered up had she been wearing sensible knickers like Stella's.

Thank God I didn't tell Stella about That Woman's vow of revenge, or she'd be straight to the cops. And then I'd have to explain everything that happened rather than the bits I thought Stella could handle. Imagine if she knew That Woman had been in her grundies – she'd have asked me if her bum was as big as hers, and I'd have had to lie. Not that I fancy That Woman in any way – far too skinny and petite, I much prefer curves. But it's just, women, well, they read stuff into things. Blimey, twenty years ago, a naked woman offering herself to me would've been the stuff of my dreams! Nah, it can't be her. Let's face it, Stella isn't exactly universally loved, is she? She's always on the telly and in the papers, stoking the fire. There are plenty of weirdos out there. And it wouldn't be hard to find out Stella's age or address.

Next track – 'White Riot' by the Clash! Get in. If I seriously thought we were in danger, I'd go to the police. But I'm convinced it's harmless. Maybe I should get one of those CCTV camera thingies for the front. Yeah, it won't do any harm, it'll feel like I'm doing something about it.

How am I doing? Quick time check: just over halfway, not bad, on schedule. Here's the rec. Jesus, look at those scrotes smoking spliffs on the swings. Better keep away from them or they'll chuck their Strongbow cans at me. Legs beginning to hurt now. Come on, son, you're doing well, you can have a fuck-off dinner tonight if you do this.

Oh shit, is that a stitch coming? Better not be . . . oh man, you lardy piece of shit, Smithy. Weak! Weak! You are weak! Keep going. Almost there, on the home straight now. Must think about setting up another game. Wonder if the IT guys will be up for it? I'll have to ask at work. I reckon we'll murder them.

Oh, I love this bit of the run, I can see the Feathers. Oh, I love the Feathers. I think it's my favourite place in the whole world. No hassle, a pint, read the paper, have a think, switch off, have a chat about football, stare at a beer mat, that first slug of a Guinness Cold – you can't beat it.

I wonder if I should pop in for a quick one? You know, just to ask the landlord if he can put up a notice to ask if anyone fancies playing Dads United? Stella won't mind, I'll only be ten minutes. They do say you need to rehydrate after exercise. Aaaah, I can smell the ale now . . . sod it, I'm going in.

Week Thirty-eight

Back to Business

Stella's kitchen

Well, for once there are no personal dramas to report, so let's get on with club business. First up, apologies. Mags can't be here because she's been called in on her day off, poor cow – such is the life of a breadwinner. I don't know how she manages to juggle everything. By all accounts, Si is pretty useless. He can just about look after the kids, but when she gets home, the house is a total tip, there's no dinner made and he then says he needs an hour off because he's had a hell of a day. Honestly, what Mags needs is a wife.

Anyway, moving on, our next item on the agenda is very exciting. We've been asked to appear in a major supermarket's Christmas ad campaign! The PR company that approached me hasn't told us which one – it's that confidential. Apparently the retail sector is paranoid about leaks and ideas being nicked and all that, so they keep everyone in the dark until the morning of the shoot. We'll get loads of cash if we agree. Mags reckons it could pay for a significant chunk of our antenatal class set-up – more on that later.

Anyway, the storyboard goes like this: us lot are gathered outside the front of the supermarket singing 'We Wish You A Merry Christmas' with Gareth Malone as our choirmaster. Yes, lovely Gareth off the telly. We'll be in choirgowns and there'll be one of those fake snow machines to make it feel festive. Then cut to Gareth doing his Christmas shopping in store. He's seen perusing all the goodies on sale, such as, 'Ooh, that jumper dress will do for the wife', 'I'll get a Wii for us to play on Christmas day', 'Mum will love Nigella's latest cookery book' etc., all as scenes that are played out in bubbles above his head, like he's imagining what joy abounds. Then cut to the real Christmas Day, when we all arrive at his house for lunch and there's a montage of us all having champagne and opening presents and stuff, and then he opens his presents and one after another he unwraps one of our naked calendars. Oh blimey, I'm so excited. I meant to tell you that, too – our calendars have been snapped up by all of the big chains and they go on sale in a few days. I've got one hot off the press – it arrived this morning – so I'll pass it round after the meeting. I tell you what, we might look a bit wobbly, but my God, we look like normal women. We should give ourselves a pat on the back fat. My personal favourite is the Season of Plenty picture for December with all of us covered in grapes and cakes and meats and stuff, it's really Ghost of Christmas Present, really fountain of plenty and decadent. I've still got some of that food in my freezer from the shoot if anyone wants some. My plan was to dish it out at our Boxing Day meeting, but if anyone's stuck for something for tea, have a root around in the top and middle shelves.

Filming for the ad takes place the day after the day after tomorrow. It's short notice, because a major celeb let them down at the last minute, so that's why we've been roped in. Their loss! The PR woman said child-minders would be there if you can't dump the kids elsewhere. Plus there'll be complimentary pastries and sausage and egg baguettes and all that waiting for us. I need everyone's size written down to pass on for our costumes, so email those over if you can make it. No idea where it's happening yet but it will be a local store, she said. Sounds like it'll be a right laugh. I can't wait to tell my mum – she loves Gareth.

Are we up for it? A show of hands in favour . . . that's a yes, then! It's all very cheesy, but you can't buy publicity like that. I'm so thrilled. Compare where we were this time last year – this club was just a twinkle in my eye then, and now we're bloody national. Scrub that, we're international.

OK, the next item is our antenatal classes. Lucy is taking charge of these. She's been working on the content and she'll be holding a dummy run in a few weeks, so if we can all prepare a few questions for her when the time comes – I've already bagsied the brilliantly unsuspecting 'Do contractions feel like period pain?' question, which we all wonder the first time around, believing labour can't be THAT bad. If you feel the need to stick a pillow up your jumper to get into the character of an unsuspecting, clueless, 'it can't be as bad as all that' mum-to-be, then go for it.

We hope to start the workshops in the new year. I really think if we were more honest and realistic about labour, childbirth and the first few months of mother-hood, plus we banned the birth plan, then perhaps – and obviously this is just a sweeping, unsubstanti-ated generalisation, but I'm good at those – we might see a reduction in post-natal depression. I can't wait to see what the Nasty Childbirth Trust makes of it.

Right, next item is a heads-up for next week, when the club reveals the findings of some research we commissioned on the website. I hope you've all taken part – lots of you have said you keep meaning to but haven't done it yet. I know how it is: not another of those bloody surveys that make you want to smash things up. But trust me, and those of you who are nodding because you've done it, this one is worth the five minutes. You've got until the end of the week, so please, please, please try.

The results of the survey will be distributed to the press in a release at the same time as we launch them on Twitter under the hashtag #bollockstoresearch so our followers can join the debate.

OK, our final thing for today, we should start thinking about where we're going to have our Christmas party. Perhaps you fancy a meal out, a trip to the dogs, an overnighter, an all-dayer, wine-tasting, a club, a cocktail-making class, whatever, suggestions, please, as ever, to any of the committee.

That, lardies, is all for this week. Hope to see you at the shoot.

Now, I mustn't forget to ring my mother to tell her she is completely not allowed to talk to Gareth Malone. Bye!

Dads United

www.dadsunited.co.uk

MATCH REPORT: Dads United v. the IT Boys

Our first game against the IT Boys saw Dads United produce a rare and stunning display of total football, reminiscent of the World Cup Holland side of 1974.

While all the lads reckon the 'total' label is stretching it a bit ('total chaos' would be a more accurate way of summing it up, because no one knew what position they were supposed to be playing), the skipper stands by his assessment of the match, which the Dads won 33–0.

To be fair, the Dads could have failed to turn up and the IT Boys would've taken a beating. They were that bad. But we don't want to take anything away from the middle-agers who ran rings round a bunch of geeks who have never seen daylight and survive on bowls of cereal at 2 a.m. because they get carried away playing computer role-play games and forget to eat.

The visiting weedy XI arrived in average-sized executive cars, suggesting they were doing quite well in life, probably because none of them has had the expense of pulling, getting married or reproducing (in real life, not online, because in cyberspace they're probably killer warlord sex animals). Their kit was tracksuit bottoms – because they're all paranoid about their skinny legs – and Atari T-shirts.

Winning the toss, their skipper kicked off, passing the ball by mistake to Dads United. From that moment, the visitors were under pressure, losing possession at every opportunity.

Dads' first goal came after three minutes, scored by Matt after he dribbled the ball past four defenders and shot at close range. The IT Boys' goalie actually shut his eyes when he saw him coming, so he had no chance. After that, no one can remember how many goals each player scored because they came that thick and fast.

The game was abandoned at half-time because the visiting skipper admitted they had never played football together before.

The Dads paid tribute to the opposition by clapping them into the changing rooms in the style of robots speaking binary, and they proceeded to get completely shitfaced at the Feathers.

Man of the Match: The IT Boys' skipper, Comedy

Pete, for graciously calling it a day so we could go to the pub earlier.

Donkey of the Match: Matt for his deadly serious post-match analysis, claiming we were just like Ajax, the big twat.

Week Thirty-nine

PRESS RELEASE ... PRESS RELEASE ... PRESS RELEASE

Studies talk bollocks, Mums Like Us research reveals

FAO: News Editors, Features Editors, Family Affairs/ Social Correspondents

Studies on motherhood are total bollocks, according to research by Mums Like Us.

An independent survey, commissioned by the world's biggest support group for women who don't dress up for the school run, reveals every single piece of research examining the impact of modern motherhood on children is LIES designed to make us feel even more inadequate than normal.

What's more, a poll of millions of members shows 100 per cent of mums read these studies, reflect on their own failings and then think, 'Oh bugger it, I'm doing the best I can in the circumstances, and I bet none of the scientists who carried out said research have children of their own because their findings are so unrealistic.'

The MLU study shows:

- Fish fingers and oven chips and beans and peas once a week is a wholesome meal containing protein, carbohydrate and two servings of veg, so knob off;
- Kids' television is educational, relaxing and the only way to get everything done;
- Working mums and stay-at-home mums empathise with one another and are not at loggerheads as divisive studies have suggested;
- Breastfeeding and bottlefeeding mums are perfectly capable of accepting one another's position without slagging the other off behind each other's backs;
- Celebrity mums who go evangelical about baby sick and use nap time to do a two-hour workout make us feel like crap. Pregnancy isn't sexy, new babies don't fix rocky relationships and crowing about the 'distressed antique' look of your nursery is just distressing.
- Whether we cotton-wool our kids or push them out to play in the rain, we know we will be accused of doing the wrong thing;
- A meal round the table is what we aim for, but

seriously, shut the fuck up about tea on a tray
– there are worse things to worry about;

- Yes, we know wine o'clock is a bit naughty, but
we've had a pig of a day and we want to chill
out, OK?;
- Having a picky eater is not our bloody fault –
we've tried everything to get them to eat
butternut squash but they still won't eat it.

Club chairwoman Stella Smith says, 'Our research flies in the face of every piece of research going, pouring not just doubt but full nappies on their conclusions. Our message to mums everywhere is to ignore any research that makes you feel rubbish.'

If you would like to speak to Stella, feature a case study or find out more about our projects and activities, click on the link below to get in touch with us. Please note, the best time to reach us is during school hours. And don't even bother calling after 7 pm because we've sat down in front of the telly by then and all we want is some peace.

ENDS . . .

Twitter Launch #bollockstoresearch
Mumslikeus @mumslikeus
Hi, tummies. Our new research is out! What do you think? #bollockstoresearch
Fishfingers @ilovefishfingers
@mumslikeus Glad to see fish fingers get a mention. What's your fave?

Mumslikeus @mumslikeus
@ilovefishfingers salmon ones because equals oily fish portion *winks* #bollockstoresearch
Miserable Cow @miserablecow
@mumslikeus At last! A piece of research I can read and believe! #bollockstoresearch
Working Mum @workingmum
@mumslikeus posted the research on my fridge to remind me im good enough :) #bollockstoresearch
Mumslikeus @mumslikeus
@workingmum @miserablecow yay! Keep the faith #bollockstoresearch
Nasty Childbirth Trust @nastychildbirthtrust
@mumslikeus
#bollockstomumslikeusresearch
Mumslikeus @mumslikeus
@nastychildbirthtrust how very constructive #bollockstoresearch
Nasty Childbirth Trust @nastychildbirthtrust
@mumslikeus breast is best, don't deny it #bollockstomumslikeusclubresearch
Mumslikeus @mumslikeus
@nastychildbirthtrust not denying it, too much pressure on new mums to add breast v bottle on their poor tired shoulders #bollockstoresearch
Mothers Superior @motherssuperior
@mumslikeus darling, a gorgeous work of fiction
Mumslikeus @mumslikeus
@motherssuperior Hattie, shouldn't you be at the gym?

319

Mothers Superior @motherssuperior
@mumslikeus how funny, I am! Tweeting on the cross-trainer
Mumslikeus @mumslikeus
Sleb mums don't eat #bollockstoresearch RT'@motherssuperior: celeb mums are an inspiration'
Mumslikeus @mumslikeus
Ooh #bollockstoresearch is trending already, we've only been going 5 minutes
Tattoo @tattoo
@mumslikeus seems you've forgotten your roots *slow hand clap*
Mumslikeus @mumslikeus
@tattoo was wondering when you'd appear. Booked in for roots a week on Wednesday
Tattoo @tattoo
@mumslikeus ha ha. Meant how your main emphasis these days is courting the media
Mumslikeus @mumslikeus
@tattoo how else do we get the message across? Suggestions v welcome
Tattoo @tattoo
@mumslikeus had any Botox recently?
Mumslikeus @mumslikeus
@tattoo no, as I revealed in interview with the *Daily Mail*, never again. Why bring that up? We're talking #bollockstoresearch
Tattoo @tattoo
@mumslikeus Stella, it's always about *you*

Mumslikeus @mumslikeus

@tattoo if only you'd reveal yourself, then we could sort this out

Mumslikeus @mumslikeus

@tattoo how funny. Radio silence. You, tattoo, are blocked

Mumslikeus @mumslikeus

Right, lardies, thanks for your trillions of messages of support – got to go, work to do #bollockstoresearch

Dads United @dadsunited

@mumslikeus Stel, do we need anything on my way back from work tonight?

Mumslikeus @mumslikeus

@dadsunited *sighs* why couldn't you just check before you left for work? Oh I forgot. I have a womb. Therefore I know if we need milk.

Dads United @dadsunited

@mumslikeus ha ha! I'll get milk, bread, wine and chocolate then

Mumslikeus @mumslikeus

@dadsunited *ears prick up at mention of chocolate* you're forgiven :)

Week Forty

Tackling Tattoo

Stella's kitchen

Hi, everyone, come in. Keep your shoes on – we had a spillage of orange juice this morning so the floor's sticky, even though I Dettoxed the area.

Park your arses. How was your weekend?

We had a lovely one; it was our sixth wedding anniversary last week so we went out Saturday night, just the two of us. We couldn't remember what the tradition was for the sixth year of marriage. You know, paper is the first, silver is twenty-five years. So we decided it was 'curry' and went out for an enormous one after a few drinks at the pub where we had our wedding reception. Matt had told the landlord we were coming, so there was a bottle of bubbly on ice for us. Usually we don't go in much for the whole wedding anniversary thing, but subconsciously, because of all the ups and downs we've had of late, we were both really up for it. When I suggested a meal out on Saturday rather than a takeaway, Matt was really enthusiastic, which is not like him, because he lives for his Saturday-night bottle of wine, box set and *Match Of The Day*. And get this, Matt didn't go to the football in the afternoon, saying he wanted to hang out with me, having despatched the little one to the mother-in-law for the night. I told him I was only planning on going to the garden centre to get some bulbs – how dull – but he came with me. He did spend most of the time not-so-surreptitiously checking the score on his phone, but top marks for effort.

We even had sex when we were getting ready to go out. Really good sex, including foreplay – rather than just we-should-do-it-sex and discussing getting the washing machine fixed in between thrusts.

But then, before we left for the pub, he dropped the loo roll in the bath and put it back on the cistern without putting it on the radiator, so I found it all soggy. And over our jalfrezi, he mentioned going to the Feathers for the lunchtime game the next day. I was secretly relieved that he was still the Matt I'd married. 'Yes, go,' I said, 'I can't really cope with you being so thoughtful and lovely.' It was all a bit too much, him being the perfect man.

Anyway, there was something I wanted to do while he was out before the little one got back. I'd had enough of Tattoo and thought it was about time I tackled the issue. So I rang Hattie.

She picked up after seven rings, enough to make me start panicking, wondering what I was going to say.

'Hello, hang on. I'm just in the health club, on the running machine, let me switch it off or I'll be heavy breathing at you . . .' she said.

'Hattie, it's me, Stella,' I said.

'Darling, how are you?' she purred.

'Erm . . . fine – well, not fine, actually. You?' I said.

'I'm fantastic, just burnt off brunch. Why are you not fine, Stella? Are you having doubts? Come on, sweetie, it's not too late to join us,' she laughed.

'Oh, not that again. No, nothing to do with that. Listen, this is serious. Is it you? Because if it is, I will go straight to the papers and tell them.'

'Is it me what? Goodness, Stella, you are funny. What on earth are you talking about?'

'You know. The doughnuts, the tweets, the nasty trolling,' I said.

'I beg your pardon! Are you accusing me of something?' she said, coldly.

'No. I'm not accusing you of anything. I'm simply asking if you are the person behind Tattoo,' I asked, and then went into my birthday 'surprise' and all that.

She paused before she said, 'Stella. Number one: if I have any bones to pick, I do it directly, you should know me better than that. Second: I would never have sent doughnuts. They're far too common. I would've plumped for bespoke fat-free pastries. Why did you suspect me? Oh . . . Stella! Is it because of my dolphin? Ha! You really are insane. Do you think I would be that obvious? Do you think I have the time to conduct this seedy little campaign against you? Let me tell you, if I was trying to get at you, I would be wanting to claim the credit myself,' she snorted.

She told me to ignore it, move onwards and upwards, and then she had to go because her personal trainer was getting twitchy, something to do with 'resting her pulse for too long'.

I believed her. It's not her; it's someone close to me, definitely, I can sense it. I'm not being funny, but you know Harry Potter's scar gets inflamed whenever he is in danger from Voldemort? The same thing happens with my episiotomy scar. I will get to the bottom of this – excuse the pun.

Right, club business to attend to: our Christmas do is booked for a month's time. Lucy collected all the suggestions and took one out of the hat: cheap buffet at that karaoke bar. We will live-stream over the internet to members worldwide so they can join in. And Dads United have asked if they can come too, because they can't be bothered to organise anything themselves.

How's that, everyone? A show of hands . . . motion carried.

Next week, I have an exciting new campaign to launch. It's called Mother Christmas.

Cheers all, see you then.

Dads United

Matt rings That Woman

'It's me.'

'Smithy . . . hi . . .'

'Can you talk?'

'Er . . . yes, I can. Everything OK?'

'I was just ringing to see how you are. The grapevine says you've gone off sick.'

'Oh. I should've known. Nothing is sacred, is it? Yeah, I'm having a bit of a crisis. It started after, well, you know, after that thing that happened.'

'Oh . . . right. That thing between us?'

'Yes. It's fine, I'm fine, I just had a funny turn. That night, after you left, I raided the minibar and was found passed out the next morning. I was still drunk and refused to leave the room and they had to call the manager, who rang the police, who rang my mum, and she had to come and get me. The doctor says I've been working too hard. The therapist says I have . . . some issues. Which I'm working on. In fact, I'm selling my company as we speak. I was ploughing all my energy into work and became delusional and . . . well, I was lonely and I thought you and me . . .'

'Oh, God, I'm so sorry. I feel like a right shit. We're supposed to be friends. Why didn't you tell me?'

'Because we're not friends, because we never were. You thought we were, but I knew it wasn't friendship I wanted, it was a . . . relationship. Whatever. It doesn't matter any more. I'm much better now. It goes without saying that I'm mortified about that night – I'm so sorry I put you in that position, let alone exposing myself the way I did. I've tried to blank it out – luckily I was so drunk I don't remember much – but even so, knowing you remember it all is just as bad. It's been really hard, facing up to things, putting my shit on other people and . . . well, I've come to a decision that I need to get out of IT and go and do something different.'

'At least you'll make a packet out of the business. I'd offer to buy it but we're skint. What are you going to do now?'

'I'm going to start with a month-long holiday in India, staying at a yoga resort, to try to clear my mind and chill out. Yes, I know it's a cliché, but I need to sort myself out. I'll probably end up with a shaved head and covered in Sanskrit tattoos!'

'Tattoos? Funny you should bring that up . . .'

'Why?'

'It's not you, is it? Tattoo?'

'What?'

'Well, we've had some . . . er . . . some contact from somebody calling themself Tattoo, someone who is a bit . . . unhinged, and the last thing you said to me that night was about getting at Stella. Look, I wish I'd never asked. I know it isn't you. I know you've got a tattoo, I saw it that time . . . and ever since, it's been in the back of my mind. But, having spoken to you now, I know it wouldn't be you. I'm sorry.'

'Jesus, of course it isn't me. I've been plugged into daytime TV and lying in bed for the last God knows how long, with not enough energy to switch off Jeremy Kyle. Look, I wasn't myself. I know I looked a total loony, I was a loony. But it's not me. I'm not being funny but . . . er . . . from what I've gathered from having all this time to read and stuff over the last few weeks, Stella isn't the most popular person on the planet. I think she's fab – I was always jealous of her, for having you, but honestly, she might just have to accept this is what happens when you put your head above the parapet.

'Listen, I'm going to have to go. The landline's going and I'm waiting to hear from my therapist. It could be her. But before I go I want to thank you. If it hadn't been for you, I wouldn't have had a breakdown and I wouldn't have realised that you're just not the one for me – you're too . . . boring, no offence – and I need to look at what I have rather than moaning about what I want. I'll keep you posted on Facebook with my travels. Bye, Matt.'

Click.

Week Forty-one

Mother Christmas

Stella's kitchen

Order! ORDER!

Right, now that you've stopped pissing yourselves at my outfit, could we start the meeting? So, you'll all be wondering why I'm dressed as a transsexual Father Christmas in a Santa skirt, jacket and beard. It's all part of the new campaign we're launching today, the first of December, which is called Let's Hear It For Mother Christmas!

An agency photographer is coming later, then the pictures will be sent to all the papers and I'll be issuing a press release later on after the meeting, but I wanted you all to know what it's all about before it hits the news-stands tomorrow.

So, the aim of the campaign is this: to give credit where credit is due, to let our kids know it is not just Father Christmas who sorts out the stockings. Oh no. His wife, Mother Christmas, is also involved. I will be accused of feminism and of trying to subvert a centuries-old tradition. But come on, it just makes Father Christmas more realistic.

Are we supposed to let our children believe that a man sorts out the entire Christmas operation when the vast majority of male role models in their lives haven't got a bloody clue what's in their stockings? In this day and age, how are we to answer those innocent questions from our kids who wonder, 'But, Mummy, how come it's a man who makes sure we all get what we asked for when Daddy doesn't even know we're only allowed Coco Pops at the weekend?'

This campaign builds on the truism that behind every great man is a woman. But it goes further – it informs our children that teamwork is responsible for the magic of Christmas. To young eyes, it is entirely feasible that Mother Christmas makes sure all the presents go to the right children and Father Christmas is the one who delivers them. After all, it's usually Daddy who drives anywhere on a family trip so Mummy can dole out sandwiches, tissues and threats to stop fighting in the back or we'll crash.

It's a pretty revolutionary idea, I know, and I'm awaiting a huge backlash from the more conservative sections of the press. But Let's Hear It For Mother Christmas! is not about destroying Father Christmas – it's the complete opposite; it's about making him more believable. My dream is that in the years to come, our grandchildren and their grandchildren will be told how Father and Mother Christmas work together to make it all happen. And then, ultimately, wouldn't it be wonderful if this belief filtered into the home, meaning mums and dads shared the weight of preparing for Christmas? Rather than how it is today – of Mum killing herself to get everything ready while Dad merely carries the tree in from the car or down from the loft and thinks, that's me done, then.

Imagine a world in which your other half buys his side of the family's presents.

Imagine a world in which he (a) thinks to get gifts for the teachers and (b) goes of his own accord to get them without even mentioning it to his wife.

Imagine a world in which he does not say, 'Oh, did we get you that?' when it's unwrapping time.

Imagine a world in which he writes Christmas cards, he dashes out at lunch to get stocking fillers, he makes paper chains with the kids, he buys some new decorations because a few are a bit Woolies circa 1970, he makes sure there are some emergency unisex presents for people we might have forgotten and he remembers to clean the loo just before the guests descend for Christmas drinks.

Then there's a possibility that we mums could at least enjoy Christmas.

That's not to say we don't love the build-up and the school concerts and the mince pies and the lights and the carols. It's just that if the load was shared then perhaps we wouldn't collapse on Christmas night, relieved it's over for another year.

I am fully expecting our loudest critics to be Hattie's lot, who believe Christmas is women's work. In their eyes, December is the most important time of the year because it gives them the chance to show how effortless it is to have a stylish Noel. It is their duty – no, their pleasure – to create an elegant home of such breathtaking beauty, with understated fairy lights draped across tasteful banisters and a real twenty-foot tree decorated in a minimalist fashion with colour-co-ordinated boutique baubles which set off the Farrow and Ball-painted walls, that when their husband returns from a hard day he will gasp with delight and thank his lucky stars for having such a clever wife.

While we are sweating and flailing, running around like headless turkeys as our 'Christmas Greatest Hits' plays Noddy Holder and Co., these Mother Superiors are serene as swans, offering amuse-bouches morsels and Nigella cocktails to a soundtrack of Michael Bublé. No doubt they are panicking just like us – their long legs kicking like mad under the surface to stay afloat – but they don't show it. They have perfected the art of keeping calm. And frankly, it gets on our tits.

Last Christmas Eve, we hosted a soirée with whack-in-the-oven vol-au-vents and spring rolls. Our guests helped themselves to wine from the fridge and everyone got merrily drunk, chucking as much booze down them as possible in the four p.m. till six p.m. window, before they had to go home and peel the spuds and wrap those final presents.

On Boxing Day we were invited to Matt's boss's house for midday drinks. His wife, a Mother Superior, had made every nibble herself – baked camembert, turkey pot pies in aqua blue Le Creuset ramekins, Thai fishcakes, avocado hoummos, sprout and cranberry quiche, individual cheesecakes and mini Christmas puddings, which were torched in one magnificent lighting-up ceremony to rounds of applause. Bear in mind it was Boxing Day and she had cooked a ten-course Christmas lunch the day before and held a hog-roast BBQ on Christmas Eve. She admitted she'd been up at the crack to get it all done but insisted it was worth it, 'much better than the cook-from-frozen muck'.

There were catering staff dressed in trendy black T-shirts and battered leather aprons handing out trays of food and champagne. A jazz quartet played carols. There were parlour games. The tree had been imported from a carbon-neutral Finnish forest, nourished to maturity by reindeer shit. And the decos were designer vintage, handmade and shockingly beautiful.

Matt's boss admitted he'd done nothing to help – he said his wife adored Christmas and he'd get his wrist slapped if he tried to get involved. Matt told him he'd get his arse whacked if he didn't help.

At one point, I nipped off to the loo and got lost in their mansion, a little bit worse for wear from the eggnog, and overheard some sobs and gulps coming from a room off a hallway I'd stumbled upon.

333

I pushed the door open and called out, 'Is everything OK?' – and there, sitting on a chaise longue breathing into a paper bag, was our immaculate hostess, who blinked back tears and insisted she was 'never better'. I couldn't leave her like that – I went over and asked if she was having a panic attack and she just nodded quickly, trying to control her inhaling. After a couple of minutes, she recovered and begged me not to mention it to her husband.

She told me he actually believed she enjoyed doing all of this organising, when really she wanted to punch him in his smug face for doing nothing to help. But she couldn't tell him it was causing her so much stress, because then he'd think she wasn't coping, and that was the worst sin of all to admit to. Her figure, she admitted, was down to nervous energy, what with having three kids under five and a career in cupcake-baking. Sometimes, she confessed, she went to the health club and lay down in the relaxation room and slept for an hour. She was that knackered.

Then she got up onto her killer orange Jimmy Choo wedges and brushed down her bodycon dress before inspecting her make-up in the mirror and then, just as if she'd flicked a switch, she smiled a dazzling perfect-toothed smile and suggested we went back to join the others. I went to the loo and as I sat there, with my tights round my ankles, my feet resting from the agony of wearing my H&M heels for the first time in ages, I shook my head in astonishment at the 'I'm

Coping' façade of the Mother Superior. Aside from the grotesque self-flagellation and denial it involved, it took a remarkable strength of character to carry it off. But while I respected her stoicism, I also felt desperately sad for her. Thank God I don't have this kind of pressure on top of everything else going on in my life, I thought while pulling up my regulation black M&S cotton-rich knickers.

I peered in the mirror and saw a smudge of foundation on my eyebrow, flecks of runaway mascara in my crow's feet and a blob of toothpaste where my left nipple was on my black jumper dress from Topshop. I decided to leave it all as it was – this is me, I thought.

By the time I returned to the party, Matt had started telling dirty jokes while slapping his boss on the back and I thought it was time we left. I located the little one, who was playing with the other kids who'd been invited, and bundled them both into the car. Starting the engine, I exhaled with relief and we returned to our straightforward lives.

This story shows how much we need to promote the concept of Mother Christmas; without her, Father Christmas would be nipping out at seven a.m. on the twenty-fifth of December in a desperate drive to find the only shop open in a fifty-mile radius to get some stuffing. This isn't about admitting as though it is a weakness that we need help – this is about four shoulders being better than two.

Right, the snapper will be here any minute, so I'm

going to have to end the meeting. That doesn't mean I'm chucking you out – please stay. Have a lie-down if you fancy it, or simply stare at the wall, completely up to you.

Next week, we'll have a cyber meeting covering top tips for a very Happy Christmas, so please email the committee your ideas. We'll post the top forty on the website in lieu of a proper meeting, because I've been invited to the Woman of the Year Awards. It's not really my kind of thing but it means a free meal and a night in a hotel – the Mandarin Oriental Hyde Park, which is super swanky – so I'm not going to turn that down. It's one of those red carpet thingies with loads of celebs handing out the awards, so I need to get something to wear. I believe it's being hosted by Carol Vorderman and apparently we will be graced with the attendance of Kate Middleton and the PM's wife. Obviously, I will give you all the goss the week after. I'm planning on hanging out in the loos so I get to meet all the stars – might ask them for their 'how they do it' secrets for a tongue-in-cheek feature for the website. I can see it now. Tell me, loaded-celebrity-with-a-nanny, how on earth do you stay so thin and gorgeous with four kids? Well, she'll say, I don't eat, I take diet pills, I spend all day at the gym and my children go to boarding school, so I never finish off their fish fingers.

If only one would admit it then we'd like them much better.

Oooh, there's the door, see you soon.

Week Forty-two

And The Award Goes to . . .

On the Train

www.mumslikeus.co.uk

Dear members,

It's 11 a.m. and I'm on my way up to the awards on the train. I love a train journey – in the quiet carriage, no kids, a coffee and one of those enormous Upper Crust baguettes you think you'll never eat but finish off before you pull out of the station. I could ride on here all day.

This newsletter is a two-parter. First up, your 40 Ways To Survive Christmas. Then, on my return journey I'll tell you about the bash, if I'm in any fit state, that is . . .

1. Ask relatives to make a list of three things they'd like for Christmas. If they do not respond by the specified deadline, give them vouchers. The 5p off a litre of petrol ones you get with your shopping – that'll teach them.

2. Hide the scissors from everyone. They are yours from dawn on 1 December until midnight on 26 December.

3. If your husband tries to use your wrapping paper, hiss at him like a possessed cat.

4. Roasties are healthier with skins left on. No point peeling them then. Have a drink instead.

5. Buy – do not make – Christmas cake and pudding. Get Vienetta for the kids.

6. The Wise Men should be much discussed at this time of year to make it clear to your husband that he is required to do something useful.

7. Tip your postie now so he will leave all your Amazon parcels in the bin/round the side when you're out, rather than take them back to the depot which is never open when you have a minute.

8. Get to work on the *Radio Times* with colour-coded highlighters for each family member so, officially, you don't miss recording those gems that will become part of your Christmas tradition and, unofficially, you give yourself half an hour off from overex-cited kids.

9. Insist on a Boxing Day afternoon walk for the entire family apart from you so you can 'tidy up' (watch a costume drama thing you recorded).

10. Nurofen Express is the only way to deal with a hangover.

11. Christmas chocolates must not be opened until 24 December. However, Mum's Unofficial Christmas chocolates can be opened whenever you like.

12. Remember how many guests you have for Christmas lunch and plate up accordingly, or you will have to ask everyone to donate a roastie, slice of turkey, pig in blanket and stuffing ball at the table.

13. Advent calendars. The Lego ones are £25. £25! Don't go there or you'll be expected to repeat it forever.

14. Gravy. Tell everyone you're doing your own if you have those sorts of relatives. But use the M&S turkey gravy – much easier.

15. Have a help-yourselves policy. And a Post-it-note-do-not-touch policy on food in the fridge that is for Christmas Day.

16. If you've got an office party, book the day off afterwards but don't tell your husband or kids so you can recover in peace.

17. Don't bother cajoling the kids to try Brussels sprouts – to the under-thirties they taste of farts.

18. You can never have enough bin bags, sausage rolls, mince pies and kitchen roll at Christmas.

19. Get a special ring tone for when your mother calls so you know not to pick up.

339

20. Tell the kids Father and Mother Christmas have a cut-off date of 1 December for requests.

21. A real tree is lovely but pine needles trapped in the sole of your tights are not. Fake trees are a must until the kids know how to use the Hoover.

22. Fairy-light anything that doesn't move. More is more. And it distracts from the dust.

23. There is no point doing any housework in the run-up to Christmas because visitors will only tread mud through the house anyway.

24. If you let the kids decorate the tree, be aware you will have to spend two hours once they've gone to bed redistributing 500 decorations from the bottom right-hand branches.

25. There is no point dieting in the run up to Christmas because the hunger will be the straw that breaks the camel's back and you'll end up crying in the veg aisle in Tesco when there are no parsnips.

26. Perspective. If you don't have bread sauce, it's not going to ruin Christmas. And anyone who claims it does can get a life. Or make their bloody own.

27. Anyone who accepts an invitation for Christmas lunch must take home leftovers. That's the deal.

28. Agree amongst friends not to buy the kids presents – spend the money you save on a

seven-star four-month holiday in Mauritius instead.

29. Delegate. Husband should be in charge of disposing of ripped-off wrapping paper, serving drinks, stopping arguments and putting drunken relatives to bed.

30. Should a guest wonder if the sprouts will be served with cranberries and bacon, kindly inform them that yes, they will be, if they are prepared to hand over £50 for the meal, plus tips.

31. Ban party poppers at the table, otherwise you'll have a soggy pink, green, blue and white garnish on your plate. They don't taste very nice either.

32. Save the Christmas cracker gifts for party bags of the future.

33. Make lists for everything you need to do. But don't cry when you lose them, because there was no way you were going to manage everything anyway.

34. Candles on the Christmas table look nice but you risk a trip to A&E when Uncle John sets his nasal hair alight as he reaches for the salt.

35. Set up an elaborate tripwire system so if the kids move before 6 a.m. on Christmas morning they lose a present every time the bell goes off.

36. Have some emergency Ikea meatballs in the freezer just in case the turkey smells weird.

Then tell everyone you've gone for a Swedish theme this year.

37. Practise patiently agreeing with extremist views so you don't punch your in-laws in the face over a discussion of 'Muslins'.

38. A real sanity saver is to tell everyone you're going to do some secret wrapping upstairs and no one is to disturb you. Then get into bed for an hour with the unofficially opened Christmas chocs and a sherry.

39. Compile a list of obscure things you have 'forgotten' to buy but can cope without then every time you need a breather, ask your other half to pop out with the kids to get it. As in, 'Oh, damn, I've forgotten the jellied fruits and they're Aunty Barbara's favourite!' To maximise the time to yourself, chuck a red herring by adding you think you've seen them for sale in the big Tesco half an hour away.

40. Invite yourself to someone else's for Christmas.

Okeydoke, I'm going to have a read of my book so will speak to you on the other side. Fingers crossed for us!

Your chairwoman,

Stella

www.mumslikeus.co.uk

Dear members,

WHAT A NIGHT! What a bloody night.

It's 4.17 a.m. I'm on a complete high and can't sleep, so I thought I'd fill you in so I can have a snooze on the train on my way back later.

I'm sitting in my bed in the most amazing hotel suite I've ever seen – I wish you could all have been here, you just wouldn't believe how posh it is.

There was pink champagne on ice in my room when I got here. The bed is the size of my bedroom at home, there are his and hers sinks in the marbled bathroom (I wash one hand in each just because I can), and there were handmade chocolates on my silk pillows when I came up. They've gone now, obviously, because I scoffed them the second I saw them. There's a flatscreen telly and a DVD player, even complimentary mineral water, the very latest stuff going, yet the décor is Victorian, elegant and plush.

I don't know where to begin with all of this – I'm so overwhelmed.

The start is a good place, I suppose! So once I'd checked in at 2ish, marvelling at the giant, twinkling Christmas tree in the lobby, I came up to my room to get ready. I had a quick glass of bubbly while enjoying the view of Hyde Park then jumped in the bath for a soak (in Ormonde Jayne products – nope, never heard of them either, but bagged a few for you to try).

I lay there thinking, if I was at home now, I'd be doing the tea, hiding in the kitchen, praying I wouldn't be asked to play tag. Instead, I was in the lap of luxury, preparing a speech in my head should we win an award. Every five seconds, I'd do a goldfish, noticing the gold-plated flush on the loo or gasping at the quilted toilet roll, and think, oh, wow, what on earth am I doing here?

Once I'd heaved myself out of the bath – the towels, oh God, the soft, soft towels – I got into a fluffy dressing gown, then flopped onto the bed and propped myself up on the pillows to shut my eyes for a few seconds.

Suddenly I came to. It was dark and I scrabbled around for my phone, which told me it was 5.45 p.m. I had fifteen minutes to get ready for the reception in the hotel's ballroom. SHIT.

It was then I opened my bag and, horror of horrors, I realised I'd picked up my mum's overnight case, which she'd left by the door when she'd arrived to look after the little one for the night because Matt was working late. I'd put my bag by the door so I didn't forget it, and in my haste to leave to catch the train, I'd grabbed the wrong one.

Why hadn't I realised on the way up? I was too bloody busy being smug and delirious about being on the quiet carriage. Oh God. It was too late to go shopping for a dress – my dress, my beautiful dress, the first thing I'd treated myself to in ages, it was a floor-length black halter-neck thing, with a swirl of sequins on the stomach area to highlight my tummy.

Fuck's sake, what the hell was I going to do?

There was nothing for it – I rifled through Mum's

case and started chucking out her stuff to see if she'd miraculously packed something I could wear. A pair of humungous white pants, a supportive and practical white bra, some knitting, her wash bag and then . . . from the depths of the bag I pulled out a mint-coloured nightie, one of those long mumsy M&S cotton ones with cap sleeves and a couple of buttons on the sensible neckline, the kind menopausal women wear so they can throw off the duvet and not freeze to death.

I was going to have to brazen it out.

Shoes? I couldn't wear my boots, that would look even more ridiculous, so I kept searching and prayed she'd packed some slippers. Bingo! There, nestling in the depths, were her dainty pink ballerina slippers, which I could just about squeeze my size fives into.

I glanced at my face in the beautifully ornate round mirror on the dressing table and thought, what the hell. I backcombed my hair a bit so it looked even more like I'd just woken up and licked a finger to smudge what was left of my mascara to give myself panda eyes.

I downed a glass of champagne and told myself to just go NOW. So I marched out of the room, into the lift and gave myself an 'it's what's inside that counts' pep talk.

The doors opened and there before me was the entrance to the ballroom. The smell of hundreds of different perfumes hit me. I was blinded by dazzling diamanté accessories glinting off candlelight, spectacular chandeliers and twenty-four-carat gilding. There were festive woman-sized floral displays at every corner, waiters were scurrying around carrying trays of champagne and canapés, and the noise was incredible, with the sound of women laughing and debating and gossiping and networking.

I stepped out of the lift, my heart going like the clappers. An immaculate head turned to look at me, then another, then another and another, until a sea of foundationed faces framed by blow-dried shining locks, luscious eyelashes and painted pouts were staring, open-mouthed, slack-jawed. There was total silence. For ages.

'Good evening, lardies!' I said, my booming voice covering up my inner squeak of OH SHIT. 'So . . .' I smiled, before necking a glass of champagne and wiping my mouth with the back of my hand, 'who's up for it then?'

The crowd parted as Hattie came forward in a swishing ivory strapless gown, her mane bouncing as her slender arm, decorated with an understated but glittering platinum cuff, reached out for my hand.

'Darling,' she said, air-kissing me on both sides, 'come and meet some people. You look divine. Where on earth did you get that dress? It's simply spectacular.' Then she whispered through gritted teeth, 'Stella, you are quite mad. Hold your chin up, smile and glide.'

I did as I was told and followed her through the

throng, the volume instantly returning to maximum to, no doubt, discuss my arrival.

I met a blur of women – the PM's wife in an orange shift dress courtesy of a British designer, various celebs and a number of well-wishers who told me they loved our club. As the alcohol settled my nerves, I began to relax and enjoy myself, forgetting I was in a nightie and slippers.

The master of ceremonies then announced it was time for dinner. Our tables were all named after iconic women – bit of a shame I was on the Margaret Thatcher table, furthest from the stage and closest to the toilets. But my fellow diners, who were a couple of charity bigwigs, an MP, an underwear magnate and a celebrity from one of those new 'structured' reality shows with tits up to her scousebrows, all bonded over the old bag straight away (except for the MP, who was a trendy Tory, one of the PM's babes who was frighteningly pro-Thatcher). Obviously Hattie was sitting between Kate Middleton and the PM's wife on Princess Diana, right up at the front. Then dinner was served – thank God, we needed some sustenance to soak up the booze.

Unfortunately, the organisers of the awards wanted to impress rather than feed us, so we had three courses off a specially created Diets Through The Ages menu, devised by one of those trendy TV chefs. For starters we had 1970s Vintage, which was a Ryvita with cottage cheese. For mains, we had Dukan Breath, which was crab sticks sprinkled with oat bran. And afters was Six Weeks To OMG, which was a cup of black coffee. Not a fucking bread roll in sight. Consequently, everyone became very, very drunk – you could tell, because the live jazz band playing in the background informed us that no, they didn't do requests, but even if they did, they'd never do a song from *Mamma Mia*.

Then the awards began.

Vorders was compering, and at the beginning we all had to stand up and sing 'God Save The Queen'. Some of the guests were propping themselves up on the table by this point, though. The next two hours were spent handing out Oscar-style statuettes to winners of categories such as Best Businesswoman, Best Politician, Best Dressed Woman and Best Charity.

By ten p.m., it became clear we weren't up for anything, so I wandered off to the loo, where I heard someone sniffling in one of the cubicles. I had a quick wee and was washing my hands – with posh soap and individual towels to dry off with, naturally – when the loo door opened and a beaming Hattie wove her way out and gave me a huge hug.

I pulled back to ask if she was OK and then saw some white powder on her nose. Oh God, I realised I hadn't heard sniffling – I'd heard snorting, and Hattie was clearly off her face on something.

'Jesus, Hattie, look at the state of you! What on earth have you been doing in there?' I asked her, hoping she'd come up with a brilliant explanation involving talc.

She sniggered. 'Stella, darling, you are such a square. It's only a bit of Charlie, just to liven things up, it's no biggie.'

'What do you mean, no biggie? You're on the same table as royalty and you're gurning – did you know that? Look in the mirror, you're chewing your bloody tongue off. If anyone gets wind of this you are dead. Oh fuck, you can't go back in there, look at you,' I said as Hattie slumped in front of the basin and started throwing up.

And then one of the organisers, a 50-something with a hairsprayed-solid brown Lego bob, burst in. 'There you both are,' she said, throwing her magnificently French-manicured hands in the air. 'Quick, get out here now, you've won!'

I asked her what the hell she meant while trying to dab vomit off Hattie's chest.

'You've both been awarded Woman of the Year! It's the first time the award has been shared, but you've both done so much to highlight women's issues this year we decided to give it to you both!' she explained, her statement jewellery-covered chest heaving with excitement.

Hattie turned her head to stare, with one eye screwed up as she tried to focus.

'Well, there's no way Hattie can go up in this state – it's . . . er . . . food poisoning. Yes, now I come to think of it, that cottage cheese tasted a bit off. She's going to have to be escorted to her room immediately

– call a member of staff and I'll be with you on stage in a sec,' I said, desperately trying to support Hattie, who had crumpled to the floor and was now sleep-puking onto the very expensive carpet.

The organiser dashed off, a bellboy came in and we hoisted Hattie onto one of those luggage carriers and I told him to take her to her room via the service lifts – if anyone saw her like this, she'd be ousted from her circle. Not that I give a shit about her shallow circle, but Hattie had shown she was far from perfect tonight and I had this urge to protect her.

Then I ran towards the ballroom, pushed open the grand double doors, and there before me, for the second time that night, were hundreds of pairs of eyes watching me in silence. As I began my walk towards the stage, negotiating a route through the tables, applause broke out. They were giving me a standing ovation! It was unbelievable! There were cheers and huge smiles and it felt like I was floating when I climbed the stairs to receive the award.

Vorders, who looked sensational with her curves squeezed into a red bodycon dress, wolf-whistled me as I took my place beside her and announced me as this year's co-winner, which was awarded 'for services to motherkind'.

'Sorry for keeping you all waiting,' I coughed into the mic. 'Hattie was suddenly taken ill and I'm up here to accept the award on behalf of both of us. Erm . . . well, I'm stunned to win. Hattie would be stunned, too, if she wasn't throwing her guts up. Despite our differences, we have an enormous mutual respect and without one another we would be less potent, which is why we won, I guess.'

Clutching at the two statues, I continued: 'Some of you may be wondering why I'm in a nightie and slippers. They actually belong to my mum – I had a bag malfunction – but in hindsight, I can think of nothing more fitting than wearing her stuff. Because I want to dedicate my half of the award to my wonderful mum and to all the wonderful mums like us out there who keep going, who grit their teeth and get on with it, who keep calm and carry on whatever kind of shit hits the fan.

'I know Hattie will be devastated not to be up here. She is a tireless Mother Superior who believes completely in her politics, as do I in mine. Never the twain shall meet sums us up, the odd couple, but tonight I salute her and every single mum out there for making us that little bit less invisible and bringing our plight to the attention of the world.'

With that, I held the awards aloft above my head and stepped away as a thousand gold-leaf balloons fell from the ceiling.

Then I got drunk with Vorders at the bar for a few hours and someone from *Elle* came over and told me straight-faced that I might just have launched a new nightie trend, but I sprayed my drink all over her because I was laughing so much.

Right, really must go to sleep, my head has started to bang. I need water – none of this fancy fizzy mineral stuff – good old tap water. Will see you next week if I ever get over what I expect to be the worst hangover of my life.

Your chairwoman,
Stella

Dads United

Email to: davidsmith70@hotmail.com
Subject: CCTV
Date: 8 December, 13:47

All right, Dave?

Brilliant news you're coming home for Christmas – Mum is beside herself, already ironing the posh pillow cases and sheets for your arrival. I'll pick you up from the airport – let me know all the details and I'll be there.

I'll also get us some tickets for the Boxing Day match – we can take Dad, like the old days before you buggered off to America. Did you manage to watch *Match of the Day* on the iPlayer last week? It's only December but title race is hotting up already.

On a train, heading back home after an overnighter for a meeting yesterday. Can't wait to see my boy, he's growing so fast now, even a night away and he's done something new. How's it going with that new bird? Is she one of those Californian beach babes? I would

353

expect nothing less. About time you thought about settling down. This is your big brother speaking – you're missing out, mate.

Stella's on a bit of a high – she won an award yesterday. She rang me at two this morning to tell me. She was totally shitted – she didn't remember ringing me when I spoke to her later. So proud of her. Mind you, doesn't come without a cost – there's this nutter who keeps sending hatemail to Stella. No death threats or anything, so it's not serious, but just general nasty comments. I've had CCTV installed in the outside porch over the front door so we can see who is doing it if it happens again. Stella doesn't know, didn't want to worry her.

It's really cool, though, the CCTV. I felt like I was in some spy thriller when I was fixing it. It's got a tiny 'eyeball' camera lens and it's weatherproof and is controlled remotely, so there are no wires. It's triggered by movement, so anyone coming to the door gets recorded. I get an email when it's recorded something, which is funny, because it's either Stella coming or going or the postman. This bloke knocked at the door the other day and picked his nose and ate it while he waited for Stella to open the door. He was one of those doorstep veg box sellers, and thank God she turned him away, or I'd have had to tell her not to eat any of his bogey turnips.

It's also got night vision, so you can see me lurching in, fiddling with my keys for ages when I'm home from the pub after a few. Unfortunately it's also revealed I'm thinning on top – you can see a circle of my scalp at the back of my head. Jesus, I'm going to end up like Dad. Quite pleased with my paunch, though – it's not as big as I thought it was.

Right, got to go, coming up to my stop. Let me know your flight number and all that. Mum says can you ring her – she wants to know if you like parsnips because you used to pull a face and make fake retching noises when they were on your plate aged twelve. It's all right for you – you're miles away, I have to listen to her banging on about the prodigal son's return every time I see her.

Cheers,

Matt

Week Forty-three

Stella Goes Stellar

Stella's Kitchen

Morning, lardies! How are we all?

I am bloody marvellous. Not only did I get to scoff four chocolates from the advent calendar this morning because matey was blissfully unaware we'd missed five windows (he had one and I opened the rest after I'd dropped him off at Mum's so I could hold the meeting) but today I received some really exciting news.

You may remember I was asked in the autumn for my comments on two policy matters: the regulation of airbrushing by the Department for Culture, Media and Sport, and research into the state of modern motherhood by a cross-party group of MPs.

I am delighted to tell you the Minister for the Department is working on introducing a Bill to make adverts, magazines, newspapers, trailers and films tell us if they have used airbrushing or body doubles. It means there will be a disclaimer at the bottom of the page or a line at the bottom of the screen to say if someone's appearance has been altered. It's a long way from what I would personally like to see – the banning of catty pieces of journalism which point out a celeb's mummy tummy as if it is a bad thing. But it is a start.

Real images of real women can only help mums like us who reflect on our own bumps and lumps and feel a sense of inadequacy when our bodies do not match up to the 'perfect' poses of superwomen in a fashion shoot minus stretchmarks or moles or spots or whatever is deemed by the industry to be unsavoury and ugly. When we can begin accepting ourselves as we are, without being hoodwinked into believing we are somehow failing because we have a saggy pair of tits, then we'll be happier.

In essence, we'll feel good enough. And if that isn't good enough, the PM has been back in touch to ask me to take on an advisory role in his government. This is top secret, so I need to remind you of the confidentiality agreement we all took when we became members.

Just like Gordon Brown wanted Fiona Phillips to get on board during his tenure – an offer she turned down – the current PM called me yesterday via his private line to see if I'd consider talking up the Minister for Motherhood idea to gauge public opinion. It was very odd; I thought his secretary would be there to put him through, but no, my landline rang and he just said, 'Stella? It's the PM. The one you told to eff off when I asked to come to one of your meetings.' I started blustering and he just cut in and told me not to worry, he was used to being unpopular and he had something he wanted to run by me.

He was very upfront, telling me he needed the female vote and our membership could play a vital role in the run-up to the next election, and that he wanted to find out whether mums would vote for him if he appointed a Minister for Motherhood. He's not my cup of tea, but I was impressed with his directness; at least he didn't smarm around. And if I'm honest, it doesn't matter if he is doing this for political gain; we have a chance to improve the lot of women now and in the future if the ministerial position has legs.

A million thoughts circled round my head. What if we could subsidise and cap nursery fees?

What if we could set a ceiling on the price of summer holidays so we weren't forced to take kids out of school during term?

What if we could ensure a woman has the same midwife throughout her pregnancy and labour?

What if we could establish a free, non-judgemental, practical helpline and home-visit system to go along with what a new mum wishes rather than what she feels she ought to do, by, say, offering breastfeeding AND bottlefeeding advice?

What if we could set up a 'work-from-home bank'

so we could matchmake mums who want to get back into their careers or just earn some money from their kitchen table during school hours with companies that can dish out jobs and projects online?

What if we could limit the amount spent on end-of-term presents for teachers so Mother Superiors can't try to influence them with the loan of their Tuscany holiday villa?

And what if we could ban party bags?

I said I'd be delighted to get involved – on two conditions. Should a Minister be appointed, all of the above ideas should be examined in the future and our club would produce a Good Enough Bible for new mums, which would be given out by midwives to every pregnant woman up and down the country. It'd tell them not to give a shit about putting on weight over those forty weeks, not to worry if you find yourself weeping over your newborn because you're so bloody tired and it all seems so relentless, and not to fret if you sometimes wish you could escape your kids for however long it takes for your stress levels to return to normal.

I warned him that if he went back on this I'd mobilise our members to switch sides and his political career would be over. He agreed. Just like that. Man, he must be desperate. Then I heard voices in the background – his wife and kids, I think – who told him 'supper was ready', so he quickly gave me his mobile number should I want a chat, their hurried off. If I'm happy about going ahead, I'm to call his secretary, who'll set up a face-to-face in the New Year.

How mad is that? I'm so happy. Who'd have thought almost a year ago that we could be faced with such an opportunity? It goes without saying: bombard me with your thoughts and ideas – not now natch because we've got loads on at this time of year, but in January, once all the festivities are out the way.

If that wasn't enough drama, I'll finish the meeting by telling you about a bit of a scare I had the day after the day after the awards ceremony. There I was, still hungover, a shade of grey and finishing off a pint of tea and loaf of toast when the door went. I peeked out of the spyhole because I looked like shit and didn't want to scare anyone, and there, right in my eyeline, was the most exquisite floral arrangement I'd ever seen. An enormous, waist-high, bulbous glass vase had been wheeled up the path, filled with orchids. My first instinct was, oh no, it's Tattoo again. I shouted through the door to the delivery woman to post the card through the letterbox, claiming I was allergic to flowers. She laughed and a silver envelope popped onto the mat. 'To my darling Stella,' it read. 'Thank you for saving me. Hope I didn't get up your nose too much. Learnt my lesson. Owe you one. Hattie xxx'

Bless her, I thought. Despite her flaws – and I'm hardly one to talk – she really is a class act. Then I told the woman to take the arrangement down the road to Mags's house because I couldn't go back on my bullshit and, as we all know, she has been having a hard time of it lately. I told the delivery lady to expect a man at the door because Mags is always at work. Which, incidentally, is why she isn't here again. She sends her love. She was thrilled with the flowers, but when she rang to say thanks I could hear a few gulps in her voice. I can't imagine what it's like being the breadwinner with a useless house husband who attains the bare minimum with the kids and then collapses on the sofa when she gets in, the house a mess and no tea on the table, saying he's exhausted and could she bring the washing in? Seriously, whoever is at home has got to pull their weight. Mags told me Si was concocting a plan to set up his own business, which means he escapes to the spare room most nights and weekends to 'work' on his laptop. What a twat.

Anyway, I'm sure Mags will make it to the party next week so we can give her loads of love and support then.

Right, meeting over – I've got masses of prep to do for our Christmas party. I haven't shaved my legs since October, so I need to make a start on hacking back the Amazonian hair forest which covers my body from toes to armpits. It'll take days.

See you at Karaoke Krazy next week. Put your glad rags on and don't forget to have a cheese sandwich and a pint of tea before you come out, or it'll get messy.

By the way, everyone's welcome for Boxing Day drinks at ours, three p.m.

Bye!

Dads United

www.dadsunited.co.uk

Please note our hijack of the Mums Like Us' Christmas party follows training next week at the karaoke bar in town.

The do starts at 7 p.m., so training is an hour earlier than usual at 6 p.m. in the leisure centre. I'll get us a minibus – we'll leave the leisure centre at 6.45 p.m.

Please bring a list of songs you'd like to sing – we do not want to let the women take over because we haven't prepared. Otherwise it'll be 'Like A Virgin', 'California Girls' or 'Girls Just Wanna Have Fun' all bloody night.

Much appreciated if you can print out your list in chronological order of release rather than applying the plebeian alphabetical method.

See you there.

Week Forty-four

Let's Get This Party Started

Stella's kitchen

'Hello?'

'Stel, it's me, Mags . . .'

'You all right? You sound like you've got a cold.'

'No, I'm not all right. I've been crying. I've done it. I've kicked him out.'

'Oh fuck, what's happened?'

'We've just had a chat, he's packed a bag and gone. I've had enough of him.'

'Let me come over. The members will understand if I don't go to the party, I've got a sitter anyway so I can be there in five minu—'

'No, don't. You've got to go to the party. I'm fine, honestly. Strangely fine. I feel like a weight's been lifted off my shoulders.'

'I can't leave you like this. Why don't you come round? Bring the kids, they can sleep in the spare room. There's a double bed and we've got a put-you-up thingy so you can all go in together.'

'No. Thanks, Stel, you're amazing, but no. I'm a grown up. I pay the bloody bills, the mortgage, everything, and this is my home, their home. Just not Simon's any more.'

'No. Quite right. If that's how you feel. Are the kids OK?'

'Fine. They're plonked in front of the telly with a Domino's pizza so they think it's bloody marvellous. Me and Si both sat them down and told them Daddy was just going away for a while to find a job and they accepted it. It was very calm – even Si failed to deliver any histrionics. It's as if he's been waiting to get his marching orders, like he knows the game's up. We had a talk just after I'd got in from work – it came out of nowhere. We were in the kitchen and I asked Si what the kids were having for tea and he said he hadn't had time to make anything because he'd been rushed off his feet with this business idea he's got, to set himself up as a consultant, and I just realised then and there that I didn't love him any more. So I told him. I told him he was a selfish bastard who contributed nothing to the household. I told him that if I was in his shoes I'd have got a job, doing anything, stacking shelves or whatever, anything to bring in some money. Instead, he's farting around on his laptop doing "research" and in the meantime his kids are hungry.'

'Are you sure about this, Mags? Have you thought it through? You know I'll support you whatever, but I just wanted to check. You do sound very rational, mind.'

'I am. I've had months of thinking things through. I've been through the finances and I can just about afford everything on my wage. There won't be treats or anything, but I couldn't give a shit. I might need you at some point to give the kids tea every once in a while if my childcare falls through or Mum can't help out . . .'

'Yes, of course, you don't have to ask.'

'Thanks. Simon will still help with the childcare, he agreed to that, but he won't be living with us. It'll be better for all of us. The kids won't respect their dad if he doesn't pull his weight. I don't mean a job, to be honest, I mean him not doing his share of the house stuff because he's chasing some dream. I know it's been hard for him, but there comes a point when he needs to turn words into actions, and despite his promises, they've amounted to nothing. I don't want the kids thinking it's OK to put up with shit like that. I'm exhausted and this stuff with Si wasn't helping; he's been selfish for years. When he had a job, he always made out he had so much on, and he wasn't even the breadwinner. It was me who had to get the kids if they started puking up, it should've been him, but I'd do it, taking home a pile of work to do in the moments when I wasn't holding one of them over the sick bowl.

I'd be up at two a.m. sorting out paperwork and he would be lying there snoring as though he didn't have a care in the world. Ridiculous as it sounds, the straw that broke the camel's back was the kids' tea being an afterthought for him. I've just had enough.'

'Where's Simon gone?'

'To his mother's.'

'Do you need anything?'

'No. I'm fine. I'm going to talk to the kids now, do the old "Daddy still loves you" routine. I never thought this would happen to us, really. We had the most perfect relationship, we were so happy. Then the kids came along and he just seemed to change. Once, just after I'd come out of hospital with the first, he asked when things were going to get back to normal. I told him, "This is normal, Simon", and this look came across his face, like it suddenly dawned on him there'd be no "us two" any more. I'll never forget it. I ignored it, put it to one side, but more and more, he'd do stuff for himself and not for us. He'd get his own breakfast and leave me to sort out the kids. We'd have family round and he'd spend the whole time on his phone, and it was like he'd put up a Do Not Disturb sign.'

'Well, you've done what's right for you. You deserve a pat on the back. You're amazing, Mags – so strong, and you deserve better. You deserve an equal, not another child.'

'I've got to go. Tell everyone I wish I could be there

but something's come up. In fact, tell them why, they'll find out soon enough. I don't want sympathy, though, tell them. I want offers of practical help instead! Like cakes and wine.'

'OK, Mags. I'll dedicate a song to you tonight. Probably Gloria Gaynor or something naff like that. Ring me anytime, come and stay whenever. Take care, lovely.'

'Bye, Stel, see you soon.'

'Bye, Mags.'

Dads United

In the supermarket

Fucking women. Stella knows I've got loads of work on before I finish for Christmas. Why the hell has she asked me to do this bloody shop? Well, I know why – she wants to make a point with this stupid Mother Christmas campaign thing. Sometimes she really pushes it, she really pushes me. She knows I'm shit at all this domestic stuff. I never know what she means when she asks me to get something like pasta – whatever I buy it's the wrong one – and so I have to make that call which she loves, asking what brand or box or packet I need to get.

This is basically her way of making me feel inadequate and of underlining how much she does. I know that already, I know she's amazing and all that – I know it and I tell her I appreciate it, then she gets one on her and decides I need reminding. So lucky old me got the essential non-perishables Christmas list, which is basically the booze.

369

Right, she said to bypass the fruit and veg and go straight to the cheese section. Cheese? I thought she said it was only non-perishable. Oh, well. Brie. Brie. Brie. Here it is . . . oh shit, there are different types here – did she mean Président, the own brand, English stuff or the healthy one? I'm not going to phone her, no way, not going to give her the satisfaction. I'll get the expensive one, she can't moan about that.

Stilton, that's easy, she doesn't like it so I'll get what I want. Cheddar, mild and mature, check.

Ham. Oh shit – does she mean slices or a joint? She hasn't said. Oh God. All of the ham then, not going to risk her wrath. I'll just say I fancied having ham on the table and we can have it Boxing Day too and beyond, it'll keep. She'll love the fact I've showed a bit of initiative, never thinks I'm up to it. I mean, my cooking is amazing, she always says so when I ask her, 'Does it taste amazing?' Bugger it, I'll show her. I'll do Christmas dinner as a surprise, yes, that's what I'll do.

Gravy. This is the back-up gravy. The one we'll have just in case the home-made stuff burns. Tesco Finest Poultry Gravy, two cartons of it, into the trolley. Will chuck another in just in case. You can never have too much gravy, nothing worse than scrimping on the gravy.

Loo roll, eighteen rolls. Guests go through it like nobody's business. Bog cleaner, not the plastic thing that sits on the lip of the seat – I remember the last time I got that and she went mental, saying it was revolting because the little one uses it as an aim when he goes for a wee – the cistern stuff instead. I'll get four packets because they're on offer.

Next up, the cheese biscuits, pickles – this is a minefield. There's some on offer but if I get those will they be the wrong ones? She's written something here, can't really . . . ah, sandwich pickle, finely chopped. The small stuff, yep, there it is.

Mince pies now. Two boxes of whatever's on offer, it says here, easy. Yule log – which no one ever eats anyway, but if I fail to bring one home Stel will go mad.

Right, choccies – big tin of Roses, After Eights and chocolate coins. Sorted.

OK, what's left to get? The booze – twelve bottles of white, six of red, whisky for Dad, gin for Mum, vodka for Dave, tonic, slimline for Mum. Bloody hell, this trolley is heaving now. Fruit juice, check; lemonade, check; Diet Coke, check. Forty-eight pack of French lagers. Some Sols and Becks. Dave loves Corona too, better get them as well.

Peanuts, crisps – oh God, what do I go for? The posh ones or Walkers? Both, I think. Did she also mean Pringles? I'm confused now – what if she meant Pringles and I don't get any? I know she loves them – give her a tube and she'll inhale them – but perhaps the omission on the list is because she doesn't want them in the house because otherwise she'll scoff the lot. I'll get them, they're on two-for-one, and then hide them in the car

371

so if she asks, 'Where the hell are the Pringles?' I can produce them. God, Matt, you are super skill, a brilliant and thoughtful husband. Not like Si – I knew he was a bit useless but didn't realise how crap he was. You never know what's going on behind four walls. Can't believe Mags and him have split up, just before Christmas, too, those poor kids.

OK, that's it. Where's the checkout with the smallest queue? Up the end, ooh, there's some chorizo, that'll do nicely, that's for me, and some Aero minty chocolate, I'll have that. And a Cornish pasty – that'll settle my stomach after last night's karaoke. Throat's a bit sore from all the singing, too, I'll get myself a Dr Pepper. I was definitely the best of the blokes, my rendition of 'Heaven Knows I'm Miserable Now' was amazeballs. Stella's 'Let's Talk About Sex' by Salt-n-Pepa was truly awful – she is such a legend.

Jesus, come on, you silly old cow, why don't you have your Clubcard ready? Some of us have stuff to do, you know. This is my bloody lunch hour, get a move on. Oh, hurry up. That checkout girl is cute, lovely eyes. Seriously, Matt, you're old enough to be her father, don't be a perv. Concentrate on something else. Your gut, for example. That chorizo isn't going to help that. Oh shut up, it's Christmas. And to be honest, you've done a cracking shop. You haven't had to ring home once to check what Stel meant. She'll be secretly annoyed at that.

Mother Christmas, my arse.

Week Forty-five

Boxing Day

Stella's kitchen

Quick, quick, in you come, it's freezing out there. Hi, everyone! Happy Boxing Day! How did your Christmases go?

We had a brilliant time. Matt's younger brother Dave is visiting from America. He's hilarious, much better looking than Matt. He isn't thinning on top like Matt, he's got a proper dark brown mop of One Direction hair – I think he's had implants. He's also really toned and healthy-looking. And of course he's loaded. He's in computers, too, but proper California Apple computers, so he's dead trendy, but obviously completely unreliable when it comes to women. He's seeing a model-stroke-actress and they've been Skyping, so we all had a look at her – all tits and plumped up lips, but if you were him, you so would. The little one is obsessed with him, keeps asking to see his teeth because he's had them done and they're

373

all perfect and white and make him look even more tanned than he is. He's also totally taken with his top-of-the-range iPad and techy knowledge, it's kept him quiet for hours.

My sister, Soph, got drunk and started flirting with him over the dinner table, it was really embarrassing. Luckily her husband was too pie-eyed to notice.

I'm afraid you won't get an eyeful of six-foot strapping stunner Dave because he's gone to a football match with Matt and their Dad, a bit of bonding. I've sent all the rellies out for a bracing walk, and Soph has got the little one, so we could have an, ahem, meeting. My mum rang from her cruise. She's having a brilliant time – it's twenty-five degrees Celsius where she is and she's made friends with the people on her table. It's so good to hear her happy.

I tell you what, all that rushing around and hernia-inducing stress beforehand totally makes up for the magic of Christmas morning, doesn't it? My son ran into our room – not too early, half seven, which is fine – and said breathlessly, 'He's been, he's been!' and dragged in his stocking and unwrapped everything in front of us, his little hands trembling as he pulled out chocolate coins and Ben 10 figures and Star Wars Lego and all that.

It was downhill from then on, really, with all the cooking and organising and making drinks and stuff. When Soph arrived, all hell broke loose because her kids had got rollerskates and they were bashing into everyone and everything round the house. Then Matt announced in this 'you-lucky-lucky-people' fanfare way that he was going to cook the dinner. He'd been hoarding the stuff in the garage and was all 'just you wait till you taste my cranberry-stuffed pigs in blankets'. He produced an enormous turkey from the back – he'd done the Nigella stick-it-in-a-bin-with-an-orange-up-its-arse – and he was expecting a round of applause, but what the fuck were we going to do with two turkeys and twice the trimmings? We had a bit of a set-to – he was quite a sight, acting all huffy and defensive in his mankini pinny and faux-fur-trimmed rubber gloves, which his mother had offended me with for a birthday present.

This, by the way, is why there are turkey sandwiches piled high on the table for our delight, along with cold roasties and parsnips and stuff.

Just to let you know, Mags isn't here because she's doing her annual Boxing Day swim – it was a family thing they used to do, Simon and the kids cheering her on as she and her swimming club mates ran into the sea in just their swimsuits. Today Simon has the kids and she's gone with her friends.

I'm a bit worried about her. She came over on Christmas Eve with the kids and was high as a kite. She seemed like she didn't have a care in the world – maybe it's the relief of Simon and her finally coming to a decision about their marriage. Even so, I was expecting her smile to slide off when the kids went off to play and we were alone, but every time I asked her if she was OK, really OK, she snapped at me, telling me to stop trying to bring her down.

She was fine, she said, never better, as she got up to leave. Then Dave walked in and her body did this amazing feline bridle, as if it was saying 'helllll-loooooo', and she shook her red curls at him and he asked for a kiss under the mistletoe. I can see why. She looked fab – she was wearing an emerald-green wrap-over printed dress, and her bosoms looked like they were trying to escape – she was completely Jessica Rabbit.

I tell you what, there was definitely chemistry between them. He put his arm round the small of her back and tilted her hips up and into him; she was all damsel-in-distress and complied and left her arms hanging by her side. Then their faces came together really slowly, both of them staring into each other's eyes, then at their lips and then back into their eyes again, and they started kissing, completely oblivious to the rest of us stood round waiting to wave her off. It was like we didn't exist. It lasted a very awkward ten seconds or so. I made her kids go and check they hadn't left anything behind, then Matt intervened and told them to stop eating each other because it wasn't past the watershed yet, and the two of them pulled apart, reluctantly, may I add, and we all stood there coughing and blushing and in shock – it was so bizarre.

After that, Christmas just seemed a bit dull. I'd be

stirring the gravy – the Tesco one, because Matt's burnt – or I'd be laying the table or clearing up discarded wrapping paper, and I'd have a flashback of Mags and Dave snogging by the door. It's years since Matt and me actually snogged like that without it leading to sex. You just get to a point when snogging for the sake of snogging doesn't happen any more. And if Matt tried to snog me like that apropos of nothing I'd probably smack him one and accuse him of molesting me.

The only other thing of note was a present I received from Tattoo. The little one found it on the doorstep in all the hustle and bustle of people coming and going on Christmas Day. My heart sank when I saw the label.

It was beautifully wrapped, as ever, with embossed velvety silver holly leaves on it and a red ribbon tied round the parcel, which was the size of a book. I didn't want to ruin anyone's day so I snaffled it and went to the loo to open it. Matt still doesn't know I got it; it'd upset him – he's so happy with Dave here. Inside there was a L'Oreal home hair-dye kit, the exact shade I use, with the words: 'Because you're not worth it. Why are you so ashamed of your roots?'

My first thought was, bloody cheek, I had my hair done two weeks ago, then I realised it was another coded dig at how I've apparently betrayed myself or you or the club. I chucked it in the bin and gave myself a good talking-to in the bathroom mirror – there staring at me was the same old face, red-cheeked from the kitchen steam, nicely highlighting my sweaty temples. How on earth could I be accused of turning my back on all of you? I live for this club – I live for the Good Enough movement. Someone clearly is seething inside at how things have turned out for me. Could it be jealousy? Hardly, I thought. I'm the same Stella I always was: harassed, exhausted and a couple of stone overweight.

Yes, this club has achieved many things in its debut year. And yes, I have rubbed shoulders with celebs and VIPs and politicians, which I'll admit has been fab. But how could we change things, how could we campaign about being good enough if we didn't get out there?

And then I had a light-bulb moment: whoever is behind Tattoo knows me because they have identified my Achilles heel – they know how much this club means to me. However, I'm not so up myself I can't recognise that this troll is pointing out what I'm already aware of – that I have been too focused on myself rather than the club recently.

That is all I'm prepared to say on the matter today, because it's Christmas and I love Christmas. I love the shit presents you get from aunties, I love the gaudy baubles and tinsel, I love the look on my son's face when yet another present is produced for him, I love the overeating and I love the rubbish Christmas specials on telly. So I won't let Tattoo win.

Help yourselves to turkey and drinks and chocolates

and sausage rolls and crisps – no Pringles, I'm afraid, because I've eaten them all. One thing Matt did do right was to stockpile some on his shopping expedition when I'd forgotten to put them on the list.

Let's raise a glass, everyone. Fat bottoms up, lardies!

Lots of apologies from members ahead of next week's meeting because we're anticipating being on our knees after New Year's Eve. It's one party too far after Christmas, isn't it?

We may as well postpone it – so see you next year!

Week Forty-six

Note to Self #2

Stella in bed with New Year flu

Oh God, I feel awful. Why is it I always get flu on New Year's Day? It's not as if I went out – I was in bed by nine p.m. after a Chinese with Matt. He went out and didn't get back in from the Feathers until four a.m. and he's fine, how unfair is that? I need a bell to ring to get him to bring me some Lemsip Max. I'm freezing, shaking and . . .

Don't cry, Stella, you big wimp. You're just ill, it'll pass. Look, this is just your body telling you to slow down. You've been buzzing around like a fat-arsed fly this last twelve months – this is why you're in bed. Mum's away, too – not that you're moaning, because she really needed the break, but it makes a difference if she's not around when you're ill.

No, I'm in bed because I'm weak and stupid and being punished for my club catastrophes – Tattoo is just saying what everyone thinks. I'm beginning to see I've been a bit 'me, me, me' when it comes to the movement.

Will you stop it! You're just feeling sorry for yourself because you spoke to the Man of Your Dreams on New Year's Eve.

Yes, you're right. But I had to. I had to ring him to find out if he was Tattoo, and to know what really happened that night. It just seemed the right time to ask – the last night of the year, a chance to start the new with a clean slate. Yes, I'd had a couple of glasses of wine on top of a Lemsip, thinking it was just a cold before the shakes and shivers started shortly after midnight. And so when I received a round robin text from him at half nine saying, 'Happy early New Year, everyone – my missus won the toss and got to go out and I'm in with our daughter so I won't be up late', I seized the day – well, what was left of it – and rang him.

So why are you feeling so down? Now you know.

Yes, I know. Thank God. We didn't have sex, we didn't even have a snog. He put me to bed and left – I'd just read the letter the wrong way. I should've known that he'd never have taken advantage of me in that state – he'd never done that in the past and he wouldn't start now. He said he'd had a long think after coming to my house for the interview and real-ised he'd been a twat, trying it on and chasing his youth, when he had so much to be grateful for. He'd come over that night because he wanted to help me sort myself out, he said. He'd been worried about me and was trying to sober me up, but I was having none of it. Apparently I started shouting, 'I love Matt, not you,' and waving my arms about, knocking a glass of wine over him, so he carried me upstairs. In the bedroom I started chucking off my clothes, which is how my knickers ended up dangling, and he put me to bed . . . so nothing happened. I can't tell you how relieved I was: I haven't been unfaithful, my marriage is intact and I've laid the Man Of My Dreams ghost to rest. I'm just feeling flat because he'd been on my list of suspects, but he isn't Tattoo. He laughed his head off when I asked if it was him. He said he isn't that clever. And the thing that convinced me was that he said he didn't even know I dyed my hair – typical bloke, they're so clueless. It's because they want to believe we're natural blondes or redheads or brunettes; it fits their very unsophisticated fantasies. Then he had a good laugh and said, come to think of it, my collars didn't match my cuffs. Knob.

That's good, though, isn't it, Stella, another suspect crossed off the list?

Yes, but it's leading me to think some really disturbing thoughts. That Tattoo is a friend. Someone who is watching me and enjoying all of this. It's starting to freak me out.

There you go again. Your mind spiralling off, convincing yourself you know something to be fact when you have no fucking idea. Why are you letting it get to you, Stella? It doesn't matter.

I know, I should forget it. But when I'm feeling down, it just preys on my mind. Oh, God. I suppose this is just one of the consequences of becoming a somebody rather than a nobody. I'm going to make it my New Year resolution to push on, be brave and keep fighting. There is no way I'm going to stop now. But before I start, I think I need a sleep, all this thinking has tired me out. Matt won't be home from his mum's with the little one until after teatime, so I need to make the most of the peace. I'll just have a couple of paracetamol and put on an extra three layers because I'm so cold. Cheers, Stella, you're the best.

No problem. Go to sleep, you silly moo.

Dads United

MATCH REPORT: Dads United v. California Dave's All Stars

Our New Year's Day fixture saw the Dads play a friendly against a team put together by the captain's brother, who assembled all of his mates to give Matt a good hiding.

The match was organised last-minute after California Dave, who was back from the West Coast for a fortnight, challenged Matt on Boxing Day night after a 12-hour session to a duel to finally sort out which brother was better at football.

Matt claimed he might have a wider girth than Dave but he possessed inner strength, while Dave laughed in his face. A quick ring-round of all his mates, and California Dave's All Stars were born.

Meeting at the rec because the leisure centre was booked out for a saddo war games convention, the difference between the two sides was instantly visible.

The Dads – whose average age is 43 – huffed and puffed during the warm-up, while the All Stars, sporting old school trainers and full heads of hair, sprinted up and down the park to demonstrate their youth.

The two captains shook hands, sealing a bet that the losing brother would forever defer to the winning brother's sporting prowess in future arguments, and it was game on.

Ten seconds in and California Dave scored a stunning goal from the halfway line after Matt lost possession when he tripped over his laces. The All Stars celebrated with a riotous bundle, which came to an end when Dave complained his new Superdry shorts were going to get all muddy.

The next 15 minutes saw the Dads chasing the ball as the younger side took the piss, passing it between their players while shouting, 'Come and get the ball, granddads.'

The All Stars went on to score twice more in the first half; one from a penalty awarded by the ref following a dodgy tackle by Dan on Dave, who took the pen and did 50 press-ups to show how fit he was compared with his brother. The second came from a corner, which was headed in by All Stars 6ft 5in beast Scotty Boy past Dads' goalie Stu into the top right corner.

In the break, the Dads got really angry as Matt accused them all of playing crap. The All Stars drank

Lucozade and discussed 4G as opposed to 3G.

The second half started much better for the Dads, with Matt dribbling the ball up the left wing, past two defenders, and scoring a beauty with his left foot. Matt ran up to his brother and screamed in his face, 'How d'ya like that, twat?'

Unfortunately, Dave didn't like that very much.

He shoved Matt backwards onto the floor and just as the ref was about to show him a red, Matt got up and did a running karate kick into his brother's back. Dave fell forwards, recovered his composure and lamped his brother one, and the pair began brawling in the dirt.

As both teams piled in to break up the siblings, Matt could be heard shouting, 'You wanker, I'm going to fucking ruin your shorts,' which infuriated Dave, who yelled back, 'You are such a bad loser, you always were, you just can't take it that I'm better than you. No wonder That Woman preferred me.'

The ref had no choice but to abandon the match, and after much persuasion, the brothers were forced to shake hands. They eventually made up in the Feathers and issued a joint apology to their teammates, who were still really fucked off the game had been called off.

Man of the Match: The ref for giving Matt and Dave an earful.

Donkeys of the Match: Matt and Dave for being complete twats.

Week Forty-seven

New Year Address

Stella's kitchen

Happy New Year, everyone! Our first meeting of January and we're all here – no apologies from anyone, which is fab. It shows how much we still need each other after nearly twelve months of this club.

For those of you on diets, there are WeightWatchers biscuits. As you know, the club only condones dieting if you don't lose any weight, so make sure you eat three times as many as you're allowed.

Over the last fortnight, I've had a really good think about things and so today's meeting should be about looking forward. Recognising how far we've come is important, but it can be distracting; we don't want to become complacent, for that could destroy everything we've worked so hard to achieve. We need to keep our ears and eyes open for opportunities to counter the new threats we face every time we turn on the telly, read the female sections

387

of newspapers, browse a magazine and step outside our front doors.

The competition is hotting up; there is no doubt about it. I speak of the seeping normalisation of all things Mother Superior – this is our biggest enemy. For example, I'm thinking of the coverage and positive spin given to famous mums who go back to work two weeks after having their fourth baby. If this is what they are happy to do, then brilliant, but for us mere mortals, this is unachievable unless we have a network of support funded by a multi-million-pound career.

Then there are the pieces devoted to mumpreneurs who have set up a business – funded by family money – from their kitchen or studio, selling bespoke cupcakes or delicious trinkets, while breastfeeding the baby and teaching Mandarin to the toddler. Or how about the half-naked 'I got my body back three days after giving birth' fashion shoots which are presented as a Good Thing? This is not normal. I doubt it's healthy, either. Nor are the articles on how to rustle up a kitchen supper in twenty minutes for friends who drop in. If you have young kids, this is impossible. It's a takeaway once they've gone to bed or a running buffet of carbs and carrot sticks. More likely, your friends will never just drop in because they know six p.m. is the start of the witching hour. Travelling to far-flung places with two preschoolers is not normal, either. Those features we read of the family of four jetting off with their backpacks and the kids wolfing down local delicacies are an insult, too.

If you can do any of these things, then fantastic – but it is not the norm, and it shouldn't be held up as an example to aspire to. Being Good Enough – providing a nutritious tea, being able to afford a week away self-catering in Majorca, losing a few pounds and feeling chuffed with that, returning to work with some marbles intact – this is what we should aspire to. That's why we are here.

The committee got together this week and came up with a list of things we should aim for this year.

The first is to live-stream our meetings over the internet so our members across the world can listen in. We now have more than 500 branches of the club operating in this country and abroad. We intend to do this when we can work out how to live-stream, which could take a while. I've had a look at webcams and stuff, but I'm not very technical, so Alex, being a teacher and clever and all that, says she will take charge of this. Anyone who can help should contact her.

Second, campaigns. Our Good Enough work is far from done and we need lots of suggestions on how we can reach more mums. So far, Lucy has come up with a Good Enough range of merchandise, from which all proceeds will go to a charity of our choosing. We're thinking Good Enough T-shirts, badges, key rings, etc. with a tie-in at the supermarkets, which would see a surge of interest. Also we have an idea to make a Good

Enough app so mums on the run can access our website and advice on their smart phones. Other ideas include a Good Enough sit-in outside Parliament – with no arrests this time, I hope; a weekly Good Enough slot on *This Morning*, which would see one of the committee discussing the parenting topics of the last seven days from our perspective. And how about this: a charity *It's A Knockout* against the Mothers Superior. That could be brilliant fun. I'm yet to approach Hattie and it's very likely we'd be rubbish, but everyone loves a loser, don't they?

Third, appointing a patron for the club. This would be an excellent way to get press coverage. The trouble is, it's very hard to think of any famous mums who admit motherhood has some really shitty bits and would be prepared to pose minus make-up in their pyjamas, with a cake, putting two fingers up to the gym. But if we can find one, if we can persuade a celeb to admit to being normal, then bingo.

Fourth, we could set up our own club playgroups so mums like us don't have to put on a smile if they're crying inside because the baby is teething, they're going back to work in a week, they're still leaking through their bras, weaning is going really badly and they feel so alone.

Fifth, Alex has proposed holding an annual election, which the committee overwhelmingly supports. We love representing you, the members. We always have and we always will. But in the interests of democracy, transparency and fresh blood and all that, we wish to introduce an annual poll of members whereby anyone can stand for the committee. We will hold a vote, in secret, of course, and whoever gets the most votes gets to lead the club. We won't lie – we'd be devastated to lose our positions, but the Tattoo hatemail thing has made me realise you can't please all the people all of the time. So if you feel you can do a better job than me, Lucy, Alex or Mags, please nominate yourself and we will draw up ballot papers. Probably on scrap paper, with a few mug stains, but that's OK, isn't it?

I don't know about you, but I'm still knackered from Christmas. All I want to do is crawl up into a ball and watch crap telly. The only good thing about this time of year is being able to wear loads of layers to hide how much weight we've put on. Matt suggested a holiday a while back, to get some winter sun, but no thank you. I don't want to get my body out for months yet. Perhaps it's the fall-out from coming off my happy pills – I've felt stable enough to stop them, and it's inevitable it'd have an impact.

Oh, I dunno. Sorry, I'm yawning, it's nothing personal. This is not a hint to get you to leave – you're all welcome to stay as long as you like – but I'm going upstairs for a lie-down. I love a daytime nap.

Until next week, my lovely lardies.

Dads United

Email to: davidsmith70@hotmail.com
Subject: Christmas
Date: Jan 9, 08:46

All right, Dave?

I'm not. The boys have stripped me of my captaincy after that fight we had. I tried to tell them it was just what brothers do, all that testosterone, and how we always used to scrap when we were kids, but they were having none of it. I'm well fucked off.

It's my bloody club, I started it. I am gutted. They're still letting me play but they won't let me be captain. Stu is captain now, which is bollocks because he hasn't got a bloody clue about all the organisation it takes to get the lads together.

I know we were arseholes, I know that, but I can't believe they're taking it so seriously. They said I brought the team into disrepute, and by the way, they think I haven't been ambitious enough and it's time for a change and we need to be focusing on getting

392

into a proper league rather than just having a knock-about.

I tell you, I'm not happy. I was thinking about resigning from the team but they're my mates and I love my football. Stel thinks it's funny, that grown men are arguing over a shit team, but she just doesn't get it. Maybe I should take up golf. What do you think? I dunno. Maybe I'll calm down, do my time and try my best, and see if they'll take me back as skipper in a few games' time, when they see how shit Stu is.

Anyway, gutted you had to go back to America, mate. We had a brilliant Christmas, didn't we? Thanks for the invite to visit you but there's no way we can afford the flights at the moment, we're skint. Maybe in a few years. Sure you'd rather get Mags over anyway! HA HA.

Back at work today after the break. Glad to be at my desk, actually. Stella's been high maintenance lately, really knackered and feeling the effects of the flu she had. It's great being round the family for a fortnight but it's easier being at work.

Hey, you know that hatemail stuff I told you about? Stella never told me but she had another malicious package arrive at Christmas. I found a note in the bin – I'd dropped my razor in it and pulled it out and it had a label hooked to it, the ribbon had got caught on the blade, so I read it and it was just some nasty comment about Stella.

Anyway, I went to check all the email notifications I'd had in the week leading up to Christmas – I was in such a bloody rush then that I'd ignored them all, thinking Stel would tell me if she'd had another parcel. There were masses of notifications of recordings, so I started ploughing through them, but it was impossible to know who was behind it. We had so many visitors coming and going, and loads of them were carrying presents and stuff, so it revealed nothing. I was really disappointed but at least I know it's working. I reckon whoever is doing it will slip up eventually.

Right, got a meeting to prepare for at 11 a.m., so speak soon.

Can you give Mum a ring? She said she needs to talk to you about the Kindle you bought her for Christmas. I offered to help, but she seemed to think you'd invented the Kindle and only you could sort it out. That'll be an interesting conversation for you, explaining how to work it over the phone.

Serves you right for showing up our gardening vouchers and for being so flash.

Cheers,

Matt

Week Forty-eight

Bun in the Oven

Stella's kitchen

Come in, everyone, here we are again.

Yes, I know I look dreadful. I've been puking non-stop this morning. No, it isn't a bug or I'd have called off the meeting. It's because . . . wait for it . . . I'm preggers!

We found out last night. It explains why I was feeling so tired and grumpy and hormonal. I was a couple of days late – usually I'm like clockwork – so I did a test and clear as anything, the line popped up within a few seconds. Matt almost had a heart attack. I must admit I was a bit shocked, too – we'd assumed it'd take ages to get up the duff.

I mean, we'd only just agreed to start trying for another. Matt told me he was a bit disappointed because he'd hoped he'd get some more sex, which is basically why men agree to have more kids. On the other hand, I'm delighted because we don't have to keep doing it. With the first, it's so different – the men are proud as punch if they score on the initial attempt because it's like a show of their fertility.

So while he's grieving for his dick, I'm now already wondering how the hell I'm going to do the school run with a puking, pooing baby, because they always do that two seconds before you leave the house. And I'll never remember all the stuff about weaning and I'll end up giving the baby chicken nuggets at four months.

I must've conceived over Christmas. God knows how that sperm found my egg. Matt spent most of December pissed! I can imagine the plucky little tadpole weaving its way drunkenly up my tubes, in the hope it'd find a can of Coke and a pasty.

I didn't have morning sickness too badly last time but now, oh my God, I spend most of the day with my head down the bowl. I can't even eat cakes – they make me feel worse, this is the cruellest thing of all. Just when I need fortifying with all these toenails and heart valves that I'm making, I can't keep anything down.

It means we'll be having a September baby, so I'll be sweating like a pig in the summer, which is always a nice look. Mind you, it's early days and you never know if we'll make it to the scan, but fingers crossed. We haven't told anyone yet, apart from you lot, obviously, but I know you won't say anything.

It feels like a new chapter for us as a family. After

all the crap we've had this last year, it's so nice to have some good news. And that's why I wanted to share it with you. And of course, it opens up a whole new avenue for us as a club – I was thinking last night we could diversify into books.

I can see it now, *The Good Enough Guide to Pregnancy*, which will underline how pointless it is to worry about 'losing your figure' because it's going to happen. And stop putting yourself under pressure to have a good birth, because your body, not you, is in control. Take the drugs, don't take the drugs – do what you can manage. This book will be the antithesis of that ridiculous industry telling pregnant women they need to build mood boards for their baby's nursery, compile baby preparedness kits of swaddles and kooky Babygros, hire a doula, attend antenatal bellydance classes and use organic nail varnish. As if we can afford any of that or have time to do it.

And *The Good Enough Guide to The First Year*, which'll be sleep as much as you can for the first six weeks; breastfeed if you can but don't beat yourself if you can't or don't want to; don't bother waving those educational polka-dotted fabric books in front of baby's face when it's three days old because baby still doesn't realise it has arms, let alone a brain; and accept as much help as you can because this is not a competition.

I think the best format will be for all of us to chip in with bits of advice so the books don't feel prescriptive. There was a study that said parenting books make mums feel confused and inadequate because they lay out unattainable standards and opinions that sound like orders. Well, tell you what, we can change all that – we can make our books the complete opposite. We can present our experiences and the options available to them and then tell the reader DO WHAT YOU FEEL IS RIGHT FOR YOUR BABY AND BOLLOCKS TO THE EXPERTS. If you like, I'll get in touch with some publishers straight away and see if there's any interest.

OK, some quick club business. The sales of our naked calendars have raised in excess of one million pounds for charity, and we can stick a load into our antenatal courses, which Lucy is set to launch in the spring. Yay! The PM has scheduled me in for a meeting at the end of February, which I'll be releasing a statement to the press about later today. Double yay! The live-streaming of meetings is set to start in four weeks. Triple yay!

I'm afraid that's it for this week because I'm about to vom. Really sorry, my boobs are killing me, too, and I am so constipated it's untrue. Funny how you never hear Mother Superiors moaning about their bowels.

See you all in a fortnight – got an appointment with my accountant on the day we usually meet because I have to do my tax return.

Really hate this time of year. Can't wait for the spring.

Dads United

www.dadsunited.co.uk

Dear lards,

I have devastating news. It has come to my attention – i.e. the landlord told me – that our beloved local, the Feathers, is under threat. Due to rising costs and more people getting lashed at home, he is considering taking up an offer from a chain pub which wants to turn it into a gastro thing.

Yes, I know – I had to have three pints in an hour to deal with the shock. No more sticky floors, no more Sky, no more real ales, no more pork scratchings. Our way of life is under threat and I suggest we get together – at the pub, obviously – to work out how we can campaign to save our second home.

I'm thinking fundraisers, sponsored events, a petition to the brewery – whatever it takes to ensure our local remains ours. The Feathers is the heart of our community; it is our bolthole and our escape from the stresses and strains of life and our families. And it's

where I've dreamt we'll take our children for their
first illegal drink when they're 15.

Anyway, the upshot of this is that I have decided
to quit the team to focus on the Feathers. It was not
an easy decision to make – but the pub needs me.
Also, Stella is expecting again – she's in bed at 6 p.m.
every night, so training's out of the question.

I hope we can remain drinking partners.

Matt

Week Forty-nine

The *Guardian*: Secret Plot to Oust Stella

Stella Smith is the target of a conspiracy to force her to quit Mums Like Us, it has emerged. The club chairwoman, who has been at the helm of the organisation she founded almost a year ago, is facing a challenge to her leadership over concerns about her integrity.

Sources within the club say some members are disgruntled at her style of administration, which they say freely courts the opposition, the chairwoman of Mothers Superior Hattie Hooper. Critics not only accuse her of betraying the roots of the club but also believe Mrs Smith is a self-serving, self-publicising totalitarian commander who places herself at the centre of club business.

Her supporters say her achievements speak for themselves: she has challenged the 'having it all' mantra by placing the club's Good Enough philosophy at the heart of the debate about motherhood.

During her 11-month tenure, the married mother-of-one has been arrested following a scuffle with Mrs Hooper at a club-organised march in London, co-won Woman of the Year with Mrs Hooper, posed naked for a fundraising calendar, stripped off to her underwear at the White House, successfully lobbied the Government to regulate the use of airbrushing in the media and is in talks with the Prime Minister to become a special adviser on motherhood. Subsequently, she is a hugely influential figure, followed by millions on Twitter around the world, many of whom have set up their own branches of her club.

But some members believe the time is right to replace Mrs Smith. One told the *Guardian*: 'Stella has lost her way. She has been seduced by the fame, seduced by the Prime Minister and seduced by Hattie Hooper. Increasingly the club has become all about her rather than our Good Enough ethos. There will be a challenge to her leadership very soon and we are working hard to rally support for a new chairwoman, the identity of whom is still under wraps because we need to move swiftly when the time comes. We would like to go back to basics and focus on the Good Enough movement as a cause rather than as a cause célèbre.'

Yesterday Mrs Smith said club members were perfectly entitled to their opinion and she would love to comment further on the imminent power struggle, but she was too knackered, and anyway, she was making tea and the chips were about to burn. 'I will raise the issue with members at our next meeting once we have devoured a tray of rocky roads,' she added.

Week Fifty

The Sex Tape
Stella's kitchen

Blimey, if I'd known so many of you were coming along, I'd have got in extra cakes. I thought I'd be standing here like a lemon today after all those stories about a plot to chuck me out. My default button is to assume the worst.

Obviously, this is a bit awkward, particularly if the story is to be believed that there are a number of members amongst us who are unhappy with the way I've been leading the club. I thought they would make themselves known to me, or I'd be able to work out who they are by their absence today. But I haven't heard a peep from any dissenters and you're all here, so I can only assume they're still undercover.

This is truly bizarre – I thought long and hard about whether to cancel today's meeting or to quit outright. But I've decided to keep calm and carry on as usual. It's a lazy defiance, I suppose. I can't be bothered to get upset about it, I refuse to get worked up when I'm only seven weeks pregnant. I'm proud of this club, and until my enemies make themselves known, I'm going to continue as I am.

I do have some news for you, which may or may not be related to this plot. It concerns Tattoo. Unbeknown to me, Matt was a complete genius and installed CCTV at our front door and only told me the other day after we received another package. This time, it was addressed to Matt, a normal looking jiffy bag which contained a DVD. There was nothing written on it so he mentioned it to me over lunch, when he'd got round to opening it, and asked if I was expecting anything.

Nope. Then he joked it was 'probably a sex tape' and we had a laugh about what it'd show – me and him eating biscuits in front of the telly deciding not to do it because we had loads to catch up on on Sky Plus. It hadn't clicked by this point that it was from Tattoo; Matt gets computery stuff delivered all the time. He stuck it in his laptop and after a few seconds, he groaned.

I leapt off my seat and stood behind him – there, on the screen, was one word: TATTOO. Nothing else. Then it flickered to life. My heart sank. What on earth was going to happen now? The picture was quite dark, something half-covered the lens and there was a bit of writing in focus, large letters, and it took us ages to work out it was the inside of a handbag. There were voices, laughter and muffled coughs and things, and then I froze.

I heard my own voice. 'That's me talking,' I said.

Matt switched the volume up to max and we craned our heads towards the sound, trying to catch everything. Occasionally the picture would shake as though the camera, or whatever it was, was being shifted.

'It's a phone,' Matt said. 'It's videoing something. Whoever did this burnt it onto a DVD.'

'Shhh,' I shushed. 'Let me hear what's going on.'

There was a bit of mumbling then my voice, saying, 'Matt and I are separated at the moment . . . the other night . . . I did something so stupid and so selfish . . .'

Oh. My. God. It was a recording of a meeting, the meeting when I told everyone I'd got really pissed and spent the night with the Man Of My Dreams.

I could feel the blood draining from my face. Matt was going to find out. Well, he was going to hear what I'd said at the meeting, not what had actually happened – that nothing had happened. I panicked but I couldn't move and the words kept coming from the computer. Matt saw me raise my hands to my face and cover my mouth and he looked confused, he had no idea what was coming. I wondered if I should just stop the DVD, but it was too late – he would know I was trying to hide something – so I crumpled into a heap on the chair and sat down and cradled my head in my palms. Thank God the little one was having lunch at a friend's house before going to nursery – if he'd been here, if he'd wandered in and heard this . . .

The words kept coming. 'I hit the bottle big time . . . I have no recollection of what happened next. All I know is I woke up naked in bed with a note from the Man Of My Dreams on my pillow . . .'

Matt turned white and gulped. His brow creased and he stared at me, looking as if he was about to cry.

The DVD kept going.

'There were a load of texts I'd sent the Man Of My Dreams – awful, cringey, desperate, self-absorbed and needy texts.'

I knew what was coming and braced myself. The letter and those damning words.

'. . . don't get your knickers in a twist. That's if you can find your knickers.'

Then all the stuff about me not knowing if we'd had sex and how awful I felt. I have never felt so ashamed in all my life. The DVD ended and Matt stood up, his back to me, ruffling his hair with one hand and rubbing his eyes with the other.

I began whispering, 'I'm so sorry, Matt, I'm so sorry.' He didn't respond. My voice got louder. 'Nothing went on. It was all a misunderstanding, I promise you.' He whirled round, his eyes accusing me of treachery. I started crying and begged him to listen to me. He exhaled loudly, his shoulders drooped and he sobbed. Nothing is worse than a man sobbing; it's soul-destroying.

I started talking. I explained everything and tried to put it into context – how it'd been a mistake, how

I hadn't so much as touched him. I knew it didn't excuse me, because there'd been some kind of intention there from me, having pursued him that night. I told him to cast his mind back to the time when we were apart – I had assumed he'd been having an affair and I'd been devastated and I was drinking heavily and I was desperate.

I was going through a crisis, I told him. The relentlessness of motherhood and marriage had sucked me under – I found myself in mourning for the time in my life when I had no responsibility, when the only person I had to please was myself, and sex – well, sex was about instant desire rather than a slow-burning sense of love and, I admit, duty. I'd felt taken for granted – doing all of this club stuff, running the house, being expected to do everything.

I hadn't told him about that night of madness when we'd got back together because I didn't want to confess just so I'd be absolved of my guilt – I wanted to deal with it alone and I had. Until now. Then I carried on – in for a penny, in for a pound – and told him about the time the Man Of My Dreams came to interview me and, well, almost came in his pants. I could see the hurt in his face when I said I'd felt something in my groin which I hadn't felt for years – but I begged him to at least try to understand.

Matt thumped the kitchen worktop and a glass toppled and fell, smashing across the floor. I was grateful for the diversion and began sweeping it up.

He joined me on his knees and grabbed my shoulders and took a huge breath.

'I believe you, Stel. Yes, I'm angry and hurt – I'm fucking furious, actually. I'm going to kill that twat. It was that ex of yours, wasn't it? Arsehole. But I'm not going to risk this baby, or us, or tear up this family. We've been through that before and it was shit. You're everything to me,' he said.

'What? Do you forgive me?' I asked, my make-up running down my cheeks, unable to believe Matt was being so rational and understanding.

'Don't expect me to be all happy and jolly straight away, I'm not a fucking emotional robot. It could take a while, but yes, I'll forgive you.'

Then it all came tumbling out – how he'd felt ground down by the whole marriage and fatherhood thing, too. When he left after I'd come back from Ibiza, he said he'd felt under so much pressure to be here for his family while trying to work his arse off at a critical moment in his career. He said he was trying to be in two places at the same time – dealing with deadlines and calls from his boss and trying to work his way up just at the time when I was nagging him to please come home in time for the little one's bedtime. I can't blame him at all – he felt like he was being pulled in two directions at once.

We got up and hugged the life out of each other, both of us breathing hard and me reflecting on my fortune in marrying this wonderful man.

Suddenly, he pulled me off him and gabbled at speed about the CCTV and how it would reveal who'd posted the jiffy bag, and we ran like kids back to the table and Matt started searching through his emails and found the alert. We waited while the CCTV footage loaded, but of course, it turned out just to be the postman.

And then we decided to go to the police. We'd had enough. So we went through all the channels, filled in the forms, made a statement and just went through the whole thing. It felt like we'd drawn a line under it. Christ, we've had enough to contend with and now with this baby coming . . . yeah, well, that's that then.

Right. So . . . next week's meeting is same time, same place. Well, what I mean by that is, I'll be here regardless. Whether the rebels emerge by then or not. Perhaps they'll keep their powder dry for another week so they can stand against me in the election in a fortnight? I just don't know. Whatever happens, this is a democracy and fighting over the cakes is not the way we do things.

So as I said, I'll be here next week. I sincerely hope you are too.

Dads United

Email to: mlumembers@yahoogroups.co.uk
Subject: Stella
Date: 1 February, 19:46

Dear all,

It's Matt here, Stella's husband. She's fast asleep, going through that exhaustion bit of the first 12 weeks, bless her. Hideous to be around, unfortunately – she's really grumpy and pale and tired all the time, so it's always a relief when she goes to bed.

I hacked into her emails and found your group address, apologies for being underhand but I've got something to say to you all. She will definitely kill me when she finds out but I don't care. Yes, I have had a bottle of wine to myself already – I'm drinking for two now.

We've talked at length about the supposed plot to chuck her out of the club. Well, she's talked at me and I've nodded, as you do with Stella. And while she's pretending to be fine about it, I know she is very hurt.

411

This club means everything to her. She knows she's cocked up a million times, but for God's sake, she's only human.

You have no idea how hard she works behind the scenes on the club. Every spare minute she gets, she's bashing away on her computer, sending emails to important people, trying to arrange sponsorship, contacting international branches, writing pieces for the website and answering queries which come in from all over. She often wakes in the night with an idea or she'll remember she has to message someone over the other side of the world about something. She pours her heart and soul into it.

I can't deny there was a stretch when I just wanted her to pack it in. God knows it'd be easier for us if she did. But over the last year, she's found something other than her family and her job to get excited about. Something outside of her responsibilities as a mum and wife. Something that gets her leaping out of bed, that inspires her to dig deep.

And that something is you lot.

She's the right person for the job. And I can't believe there are people out there who want to depose her because she's shown herself to be fallible. The worst of it, though, is that this is being done behind her back. Talk about cowardly. Which is why I'm supporting Team Stella. I will leave her to the specifics about why you should vote for her.

If you'd like to join me, then feel free to contact me for her election campaign posters and badges and stickers to Save Our Stella.

Cheers,

Matt

Week Fifty-one

Tattoo Uncovered
Stella's kitchen

You're all here! And, my God, check out your stickers!

That's so touching. I started to go mad at Matt over his email but I was so knackered I gave up the rollicking halfway and had a cup of tea and a biscuit instead. Then I had a snooze and decided his intention was good and I'm really lucky to have him. I suspect he's trying to earn a few points because he's got a load of meetings to go to about saving his local but still, it was nice he bothered.

Anyway, how are you all?

I'm OK, still feeling sick – everyone keeps giving me irritating advice, like eating ginger biscuits every twenty minutes, or sipping flat Diet Coke, or tying a sweaty sock round my neck. The only thing that works is to keep eating all the time, even when I'm not hungry. It's like a hangover but without the laugh the night before.

Got some lovely goss for you – my mum's met a gentleman friend, as she puts it. How sweet is that! Apparently they were both on the same table every night on the cruise. He's a widower and lives twenty miles away and his kids are grown up, and she says he's charming, funny and very well-mannered. Not remotely upset by my dad 'being replaced' because he never will be, and Mum looks happier than she has done in years. We're due to meet him at hers in a couple of weeks and I'm dead nervous – don't want to frighten him off with loads of questions.

So. I have news. You know I said I'd gone to the police about Tattoo? Well, I lied. Before you say 'oh, not another porkie', I have a very good reason.

Last night, I held a top secret CrAP meeting with the committee regarding Tattoo. You will note none of them are here. This is because of what happened in this very room a little over twelve hours ago. I summoned them here under the pretext of club business regarding the election.

Lucy was the first to get here – Dan was home early from work and so she made her excuses and left bath and bedtime to him. Then Mags turned up, having dropped the girls at her mum's, huffing and puffing about dying for a wee and a drink. Last was Alex, who'd spent the witching hour doing that military fitness thing in the park, so she was in fatigues and covered in mud. Each brought a bottle – I was left to sniff their wine glasses and nurse a cup of tea all night.

It was all small talk at first, as we sat round the kitchen table – what we'd been up to at the weekend, and how knackered we were and it was only the beginning of the week. Then I said it was time to crack on with the CrAP.

'You'll be wondering what's so urgent and confidential that I asked you to come round,' I began.

Alex snorted and said, 'It's a good excuse to get out of the house?'

'Well, yes, apart from that,' I said. 'You're all here because of the troll who's been making my life a misery.'

Lucy raised her eyebrows. 'Oooh, what's happening, Stella? Have the police got him?' she asked.

'No,' I told them. 'The police haven't got him. And it's a her, by the way. And she's sat in this very room.'

The perpetrator kept very still. The other two, who didn't notice because all eyes were on me, dropped their jaws to the floor.

'This person has been responsible for a great deal of upset,' I went on. 'This person has, for some reason, waged a campaign against me and Matt and the little one. And she thought she'd get away with it. But she made a fatal error with her last vicious little parcel, the recording of me telling the meeting that I'd been unfaithful.

'I've brought you all together here tonight to ask her why she did it. Now that I know who it is, I'm not angry or scared, I'm just confused. Why would a friend turn on another friend like she did? Did it start

416

off as a joke, a little fun at my expense? Was it a message to say "keep in line, you're going off-message"? Was it a reaction to a crazy life crisis? Or was it a genuine bit of trolling, someone who hates me so much she wanted to undermine me and turn me into a nervous wreck so that she could step in from the wings and take over the club?

'Lucy. I knew it wasn't you. You're far too honest for your own good – knowing you the way I do, any problems you would've brought up face to face and we'd have sorted them out. Besides, your tattoo – that beautiful little rose on your left hand, a reminder of the summer you met Dan and fell in love – is highly visible, far too obvious to be the troll. And you wouldn't hurt a fly.

'So that left Mags and Alex. Hmmm. Now which one of you was it? Wait . . . no confessions are needed, I'll get there in a minute. Was it you, Mags? Fiery, full-on, going through a marital breakdown, stressed out, the owner of not just one but two tattoos – a Celtic band on her ankle and a winking sailor girl on her lower back. Or what about Alex? On the outside, no nonsense, practical and as perfect as a wife and mum can get without being all smug about it. But no tattoo.

At least, not on her body. But in her handbag, yes. On the label, you'll see the letters T-A-T-T-O-O, some random make from somewhere. Those letters were caught by the iPhone recording from inside your bag. I knew who it was the second I saw that bit of the recording – I hoped it wasn't, my oldest mummy mate, the one who'd saved me on many occasions with a hug and a spare nappy. I told the meeting last week that I'd gone to the police – it was a cover. I was actually hoping for a confession. But it didn't come.

'Now,' I paused, stopping just a second to take in the silence, 'would you like to explain why you did it?'

All three faces turned to Alex. Lucy and Mags's eyes were wide with disbelief. I sat and waited for Alex to speak.

Her head bent, she bit her bottom lip and after a few seconds, she started nodding and raised her chin at an angle, her head tilted, still nodding. She said, 'It was me. Look, Stella's right, here's the handbag with the label on it. I don't know what to say. It wasn't anything personal. Well, it was, I suppose. What I mean is . . . I think this club is at a turning point. I think my friendship with Stella is over. It was meant to be a joke. At first. A reminder of who you were when you started this club, and how your head got turned by all the interviews and the newspaper articles and the makeovers and the Botox and the teeth and the march and Hattie and the Prime Minister. I didn't feel I could bring it up because you were so immersed in it and I was worried we'd fall out.

'It was supposed to be a gentle mockery,' she said, showing no sign of an apology or being ashamed of what she had done. 'But the more I did it, the more angry I became, at how you had departed from the foundations of it all. It's always been about you. Not the club. You. In twelve months of meetings, not once have you tackled the issue of guilt – the one thing that stands in the way of achieving this Good Enough status that we're all seeking. 'If we campaigned against maternal guilt then just imagine how easy it would be to be Good Enough. But I know why Stella would never do that.'

And then she did this impression of me, waving her hands in the air and saying in a stupid voice, 'Guilt's shit, isn't it? I feel guilty every time I fob off my son with the telly because I'm making the tea. But having said that, I believe guilt is an instinct, part of what makes a mum a mum, makes us protective and all that stuff, blah blah blah. Let's have a cake.'

I was quite annoyed at that – she was right; that's what I would say about guilt. But I don't wave my hands like that, do I? Oh. I do. Apparently.

Then Alex, all steely-eyed, continued. 'I suppose what it comes down to is this: I'm more hardline than you. I believe we should be pushing on a daily basis for better flexible working conditions to free up mums from that work-life nightmare. We need to teach dads they are half responsible for their kids, not just when mum's getting her hair done; and to pay mums to stay at home, should they choose to. There's even an argument for letting dads in – it's rather sexist of us to be women-only.

'Stella, we need a serious debate, not more of your

haphazard meanderings. I'm all about militarising this. I suppose the seeds were sown when I found myself befriended by those Mother Superiors at that baby-signing group. I just think this club, you, Stella, you're too . . . middle-of-the-road. It's not just me who thinks it – several others have come to me, expressing concern over the club's direction. So I started thinking, mulling over a few things, realising there was room for a third way – there was a need for it.

'It was me who told the *Guardian* about the coup to overthrow you. And that's why I'm standing against you next week under an electioneering platform of Not Guilty! – in fact, I've got a load of badges and banners waiting to be picked up with that very slogan on it. If I lose, which I don't believe will happen, I'll form a splinter group and I will be aggressively recruiting those mums who are dissatisfied by your shambolic and disorganised style.

'I'm sorry it turned out like this. I tried to keep the faith. We had a very special bond, Stella, but the more ridiculous your antics became, the more I started to dislike you and what the club stood for. No wonder Hattie loves you, you're no competition at all.'

I asked Alex why she hadn't talked to me. She said she'd tried to, at first. I do remember she texted me a few months ago, after the march, for a chat, one to one, and I'd meant to reply but I'd been in too much of a whirlwind. I completely hold my hand up to that. But even so . . .

Alex just shrugged and told me our friendship had run its course and she'd buddied up with me at that playgroup where we'd met because she thought I was like her, but then as the years passed, she realised we weren't the same people. Fair enough, we've all made friends with mums that haven't worked out.

Mags had had enough. 'Now hang on a minute . . .' she started. 'Fair enough, you don't like the club, but to behave like that with Stella – that's so mean! Do you know what? I always wondered about you; a bit too bloody earnest for me. Can't you see what Stella's achieved?'

Lucy was really flustered by this point. So she started offering snacks from the cupboard. Crisps and peanuts. Asking if anyone wanted a refill. Bless her.

By this stage, Mags was squaring up to Alex, demanding an apology because she was yet to hear one.

I just felt washed out by it all, stunned by her words. I mean, I knew I couldn't possibly be everyone's cup of tea, but I had no idea I could be so hated. Especially by someone I thought was a best friend.

Then Matt bounded in, telling us to keep it down or we'd wake the little one, but Mags blurted out, 'It's her, Alex is Tattoo.'

He yelped then tried to cover up his girly tone with a cough and a deeper yelp. He gave up and simply pointed at the door.

Alex delivered a quite spectacular final flourish.

'You, Matt,' she said, as she clutched her bag and her coat, 'you're pathetic. You're hardly whiter-than-white, are you? I bet you haven't told Stella about THAT!'

She left, slamming the door, then when she realised she'd forgotten her camouflage training water bottle and matching knuckledusters she had to come back in, and she was all polite as I handed them over. 'Thanks, Stel, see you later,' she said, forgetting we'd just had this massive fall-out. I did the bloody same too! 'Yeah, cheers, Alex, bye!' before I remembered I was angry, and giving Matt a grilling. Turns out he'd seen That Woman in the buff and he hadn't told me! That night he went for that supposed interview, she was waiting for him completely naked. Stu, Alex's husband, had known about it and told Alex, who then used it as her last hurrah! I didn't bang on about it much – just an hour or so – I hardly had a leg to stand on, did I?

The rest of the evening was spent piecing together any titbit of evidence we had seen in the preceding months of indicators that Alex was unhappy. There was the time she'd said she wished she'd been charged with a public order offence at the march – well, yes, but we all thought that was her showing some soli-darity not a desire to be a martyr. There was the personal attack on Hattie during the march, when she ground a dougnut into her trousers. Another occasion, on the holiday in Ibiza, she'd said we weren't 'militant mummy' enough. No wonder she'd suggested an election. We even wondered whether Alex should be disciplined for breaking the club's vow of secrecy – but then what was the point?

The main thing, my dear members, is that she lost faith in me. She was pissed off and thought I didn't take the club seriously enough and spent too much time messing about. I'm not going to brush off her comments and dismiss them as if they are a bit loony or left field. As chairwoman I have to take them on board. Perhaps she's right in a sense. Perhaps the club has lost its way.

Whatever, it is clear I have much to think about before the election. Both Lucy and Mags decided not to come today because they're still very upset. But they will be back, I guarantee you. Alex was too busy to come due to her campaigning. I spotted her earlier knocking on doors, handing out leaflets – her strength is clearly her organisational skills. Obviously I'm far too slapdash and caught up with the washing and eating chocolate to have a strategy. But then that's who I am, and I think my record of the last year speaks for itself. At least I care. I really, really care.

So next week will not be the happy-clappy hurrah of an organisation about to celebrate its first birthday. There will be an election. And it'll be live-streamed to all our clubs across the world – details of which will be on the website. Funny how Alex managed to fix all that up for her big moment. Sorry to sound bitter, I'm still very upset about losing her friendship.

Right, that's it. I've got to rush off to Tesco Extra to do the rubbish-mummy packed-lunch crawl of shame because the little one is off on a trip to the zoo tomorrow and I've only got mouldy bread and Marmite. I'm going with him as one of the nominated parents – God help me. Especially because I just know I'm going to be paired up with Passive-Aggressive Mummy, who likes to express her feelings through her son, as in, 'It's OK to turn down one of Stella's yucky Scotch eggs. Mummy doesn't like them either, they're common. Just be polite and say "no, thank you".'

Wish me luck. See you next week.

Dads United

www.dadsunited.co.uk

Dear lards,

I am very touched by your decision to chuck Stu out of the club and reinstate me as captain. It just goes to show that our 'what goes on in football training, stays in football training' ethos has been applied to the letter after he grassed me up to Alex about That Woman.

Looks like Stu and Alex aren't quite the people we thought they were. First, Alex with the Tattoo campaign and now Stu. I gave Stu a ring the other day to ask why he did it and he told me straight: he thought I was a twat who needed to grow up and stop messing about. Fair play, he came out with it, there was no 'sorry, mate', but he just said he'd had enough of my flip-flopping and what he called 'amateur leadership' of Dads United, and it just slipped out when he was slagging me off to Alex. Yeah, cheers, mate.

He started telling me what he'd subjected you lot

to – twice-weekly training, a diet sheet and a beer ban. You lot would've hated that. Talk about taking it seriously. Not that I don't, but you know what I mean – a beer ban? Was he mad? Worse news, Stu said he didn't give a shit about being kicked out because he was going to train as a referee. I bet we end up with him at some point.

Anyway, glad you've seen sense. I accept I was a right twat when I had that scrap with Dave. Won't happen again. Mainly because he's thousands of miles away.

Having chatted to you all over the Feathers, I've done what you wanted, what we all wanted, and applied for Dads United to join the Sunday League for next season. Division Four, obviously.

Haven't told Stella yet that I'm back in the game, because she'll go mental. She was really happy I'd thrown in the towel because of number two coming in September and she was looking forward to me being around more. But I bet you, once I've convinced her that Dad and me can take the little one – who will be the big one come the new season – to his football on a Saturday and then to watch me play on a Sunday, if we make it into the league, then she'll be happy as Larry.

Or not. You know what women are like. I tell you, I still don't get them. Stella hasn't kicked Alex out of the club – unbelievable. I thought all those women would be baying for Alex's blood after what she did, but no, they're being all rational and spouting, 'This is a democracy.' Stella is pretending she's cool about it all, but I know she's devastated about Alex going nuts. They used to be so close. But I guess parenthood does that to you – sends you a bit mad. Those similarities you share at the beginning with mates who have kids can easily become differences. At the start you're so desperate to compare notes with new parents and get on and share stuff about poo that you don't see the fact they're bloody mentaloids.

Right. Training this week – the usual followed by the usual at the Feathers, when we can work out our plan to save the pub from the clutches of pricks in suits.

And thanks again,

Matt

Proudly Your Captain

Week Fifty-two

Stella's Swansong?

Stella's kitchen

Lardies, I stand before you today in my grottiest joggers, crunchy with snot because my son thinks I'm a human tissue. I have unwashed and unbrushed hair, my deodorant is yesterday's and my make-up consists of clumpscara, the remnants of two days ago when I last left the house. This is because I've been up most of the night with a boiling hot boy who puked up over his bed, our bed, him, me, the hall carpet on the way to the bathroom and everywhere but the loo.

But this morning, on one of the most important days of my life, I offer no apology for my appearance to those in my kitchen, which is packed to the rafters, or to the millions of members who have tuned in to watch our website's live-streaming of the club's election. Indeed, the way I look, thanks to bugger all sleep, is completely in keeping with what we have created together: that of being good enough. Yes, I might look a state, but I'm a good enough mum regardless. And this is the platform on which I stand as I fight for my life to remain chairwoman.

You've just heard Alex on the hustings calling for a radical revamp of this club based on her Not Guilty! regime. Her speech was amazing, and I applaud her zeal, but I do not share her vision. How can I when I feel guilty for handing over my poorly son to my mum while I ask for your support? Yes, I know I shouldn't, it's only for a bit, my mum is capable and I am entitled to my own pursuits. But I am a mum and guilt is the ying to the yang of all that love you feel for your kids. It's an integral part of mothering – not something I like, but it's there. To speak of it as though we can turn off the guilty switch is a nonsense.

If you vote for Alex, then I can only see division after division down the line. You will be polarised into two groups: the hardline Not Guilty! versus what will be considered the weak Guilty. That's if anyone dares admit to it for fear of getting a verbal kicking.

But if you vote for me, you will be voting for a big, welcoming, non-judgemental hug. Our dissenters will depart to join Alex's splinter group, which she has said she'll set up if she loses the election. And we can get on with the business of encouraging mums to be good enough.

What can I offer you? More of the same. I don't blame you if your first reaction is 'Oh God, not more bumbling shenanigans.' Yes, there were plenty of them.

I was sucked in by Botox, the Man Of My Dreams and fame. Up to my elbows in plastic toys, tantrums and tidying up, my head was turned. But I have paid the price with Tattoo and lost a friend – I promise you there will be no more 'me, me, me'. I have apologised and learnt my lesson.

What I mean, instead, by 'more of the same' is our achievements. Sticking up for mums like us, taking on the Mother Superiors, staging an incredible march and getting the Government to listen to us. If you choose me, you'll continue to have a voice. And I'll represent you with a heady passion as I've always done. I love this club and its members – you are the ones who inspired this kitchen-sink revolution – and it is a privilege to have led you for twelve months.

If Alex wins, there will be no sour grapes, because I respect the democracy that runs through the Mums Like Us club's varicose veins. I will remain a member and keep shouting the Good Enough mantra because I could never leave you. But a vote for me is a vote for progress, unity and, most of all, yourselves – I really couldn't have done any of this without you all, you flabulous, flabulous lot.

There are many great things ahead of us – you've all heard the plans about our antenatal classes and books and stuff – and I only hope you will permit me to be at the helm . . . and . . . oh, goodness . . . I promised myself I wouldn't cry . . . but my mum has just come in at the back with my son, who looks a lot perkier . . . hello, poppet . . . and there's Matt with . . . Christ, it's Hattie and they're all wearing Save Our Stella T-shirts! That is so touching, thank you so much.

Well, that's just about finished me off.

One last thing, lardies, and I've been wrestling over whether to tell you because it's such a biggie and today is about the election, and I don't want to influence you either way. But, get this, just last night, I had an email from a major director who wants to make a film about our club. To tell the story of how we began, in this very room, and became a worldwide movement for mums who were fed up of the pressure to be perfect.

I KNOW! I can tell by your gasps that you're as gobsmacked as me. I checked my email at about two a.m., in between bouts of my son throwing up, while he was sleeping and I was on that red alert status of watching his every breath and feeling his forehead – you know what it's like. I couldn't sleep, even though I was dog-tired. Anyway, there, in my inbox, was an email with the subject line 'Hollywood calling!'. The time difference explains why it popped up in the early hours – it came from California, after all.

He says he wants to meet us, the founding club, to discuss a screenplay. I couldn't believe it either but I checked online with the studios and it's bona fide. And you'll never guess who he's got in mind for the lead role – only Gwyneth bloody Paltrow! Blimey, she'll have her work cut out to turn into one of us.

What's more, he mentioned a multi-million pound deal. But it all depends on me staying chairwoman, that's what the director stipulated. On the surface, it all looks amazing, yet the irony hasn't escaped me: we'd be so rich, it could tempt us into having a nanny, a holiday home and a personal trainer!

However, I can see by your faces that you're excited – if anyone's got any Tena Lady pads, please pass them round. It looks like you have a big decision to make: no film and Not Guilty! if you choose Alex, or the Mums Like Us blockbuster if you pick me. So, should I stay or should I go?

It's time to vote. All those in favour of re-electing me as chairwoman, please raise your hands . . .

LOOK OUT FOR LAURA KEMP'S NEW NOVEL, COMING IN 2014

Mums on Strike

It was just a squashed grape on the kitchen floor. Hardly a reason to get upset, right?

But six years of motherhood has left Lisa Stratton feeling like the skivvy.

Every morning before she's opened her eyes, she starts her mental inventory of jobs to do. And just like yesterday, the day before and every day since she became a mum, she's woken up knackered.

So when Adam deliberately steps over the grape because it's 'her responsibility' to run the house, it tips her over the edge.

He wasn't always like this – they used to share everything.

Then the kids came along.

On the third day she rose again. And this time things are going to change. She's made a decision. She's going on strike...

arrow books